Underneath her schoolteacher starch, Katherine Taylor was a lovely, courageous bundle of beauty.

Even when they clashed, Trey admired her moral fortitude and persistence. She'd triumphed over a scandalous childhood. She was, quite frankly, a woman worthy of his respect.

With the wind snapping tendrils of black hair from her confining hairstyle, she looked like an avenging angel sent to demand his reckoning.

It was always like this between them—volatile, unpredictable, confusing—but more so over the last few months.

Alarm spread through him, the reaction shocking him. The corresponding ache in his gut warned him that he'd made a mistake challenging Miss Taylor this time.

"Relent…*Marshal*," she said.

The impossible had happened. Trey Scott, defender of justice, protector of women and children, had just suffered defeat. At the hands of a schoolmarm.

Renee Ryan
and
Jane Myers Perrine

The Marshal
Takes a Bride
&
Second Chance Bride

◆**H HARLEQUIN**® LOVE INSPIRED®CLASSICS

LOVE INSPIRED BOOKS

Recycling programs
for this product may
not exist in your area.

ISBN-13: 978-1-335-45449-2

The Marshal Takes a Bride & Second Chance Bride

Copyright © 2019 by Harlequin Books S.A.

The publisher acknowledges the copyright holders
of the individual works as follows:

The Marshal Takes a Bride
Copyright © 2009 by Renee Halverson

Second Chance Bride
Copyright © 2009 by Jane Myers Perrine

www.Harlequin.com

Printed in U.S.A.

CONTENTS

Renee Ryan grew up in a Florida beach town where she learned to surf, sort of. With a degree from FSU, she explored career opportunities at a Florida theme park and a modeling agency and even taught high school economics. She currently lives with her husband in Nebraska, and many have mistaken their overweight cat for a small bear. You may contact Renee at reneeryan.com, on Facebook or on Twitter, @reneeryanbooks.

Books by Renee Ryan

Love Inspired Historical

Lone Star Cowboy League: The Founding Years

Stand-In Rancher Daddy

Charity House

Visit the Author Profile page
at Harlequin.com for more titles.

THE MARSHAL
TAKES A BRIDE

Renee Ryan

Avenge not yourselves, but rather give place
unto wrath: for it is written, Vengeance is mine;
I will repay, saith the Lord.
                                        —*Romans* 12:19

To my critique partners, Cindy Kirk and Terry Hager. You have no idea how much I appreciate you both. And to my twin, Robin. Thank you for showing endless mercy and forgiveness to a sister who loves you dearly but fails you often. And to my mother, Elsie, who went home to the Lord before she had a chance to read this one. I miss you, Mom!

Chapter One

Denver, Colorado, June 1880

Cornered and nearly out of ideas, U.S. marshal Trey Scott refused to consider retreat. Not while he had a five-year-old little girl counting on him to triumph against the misery that assailed her. What had started as a mere game to the others was a matter of tragic proportions to the child.

Trey would *not* let her down.

Shivering, Molly Taylor pressed her tiny body closer to him. "You gotta save me, Mr. Trey."

Those big round eyes and that trembling lower lip punched through the last remnants of his resolve to remain neutral in this standoff. He would stick by the kid throughout this battle of hers.

Softening his expression, Trey knuckled a long black braid off her shoulder. "I won't let them get you, kitten. Just stay close."

He scooted Molly behind him, mutiny twisting in his gut. No one would stand in his way as he protected the girl from her dreaded fate. The troubled child deserved some peace and joy in her life.

"Leave this child alone." He fixed an uncompromising glare on the leader—a woman of uncompromising valor—and ignored the half dozen or so others crowding closer.

The pale-eyed, persistent female held firm against him in their battle of wills. Apparently, this was no game to her, either.

Trey widened his stance and folded his arms across his chest, settling into the standoff as though he had all the time in the world. He wrestled against the knot of regret tangling inside his anger. At one time, he'd considered this woman beautiful, godly—even fair-minded.

He'd woefully miscalculated.

At least Molly had *him* on her side. A swift glimpse to his left revealed an opening in the hedge that ran along the perimeter of the yard. Mentally, he measured the dimensions and came up victorious. The hole was the perfect size for a forty-pound slip of a girl to glide through to freedom. He'd catch up with her before she made it halfway down Larimer Street and long before she hit the bedlam of horse-drawn taxis on Tabor Block in the business district.

Comfortable with his plan, Trey inched across the grass, tugging Molly along with him.

The *boss* matched him step for step.

Shooting the woman a warning glare, Trey then turned to Molly and cocked his head toward the thicket. "You know what to do," he whispered.

Tears wiggled just below long, sooty lashes. "What if they catch me?"

He lowered his voice. "I'll create a diversion."

"What's that?" Molly asked in a whisper loud enough to be heard two counties over.

"Never mind. When I say run, you run."

But the leader—wrapped in that deceptively feminine package—pulled around to the left, effectively closing off the escape. "Don't even think about it."

At the end of his temper, Trey swallowed back a bitter retort.

As though hearing his unspoken words, inflexible blue eyes cut through the distance between them.

"The game is over… *Marshal,*" the woman said.

Although he had at least a hundred pounds on the stormy-eyed sprite, Trey had to stifle the shocking urge to withdraw. He'd stood up against cannons, gross injustice, crooked judges and vicious criminals, but nothing compared to the disapproval of Katherine Taylor—schoolmarm, official custodian of the Charity House trusts and Molly's overprotective sister.

With that inflexible look on her face, Trey knew he could no longer count on the fact that Miss Taylor would set aside her volatile feelings for him and be reasonable, for Molly's sake.

So be it.

He had to delay. Procrastinate. Postpone the inevitable.

But how?

The late afternoon heat pulled sweat onto his brow. He'd lost his hat long before the battle had begun. A light breeze lifted the hair off the back of his neck, the comforting sensation mocking his inability to think straight.

He circled his gaze around the perimeter of the yard, taking note of the snowcapped mountains in the distance. *Too far away.* Growing a little more apprehensive and a lot less confident, he focused on the brick, two-story mansions running shoulder to shoulder for several blocks off to his right. *Too many questions.* As a last resort, Trey shot a quick glance past the manicured lawn and blooming flowers to the large, fancy home behind him. *Too risky.*

His only hope was to take the woman by surprise.

As covertly as possible, he inched toward the hedge, but an irreverent growl wafted on a cloud of threat. A quick look to his right and Trey's gaze connected with two more villains joining the foe's ranks. Shifting to face these newest threats, he snarled at the man he'd once called friend and the woman who co-owned the Charity House orphanage with him. "Marc and Laney Dupree, this is *not* your fight."

A grin slid between the two. "It is now," Marc said for them both.

As one, they glanced to Katherine, then separated, covering the gaps she'd left when she'd moved in front of the hedge.

Blowing out a hiss, Trey lowered his head to Molly's. "Don't worry, kitten. I have everything under control."

Various snorts and snickers cut through his words as more joined the enemy's ranks. Katherine spoke for the group. "Just hand her over, and no one will get hurt."

Wrapping all four feet of trembling little girl in his arms, Trey darted a quick glance to the house in front of him. "Not a chance."

"This is ridiculous. Surrender the child, now." Katherine spoke in a flat, no-nonsense tone that made him bristle.

Marc took two steps closer. "Enough, Trey. Hand her over."

Trey eyed his friend turned traitor. Clean-shaven, dressed in a fancy vest and matching tie, Marc Dupree didn't look much like the tough, hardened man Trey had once known, a man who had overcome poverty and…worse. In fact, with the sun winking off the dangling watch fob, Marc looked more like a dandy than a threatening opponent.

But Trey knew the man had hidden skills. Came from living with that wily, unpredictable wife of his, the same woman who was now conspiring openly with the enemy in this standoff.

"All right, Molly," Trey whispered in her ear. "We're going to make a run for it."

Another low whimper slipped from her lips. "But, Mr. Trey, I'm not fast."

He folded her deeper into his embrace. "Don't worry. I'll carry you."

She wrapped her spider-thin arms around his neck, nodding her head against his chest.

Shifting her to a more comfortable position, he studied the biggest threat to the child. Her sister.

Just looking at the woman made his throat ache. Underneath all that prim schoolteacher starch, Katherine Taylor was a lovely, courageous bundle of feminine charm and beauty. Even amidst this contest of wills, Trey found a part of him admiring her moral fortitude and persistence. She'd triumphed over a scandalous childhood and the unspeakable violence committed against her. She was, quite frankly, a woman worthy of his respect.

Then again…

With the wind snapping tendrils of black hair free from that hideously confining hairstyle, she looked a lot like an avenging angel sent to demand his reckoning.

It was always like this between them—volatile, unpredictable, confusing—more so over the past few months.

Alarm spread through him, the physical reaction shocking him. The corresponding ache in his gut warned him that he'd made a mistake challenging Miss Taylor on this matter.

Seeking compassion, Trey pivoted to his right. But another glare of disapproval angled back at him. Carrying thirty or so extra pounds and a rounded belly, Laney O'Connor Dupree was just as relentless as Katherine.

"No way out yet, Molly. The flanks are too formidable for a quick escape."

"Don't let them get me," Molly wailed.

"Don't you worry. I'm a United States marshal. They wouldn't dare take me on."

The scoffing and giggles coming from the crowd behind Katherine didn't seem to fill the little girl with confidence. "They don't sound very worried."

"They are. They just don't know it yet."

Balancing on the balls of his feet, Trey tucked Molly firmly in the crook of his arm. Leading with his shoulder, he charged through the front line. With the element of surprise on his side, he knocked his big, overdressed friend back a few yards.

Marc recovered quickly, and while Trey battled with his childhood friend, two pairs of persistent hands worked from behind to wrestle Molly free.

She kicked and squealed. "No, I don't want to go!"

Trey ground his teeth together and dug his heels into the ground.

"Relent... *Marshal*," said Katherine.

Trey pressed Molly tighter against his chest.

"You've taken this too far already," Marc said.

Trey dodged a flying elbow. He spun to his right but slipped, dropping to his knees. Next thing he knew, Molly was wrested out of his grip, and he was lying flat on his back.

The impossible had happened. Trey Scott, defender of justice, protector of women and children, had just suffered defeat. At the hands of a schoolmarm, a dandy and a pregnant woman.

"Attack," yelled the fancy man.

High-pitched squeals lifted into the air.

"And, this time, finish him off."

In a blur, seven children jumped on him, fingers jabbing in his ribs and stomach. Trey clamped his teeth together. "I'm not ticklish."

Undaunted, fourteen miniature hands worked quicker.

Trey finally let out a hoot of laughter. He rose to his knees, just in time to see Molly ushered up the back stairs, caught in the clutches of her relentless big sister. "Mr. Trey," she yelled, "save me."

She reached her thin arms out to him.

Trey hopped to his feet and then darted toward the back porch, but he was held back by the Charity House orphans. One by one, he peeled away hands and feet. A particularly persistent little boy rode on his leg, clutching with the grip of a full-grown man. It took considerable maneuvering to release the kid without hurting him. Trey could use such a man on his side. He nearly considered swearing the boy in as a deputy.

Too bad the brute was only eight years old.

"Mr. Tre-e-e-e-ey..."

Trey raced up the back stairs, then shot in front of the door, barring entrance with his hulking frame.

He looked from one woman to the other. "Laney Dupree and Katherine Taylor, I'll not stand by and watch you degrade this child."

Katherine narrowed her eyes, depositing every bit of the formidable schoolteacher in her expression. "A bath is not degrading."

Trey dropped his gaze to Molly, and his gut twisted. She looked so sad and pitiful with her lower lip trembling. "It can't wait until tomorrow?" he asked.

Katherine pulled her lips into a tight knot of disapproval.

Sensing a stalemate, he appealed to the wisdom of the group. "Laney, do something."

Marc's wife shook her finger at him as though he was the one who'd committed a terrible wrong. "I'm going to have to agree with Katherine. The child needs a bath."

"No," Molly cried. She twisted out of her sister's grip, rushed to Trey and hooked her hand in his. "Mr. Trey says I don't have to if I don't wanna."

Laney chuckled, instantly sobering when Katherine leveled a glare on her.

Sighing, Katherine spun back to look at Molly, the first signs of frustration flushing in her cheeks. With fists planted firmly on her hips, she said, "A bath is not going to kill you, young lady. Just look at you. Not a clean spot to be found."

In a gesture identical to her sister's, Molly jammed

her balled fists on her hips. "We was playing marshals and bank robbers with the other Charity House kids."

"And losing, from the sight of you," declared Katherine.

Trey took exception.

"We were just letting them win." He winked at the little girl. "Isn't that right, Molly?"

She favored him with a big gap-toothed grin. "*Right.* We can't never, not ever, let them stinkin' outlaws get the best of us."

Katherine gasped. "Did you teach her that?"

Trey had the presence of mind to cast his gaze to the sky before he responded. "Maybe."

Marc joined them on the porch, turning into the voice of reason. "It's over, Trey."

Trey looked from Katherine to Marc to Laney, then back to Katherine again. Ignoring the satisfied expressions on the faces of the three other adults, he crouched down to the five-year-old little girl's level. Plucking at one of Molly's braids, he said, "Sorry, kitten. Looks like you're taking that bath today."

Her eyelashes fluttered, and one fat tear rolled down her cheek.

Before he gave in to the pleading look, Trey squeezed his eyes shut, rose and shifted out of the way. He opened his lids in time for Katherine to link her disapproving gaze with his. "Stick around… *Marshal.* I'm not through with you."

With that, she spun around and marched inside the house, Molly in tow.

Laney poked him in the chest. "You just made a big mistake, my friend. *Big* mistake."

Chapter Two

With her resolve firmly in place, Katherine marched up the back stairs of the twenty-year-old mansion turned orphanage, tugging a reluctant little girl along with her. The moment her gaze landed on Molly's tear-streaked face, Katherine's determination turned into heart-wrenching guilt.

By engaging in that senseless battle with Marshal Scott, she'd hurt the very person she'd set out to protect.

What kind of big sister did that make her? Usually, she turned to God to help her with the overwhelming task of raising her newfound sister.

Today she'd allowed emotion to get the best of her.

Sighing, she caressed Molly's hair and steered her into the recently refurbished bathroom, where Marc had installed multiple basins for the home's many children to wash up for the evening. On the outside, Charity House looked identical to the rest of the fancy homes on Larimer Street. But inside, the mansion had been perfectly altered to house forty special children and the adults who cared for them.

"Come on, Moll." Katherine clicked the door shut behind them. "Let's get you out of those filthy clothes."

Molly crossed her tiny arms over her chest. "I was having fun, Katherine."

Inhaling a deep, calming breath, Katherine knelt on the floor and cupped the child's cheek. "I know you were. And you can go back outside—"

Molly darted away from the claw-foot tub, but Katherine caught her by the sleeve. "*After* we get you cleaned up."

"But Mr. Trey said playtime was more important than a bath."

"I just bet he did." Frustration speared Katherine's previous remorse into something deeper, darker. Uglier...

Take captive every thought and make it obedient to Christ.

Katherine swallowed back her rising annoyance and forced her voice into an even tone. "Let's leave Marshal Scott out of this for now."

Molly scrunched her face into a frown, her expression reminiscent of one Katherine had seen in her own mirror often enough before she'd made peace with her past, the same one permanently stuck on their mother's face every day before she'd finally succumbed to tuberculosis.

"Don't you like Mr. Trey?" Molly asked.

Katherine's throat tightened. Her feelings for the U.S. marshal could never be classified as something so benign as "like." Explosive, precarious, frightening—those were far better descriptions for the disturbing emotions the man brought out in her.

She closed her eyes and took a deep breath.

Perhaps he'd had good intentions at first. But there was no question in her mind that Marshal Scott was a difficult man, with his own personal demons to battle. Katherine knew, to devastating ends, what such a man was capable of doing when a woman let down her guard. She absently touched the top button of her blouse, made sure it was fastened.

Truth be told, Trey Scott was too dangerous. Too bold. Too *everything* to trust. He simply had to go. Especially now that God had given Katherine the gift of finding the little sister she hadn't known existed until six months ago.

Straightening her shoulders, Katherine turned her attention back to Molly. "Let's get you into the tub, pumpkin."

Molly arranged her face in an expression identical to the one Trey had leveled on her just moments ago on the back porch. "Don't wanna."

Katherine was long past being amused. "Well, sometimes we have to do things we don't want."

"That's not fair to me."

"Life's not fair," Katherine said, with a sigh.

A heart-wrenching sob flew out of Molly. "I wish you'd never come for me. I *hate* you."

Holding back a sob of her own, Katherine prayed for the right words to ease Molly's resentment. The set of the child's jaw was so similar to the look on her face the day Katherine had found her in that bleak mining camp, with only a threadbare blanket on a dirt floor as her bed. The child had been so quiet, so…alone and scared, having been left to fend for herself after her father's fatal accident in the mine.

Katherine pushed a lock of hair off her sister's forehead, praying she could offer her sister a good life here at Charity House. "I know you think you hate me now, but I'll always love you, Molly. You're my sister."

The five-year-old responded with a hiccuping sigh.

To keep from speaking out in anger, Katherine bit down on her lower lip. The realization that her sister blamed her for what had happened today wounded her far more than the child's hurtful words. Before Trey Scott had entered their lives, Molly had never openly challenged her authority.

As though sensing her misery, Laney chose that moment to duck her head into the room. "Want me to take over?"

Katherine peered at her friend. The sympathy she saw staring back at her clogged the air in her throat, reminding her of the dark night when Laney had wrapped Katherine in her arms and held her until the tears had eventually stopped flowing.

Her friend had made things easier for Katherine then, and she wished she could give in to the offer of help now. "I have to do this myself."

Angling her head to the side, Laney looked at Molly's mutinous expression. "Are you sure?"

Katherine focused on her little sister. The childish rebellion brewing in her gaze warned Katherine the fight wasn't over yet. Perhaps taking a moment to strengthen her resolve would do them both some good.

"Molly, I'm going to step in the hall with Laney for a few minutes. When I return, I want to see you completely undressed and sitting in that tub."

The little girl opened her mouth to protest.

Katherine stopped her with a warning look.

The angry child paused, made a face and then stomped her foot. Hard.

"Molly. Grace. Taylor. That's enough. Get undressed, *now*," ordered Katherine.

Two scrawny shoulders hunched forward, and tears began pouring down the dirt-smudged cheeks. Sniffing loudly between sobs, Molly plopped onto the floor and started tugging off her shoes.

Katherine winced at the pitiful sight her sister made, but she wouldn't give in to the tantrum. Molly needed to learn respect for the new life she had at Charity House. How could Katherine explain to the child just how blessed they were to be living at the orphanage, instead of above some filthy saloon? Or worse.

With unshed tears burning in her own eyes, Katherine motioned Laney into the long hallway that led to five bedrooms and a sitting chamber, then shut the door behind them.

As Katherine turned to look at her ally, her heart swelled with renewed gratitude for Laney's kindness. The woman had virtually saved Katherine from the life that could have been her legacy as the daughter of the most notorious madam in town.

She opened her mouth to speak but Laney beat her to it. "That is one upset little girl in there. Are you sure you don't want me to help you?"

Katherine shook her head. "Molly and I are still trying to get used to one another. I have to put an end to this blatant disobedience, before it goes any further."

"I understand." Laney headed toward the stairs, then stopped and looked back over her shoulder. "If you change your mind, I'll be in the kitchen, helping Mrs. Smythe with supper."

"Laney, wait."

She pivoted around, her eyebrows lifting in inquiry. "Yes?"

While trying to gather her swirling thoughts, Katherine studied her friend. Even at eight months pregnant, her thick mahogany hair and creamy skin glowed with good health. Inside that beautiful exterior, Laney O'Connor Dupree carried a fiercely loyal heart. And Katherine never took that blessing for granted.

"Thanks for—" Katherine cocked her head toward the back of the house "—taking my side out there today."

Laney's amber eyes crinkled at the corners. "Think nothing of it. Trey may be Marc's family, but in all the ways that count you're mine."

Katherine didn't have the words to express her love for this woman, her sister in the faith. She had given Katherine far more than a home on that horrible night two years ago. Her friend had given her an opportunity to start over and had provided a place in the world where Katherine could exist without shame. "I…well, I just want to say thank you for supporting me."

"Always." Laney regarded her with a kind, patient look. "And we both know it goes both ways. I wouldn't have Charity House if it weren't for your help."

Year-old memories pushed to the front of Katherine's mind. Laney had nearly lost Charity House to a shady banker when he'd called in the loan six months earlier than the agreed-upon date.

Yet Katherine had never blamed her friend for her rash actions in trying to save their home. How could she? Laney had given her a safe haven when she'd been attacked by one of her mother's former customers. Even when the townspeople had blamed her, rather than the man who had forced himself on her, Laney had taken Katherine in and had given her a job—one that had allowed her to give back to Charity House.

Katherine might be tainted forever, but God had blessed her. By being given Laney and the Charity House orphans, Katherine had learned she was not without worth. Thus, it was with a cheerful heart that she had helped her friend raise the money needed to save the orphanage. In the process, the other woman had found the love of her life in Marc, and because of his help, they all still had a home.

"Even if you had lost Charity House, I'd have never blamed you, Laney. You helped save my life, you—"

The sound of hiccuping sobs cut her off.

"This isn't the time to look backward." Her friend slid a glance toward the closed bathroom door. "Right now, you need to focus on your sister."

"You're absolutely correct."

Laney squeezed her shoulder. "Hold firm, Katherine. Remember who's in charge."

"Yes. Yes, I will."

Oh, heavenly Father, please give me the wisdom and strength to face this challenge. Make me a good sister to Molly.

With renewed strength, Katherine turned the doorknob. No matter what else happened today, big sister *would* prevail over little sister. And once she was finished with Molly, she'd turn her attention to a United States marshal who thought he could disrupt her orderly life by pitting one Taylor female against the other.

There was a lesson to be learned here today. And Trey Scott was going to learn it.

* * *

Still stinging from his unprecedented defeat, Trey stared out the window of Marc's study, where he'd spent plenty of hours whenever his duties brought him to Denver. The former prairie town had grown since Trey first pinned on a badge, becoming a city that lured people with its promises of riches and opportunity. Unless, of course, the one seeking said opportunity was a five-year-old child with a rigid schoolmarm for a big sister.

Feeling his temper rising, Trey inhaled a slow breath and slid his glance along the rooftops peppering the nearby horizon. It struck him as somehow fitting and yet also ironic that a home for orphans sat in the middle of a neighborhood designed for the supremely wealthy. A few of the snobbier neighbors still filed complaints, always unfounded and *always* thrown out of court. In the end Charity House was here to stay.

Although Marc had always made him welcome here, Trey's trips had gotten decidedly less restful since Katherine Taylor had taken on the role of zealous protector to her troubled little sister.

As he watched the Charity House orphans play a game of tag in the backyard, dark, angry thoughts formed into one bitter reality. He'd failed little Molly Taylor.

"You through brooding yet?"

Trey spun around and nailed Marc with a hard glare.

"Blast you, your wife and that woman she put in charge of the Charity House School." He slashed his hand in the direction of the window, unwilling to dig deeper into the reasons for his dark mood. "After everything that child's been through, she should be playing."

Hitching a hip onto his oak desk, Marc considered

Trey for a long moment. "Perhaps. But one bath does not make an unhappy child. I think she'll survive the disappointment."

Trey paced to the opposite end of the room. Leaning against the mantel, he dug his toe at the stones in the hearth. "What possessed that woman to turn a bath into grounds for war?"

Lifting an ironic eyebrow, Marc angled his head. "I think she had some help."

"The poor girl just wanted to stay outside and play with the other children."

"Katherine is pretty rigid about schedules."

Trey made a face. "Boards are more pliant."

Obviously finding some dark humor in the situation, Marc chuckled. "You realize, don't you, that you're in for it now? Katherine won't let this one drop."

Trey was well aware that the prissy schoolmarm was gunning for him. In the cold aftermath of their battle, he actually relished the ensuing confrontation. It was long past time he set the woman straight on a few things, like the value of putting the priorities of a five-year-old child ahead of an unreasonable schedule.

After striding back across the room, Trey sank into a dark blue wing chair opposite his friend. The smell of rich mahogany paneling did nothing to soothe his temper. A vision of Katherine Taylor in the role of avenging big sister scooted frustration deeper. For well over a year now, ever since Marc had married Laney, Trey had found himself on the opposing side of every argument with the schoolmarm. It had only gotten worse with Molly's arrival.

Scrubbing a hand down his face, he said, "I don't

understand why that woman treats me like I'm evil incarnate."

"I'd say you give her good reason."

Trey opened his mouth to deny his friend's accusation but shut it without speaking. Looking back, he realized that in his misguided attempt to defend the girl, Molly had ended up hurt.

Guilt gnawed at him, making him jerk out of his chair and start pacing again. Quite frankly, now that the emotion of the moment was gone, he was ashamed of how he'd behaved today.

"Why'd you take it so far, Trey?"

Ah, the real question at hand, and one he couldn't fully explain. "Something about Molly gets to me. Has ever since her sister brought her to live at Charity House with all of you."

"Granted, no child should have to lose both her mother and father at such a young age, or suffer the ridicule of her mother's profession. But there are forty other...*orphans* in this home with similar stories. Why Molly?"

Trey stopped, turned and then dropped slowly into the chair he'd occupied earlier. "I can't explain it."

Marc kept his gaze focused and direct, looking at Trey with a quiet intensity that warned him he wouldn't like what was coming next. "Why do I get the sense that your dedication to Molly has to do with your need to avenge the loss of your wife and child?"

Caught off guard by the unwanted reminder of his dead wife and the baby she'd carried, Trey clenched his fist. "You're wrong."

"Am I? Everything you do is about your quest for

vengeance. Let's see. How old would your child be now? About Molly's age?"

Bitterness nearly choked him, the emotion so strong, Trey hadn't realized how deep it ran until this moment. But now that the subject was broached, he couldn't let it pass. "You know I can't stand by passively and allow Ike Hayes to run free. His killing has to stop. No matter what it takes."

Marc leaned forward, a perceptive look blazing in his eyes. "And because he murdered your wife and unborn child, you're now the God-appointed agent for justice, is that it?"

Trey swallowed an angry retort. As far as he was concerned, God had nothing to do with his quest. "I *will* take Ike down."

"It won't bring Laurette or your baby back."

Trey squeezed his eyes shut. "I know that."

How many nights had he lain awake, alone? Always alone, always grieving. Only for a few brief moments, when he was championing little Molly Taylor, had he felt a little less empty. It wasn't something he could put into words. It just…*was*.

As if his friend could read the direction of Trey's thoughts, he said, "Well, singling out Molly won't bring her parents back, either."

Trey struggled to find his breath, his control. His reasoning. "I can't explain how I know this, but Molly needs me more than the others do. And for the first time since I failed Laurette, the fact that another human being requires my protection doesn't scare me half to death."

Leaning back in his chair, his friend steepled his fingers under his chin. "Want to know what I think?"

"No."

Marc continued as though Trey hadn't spoken. "I think it's time you moved past this poisonous need for vengeance. Start over. Begin a family of your own."

Rebellion swept through him, and Trey had to swallow the fresh agony rising out of his grief. He couldn't start over. Not yet. *Not ever.* The memory of his wife and unborn child deserved his total devotion, his complete concentration. And until Ike Hayes was made to pay for murdering Trey's family, there could be no talk of starting over. "It's too soon."

"It's been four years."

Trey grimaced. Had it been that long since he'd held his wife in his arms, since he'd smelled the fresh scent of her hair? Four years since the soft lilt of her laughter filled his home? "I still miss her."

"Me, too." Marc's face softened, and Trey knew his friend was remembering his sister, the one he'd entrusted to Trey's care. The one Trey had failed.

"No one can replace Laurette," Trey said, his voice thick with familiar emotion. "She was sweet, innocent, compassionate. Gentle, through and through."

"Careful, Trey. Don't rewrite history with the prejudice of your guilt. As her big brother, I agree that Laurette was special. But she was human, too, a woman with flaws."

"I don't remember any."

"Maybe you should."

Trey's chest ached too much to respond. Even after four years, he couldn't think of his wife without his mind filling with the image of the last time he'd held her in his arms, pregnant and dying from a bullet that should have found him.

At Laurette's funeral, several members of his church

had spoken of God's will. They'd told him Laurette was in a better place, free from the pain and sorrow of this world.

Trey hadn't believed their words for a minute. He would *never* accept that his wife's senseless murder was part of some divine plan for his own life. And with every additional murder he had to investigate, the chasm between him and God widened.

Settling his head into the cushioned softness of the chair, he tried desperately to free his mind of the painful memories. But intense longing for what he could never have again tightened in his throat. The ugly role he'd played in Laurette's death waged a battle inside him, choking the breath out of him. "If only I had been there to protect her and the baby she carried, maybe then—"

He broke off, unable to put into words the self-condemnation that haunted him still.

As though sensing his inability to continue, Marc changed the subject. "How long will you be in Denver this time?"

Thankful for the reprieve, Trey lifted his head and focused his thoughts on the present. "At least a month, maybe two. I don't plan to leave until the trial is over."

"You think you'll get a conviction?"

Uncompromising resolve spread through him. A month ago, Trey had caught Ike's younger brother, Drew, and had brought him in for trial. With one Hayes in custody, it was only a matter of time before Trey captured the other.

"I'll get the conviction *and* I'll find Ike," he said. Laurette deserved nothing less from him. "They don't call me 'Beelzebub's cousin' for nothing."

Marc's lips twitched. "Oh, you're dangerous—except when you're up against a ferocious schoolteacher."

"I can handle Molly's big sister."

"Like you did today?" Marc's expression was too innocent, deceptively so.

Trey ground his teeth together and dug his heels into the rug. "Yeah, well, she got lucky."

As if she'd planned her entrance for effect, the object of their discussion marched into the room, arms wrapped around her waist. Her glare pinned Trey in his chair.

Well, now. If that's the way she wanted to play it. His earlier feelings of shame at sparring with this woman instantly disappeared. Perhaps it was time to put Miss Rigid-Rule-Setter on the defensive for a change.

With deliberate slowness, he took in her appearance, concentrating on the streaks of dirt on her cheek, the smudges on her once-crisp white blouse.

So Molly had fought to the end.

Good girl.

As he linked his gaze with Katherine's again, he noted the sudden flicker of uncertainty flashing in her eyes before she covered it with her usual prissy determination.

Interesting.

She squared her shoulders. "I'd like that word with you, Marshal Scott. *Now.*"

Trey didn't like her attitude, nor was he overly fond of the riot of emotion spinning in his gut. "I'm not in the mood for a discussion."

"Perfect, because I plan to do all the talking."

Marc rose and slapped Trey on the knee. "Go get her, *Beelzebub's cousin.*"

Chapter Three

By the time Marc left the study, Katherine's frustration threatened to steal the remaining scraps of her composure. Trey Scott, with his challenging stare and unyielding presence, didn't help matters. He looked too masculine, too intimidating for someone who had just championed a five-year-old over a bath.

With the arrogance only a lawman could pull off, he lifted a single eyebrow, relaxed back into his chair then propped a foot on his knee. "So talk."

His attitude made Katherine forget all the reasons why this big, hard man alarmed her. "Marshal Scott, you are a disreputable, ill-mannered disturber of the peace."

There. Very pleasant under the circumstances.

He returned his foot to the floor, then leaned forward to rest his elbows on his knees. "Don't hold back, Miss Taylor. Tell me how you really feel."

His gray eyes regarded her without a sliver of amusement, while the rich Southern drawl rumbled across her tight nerves.

"Oh, I've only just begun," she said, allowing her

growing resentment to take hold. She found it much easier to deal with the large, dangerous lawman when she thought of him as nothing more than a disruptive troublemaker.

Unraveling his hulking frame from the chair, he rose and began striding toward her. "By all means, go ahead and give it to me."

Guard what has been entrusted to your care....

The Scripture from 1 Timothy gave her the courage to hold her ground as he approached. For Molly's sake, she had to stand firm. "Stay away from my sister."

Thankfully, her words stopped his pursuit, and two matching black brows slammed together. "Why? What is it you have against me?"

Katherine ignored the twist of unease in her stomach and concentrated on an image of Molly's tearstained cheeks. "Must you ask after your behavior this afternoon?"

"I didn't work alone out there." He pulled his lips into a sarcastic grin. "Or don't you remember that part?"

Swamped with regret over her own role in Molly's distress, Katherine slapped her hands onto her hips. "Molly has been through too much trauma already. When our mother became ill, instead of contacting me, she sent the poor child to live with her father in a remote mining camp. From all accounts, he did his best, but he still died in an accident, which left Molly all alone."

A wave of regret pressed inside her chest. Katherine hadn't even known of Molly's existence until the letter from the mine's foreman had arrived at Charity House. Why her mother hadn't told her about her baby sister was a mystery that would never be solved. And by the time Katherine had rescued Molly from the mining camp, the little girl had been on her own for two weeks.

After all her losses, will the child ever believe I'm here to stay?

Katherine shoved the worry aside. If Marshal Scott kept undermining her efforts, it would only destroy the fragile bond she had with Molly. "I don't want my sister hurt further."

Genuine shock rippled across his features. "You think I'd intentionally harm that child?"

Surprised by his vehemence, Katherine shook her head. "Not intentionally, no. But singling her out from the rest of the children will only make her feel different from the group."

"Don't you think you're being a bit overprotective?" He crossed his arms over his chest. "Molly is too timid, too closed off from the others for a normal five-year-old. The child needs shaking up."

Katherine didn't like how he summed up her sister's problem so accurately, nor did she trust the look of genuine distress she saw in his eyes. Finding common ground with this man, especially where her sister was concerned, brought matters to a dangerously personal level. And that simply would not do.

She had to remember he was her adversary. "And you're the man to do the shaking up, is that it?"

He lifted a shoulder. "Why not me?"

Oh, she could give him several reasons, but she focused on the main one. "You treat her like a toy you can play with whenever the mood strikes, and then off you go, back to your...*marshaling.*"

"You mean off I go, *pursuing* men who kill innocent women and children."

And therein lay the real issue between them. Trey Scott's drive for vengeance was in direct conflict with Katherine's need to forgive, even—no, especially—the unforgivable.

"Your actions send the wrong message," she said. "They teach her that it's acceptable to trust in her own power instead of relying on God's."

He gave her a mutinous expression. "Maybe that wouldn't be such a bad lesson."

"I don't want her to think revenge is the answer. Because of her circumstances, it would be too easy for her to hate. I want her to learn God's healing power of forgiveness." Katherine knew better than most just how hard that lesson was to learn, but she also knew the peace that came with offering absolution where it wasn't deserved.

"There is *no* forgiveness for senseless murder and violence," he said. His expression hardened as he spoke, but not before Katherine caught a glimpse of real pain just below the surface.

In that moment, she realized he would never understand her point, not with his own grief still so raw. Overwhelmed with emotion and consumed with compassion for his terrible loss, Katherine reached out and touched his arm. "What happened to your wife was horrendous. If only you could learn to let God—"

He jerked away from her and strode to the window. "This isn't about me."

"Yes, it is. At least, partly."

He paced to the desk on the opposite end of the room but didn't meet her gaze. "How do you figure that?"

"Ever since Marc married Laney, you've been coming around here a lot." She lifted her chin at him. "Of course, you would. In fact, I think you should. You're Marc's brother-in-law. Nevertheless, I won't stand by and watch you give my sister the wrong message every time you go after another outlaw for your own personal reasons."

He clenched his hand into a fist. "You know nothing about what drives me."

"Oh, but I do."

He locked his gaze with hers and studied her with his hawklike eyes. The day-old growth of stubble on his jaw added a sinister look to his already hardened expression.

Katherine swallowed her own trepidation and dropped her gaze to the tin star pinned to his shirt. "Try to understand, I don't want Molly to suffer another loss. Even if I were able to put aside the reasons *why* you hunt those criminals, one day you will leave and never come back. And the fonder she is of you, the more it will hurt."

His eyes turned sad, haunted. "One day we all leave and never come back."

She knew he was still thinking of his wife. "That's not what I meant."

His expression cleared into a blank, unreadable glare. "You certainly seem to know a lot about what you *don't* mean."

Struggling for control, Katherine whirled away. How could she explain the pain she had suffered as a child and subsequently as an adult without baring her soul? He wasn't the only one who'd known suffering.

When she was Molly's age, her own father had died a dedicated lawman, killed by an outlaw's bullet. He'd left his family penniless, and as a result, Katherine's mother had looked to a life of prostitution for her answers. Even after Sadie Taylor's death, men still came looking for the infamous madam. Two years ago, one mean-spirited ranch hand had found Katherine instead.

In a rational moment, she knew linking her attack back to her father's murder was defective thinking at best. However, she couldn't deny that her father's death had been the first in a long line of other tragedies in her life.

"Men who wear badges die. That is—" She broke off, swallowed. "Just stay away from Molly."

He pushed away from the desk, his gaze dark and serious.

She fought the urge to turn tail and run. "I'm warning you…"

He halted several feet in front of her and waited for her to finish her threat.

As the silence grew heavy between them, Katherine's heartbeat picked up speed, and she dropped her gaze to her toes. "Please, Marshal Scott, don't champion my sister anymore."

She hated the desperation in her voice. But now that she had Molly with her, all Katherine wanted for them both was a safe, orderly life that honored God.

Why was that so hard for him to understand?

He closed the distance between them until he was towering over her. "Look at me, Miss Taylor."

Katherine jerked her gaze back to his. The sight of his inky-black hair, day-old growth of beard and fierce gray eyes sent a wave of fear through her.

"You're standing too close," she whispered.

"Is this really about Molly?" he asked as his hard, callused hand closed over hers.

His touch was surprisingly gentle. And…and…*terrifying*. She yanked her hand free, flinched two full steps back when he tried to touch her again.

"Of course it's about Molly," she said.

"You don't think it's about you? Me? Us?" He took a slow, careful step in her direction. "And the antagonism you have toward me?"

"Please." A shudder shot through her. "D-d-don't come any closer." She had to squeeze her hands together to keep them from trembling.

He froze in midstep, dropped his gaze to her clasped fingers and then quickly moved away from her. "I'm sorry, Miss Taylor. I wasn't thinking. I didn't mean to frighten you. That was never my intention."

Why was it always like this between them? Why couldn't she simply talk to Marshal Scott like a reasonable, well-adjusted woman spoke with a friend? Why did she have to be such a coward around him?

Frustration at him, fury at her own fears, and disappointment at them *both* made her voice come out harsher than usual. "I… I know you didn't mean any harm," she said.

He pulled a deep, audible breath into his lungs. "Regardless, I only wanted to—"

"Mr. Trey, Mr. Trey, you gotta come see." Molly chose that moment to skip into the room. "Laney's talking bird said my name. Twice. He—"

As though sensing the tension in the room, she broke off and shifted her large, rounded gaze from Trey to Katherine and back to Trey again. "You wanna come see?"

Molly's devoted expression reminded Katherine just why this man was so dangerous. He held too much power over them both. In a purely protective gesture, Katherine gently pulled her sister against her. "No, Moll, Marshal Scott was just leaving."

"You are?" asked Molly.

As though the past five minutes had never happened, he slid Katherine a challenging look before smiling down at Molly. "Of course not, kitten. I wouldn't disappoint my favorite five-year-old."

Several hours after his confrontation with the prissy schoolmarm, Trey left the orphanage and headed back to his room at Miss Martha's boardinghouse. Out of habit, he surveyed his surroundings, hunting for potential danger hidden in the shadows. All he found was a kaleidoscope of yellows and gold that spilled from the streetlamps and mansion windows into a patchwork of sporadic light along the lane.

Taking a deep breath of the crisp night air, he crammed his hat onto his head and increased his pace. Various wagon-wheel tracks pointed the way toward the center of town. After passing several mansions nearly identical to Charity House, Trey eventually turned onto Sixteenth Street. A few blocks later the two-story homes became three-and four-story businesses, and Trey found his mind returning to the events of the night.

He knew he shouldn't have stayed at Charity House as long as he had, but Molly's eager devotion had torn at his heart, making him set aside his own conflicting emotions concerning her sister. The child made him want to right the wrongs done to her.

He tried to tell himself his present restlessness was due to his concern for the kid, but Trey knew Molly wasn't the real source of his agitation.

It was her sister.

He'd known there was going to be trouble the moment Miss Taylor had sauntered into Marc's study, with her self-righteousness wrapped around her like a winter cloak. She'd spoken of forgiveness. Then flinched from his touch.

The woman had genuinely been afraid of him. The shock of it still sat heavy in his chest. Once he'd recognized her terror—terror of *him*—all he'd wanted to do was ease her worry.

Trey knew her past; Marc had told him what she'd endured. Hot anger rose inside him. Considering her terrible trauma, she had every right to be afraid of men.

Yet, beneath her fear, there was a real innocence about her. She truly believed there was healing after unspeakable pain and violence. With such a naive view of life, Miss Taylor could never understand what drove Trey.

How could she? In his experience, people who spoke of forgiveness had already done their forgiving. Well, he would *never* forgive Ike Hayes. He couldn't allow Laurette's killer off that easily.

Laurette.

At the thought of his wife a swift, unrelenting wave of guilt whipped through him. He'd nearly betrayed the memory of her tonight, all because he'd wanted to ease another woman's fears.

Ripping off his hat, Trey slammed it against his thigh. He'd like to think he'd been drawn to Katherine tonight because he'd wanted to show her that all men weren't like the one who had attacked her, but he knew better. Something about the woman dug past his well-built defenses and made him want to be a better man.

A man worthy of trust.

It must have been all that talk of "moving on" he'd had with Marc prior to their confrontation over Molly. He'd been missing Laurette so much, he'd ached inside.

Still shaken from the encounter, Trey desperately tried to call forth memories of the only woman he'd allowed in his heart since childhood. Instead, images of a beautiful, spitting-mad schoolteacher defeated his efforts.

Laurette's memory deserved his total devotion. He *had* to get Katherine Taylor out of his head.

But how?

What he needed was a diversion, something that would put his mind back on important issues.

Like the whereabouts of Ike Hayes.

Changing course, he crossed over to Fifteenth Street and headed toward the jail where Ike's brother, Drew, awaited trial. It was time to focus on serving justice the only way Trey knew how.

By his own hands.

Chapter Four

Drew Hayes's rotund body lay sprawled haphazardly across the lone bed in the back of the jail cell. With his jowls slack from sleep and his face full of belligerent beard, the outlaw looked like the animal Trey knew him to be.

A jolt of anger came fast and hard, filling Trey with such hatred, his throat burned from it. This man, *this outlaw,* had played a leading role in the murder of Trey's wife and child. The reminder brought a driving need to lash out, to end the life of the man who had stolen what was so precious to Trey. He had to brace himself against a nearby wall to keep from taking action.

Breathing hard and trying urgently to gain control over his turbulent emotions, Trey forced his attention to the window above Drew's bed. The rising moon glittered through the rusty metal bars, casting a thin ray of light that led from the cell door to the foot of Drew's bed.

Trey wanted to follow that path, and end the battle with a single bullet. But as he struggled inside the blinding haze of his hate, he knew he wouldn't do it. Drew Hayes didn't deserve such an easy out.

Motioning to the deputy on duty to join him, Trey lifted the keys off the hook and then turned to enter Hayes's cell. Once inside, he tossed the keys and a warning look at the other lawman.

"Stay close," he said. "And keep your ears open. I may need your testimony, if he talks."

The deputy nodded.

Forcing aside all emotion except uncompromising resolve, Trey moved deeper into the cell, kicked the leg of the bed. "Wake up."

The body stirred under the blanket.

Trey waited, watched, gauged.

Although the man had fifty pounds on him, without his brother, Ike, by his side, Drew Hayes was a coward. He'd proven that well enough when Trey had found him in Mattie Silks's brothel on Market Street. A few threats and a cocked pistol were all it had taken to bring the man into custody without a fight.

The easy arrest hadn't been the only surprise. Trey had expected a simple admission of guilt and a full disclosure of his brother's whereabouts. Drew hadn't talked.

"I want a word with you." Trey yanked the blanket to the ground. "Now."

The outlaw lifted his head. "I ain't talkin' to no law dog."

Leaning against the wall, Trey folded his arms across his chest and clung to the last scraps of his humanity. He forced all thought of Laurette out of his mind and focused only on the most recent murders, the ones he could pin on Drew with or without an admission.

"About the night of the twenty-third, on the McCaulley ranch…"

"I ain't answering none of your questions," Drew snarled, then launched into a string of obscenities.

Trey ignored the foul language and continued. "Was it only you and your brother that day?"

Snorting, Drew sat up, swung his beefy feet to the ground. "What do you care? It was just a woman and some snot-nosed kids."

A dark rage swept over Trey, one he hadn't felt since that night in Colorado Springs when he'd found the twisted bodies of Mrs. McCaulley and her boys. The unforgettable images of blood and brutal death were still clean and sharp in his mind. The fact that the Hayes brothers had done the same thing to Trey's wife and child added fuel to his fury.

In that moment, Trey knew that Marc was dead wrong. Trey didn't seek vengeance only for his own behalf. He sought justice for all the innocent victims murdered by the Hayes brothers.

"I'm gonna see you hang for what you've done," Trey said.

"I ain't afraid of you."

"You should be."

Drew vaulted off the bed.

In a heartbeat, Trey drew his gun and pressed it against the man's temple. Death was gunning for Drew Hayes. And in that moment it didn't matter to Trey how it came about, just that it came swiftly.

"All I need is a reason." His finger itched to pull the trigger. "Just one."

Palms facing forward, Drew inched two paces back toward the bed. "I don't want no trouble."

"Then start talking."

The outlaw's small, deep-set eyes narrowed into calculating slits. "I know your kind, Marshal. You ain't no better than me."

"We're nothing alike," Trey said, holstering his gun to punctuate his point.

"You enjoy killing, Marshal." Drew dropped to the bed, and a sinister grin glinted behind the dirty beard. "Same as me."

Black crept across his vision as Trey yanked Drew off the bed and wrapped his fingers around the outlaw's throat. "You and I aren't anything alike."

"Turn him loose, Marshal. You…"

Trey couldn't hear the rest of the deputy's plea over the sound of his own pulse drumming loudly in his ears. Nor did he pay much attention to the metal click of a key turning in the lock.

"Marshal Scott."

Trey squeezed tighter, and Drew's eyes began to bulge.

"Marshal. Stop."

The urgent yank on his arm finally got through to Trey. Slowly, deliberately, he loosened his grip from around Drew's neck, then launched the outlaw to the floor.

Drew flopped around like a dying fish, clutching his throat and wheezing in between coughs.

"Don't you ever compare yourself to me again." Trey turned his attention to the deputy. "I'll be back tomorrow. Make sure he's in a more talkative mood by then."

The deputy flattened his lips into a grim line. "You can count on it, Marshal."

Without looking back, Trey walked out of the jail.

Once he was on the street, a burst of cold mountain air punched through his black mood.

He felt dirty. Contemptible.

Vile.

Was Drew Hayes right? Was Trey more like the outlaw than he wanted to admit?

No. The need to protect, especially women and children, was deeply ingrained in him—as much a part of the reason why he'd accepted President Grant's appointment to the U.S. marshal post as to avenge Laurette's death.

All Trey had to do was think back over the events earlier in the day with five-year-old Molly Taylor. No matter how silly and foolish, he'd set out to defend a little girl who'd simply wanted a few more hours of play.

Didn't that make him better than the Hayes brothers?

Perhaps. But now, with the distance of time, Trey's reasoning told him that he'd chosen the wrong path to demonstrate his loyalty to the child.

Marc's accusations suddenly shot through his mind. Had Trey silently made a promise to champion Molly Taylor for his own purposes, even knowing he couldn't give false guarantees where the future was concerned?

At least he could right that particular wrong. First thing in the morning, he would set matters straight with Molly and Miss Taylor. Perhaps with the schoolmarm's forgiveness, Trey could erase some of the ugliness from his recent encounter with Drew Hayes.

Once she'd helped settle the other children and said all their evening prayers, Katherine returned to her sister's bed for a final good-night kiss. Pulling the blanket up to the child's chin, she tucked the corners underneath her tiny shoulders. "Pleasant dreams, sweetheart."

Big round eyes filled with childlike worry looked up at her. "You still angry at me, Katherine?"

Katherine dragged her sister into a fierce hug. "I was never angry *at* you, Molly. I was only upset with your behavior. I didn't set out to ruin your fun, but rules are rules."

The little girl rubbed a wet cheek into her shoulder. "I don't really hate you, you know."

Tightening her hold, Katherine dropped a kiss onto her sister's forehead. "I know."

Oh, Lord, make me worthy of raising this child. Help me to show her Your unconditional love so she'll turn to You when times get tough, or when I fail her.

With gentle movements, Katherine lowered Molly back to the bed. "No more worries, pumpkin. All's forgotten."

Molly swiped the back of her hand across her cheek. "Really?"

"*Really.* We're family. And now that God has brought us together, I won't ever leave you or let you go."

As Molly grinned through her tears, devotion brimmed in her eyes. "You're the best sister ever."

Katherine reached out and tweaked the upturned nose. "So are you, Molly."

"Night, Katherine."

Smiling, she leaned over and blew out the bedside lantern. "Night, Molly. I love you."

"Me, too."

Katherine quietly edged out of the room, then shut the door behind her. Tiptoeing toward the back staircase that led to the kitchen below, she offered up a silent prayer of gratitude to God. She and Molly had stumbled today, but they'd avoided any permanent rift.

No thanks to Trey Scott.

The U.S. marshal had gotten in the middle of a situation where he quite simply hadn't belonged. Perhaps his intentions had been honorable, but in the end he'd caused far more harm than good.

And not just in Molly's case.

Katherine stifled a shudder as unwanted memories of their latest encounter crept into her thoughts. If only he'd agreed to leave her sister alone, Katherine might have been able to keep her precarious emotions under control during their argument.

But he'd pushed and demanded explanations that weren't easily voiced. Then he'd stood too close. And she'd become unreasonably terrified.

During a moment of clarity, Katherine knew the man would never hurt her. Not in the way her attacker had. Then why was she so afraid of him? Why did she always feel the need to run whenever Marshal Scott got too close?

Even now, hours later, the humiliation of her panicky reaction dug deep.

Collapsing against the wall, Katherine shut her eyes against the shame that still burned in her. *No.* She wouldn't take the blame this time. Her uncomfortable reaction to Trey's nearness wasn't her fault. It was the legacy of her past. Nothing more.

In fact, her fear of Marc's friend was a small annoyance compared to the importance of maintaining stability in her life. Especially now that she had Molly's welfare to consider.

With renewed determination, Katherine marched

down the stairs, then pushed through the door leading into the kitchen.

The sight of Mrs. Smythe washing dishes at the sink improved Katherine's mood considerably. Tall, broad-shouldered and gray-haired, Mrs. Smythe was the perfect adopted grandmother for forty orphans—and one grown woman in need of a friendly face. Arranging a smile on her lips, Katherine greeted the other woman. "Good evening, Mrs. Smythe."

The older woman turned, her smoke-gray eyes sparkling with pleasure. "Hello, dear."

The housekeeper's affectionate reception warmed Katherine's heart, but after the events of the day, she found she wasn't in the mood for company, after all. "Why don't you go on home? I can finish the washing."

Mrs. Smythe's face cracked into a wide smile. "Are you sure? I certainly don't mind staying until I'm through."

Katherine nodded. "I feel like cleaning tonight."

Wiping her hands on the front of her skirt, the older woman let out a hearty chuckle. "Well, then, I won't ask again."

Mrs. Smythe hurried around the chopping block in the center of the kitchen, then gathered her belongings out of the supply closet. "I'll see you first thing in the morning."

"Night," Katherine said.

Just as the door shut with a bang, Laney waddled into the kitchen, carrying an armload of dishes. Avoiding her friend's eyes, Katherine took the stack of plates and set them in the soapy water. "I sent Mrs. Smythe home."

"I see that."

"Why don't you go rest, enjoy some time alone with Marc?"

Laney blew out a sigh of gratitude. "My feet *are* hurting, and I certainly won't turn down a quiet moment with my husband. I'll just bring in the rest of the dishes before I head upstairs."

"You don't have to do that."

"I want to."

All argued out, Katherine relented. "That would be a great help, thank you."

As Laney trudged back to the dining room, Katherine picked up a plate from the soapy water, grabbed a rag and began scrubbing. She tried to empty her mind of all thought, but images of Trey's stricken expression when he'd realized how frightened she was of him kept flashing through her mind.

Just thinking of the genuine remorse flickering in his eyes made her feel so...so...guilty.

Why did she feel as though *she'd* hurt *him* when she'd flinched from his touch?

"You're going to wipe the pattern right off that china."

Katherine jerked at the sound of Laney's voice. Looking over her shoulder, she let her gaze unite with her friend's worried expression.

"Are you all right?" Laney asked.

Sniffing, Katherine flicked the water off her fingers. "Perfect."

"You don't look perfect," Laney said, her gaze sharp and assessing.

Katherine took the stack of dirty dishes, then set them on the counter next to the sink, with a thud. "I've never been better."

Returning to work, she yanked another dish out of the water, spraying soapsuds into the air.

Laney wiped a bubble off Katherine's cheek, then laid a hand on her arm. "Did you argue with Trey again?"

Katherine increased the vigor of her scrubbing, her erratic movements sloshing water and bubbles onto the floor. "Trey and I always argue."

"Over Molly?"

"I told him to stay away from her."

Sliding a look from beneath her lashes, Laney fiddled with the dishes, stacking them largest to smallest. "He's good with her, you know. And with the rest of the children, for that matter."

Perhaps. Maybe. Okay, yes, he was good with the orphans.

It changed nothing. "Ever since he started hanging around here, he's disrupted my, I mean, *our* lives. Molly never defied me before today."

"It was bound to happen sooner or later. She's a child, after all."

Katherine knew Laney was right—to a point—but she also knew that her concerns over Trey's impact on her sister's well-being were valid as well. "He's too bitter. And his anger at God is tangible. I don't want the man's influence to result in Molly's unbelief."

Laney abandoned all pretense of helping and turned her full attention to Katherine. "I'll admit Trey can seem hard on the surface, but deep down he's a good man. And none of his anger shows when he's with the children."

Katherine swung around to glare at her friend. "Are you defending him?"

Throwing a palm in the air between them, Laney shook her head. "No. No. It's just that he's—"

"A U.S. marshal."

"Yes, that's right. And although he's not exactly godly, he is a man of high morals, sworn to protect the citizens of this country. All things considered, he's an acceptable example for the children, including Molly."

Katherine dismissed the notion with a flick of her wrist. "You know what I mean."

"Yes, I'm afraid I do." Laney lowered her hand, sighed. "It's his job to hunt down criminals, Katherine, including the men who murdered his wife and child. Maybe instead of condemning him, you could try understanding him better."

Clenching tense fingers around a plate, Katherine set her jaw. "Let's say I do find compassion for his lethal quest. What if he's killed in the process?"

"Oh, honey." Laney's eyes softened. "Not every lawman dies."

Katherine shook her head, refusing to let her mind go in that direction. "Trey Scott is the embodiment of instability. I don't want Molly getting attached to him."

"In case you hadn't noticed, she already is."

Katherine cringed over the statement, seriously concerned Molly wasn't the only one growing attached to the man. "Well, it's not too late to prevent any further harm. As long as he stays away from her, everything will be fine."

"Aren't you being a bit overprotective?"

Trey had used similar words against her. The accusation hadn't sat well with Katherine then, and it didn't sit well with her now. "Isn't that the role of a big sister?"

Laney gently pried the plate out of Katherine's grip.

Steering her to a stool, she forced her to sit. "I'm worried about you. You've been on edge a lot lately, and I think it has more to do with a certain U.S. marshal than your struggle to find your way as Molly's guardian."

Katherine tried to rise, but Laney placed a restraining hand on her shoulder. "It's time we talked about what's really bothering you."

"*Nothing's* bothering me except my concern over Marshal Scott's damaging influence over Molly's life."

Laney pressed her nose inches from Katherine's. "Why don't we get to the real problem? Shall we?"

"And here I thought we had."

A shrewd look filled Laney's gaze. "I think you should admit you have strong feelings for Trey Scott, ones that have nothing to do with your little sister."

Katherine shot off the stool. "That's ridiculous."

"Correction." Laney pointed a finger at her. "*Very* strong feelings."

Chapter Five

The next morning, Katherine exited Charity House with the notion of using work to alleviate her restlessness from the night before. Unfortunately, the crisp mountain air did nothing to shake her melancholy. Perched on the top step of the wraparound porch, she looked to the heavens and sighed. Large puffs of cottony white clouds drifted aimlessly against the deep blue sky.

If only she could be that carefree. But Laney's accusation about her feelings toward Marshal Scott had put dangerous thoughts into Katherine's head, making her want to cast off the chains of her past. To start a new life free of fear.

If only I deserved a second chance.

More agitated than before, Katherine trudged down the steps and started along the sidewalk that led from the orphanage to the Charity House School two doors away. The faint whinny of a horse in the distance had her looking up.

Realizing she wasn't alone on the path, Katherine immediately stopped in her tracks. Two ladies slowly approached from the opposite direction. They were dressed in beautiful tight-waisted dresses in identical shades of pink satin. With each graceful step, their skirts billowed over their dainty feet. They shimmered in the morning light, looking like purity personified.

In spite of her best efforts to remain calm, instant trepidation sprang to life. Katherine knew these women. She had seen the two sitting together with their families in church. They were either sisters or very good friends, but Katherine had failed to find out which because no matter how often she smiled at them, they never acknowledged her in return.

The reflex to rush back into Charity House came fast, nearly too powerful to resist. But Katherine was no coward. Thus, she held her ground and took courage in the last line from Psalm 31. *Be strong and take heart, all you who hope in the Lord.*

As the two drew nearer, Katherine lifted her chin a little higher. They studied her from under the brim of their feathered hats. Their gazes were unreadable but not overly antagonistic. Pleased the women hadn't snubbed her right away, Katherine smiled.

"Good morning," she said.

The taller woman grabbed the elbow of the smaller and pulled her closer, as though she were saving her from stepping in a cow pie. A snarled lip confirmed her disgust.

Katherine swallowed down the bile rising in her throat. A shiver slithered up her spine, and her hands started to shake.

Oh, please, Lord, not again.

Her prayer went unanswered. As one, the ladies lifted their regal noses in the air, snorted—they actually snorted!—and all but scrambled across the street in their haste to get to the other side.

Stunned, Katherine's eyes began to sting, and she had to fight a wave of hysteria as their pointed whispers lifted in the air.

"Tramp," one said to the other, menace dripping in her voice. "She's just like her mother."

"I heard she led that man on," came the harsh reply.

At that comment the women turned back and stared at Katherine from over their shoulders. From the measuring glint in their eyes, it was obvious they thought very little of her.

Katherine had experienced this sort of shunning often enough before, but the pain and humiliation were still sharp, like burning shards stabbing into her heart. For several heartbeats, Katherine stood with her head high and her breath stuck in her throat.

On her left, the Charity House School stood like a sentinel, offering sanctuary. Giving in to her humiliation, Katherine rushed up the steps and quickly fit the key into the lock.

Once inside the safety of the building, she leaned back against the shut door and gulped for air. Blinking away the tears in her eyes, she swallowed hard, again and again and again, until she had her emotions under control. Katherine would not allow those cruel women's barbs to hit their mark. Not today. Not ever.

At last her breathing evened out, and she wandered aimlessly through the rooms of the school. Unfortunately, and against her best efforts, Katherine's thoughts kept circling back to what the women had said on the street.

She'd led that man on....

No. It wasn't true. Katherine hadn't asked to be forced like that. All her life she'd kept her distance from men. They'd always scared her, a legacy from the ugly side of their nature, which she'd witnessed often enough in her mother's brothel.

And no matter what people claimed about her, Katherine would never have relations with a man, not willingly. Which made Laney's accusations about her feelings for Trey Scott all the more absurd. The man was too intense, too dangerous, and…and… Katherine had worked too hard to achieve normalcy in her life to give any man—especially a lawman with a death wish—the power to hurt her again.

With her head thick and heavy from her troubling thoughts, Katherine prayed for focus. *O Lord, be not silent. Do not be far from me.*

She looked around her and studied the safe world she'd created out of an incomplete education and necessity.

No man could hurt her here.

This was *her* territory. Her home. The one place where she had complete control. Each desk, book and writing tablet had been chosen with care. She and Laney had turned the two-story brick building into a reputable school for the children banished from all the others in town.

She and the orphans might be outcasts in the community, but they had a place of belonging here.

Katherine crossed to her desk and straightened a stack of papers that didn't need straightening. The fresh smell of soap and furniture polish told her Mrs. Smythe had indulged in some deep cleaning earlier this morning.

Strolling through her domain, Katherine released a sigh. Every detail reflected her taste for precision and order.

Admit you have strong feelings for Trey Scott...

Laney's words from the night before echoed through Katherine's thoughts. Taunting her. Mocking her. Far worse than any whispered attempts at hurting her with untrue accusations.

Frantic for some relief, she wove her way between the desks and trekked toward the supply closet in the back of the building. After lighting a lantern, she carried it with her into the dark, tiny room.

Katherine's trademark military-style order was reflected here as well. Inkwells, writing tablets and fresh sticks of chalk marched in straight rows along the lower two shelves on her left. More writing tablets were stacked on the upper shelves, along with rulers and other miscellaneous supplies.

Katherine set down the lantern and breathed in the comforting scent of books and paper. She ran her fingertip across the cold inkwells, and then along the smooth book spines. But even here, in her favorite refuge, thoughts of Trey Scott threatened her peace of mind.

What if she hadn't flinched from his touch? Would such a man ever be able to give her the genuine caring and devotion she secretly craved, in spite of what others thought of her?

She was only kidding herself with dreams of the impossible. No man would give her the love and respect that another, untainted woman deserved. Her attacker, and the subsequent response from the townspeople, had shown Katherine exactly what her value was in this world.

Anyone who trusts God will never be put to shame.

The verse from Romans swept through her mind, giving her the reassurance she sought. Ever since that dark night, Katherine had turned to God as her salvation. And she'd always found peace in His shelter.

His opinion was all that mattered. Today would be no exception. Instead of feeling sorry for herself, she would take a quick inventory of her supplies.

She focused her attention of the rows of *Michel's Geography* and *The Pilgrim's Progress* on her right. Looking forward to the mind-numbing task, she dropped to the floor and began counting the books on the bottom shelves first. She had to bend all the way over in order to reach the books nudged in the farthest back corner.

"Ten, eleven, twelve." She jabbed at the last one. "That makes thirteen. I'll definitely have to order more this week."

"Well, now." The familiar drawl dropped through the stuffy air and skidded down the back of Katherine's neck. "This is by far the most interesting sight I've seen all morning."

Katherine jerked upward and promptly thumped her head against the shelf above her. "Don't you know how to knock?"

A masculine chuckle was Trey's only response.

She tried twisting around but only managed to bang her head on the shelf again.

"Careful now."

She quickly flipped over, sat up and hugged her knees against her chest. Huddled in a tight ball, she had to look up—and up farther still—in order to bestow her indignation upon the man.

"Ma'am." He whipped off his hat and bowed. "Always a pleasure."

From her vantage point, the brute appeared more mountain than man. "Isn't there a rule or code or something against sneaking up on unsuspecting women?"

He lifted a shoulder. "Probably. But I think I skipped that day at lawman's school."

"You are a mule-headed—"

"Stubborn pig." A touch of mischief danced in his eyes. "Or so I've been told a time or two."

In this lighthearted mood, with his face clean-shaven and his hair damp on the ends, Trey Scott was far more dangerous than he had been the day before.

This time, however, she would not give in to her fear of him. She would *not*. The neighbor ladies had caught her at a weak moment this morning. Trey Scott would not be given the same chance. "You've only heard that once or twice?"

He laughed, the gesture swiping ten years off his features. She didn't like the way her stomach twisted in response. But from dread, or something else entirely? Disturbed by the direction of her thoughts, she dropped her gaze and instantly noticed he hadn't worn his guns.

Come to think of it, he never wore the six-shooters when he came around the children. The consideration for their safety made him infinitely more likable.

The big, heartless brute.

It was so much easier to control her emotions around him when he acted like the mule-headed, stubborn pig he claimed to be. But Trey Scott had hidden depths that

Katherine was only beginning to notice after their year-long, precarious acquaintance.

Oh, Lord, what now?

"Are you going to sit down there all day?" he asked.

"Are you going to prove yourself a gentleman and help me up?"

The aggravating grin on his face widened as he flipped his hat onto one of the desks behind him. "Ask nicely."

What gave Trey Scott the right to look so vital and handsome, like he was a hero out of a ridiculous dime novel? "Would you stop staring at me like...like... *that?*"

He rubbed his chin between his thumb and forefinger. "Are you taking a tone with me, Miss Taylor?"

His outrageous remark pushed her to stand on her own, but her foot tangled in her skirts, and she fell back down. "Oh, now look at what you've done."

He angled his head at her. "For a good Christian woman, you have a pretty mean temper."

"How absurd. Christian women get angry, too."

"Obviously."

She didn't like this teasing side of him. What had happened to the Trey Scott who couldn't go three sentences without arguing with her? *That* man she could handle.

"You can save the snide remarks, Marshal. And. Help. Me. Up."

The light from the lantern flickered off the watch fob dangling from one of his vest buttons, blinding her for a moment.

"I wish you'd turn around again." He drew out a long, dramatic sigh. "The other end didn't bite."

A seed of rebellion took hold of her. "Don't forget, a bee keeps her stinger in her behind."

His lips twitched. "Miss Taylor, I'm shocked!"

Panicked he might start laughing, and then get her started as well, she gave him her let's-get-down-to-business look. "Marshal Scott—"

"Right, right. Help you up."

Pushing from the wall, he reached out to her. Palm met palm, and...nothing. No fear. No terror. Just a pleasant warmth.

Then, when he shifted his hold slightly, all she felt in response was...

Contentment?

At that odd thought, a riot of confusion shot through her already addled brain, and she pulled on her hand. "Either help me up or let go."

"Right." With a flick of his wrist, he yanked her to her feet.

Quickly dropping her hand to her side, she took a careful step back and then straightened to her full height. Feeling remarkably out of her depth, she resorted to the one tactic that kept her on an even footing with the man. Antagonism.

"I don't know why you're here, but I refuse to continue trading insults with you today," she said.

He had the nerve to look shocked by her words. "Is that what we're doing? I thought we were getting on rather well. For us."

She took a deep breath. "Step back please. So I can pass."

His expression turned serious, concerned even, and he quickly did as she asked. "Of course."

Right. Now he had to be heroic and honor her fears,

like he had the day before in Marc's study. Did he know that when he acted like this, with such careful consideration of her feelings, his closeness didn't frighten her so much?

But, if that were truly the case, why were her hands shaking?

In an effort to hide her trembling fingers, she busied herself with brushing off her skirt.

"I'd be happy to assist." He peered around the side of her. "Unless, of course, you brought your stinger with you."

"You, sir, are outrageous." And the more he talked with that smooth Southern drawl, the more her uncertainty increased. "Maybe you should be on your way now."

"Don't you want to know why I searched you out?"

"Not particularly." But curiosity poked through her wish to be rid of him. "How did you know I was here?"

"I stopped at Charity House first. Laney told me where to find you."

She couldn't stop a small jolt of surprise from spreading into something more tangible, more pleasant. But reality set in just as quickly. Had the two ladies from her earlier encounter seen Trey enter the building? Would they think Katherine had set up a secret rendezvous?

No, she was being oversensitive because of their rudeness. Surely they'd been long gone by the time Trey had arrived. "You came looking for me?" she asked at last, suspicion digging deep. "Why?"

"I want to talk to you about Molly." As he spoke,

everything about him turned serious—his expression, his body language, even his tone.

Surprised by the change in him, and her intrigued reaction in response, she focused on ending their discussion as quickly as possible. "There's nothing more to discuss. In fact, it's all very simple—"

"Is it? I was under the impression it was—" he blew out a slow breath "—*complicated.*"

She started to push around him, but he evened out his weight, barring the exit. He seemed to fill every available space.

He looked too big, too casual, and for a brief moment, she feared he would attack. But instead of making her shake, or even tremble, the notion made her temper flare.

Finally, an emotion she understood. "Get out of my way."

A troubled look pooled in his gaze, and he scrubbed a hand through his hair. He shifted to one side, leaving a small opening for her, but he didn't move completely away. "Not until I've said my piece."

After his earlier consideration of her fears, she knew she owed him that much. "Go ahead then. Say what you came to say."

He nodded. "I was wrong to get between you and your sister yesterday."

"You admit it?" Katherine could hardly believe her ears.

"Yes."

Blinking at this newest change in him, she didn't know what to think. Trey Scott had just given her what she wanted.

So why didn't she feel any satisfaction?

"It's not personal, you know," she said, the truth finally hitting her. "It's simply that you can't offer Molly the stability she needs, especially now."

"You're correct. I can't make promises."

She suddenly wished he would. Because she sensed, all the way down to the last hair on her head, that if Trey Scott made a promise, he would keep it.

"I won't come around the orphanage anymore," he said.

Her stomach bounced to her toes. Now that he'd given her exactly what she wanted, she realized she wasn't sure she wanted it anymore.

In truth, she couldn't bear the thought of never seeing him again. "What about Marc?"

"I can visit with him during school hours."

He looked so sad, troubled, and she found herself no longer concerned about her own fears.

She reached to him and touched his sleeve.

It was his turn to shrug her off.

"Molly's your sister. Your word stands. I won't interfere anymore. However—" he commanded her gaze with a hard, unrelenting look "—you should know that I will not stop hunting Ike Hayes until I find him and bring him to justice."

Katherine sighed, realizing he'd missed the crucial point in all her arguments. Didn't he understand that it wasn't the hunt she feared, but rather Trey's motivation? "Seeking vengeance won't—"

"*That* is not up for discussion." His closed-off expression couldn't hide his pain.

Katherine shook her head, feeling as though she'd failed him and unsure why that thought hurt so much.

She didn't want him to walk away. Not like this. With nothing really settled between them.

But before she could plead with him to hear her out, he said, "You were right all along."

"I… I was?"

His eyes clouded over. "Men with badges die."

Chapter Six

Unable to sort through his chaotic thoughts, Trey shoved his own turmoil aside and studied the myriad of emotions that swept across Katherine's face at his declaration. Dread. Pain. Sorrow.

He wanted to offer her words of reassurance, to promise her they'd figure everything out for Molly's sake, as well their own.

But he couldn't lie to her now that they were starting to have an honest conversation.

"That's all I had to say." He reached for his hat.

"Stay." She gripped his arm. "Please. This isn't right. Can't we find another way?"

He shook his head at her. "You want me to forgive murderers, while I never can."

"Maybe not on your own." She dropped her hand and sighed. "But with God's help…"

"Don't you understand, Katherine? I don't believe in turning the other cheek. I'm Old Testament. An eye for an eye."

"Seeking revenge only hurts you, Trey, not—"

"Tell that to my wife, and all the others Ike Hayes has killed. Good, decent people."

Katherine lowered her gaze to her toes. "I'm...sorry. I didn't mean to make light of your loss."

"I know."

Now was the time he should walk away, but the unmistakable sadness in Katherine's eyes—sadness for *him*—touched the part of his soul he'd thought he'd buried with Laurette. Vengeance still burned in his gut, probably always would until he captured Ike, yet Trey didn't want to walk away without attempting to assure Katherine his anger wasn't directed at her.

With unsteady fingers, he touched her cheek, dropped his hand at her flinch. Why couldn't she trust him, even a little? "I know I argued the point yesterday, but like you, I don't want to put Molly through another loss."

She blinked at him but didn't respond.

He took a step closer, determined to set aside his own bitterness for a moment so he could help her understand. Katherine was courageous and good. She deserved a future free of the fear that still gripped her, the same fear that still held her captive after two years of living in the safety of Charity House.

With slow, careful movements he shifted the long black braid off her shoulder and sent it tumbling down her back. He couldn't help but notice how her skin stood pale against the slash of her arched eyebrows. "I don't want to hurt Molly any more than you do. In spite of what my actions might have said yesterday, I only want what's best for her."

An emotion he couldn't read wavered in her eyes before she covered it with a scowl. "Then we're in agreement. Now, if you'll excuse me, I have work to do."

"Not yet. It's time we had the rest of it out between us." He shifted his weight. "*All* of it."

Her clenched fists spoke of inflexible resolve. "Now is not a good time for me."

"Nevertheless, we're going to settle this. Not only for your sister's sake, but for yours as well."

And maybe even for his own.

Here, now, in the confines of the school's supply closet, Trey finally admitted to himself that he'd been moved by this woman and her painful past long before she'd brought Molly to live with her.

The discovery sat heavy on his heart. How could he have feelings for this woman when his hate and anger drove him so hard? How could he be drawn to Katherine when his only goal should be to avenge his wife's senseless murder?

How could he betray Laurette like this, even in the secret corners of his mind?

"Please." Her trapped gaze darted to the exit. "Can't we do this later?"

He nearly relented at the sight of her unconcealed dismay, at the wave of guilt that had begun to spread through him, but it was time they addressed the real problem standing between them. Without the issue of Molly or the little girl's future as a buffer. Without his mind consumed with his wife.

He reached to Katherine, brushing aside a strand of hair that had freed itself from the braid. "We have to work through this, before our antagonism explodes in some unforeseen way, and we do something *you'll* regret."

"Me? What about you?"

"I'm long past regrets."

Trey had told himself the only reason he'd sought out Katherine today was to tell her he would honor her wishes concerning Molly.

He'd been lying to himself.

Katherine Taylor awakened tender emotions in him he'd thought dead. She gave him a glimpse of who he used to be before anger and hatred had taken root. He wanted to teach her how to trust him, as a *friend* would trust another, and that all men didn't want to use her for their own selfish desires.

"I won't hurt you, Katherine. Ever."

He meant every word, but she stiffened anyway, and then shifted away from him.

Feeling helpless, foolish, he stepped back. Focusing on her fears helped him remember why they needed to work through this awkwardness between them. He tried another topic. "I know you and Molly shared the same mother, but you had different fathers. I also know how your sister's father died. But, tell me, Katherine, what happened to yours?"

Her closed, stony expression made him fear she wouldn't answer his question, but she surprised him. "He was a town sheriff, shot in the line of duty."

His stomach dropped, and he felt like he'd been gut-punched. Why hadn't Marc warned him? Now her worries for her little sister made more sense. "How old were you when he died?"

"About Molly's age. He left us with less than nothing."

"Us?"

"Me and my mother. It's why she turned to her scandalous profession." The look in her eyes explained more than her words. "Momma didn't have any skills. When the last of our money ran out, she did what she thought she had to do. Eventually, she started her own business and, well, you know the rest."

"You admired her."

Katherine started trembling, her eyes clouding over as though she was lost inside painful memories. "No. I wept for her. She was a strong woman, capable and resourceful. But because of the choices she made, she lived a bitter and lonely life."

He reached to her again.

She shrugged him off. Again.

"You escaped her legacy."

"Yes." Her face took on a faraway look. "I guess she knew what would happen if I grew up in her brothel, so she sent me to school back East. But I had to leave right before graduation and care for her during her illness. It was an honor and a blessing to share those final days with her, and to see her come to know the Lord."

He had to swallow back his own anger at the thought of Katherine leaving the safety of school, only to have a man violate her in the most vile way possible. "You truly believe returning home was a blessing, after what happened to you?"

"Oh, Trey." She gave him a serene smile, the one he'd seen her use on the smaller children when they were confused. "Despite all the tragedy, I eventually found my real home. Here at Charity House."

Her naive response swelled a primitive need to lash out. "Good doesn't always come out of evil. Look at Molly. Tell me, what good has come out of her loss?"

Katherine sighed. "God never promised us a life without adversity. But He gave us the strength we need to bear up under it. Molly may have lost both her mother and father, as I did, but she's not alone. She has me. We have each other, and we have our heavenly Father."

"How can you speak of God as though He cares?" Trey demanded, no longer thinking of Molly now, but of his wife.

She'd been a woman of faith, too, just like Katherine. However, God hadn't given Laurette the strength to face Ike Hayes and his rotten brother, Drew. Her faith had been grossly rewarded with unspeakable violence. "Look around you. God abandons those who care for Him most."

Katherine winced, but she didn't challenge him. Instead, she reached out and placed her hand on his shoulder. "If you give it a chance, healing will come with time."

She was wrong. Time healed nothing. At least not for him. Not until he caught Ike Hayes.

But maybe, *maybe,* the future could be different for Molly. She was just an innocent child, one who deserved peace in her life. And she'd get it, too. If he walked away now.

"I've been reckless with your sister." He placed his fingertips against his temples, his heartbeat coming fast and hard under his touch. "I'm sorry, Katherine."

"Do you know, until yesterday you never used my given name?" She wrapped her fingers around his wrist. "Say it again."

Foggy memories screamed at him to stop before it was too late. He ignored the good sense that told him to pull away; instead, he touched her cheek with a gentleness he didn't know he still possessed. "Katherine."

She tilted her head at him, smiled.

All thoughts escaped him. All but one. "Am I scaring you?"

"I..." She pressed her hand over his. "No."

She sounded shocked. Puzzled.

Amazed.

"Ah, Katherine." Slowly, he lowered his hands to her shoulders. "Do you know what's happening between us?"

"No."

"Neither do I." He started to pull her closer. "But I—"

"*Mr. Trey!* Whatcha doin' to my sister?"

At the sound of Molly's voice, resignation filled Katherine. She let out a choppy breath, drew in another, and then glanced into Trey's eyes.

He dropped his hands immediately from her shoulders. His expression gave away nothing of his emotions. In fact, his face was stark, fathomless, his gray-eyed gaze guarded.

Katherine gave him an exasperated look.

He sent her a small shrug.

"*Mr. Trey!* I was talkin' to you."

Trey gently pushed Katherine farther away from him, but he kept his gaze locked with hers as he answered Molly.

"I heard you, kitten." His lips curved into a slow, sardonic smile. "We were just talking."

Molly scooted around the back of Trey and then shoved between them. "Huh?"

Trey flashed Katherine a fearless grin and then lowered his attention to Molly. "What are you doing here, kid?"

Furrowing her brows, the little girl looked from Trey

to Katherine and back again. "Laney told us to come get Katherine for lunch."

Katherine's breath caught in her lungs. *"Us?"*

Molly pointed to a spot just behind Trey. "Me, Megan and Johnny."

Leaning to her right, Katherine groaned at the sight of the older children shifting from foot to foot. Both were looking intently at the ceiling, but their smirks told her that they knew exactly what they'd just interrupted.

Perfect. Two fifteen-year-old *witnesses.*

Trey's shoulders stiffened as he pivoted completely around. "Johnny, Megan, please take Molly back to Charity House. Kath—that is, *Miss* Taylor—and I will be right behind you."

Molly marched around Trey and parked two balled fists on her hips. "We can't leave 'less Katherine comes, too."

"Go on, Molly," Katherine said, squelching her sister's mutiny with a firm voice and firmer frown. "I need to talk to Marshal Scott. Alone."

The little girl stomped her foot. "But I wanna stay."

Trey stooped to Molly's height and then plucked at one of her braids. "We'll be right behind you."

Molly cocked her head. "Really?"

"Promise. And after lunch we'll finish our game of marshals versus the big bad bank robbers," said Trey.

Molly cocked her head at him. "Do I get to be the marshal this time?"

Trey nodded. "Of course."

"Well, okay." Molly skipped over to Megan, clutched the girl's hand and then looked at Katherine over her shoulder. "Bye, Katherine."

Katherine gave both girls a shaky smile. "Bye."

With a knowing grin, Johnny addressed Trey directly. "See you in a few...*minutes, Marshal.*" He wiggled his eyebrows but followed the girls out of the room without commenting further.

"Perfect. Just perfect," Katherine said once they were alone again. "Everyone at Charity House is sure to hear about this."

She's just like her mother. The woman's words from her earlier encounter echoed through her head.

Trey turned to face her then, his gaze impossible to read. Katherine didn't much care for the tug of unease that sped up her spine. Even before he opened his mouth to speak, she knew she wasn't going to like what he had to say.

"I guess this means we're getting married," he said, with a heavy dose of resignation in his voice.

Married? Katherine couldn't breathe under the weight of her confusion. How on earth had the man come to that conclusion? It took several seconds for her pounding heartbeat to settle enough for her to speak. "Pardon me?"

In the silence that followed, their gazes met and held. And held. And *held.*

Trey blinked first. "I didn't mean to put you into this predicament." He sighed. "Not only did three children catch us alone, but a passing neighbor or deliveryman could have seen me come in here."

"Maybe not," she said, a little too desperate, a little too shrill.

"Ugly talk, even unfounded, could bring trouble to the school. Or worse, yet another complaint against the entire Charity House venture." He darted his gaze around the room, speared his fingers through his hair, then gave a quick nod. "Under the circumstances, marriage is our best option."

Tears of indignation pricked in Katherine's eyes, but her pride refused to allow a single drop to fall. Her only defense was to drop a cold chill into her words. "Stop talking nonsense. Even if someone saw us and filed a complaint, it…"

She trailed off, realizing the trouble that could come to Marc and Laney. To Charity House.

No. They were speculating now. Nothing more. There hadn't been a formal complaint against the orphanage in well over a year. The probability of a renewed grievance was ridiculous. "Let me pass."

As though he'd forgotten where they were, his gaze flicked around. "Katherine, you must realize how sor—"

"Don't apologize."

He clamped his lips shut, but his unspoken remorse hung between them.

As the silence grew, a burning throb of shame knotted in her throat. For one blinding moment, Katherine had actually wanted him to hold her. Was she leading him on?

Why hadn't she tried to stop him?

As though hearing her silent chagrin, Trey looked deep into her eyes, winced. "Let me make this right for you."

She fought the disparaging echo in her head. Too late. Too late. Too, *too* late. A blast of sunlight chose that moment to spill into the room, blinding Katherine as it chased away the dark.

She started forward, but Trey's voice, melodious and smooth, stopped her. "Marry me."

Let your conversation be always full of grace, seasoned with salt, so that you may know how to answer everyone. Even as Paul's words to the Colossians echoed through her head, Katherine could only stare at Trey, a blank, lifeless sense of doom fisting around her heart. "No."

For the first time that day, he actually looked angry, as though she'd finally pushed him past his limit. "Why not?"

Refusing to allow his bad manners to intimidate her, she stepped back, stopping his approach by shoving her palms hard against his chest. "I shouldn't have to explain myself after everything we've discussed. I won't marry a man"

"Who wears a badge?"

She let her hands drift to her sides. "That's only part of it."

He raked a tender gaze across her face, but he didn't come any closer. "I'm not like the man who attacked you, Katherine. I *won't* hurt you."

As a slice of yearning clung to the edges of her resolve, her heart hammered out her words. "I know that."

"Do you?" he asked, gripping her shoulders again.

She slapped his hands away. "I don't think I'll let you paw at me anymore today."

He stepped back and waited until her eyes locked with his. "Marriage is the only way out of this. If we go to Charity House and tell the children we're engaged, word will get out quickly. If I was seen coming here, alone, all will be forgotten with the news of our impending marriage."

At the sight of the turbulent emotions in his eyes, a spasm of longing threatened her resolve. But nothing had changed between them, and although his argument had some merit, she wouldn't marry a man simply to stave off the mere possibility of trouble.

"We did nothing wrong," she said. "But you're right about one thing. We don't need any additional talk. If we're seen leaving together, the neighbors might not be kind in their estimation of the situation. You go first, out the back door, and I'll follow out the front after a considerable amount of time has passed."

His expression turned into stone. "I won't allow you to walk into Charity House with rumors flying among the children. You suffer enough of that in town."

"So this is some sort of misguided sense of gallantry? U.S. marshal Trey Scott saves the day?"

"No." He paused, hissed. "Yes. Maybe. I don't know. I hear how they speak about you and Molly."

"They?"

"You know who I mean. The gossipmongers." His gaze softened. "You and Molly deserve better than inaccurate rumors and nasty hearsay."

"They're words without substance. Anyone who knows me will know the truth of who I am and what I stand for."

"Some claim you're Molly's mother."

For a dreadful moment, Katherine's heart skipped a beat, and another. She'd suspected this but hadn't known for sure until now. Although Trey meant well, his desire to protect her through marriage was misguided at best. It wouldn't change the reality of what others chose to say about her or her connection to her sister.

"I've never worried about talk before. I won't start now. A marriage license would change nothing. I'm still the daughter of the most notorious madam in Denver next to Mattie Silks, and I'll always be a ruined woman in the eyes of the town."

He stiffened at her blunt words. "What about Molly? Do you want to teach her that cavorting in supply closets is acceptable behavior for an unmarried woman?"

His point hit its mark. For a moment, Katherine wavered on the edge of relenting, but then reality burst through the shield of her other emotions. "I'll simply explain the truth to her."

He speared his fingers through his hair. "You're being unreasonable."

"And you're suddenly the voice of logic here? You're offering marriage on the off chance someone sees us leaving together and will ultimately file a complaint with nothing more than conjecture to base it on. I won't stand here and hypothesize about a situation that may never happen." She shoved at him again. "Now let me pass."

His expression dropped into a frown as he shifted to his left and waved her forward. Tilting her nose at a regal angle, she sailed past him. But he caught her by the sleeve.

"Let me go."

"Not yet. You throw around words like *off chance* and *conjecture,* but you know I have a point. Give me one good reason why you won't marry me." Turning her to face him, he added, "Other than my profession, and I'll leave this alone until we know for sure if there will be any consequences over this meeting of ours."

Although his words were spoken in a firm tone, the masculine confusion that blazed out of Trey touched a hidden corner of her soul.

Katherine had a sudden urge to ignore her own fears

and take a crazy chance with this man. But she had someone to consider besides herself. And Molly deserved to know that a woman never had to settle for being second best, not even one with a ruined reputation.

"I can't marry you, Trey." Katherine swallowed hard.

"Because…?" he prompted.

She met his gaze without wavering. "*Because* you're still in love with your wife."

Chapter Seven

Later that afternoon, Trey decided to use work to rid himself of the painful emotions Katherine had awakened in him. How could she speak so boldly of forgiveness given the tragedies she'd suffered?

Where did that strength of faith come from?

And why did he admire her for it?

Disturbed by his train of thoughts, he charged up the steps of the newly completed Arapahoe County Courthouse. The smell of fresh varnish hit him as he entered the building. Italian marble floors reminiscent of the Capitol in Washington gleamed white and pristine in the late morning light.

The three-story building, by its regal existence alone, changed the look of Denver from a prairie town to an up-and-coming city. Important business occurred in this building, carried out by important people. The same important people Trey didn't especially want to see at the moment.

Increasing his pace to a significant clip, Trey avoided eye contact with the various politicians, lawyers and other civil servants he passed along the wood-paneled corridors. At last, he entered his makeshift office at the back of the building and slammed the door shut with a bang.

Thin rays of light slipped through the seams of the windows, creating little pockets of warmth in the otherwise austere room. One desk, one chair, countless stacks of papers and a thick layer of dust spoke of the respect Trey had given to his administrative duties of late.

Determined to keep his mind on business, he gathered the nearest pile of papers. But as he glanced down at the writing, the black script drifted into one unreadable blur.

Accepting defeat, he tossed the stack aside and gave his chaotic thoughts full rein. What had possessed him to confront Katherine Taylor this morning, alone, in the school's supply closet no less? It was bad enough two impressionable teenagers had witnessed their impromptu meeting. Anyone could have seen him enter the building alone and then exit after Katherine.

If they were looking.

Trey knew that some of Charity House's neighbors weren't exactly overjoyed at the notion of the unique orphanage in their high-class neighborhood. Several had filed complaints about excessive noise and other ridiculous offensives.

What would they do with a meaty scandal, unfounded or not?

He'd acted without a thought to the consequences. But there had been repercussions, in the form of two fifteen-year-olds who thought they'd seen more than they had. And nosy neighbors or not, if word got past those Charity House children, the town gossips would have more ammunition in their battle to destroy Katherine's already tenuous reputation. Would they go so far as to try to shut down the school?

What would happen to Katherine then?

Why hadn't Trey forced the issue of marriage, instead of allowing the mule-headed woman to walk away with nothing resolved between them?

You're still in love with your wife...

Trey's heart weighed heavy in his chest. Even after Katherine had brought up Laurette, Trey had been more concerned over the stricken expression on the schoolmarm's face than the momentary betrayal of his wife's memory.

Given the opportunity again, would he attempt to offer comfort to Katherine and alleviate her fears?

Yes. Yes, he would, because what had happened between them in that supply closet had nothing to do with Laurette or Trey's search for Ike Hayes. For a brief moment, and he assured himself it had been brief, Trey had allowed himself to forget his hate. He'd wanted to give Katherine a reason to trust again, and to help free her from the dark legacy of her attack.

His motives had started out pure enough, yet he'd hurt Katherine anyway. He probably always would. She needed a man unsullied of heart, less broken and certainly not consumed with hate. A man who loved and trusted God as much as she did. Trey, on the other hand, hadn't stepped inside a church since Laurette's funeral.

With that thought, he circled around his desk and dropped into the lone chair in the room. The leather and wood protested under his weight in the form of a succession of creaks and groans.

He tried to call forth memories of his wife, but his

mind kept straying back to a prissy, frightened school-marm who hadn't been quite so afraid this morning.

A jolt of satisfaction passed through him. For once, Katherine Taylor hadn't flinched from his touch.

As soon as the thought came, guilt and regret lashed into one another. Katherine's reputation could be irreparably damaged. If the neighbors had seen them, had put two and two together, there could be more trouble for her than a damaged reputation. Why wasn't she more concerned?

For one dark, dangerous moment, Trey considered charging back to the orphanage and shaking some sense into the woman. Of course, he still had the obstacle of a three-inch tin star to overcome.

Yes, he wore a badge. Yes, he could be killed in the line of duty, just like Katherine's father. But his usual, day-to-day duties were far from dangerous. The biggest problem besetting him this week was the accounting of monies he'd used in the past six months to run the courts.

He would much rather be out on the trail, pursuing bank robbers and other outlaws—men like Ike Hayes—but a small army of accountants at the Justice Department had started auditing his every expenditure. They'd gone so far as to deny his last request for additional funds to run his trials properly. Hence Drew Hayes's far too lengthy stay in the Denver jail.

So here he sat, keeping track of the money used by the court, instead of enforcing the law of the land. The biggest threat to him right now was a paper cut.

Loud, insistent knocking at the door ripped Trey out of his thoughts. "Go away."

Ignoring the command, Logan Mitchell pushed into

the room, hat in hand, a wary look on his face. Trey scowled at his deputy. With his blond hair matted to his head, the man looked more like a greenhorn rancher than a seasoned lawman. Trey knew better than to believe the deception. Logan was fast and accurate with a pistol. He was also smart, discerning and mean as a snake when it came to serving justice. The younger man reminded Trey of…himself.

"What do you want?" Trey asked.

"You got a visitor over at the jail, Marshal."

Trey picked up a random piece of paper and studied it intently. "I'm busy."

With his lips curling in distaste, Logan shifted his gaze to the papers scattered on the desk. "The audit?"

Trey bared his teeth in response.

Logan lifted a shoulder. "All right, I get the hint. I'm leaving. But I think you'll want to see this particular visitor."

Trey placed the paper on the desk, picked up a ledger and flipped open the front cover. Running his finger down one of the columns, he pretended grave interest in the declining numbers. "I doubt it."

"She asked to see *Mr. Trey.*"

The ledger crashed to the floor as Trey hurled himself out of his chair. He was around the desk in the same amount of time it took his heart to take a single beat. "You left her alone? With Drew Hayes in there?"

Logan took a step back, palms in the air, his eyes wary. "I'm not stupid. She's playing checkers with Sheriff Lassiter."

Nursing his anger at the thought of Drew Hayes within fifty feet of Molly, even if thick bars did separate them, he growled. "She's inside the jailhouse?"

"They're on the covered walkway out front. The sheriff set up two chairs with a crate in between."

Regardless of this new information, Trey's temper prowled like a hungry lion seeking to devour anything in its path. Right now, that meant Logan Mitchell. To keep from taking out the other man for the sheer pleasure of it, Trey clenched his jaw until his teeth started to ache. "She say what she wanted?"

"Nope."

Shoving his hat on his head, Trey headed toward the hallway.

Logan dropped a weary look onto the open ledger. "I guess this means you'll want me to stay here and work on balancing those numbers for you."

Already out the door, Trey looked back over his shoulder. "The bean counters in Washington can wait until I get around to it."

Logan grinned as he fell into step beside him, and the two wound their way through the maze of hallways. "I like the way you think, Marshal."

Deciding his temper needed an outlet after all, Trey sliced a glare at the other man. "Where are you going?"

"With you."

"You're not coming with me."

"I'm not?"

Trey held the pause for effect, then pulled his lips into a sarcastic grin. "You're going over to Mattie Silks's place to question her again about the night we found Drew Hayes in her brothel."

Logan's expression darkened. "We both know it's a waste of time."

Trey shrugged in response, increasing his speed once they were outside the courthouse and heading toward the jail. When Logan continued to walk alongside him, he pointed to his left. "Market Street is that way."

"I know where it is."

"Then why are you still following me?"

For the first time since he'd sworn the man in, Logan looked uncertain. "Come on, Marshal. That woman won't tell me any more than she has the past fifteen times we've questioned her. She'll probably start talking in circles again." He tipped his hat back and rubbed his forehead. "It makes my head hurt just thinking about it."

"Eventually, she's going to talk herself into a corner and reveal what we want to know. And one of us is going to be the man to get her there. Why not you?"

"Are you forgetting that Mattie hates me almost as much as she hates you?"

The frustration in Logan's voice was exactly the reaction Trey had expected, but he refused to relent now that the idea had taken hold.

"She likes you just fine." Trey slapped the younger man on the back. "Except when you're asking her questions about the Hayes brothers."

A defeated hiss whipped out of Logan. "You know, Marshal, what they say about you is true. You really are Beelzebub's cousin."

Trey's grin turned into a genuine smile. "Just be glad we're on the same side."

"Yeah, well, I have my doubts about that."

Ignoring the activity around him, Trey strode purposely down the busy streets of Denver's business district, en route to the jail. A steady stream of people meandered alongside him, their murmurs indistinguishable from one another. Determined to make good time, Trey clenched his jaw and bit into some of the grit kicked up from a passing carriage. A few unsavory types made an especially wide berth for him to pass. Sometimes a badge had its advantages, he thought, with a smile.

Still grinning, he swung around to his left and crossed the street. A group of well-dressed ladies stopped in conversation and simply stared at him in a gesture just short of rude. Undaunted, he tipped his hat as he drew near. They quickly looked away, whispered among themselves and then hurried off in the opposite direction.

Although Trey thought their behavior odd, his mind was too focused on other, more important matters to be overly concerned with the particulars of the brief encounter. Logan had assured him Molly was safely outside the jail; nevertheless, Trey increased his pace. Relief speared through him the moment he turned the last corner and caught sight of two heads bent over a checkerboard.

Slowing, he focused on the little girl in the crisp green dress. Her pitch-black hair gleamed almost blue in the sun, and one long braid hung down her back. She looked too young, too innocent, for the harsh setting of the jailhouse behind her.

Trey couldn't deny the truth any longer. Molly Taylor deserved every bit of the stability her sister wanted for her. The sudden craving to be the man to make that happen nearly brought him to his knees.

He wondered when he'd gotten in so deep. In his none-too-subtle way, Marc had recently claimed that Trey's affection for the kid was directly connected to his loss of Laurette and their unborn child. Granted, his friend might have been on the right track, but Trey's paternal feelings for Molly Taylor had grown separate and distinct in the past few weeks. A reprieve, of sorts, from his feelings of hate and anger.

Unable to catch a decent breath, he continued to watch as Molly considered her next move. She chewed on her lower lip, then picked up a black checker. Grinning up at the sheriff, she slammed her wooden playing chip on an empty square in front of him. "King me."

The grizzled old man shook his head and lifted his palms in the air. "I'm all out. Looks like you win again."

"Well, 'course I did. It's 'cause I's good."

"Won't argue with that." A twinkle danced in the sheriff's eyes. "Molly Taylor, you play a mean game of checkers."

Trey could only marvel at the change in Sheriff Lassiter. What had happened to the nasty curmudgeon, known throughout the West for his lack of tolerance of anything frivolous? Right now, his hard eyes actually looked…kind.

Closing the distance, Trey called out. "Molly? You wanted to see me?"

At the sound of her name, the little girl lifted her head. The moment her gaze connected with Trey's, her face broke into her hallmark gap-toothed grin.

"Mr. Trey!" She vaulted off her chair and, with a leap, launched herself into his arms.

Unable to deny the momentary pleasure he got from her childish devotion, Trey shoved aside the ugly emotions that usually resided in him and allowed the kid's glee to fill his heart. He wrapped her tightly in his embrace and breathed in her goodness. She smelled of soap and little girl and everything innocent. A swell of protective instincts, abrupt and violent, rose inside him.

She giggled, then pulled back. "Hi."

He smiled in return, wanting very much to be the man he saw shining in her eyes. "Hello, kitten."

Giggling again, she kissed him on the cheek, then squirmed out of his arms.

"I hurted my finger." Standing tall, she thrust her hand toward him. "See?"

Trey squinted. Taking her small hand, he arranged his face into a look of genuine concern and examined the tiny slit. "Looks like it hurts real bad."

"It don't really hurt no more."

Trey kept his expression serious, intent. "Well, that's a relief."

Little worry lines dug between her arched brows as she toed the wooden slats beneath her feet. "I have a loose tooth, too."

Trey had seen his share of stalling tactics to know when he was in the midst of some of the best. He stamped down his impatience and continued to play her game. "No kidding?"

She wiggled one of her remaining two front teeth with her thumb. "See?"

"I do, indeed."

Suddenly realizing there weren't any other Charity House children in the general area, he took a quick, covert glance down the street. "Are you alone, Molly?"

Skinny shoulders hunched forward. "Maybe."

Trey's gut flipped inside itself. If her trembling lips were anything to go by, trouble lay ahead. And there was going to be one ornery schoolmarm at the other end of it. "Does your sister know where you are?"

"No." She gave him a pleading look that tore at his defenses.

"But I gotta talk to you, Mr. Trey. Really, really bad. Katherine said I couldn't come see you." Molly sighed, then puffed out her chest. "But I came anyway."

A wisp of regret expanded into soul-deep guilt. Because of him, Molly had defied her sister. *Again.* He had to put a stop to it. Now. "Let's get you back to Charity House."

"But I came to—"

"You can tell me why you're here on the way back to the orphanage."

She looked ready to argue, but Lassiter chose that moment to break into the conversation. Clearing his throat, he cocked his head toward the jail and said, "Well, I'm heading back inside."

Molly shoved her hand forward. "Good game."

The grown-up, manly gesture had the older man's lip twitching. Taking her hand in his, he pumped it up and down. "It was. But next time you won't be so lucky."

"Yes, I will."

Lassiter patted her head. "I like your conviction, kid." He glanced to Trey. "Are we gonna finalize that date on Hayes's trial soon?"

Trey shared a look with the sheriff as he spun Molly toward the direction of her home. "I'll be back in an hour. We'll discuss it then."

"Right."

Molly slipped a wave over her shoulder. "Bye, Sheriff, see ya."

"See ya, kid."

Once Trey had Molly heading reluctantly down the street, he nudged her onto the planked sidewalk and pointed her in the direction of Charity House.

She scuffed her feet, digging the tips of her shoes into a wooden seam every third plank. "Mr. Trey?" she said, keeping her gaze focused on her feet.

He ignored the foreboding skipping along the base of his spine. "Yes?"

"Will you—" She broke off and sighed. "Will you…"

"Will I what?"

Throwing back her shoulders, she jutted her chin toward the sky and turned to look at him straight in the eye. "Will you be my daddy?"

Trey's heart lifted, then dropped. Swallowing the lump in his throat, he stopped walking and turned to look at her.

She shifted from foot to foot but held his stare, with a hopeful plea in her eyes. For a long moment, a cloak of silence enveloped them, broken only by the sounds of the people and horses milling about.

For one glorious second, he wanted to tell her that of course he would be her daddy, but he hadn't settled the particulars with Katherine yet. He still had to make the woman understand that this was more than a mere discussion of stability versus her reputation.

He was afraid talk had already begun. If an unsavory scandal was brewing, Trey knew it could affect far more than himself and Katherine.

Something had to be done. Soon.

"Ah, Molly," he said. "I'd like nothing better than—"

"Good." She threaded her fingers with his and grinned up at him. "'Cause I need two parents. And I want you most of all."

Her look of absolute hero worship frightened him more than her request. What if he let this child down? What if she came to harm because of him?

And what if he hurt Katherine in the process as well?

He hadn't been able to protect Laurette. What made him think it would be any different with Molly and her sister? "You have Katherine as your big sister. That's almost like a parent."

"No." She stamped her foot. "That's not good enough. She can be my momma. And you get to be my daddy."

"Kitten…"

Mutiny swept across her features. "Well, if you don't wanna, then I'll get Dr. Shane to do it. He likes Katherine. I know, 'cause he's always around the house and he smiles at her a lot and he said so when I asked."

Trey's heart rebelled at the notion of the good doctor marrying Katherine, sharing her smiles, her future. Her life.

The rush of sickening jealousy took root, the sheer power of it dragging air out of his lungs in an unpleasant wheeze. Dr. Shane Bartlett was a perfect match for Katherine, and completely, totally wrong for her. Trey suspected Molly might have continued speaking, but his own turbulent thoughts smothered her chatter.

Panic rushed blood through his veins, pounding one thought through his head. Although he wasn't sure he wanted to explore the subject too deeply, he couldn't let Katherine marry Shane Bartlett.

Eventually, Molly's words jolted him back to the immediate disaster at hand. "So whattaya say?"

Their gazes met, hers hopeful, his unable to focus. How could he become a husband and a father with Ike

Hayes still alive? Could he live within one set of parameters, for Molly and Katherine's sake, and still pursue the most important goal of his life?

"You haven't been listening," she accused.

He shook his head. "Sure I have. You want me to... to..."

"Marry my sister. Then you can be my daddy."

"I think we better slow down here."

She gave him a look that made him feel like the five-year-old instead of the adult. "We aren't walking, Mr. Trey."

"That's not what I meant. We need to think this through."

"What's to think about? Just ask Katherine to marry you."

"Let's say I agree to this."

The air around her crackled with pleasure. "You'll do it?"

"Now wait a minute. Aren't you forgetting that Katherine doesn't like me very much? *She* might not want to marry *me*." The thought made him unreasonably anxious.

Jamming her fists on her hips, she gave him another pitying look that had five-year-old tenacity clinging to the edges of it. "Well, then, you change her mind."

Doomed. He was doomed. He knew it with a lawman's instincts. The same innate reaction that had kept him alive in deadly situations told him it was too late to stop the inevitable now. No matter his drive for vengeance on Laurette's behalf, no matter how ugly his own life had become, Trey could not find it in his heart to let this child down.

Acting as though he still held a portion of the control, he carefully said, "If I agree to this—"

Molly's flushed words cut him off. "I knew you'd say yes."

"Now let me finish. *If* I agree, I'm gonna need your full cooperation."

Her eyes lit up. "I'll do anything you say. *Anything.* As long as you'll be my daddy."

She punctuated each word with a little swish of her shoulders, each movement solidifying his resolve.

"The first thing you'll have to do is stop disobeying your sister."

"Well…" She went perfectly still. "Okay. I guess."

"I want a solid answer out of you."

"Yes. I'll do it."

"And you're gonna have to let me do all the talking."

Her face scrunched into a scowl. "You think that's a good idea, Mr. Trey? She gets kinda, I don't know… upset when you talk to her."

Ah, there it was. The truth spoken so bluntly by the five-year-old had him second-guessing himself. Talking sense, logic—or even reason, for that matter—into Katherine Taylor might prove impossible.

Then again, perhaps it was time to stop thinking in terms of logic and reason. Perhaps it was time to consider alternative weapons.

Perhaps it was time to stop playing by the rules.

As he stared into Molly's eager face, Trey realized he still held a portion of the control. No matter her arguments to the contrary, Katherine Taylor would marry him. For all the right reasons, and maybe even for a few of the wrong ones.

"Just leave it all to me, kitten. I'll convince your sister she needs to become my wife."

"Really? How?"

"I have a plan." And this time, Katherine Taylor would not get the chance to walk away from him.

Chapter Eight

Once back in the safety of her room, Katherine changed clothes and then washed her face, never once allowing her mind to think beyond one task at a time. It was only after lacing up her boots that the shock finally set in. She sank slowly to the bed and then simply sat motionless, in a state of disbelief.

Holding back a sob, she buried her face in her hands, taking only mild comfort from the black solitude she found there.

She'd been caught in a compromising position, in front of Molly, no less. And although innocent enough on the surface, she and Trey had been caught alone—*alone!*—inside the school's supply closet. Katherine had always tried to remain above reproach, and not just for Molly's sake. In spite of the whispers, and the public shunning, Katherine held herself to a high moral standard for the benefit of Charity House and the school.

Which made the whole situation so much worse. In fact, if she and Trey hadn't been interrupted, Katherine could only wonder how far things would have gone.

What must Megan and Johnny think of her? Katherine was supposed to be an example to the children. She was not supposed to be some reckless woman who allowed herself to be caught up in the moment.

She pounded her fists into the bed, stood up and trudged toward the mirror hanging over her dresser. Studying her image for a long, breathless moment, she wondered why she didn't look any different than she had before she'd met up with Trey at the schoolhouse.

Where was the remorse? The humiliation?

The fear?

Pressing her palms against her temples, she prayed for sanity to return.

On that terrible night two years ago, her attacker had claimed she'd led him to believe she was a willing partner, simply because she hadn't told him to stop. And now, another man had nearly kissed her because she hadn't told him to stop.

She closed her eyes against the sting of tears.

Was she like her mother, as her attacker had viciously claimed in front of all the townspeople, a woman with carnal appetites that made a man force himself on her?

Her heart clenched.

No. She would not torture herself with such flawed thinking. No matter what her attacker had claimed, and what others said now, she'd been the victim that night.

Swallowing, she forced all doubt to the back of her mind and went to the Bible for solace. After flipping to 1 Corinthians, she quickly found the verse she was looking for in chapter ten. "God is faithful." She read aloud, "He will not suffer you to be tempted above that ye are able; but will with the temptation also make a way to escape, that ye may be able to bear it."

Unfortunately, God's Word only brought more trepidation. Just how much temptation could she stand around Trey Scott? How long before she…before he…before they…

No.

Appalled at her own worries, she set the Bible down and took to pacing. After what had nearly happened between Trey and her, she should be staying far, far away from him, and yet she didn't want to stay far, far away. Against all signs otherwise, she was beginning to trust the man.

And wasn't that ridiculous? Nothing was resolved between them. Trey was still a lawman. He was still in love with his wife. And he was still set on seeking vengeance by his own hands. If talk began… Well, they would deal with that when and if it happened. Katherine wouldn't worry about something that had yet to occur.

At least Trey had let her walk away from him this morning, even after he'd lectured her on her reputation and the consequences of their time alone together. Unfortunately, she'd recognized the look of unyielding determination in his eyes. He wasn't through with her yet.

If only he would…

Her breathing picked up speed.

If only he would what? What did she want from him?

Determined to get her answers, one way or another, Katherine took a deep breath and pivoted toward the door. She was a grown woman. A Christian. It was time she started acting like one.

My flesh and my heart faileth: but God is the strength of my heart, and my portion forever.

Fortified once again, she sailed into the hallway, marched down the stairs and out of the house. But the moment she turned toward town, her gaze connected with Trey and Molly laughing in tandem as they made their way down the lane, toward her. With the manicured lawns and perfectly sculpted hedges lining their path, the two looked like a real father and daughter journeying home from a day of play in town.

Katherine didn't have time to wonder why they were together before a swift jolt of pleasure took hold of her.

If only Trey wasn't as driven as he was to seek vengeance. If only he wasn't so bitter toward God. As things stood, he would never be able to provide the stability Molly needed—or the security that Katherine secretly wanted for herself.

Miserable and heavyhearted, Katherine shifted out of sight and watched the two interact. Molly stumbled, but Trey caught her before she fell and scooped her up into his arms. Raising her high in the air, he spun her around in fast, dizzying circles. The little girl's childish giggles united with Trey's deep, masculine chuckles.

Katherine's knees nearly gave way, and she reached for the railing to steady herself. Trey Scott brought out the child in Molly, the one Katherine had once feared didn't exist.

In those first few weeks after retrieving Molly from the mining camp, Katherine had fretted that the little girl was lost forever inside the frightening silence she'd wrapped around herself after her father's death.

How could Katherine have forgotten the role Trey had played in bringing Molly out of that dark world? He'd been the first person to make the child laugh. It had happened several months ago, during one of the infamous Charity House baseball games. Trey had just hit a home run, but instead of running the bases alone, he'd rushed to the porch, whisked Molly into his arms and taken her with him. From that day forth, Trey had found ways to include the little girl in other games, until she had taken to joining on her own.

Oh, how Katherine wanted to believe in Trey Scott. But she was honest enough with herself to admit that her own fears and her concern for Molly's future chased away any hope. The reality of his badge and what drove him to wear it wouldn't go away.

Molly couldn't handle another loss, and Katherine couldn't bear to watch the little girl close herself off from the world again. No matter how happy Molly and Trey looked right now, Katherine wasn't going to allow the man to stand in her way of protecting her little sister.

Trey chose that moment to look up. As though he sensed her confusion, his piercing gray eyes turned serious and intent, silently demanding of her the one thing she couldn't fully give him. Her trust. As he continued to hold her stare, her head started to pound. She wanted to run, to flee.

To him or *away* from him, she couldn't say.

Maintaining eye contact, he started advancing on her, his eyes communicating his resolve. Desperate to free herself from the power he suddenly held over her, she searched for a flaw in him. Just one. But she found only masculine beauty in his fiercely handsome features, arrogant scowl and bold swagger.

Katherine couldn't remember ever having been so aware of a man before. Was she more like her mother than she thought, after all? Was she a "tramp," like the ladies had claimed earlier today? Was there something deep inside her that wanted to explore the temptation Trey Scott presented?

Ridiculous. Absurd.

Shocking.

Determined to regain control over her emotions, Katherine forced her gaze to Molly. The look of guilt in the little girl's eyes put Katherine instantly on alert.

"Where have you been, Molly?" she asked.

Shifting her gaze to Trey, Molly drew her bottom lip between her teeth. "Um…with Mr. Trey?"

Katherine angled her head and waited for more, but neither man nor child felt the need to explain further. "I see."

Trey's lips pushed into a lopsided grin. "No, you don't."

Katherine bristled, ready to do battle, until she noted the hint of worry in his gaze and the twinge of some other, deeper emotion she didn't dare name.

"Run inside, kitten. I want to talk to your sister." Trey paused and looked meaningfully at the little girl. *"Alone."*

To Katherine's utter surprise, Molly instantly obeyed. "Okay, Mr. Trey. See ya later."

Trey tugged on her braid. "Bye, kid."

He waited until the door banged shut behind Molly before joining Katherine on the porch.

"I'm not sure I have anything to say to you right now," she said.

He removed his hat and gave her a grin that had her thinking about…well, things better left alone.

"Good," he said. "Because I'm not sure I want to hear what you have to say."

Astoundingly enough, fear of his touch wasn't her first concern at the moment. No, no, it was the possibility of future happiness with the man—or rather the *impossibility*—that frightened her now.

"What do you want from me, *Marshal?*" She made sure she put special emphasis on his job title, as much for her own benefit as for his.

He inched closer. "You're looking very lovely this fine afternoon, Miss Taylor."

She took offense at his far too late attempt to soften her with pretty words. "Charm won't work on me at this point in our relationship."

His boot heels clicked on the wooden slats as he edged around her, circling her like a dog with a particularly meaty bone. "Pity."

Feeling more than a little unbalanced, she decided not to argue the point. Yet.

He stopped behind her. "What? No clever reply this time?"

"I'm working on it."

He paced to the front of her. "I see you changed your dress."

She pursed her lips into what she hoped was a mixture of boredom and prim scolding. "I felt it necessary after you pestered me earlier."

"Are you claiming I acted against your will?" His words were barely above a whisper.

Katherine shut her eyes against the implication of his question, trying desperately to keep her thoughts in the present. But slowly, oh so slowly, her mind slid back in time to a place where a man *had* forced her.

The muscles in Katherine's heart tightened from the effort to stop the memories from overwhelming her. The effort left her breathless.

Panicky.

The other man had made her feel so dirty, while Trey

never, never ever, did. She shouldn't have let him believe otherwise, not even for a moment.

Feeling remorseful, she lifted her eyes back to Trey's. His stricken expression sent fresh guilt through her.

"Against my will? No. No, of course not," she rushed to say. "I didn't mean to imply otherwise."

He nodded, relief filling his gaze. "Then let's settle down and talk this through."

"Oh, Trey, the past few times we tried to talk, we didn't do so well."

He slid her an amused grin and then waved her toward one of the chairs. "So we get back on the horse and try again."

"I don't ride horses."

"Well, then." He tapped her lightly on the nose. "That makes it more likely you'll learn something here."

She bit back a flippant retort, annoyed as much by her shaky reaction to his nearness as by the arrogance of his tone. He had the insolence to smile at her again, and everything in her softened. "Don't, Trey."

"Don't what?"

"This is hard enough as it is." Resignation tripped along her spine. "Don't make me like you on top of everything else."

He touched her cheek. "Would that be such a bad thing?"

"The worst."

He dropped his hand and clenched his jaw so hard, a muscle jumped.

Realizing she'd insulted him, she shook her head. "I'm not making myself clear. Perhaps this isn't the best time to talk."

She started to turn, but he caught her by the arm.

"No, it's the perfect time. We… Let's start again, shall we?"

"Can we do that?" She had her doubts, for very good reasons.

He steered her toward one of the rockers. "We can try."

She scooted out of his reach and perched against the railing. "How do you propose we start again when we can't have a single conversation without arguing?"

"I'm confident we can do this. I'll start. By apologizing."

He took her hand gently into his.

"I don't think this is a good idea," she said.

"The apology or—" he dropped his gaze to their joined hands "—this?"

She quickly pulled her hand free. "*This* is the sort of behavior that got us into trouble earlier. Aren't you rather forgetting yourself?"

He made a deep sound in his throat. "Seems I always do when I'm around you."

"Well, in my estimation, that makes you *very* unpredictable."

His smile never faltered. "I certainly hope so."

Resisting the urge to smile back at him, she swallowed. *Slowly.* "Your charm isn't working on me."

"So you said already."

"Keep it up and I might say it again."

"You know, Miss Taylor, there is nothing worse than when a man is trying to be sincere and the woman is not."

"This is your attempt at sincere?" she asked.

"I'm trying, Katherine." He let out a slow breath,

his eyes slightly less haunted than usual. "I'm really trying."

She shut her own eyes against the intensity in his gaze, wishing she knew how to shut out the tender emotions trying to break free from her heart. "I won't marry you." She hissed, "I *won't*."

"I didn't ask."

Shocked, she whipped open her eyes and gaped at him.

He winked at her.

"You're a skunk, Trey Scott."

"Make no mistake, Miss Taylor. I'll ask." Masculine triumph narrowed his eyes. "When I'm ready."

With that pithy remark, he placed his hat on his head, turned and sauntered down the steps, never once looking back at her.

Although Katherine would have liked nothing more than to follow after the beast and kick him in the shins, a part of her was thrilled at the way he'd once again caught her off guard with his outrageous conceit.

And that frightened her far more than his touch.

Chapter Nine

Trey met up again with Sheriff Lassiter exactly one hour after leaving Katherine on the Charity House porch. The traffic was dying down on the street, but Trey hardly noticed. A stream of tobacco juice arced through the air and landed inches from Trey's feet.

"Nice shot, Sheriff."

Lassiter ignored him.

Dropping into the empty chair that Molly had occupied earlier, Trey tried to focus his thoughts on anything other than the stubborn schoolteacher who made his blood boil with irritation.

With a shake of his head, he banished the disturbing woman from his thoughts and turned his attention to Denver's notorious sheriff. Lassiter had pulled the wide hat brim over his weather-beaten face, the relaxed posture making him appear asleep.

Trey propped his feet against the rail in a gesture identical to the sheriff's and inhaled the sharp, spicy fragrance of a coming rain. "Surveying your domain, Lassiter?"

With two fingers, the sheriff pushed his hat back,

leaned forward and spat another rivulet of tobacco juice to the ground. "You get Molly home safe?"

"Yeah, she's back at the orphanage, probably causing trouble already." His tone reflected all the admiration he felt for the little girl, and all the frustration he felt toward the older sister.

"No doubt." After a moment of shuffling around in his chair, the sheriff leveled a measuring look at Trey. "So what did our little Molly want from you that couldn't wait until later?"

Trey lifted his gaze to the heavens. As the warmth of the day skidded behind threatening rain clouds, his mood turned the same dreary gray as the sky. "She just wanted to talk."

He didn't feel the need to add the particulars of their disturbing conversation, or to reveal the resulting clash he'd had with Katherine.

Lassiter dropped his feet to the ground, then leaned forward. "She came all that way, by herself, just to talk?"

"That's what I said."

Rubbing his chin between his thumb and forefinger, the sheriff slid a shrewd look at Trey from below his hat. "Molly's a pretty little thing. Already a charmer."

Why deny the truth? "I'd say."

Lassiter shifted the wad of tobacco around in his mouth. "She's a lot like her sister. Don't you think?"

Trey knew where the sheriff was heading, knew he should put a stop to it, but he didn't have the strength to fend off the attack. *"A lot."*

Even as he spoke the admission, Trey accepted the complexity of the task that lay before him. Katherine Taylor was proving far more difficult than he'd expected. All he wanted was to secure her good reputation and protect Charity House from a potential scandal.

Or so he told himself.

But, even now, as frustrated as he was with Katherine, he could feel the pull of attraction between them growing stronger by the day. He was drawn to the way she made him feel less anger. His need to strike out dimmed when he was around her. But Trey knew the feeling was only temporary. The hate was still in him, bubbling just under the surface, festering and spreading like a cancer. Driving him to hunt down Ike Hayes and make him pay.

"Do you want to talk about the big sister?"

"No."

Trey didn't even want to *think* about Katherine Taylor until he figured out what marriage to her would mean to Laurette's legacy.

One thing he knew for certain. When he focused on vengeance, he honored his wife's memory. So Trey would focus on finding Ike Hayes. He would concern himself with the schoolmarm later. "I'm setting Drew's trial for two weeks from next Monday."

Lassiter nodded, taking up the new topic with ease. "You got the okay for the money?"

Trey snorted. "I'm through waiting for the Justice Department to approve my request. I want this trial over, even if that means using my own money to make it happen."

"Too bad it ain't a double trial. Ike is the real brains of the operation. Drew's too stupid to have planned that raid in Colorado Springs all on his own."

Trey couldn't argue with the truth. Unfortunately, after his numerous conversations with Drew Hayes, he'd decided it wasn't family loyalty keeping the man's mouth shut. The outlaw didn't know where his brother was hiding.

"At least we have one of them in custody. That's gonna have to do, for now," Lassiter said.

Trey nodded. "It's something."

Out of the corner of his eye, Trey caught sight of his deputy trudging down the street. The man's shoulders were slumped in defeat.

Scuffing his heels as he walked, Logan wended his way around a horse and rider, a carriage, a mother and her small posse of children. With his head hung low, the twenty-year-old deputy looked like one of the Charity House children after a good scolding.

"Talking to that woman was a complete waste of my time," Logan said on a wave of disgust.

Trey held back a sigh of resignation. "So Mattie won this round, too."

"I'd have had better luck getting information out of a dead mule."

As Trey listened to Logan expound on the worst of Mattie's qualities, his mind sorted through various possibilities to get the tight-lipped madam speaking.

Rising in the middle of Logan's tirade, Trey slapped his hat against his thigh and turned in the direction of Market Street. The thriving red-light district between Eighteenth and Twentieth Street had been the source of great frustration in Trey's early days of marshaling. For weeks he'd fought a losing battle in his attempt to clean up the area. The community's tolerance, coupled with the politicians' blind eye to prostitution, had been too powerful an alliance to overcome.

Today, however, Trey was not on a moral errand.

This one was far more personal. He'd had enough of women running him around in circles. At least one of them was going to cooperate this afternoon.

"Hey," Logan called after him. "Where are you going?"

"Mattie's. It's time I explained to that ornery madam the value of female compliance."

A clap of thunder punctuated his words with an ominous clash.

Resolved to get his answers, Trey stood outside Mattie's brothel and considered the heavy double doors that led into the unremarkable two-story brick building. As though to mock him, the rain began falling in heavy sheets, making him impatient to be done with this filthy business. Without waiting for a response to his knock, he twisted the knob and pushed into the gaudy foyer.

Barely taking note of the decor, Trey continued forward, bypassing several pieces of furniture, including a red velvet divan.

Although it was still early afternoon, Mattie's brothel was full of customers. Trey ignored the men, warned off Mattie's infamous bouncer with a look and then trudged deeper into the activity around him.

The magnificence of this parlor house had always struck him as off-kilter with the rest of the world. The prostitution business did a solid trade in Denver, making madams like Mattie Silks among the wealthiest in town. As he continued to study the room and its occupants, Trey took special note of the women's painted faces and their expensive dresses, designed in the latest Parisian fashion.

Circling his gaze to the back of the room, he found Mattie in deep conversation with a notable banker in town. The woman, in all her theatrical glory, was his link to Ike.

Today she would talk.

Trey moved in between the woman and her customer, not caring that he was interrupting. "I want a word with you, Mattie. *Alone.*"

She didn't respond but instead chose to continue her conversation with her customer.

Trey took the opportunity to measure his small, blond adversary. Just like her brothel, everything about Mattie Silks was overdone. Her hair was too blond, her eyes were too large, and her mouth was too red. Born to live in the sensational, moment by moment, she struck a pose after every sentence she spoke.

Apparently, Ike Hayes had a taste for the dramatic.

The notion made Trey sick. "I won't ask twice," he said. "Cooperate here, or I'll haul you down to the jail-house."

With a studied toss of her blond mane, Mattie blessed him with a hard glint in her eye. "I've already dealt with one of your kind today. Perhaps tomorrow I'll recon-sider. But, for now, if you would please leave me to—"

"It's important." His tone made his point.

Her eyes went flat, the businesswoman gliding into place. "It'll cost you."

"I figured it would."

Mattie Silks might be a well-known madam who peddled the charms of her "girls," but she was also very shrewd. Money spoke louder than a smile, a handsome face or false words.

"Perhaps this will persuade you of the urgency of my task." Trey fit a fifty-dollar bill into her palm.

With a diminutive grin, she closed her hand around

the money, excused herself from her companion, then turned her full attention to Trey. With sugar dripping in her voice, she lifted an arched eyebrow. "Perhaps you would like to follow me, Marshal Scott?"

She led the way to her private sitting room.

Once inside, Trey shouldered the door closed behind them.

Mattie slipped the money inside a small compartment in her desk. "You've just purchased a full hour of my time. So what can I do for you, Marshal?"

Trey clenched his jaw. "I want answers, nothing more."

Mattie's gaze swept over him. "I never noticed how handsome you are, Marshal." She leaned forward and trailed a finger up his arm.

Trey didn't bother holding back a shudder of disgust. While he knew many men would be eager to sample Mattie's charms, Trey was not one of them. He suddenly craved Katherine's purity and goodness, to experience relief from the dark emotions that drove him to stand in this brothel and question this madam.

"Like I said before, I want information from you, Mattie. That's all."

Unfazed by his declaration, she looked him up and down, her eyes shifting with curiosity. "I know that glint in your eyes, Marshal. You've got a woman on your mind." She tossed him a pitiful look. "Not one of my girls, of course."

"Mattie, I'm warning you. This is not a conversation you want to have with me."

The madam relaxed into a pose and summoned a faraway look to her eyes. "Now, I know you're friends with that disgustingly noble Marc Dupree. And since Marc is, well, so noble and he's married to Laney—another disgustingly noble creature—it can't be her. So who else is there…"

Trey's head spun with fury, but he held the emotion in check. He could see she was enjoying the sheer drama of her game. He would not give her the satisfaction of knowing how thoroughly she'd hit her mark.

"That leaves…" She held the pause for a long moment. "Kath—"

"Don't finish that sentence, Mattie."

"Ah, but you see, Marshal Scott—" she shook her finger at him "—I've heard all about your shameless behavior with the not-so-proper schoolmarm. It's obvious there's more to the prissy Katherine Taylor than meets the eye."

As soon as the false accusations fled Mattie's lips, Trey's anger exploded—the silvery edge of it tearing away the rational part of him. Unable to speak, he clenched his fists so tightly, his knuckles burned like fire.

"I'll say this once," he managed through his clenched jaw. "Never speak about Kath—*Miss Taylor*—in that ugly tone again."

Hands on her hips, Mattie straightened, her eyes turning frigid. When she spoke, her voice filled with the harder side of the life she'd endured for thirty years—cold and nasty and vicious. "Like mother, like daughter." She waved her hand back and forth.

In one swift movement, Trey captured Mattie's wrist and held her firmly, but not tight enough to cause harm. "I'm through playing it your way."

She held his stare, her gaze as unforgiving as he felt, but Trey saw the flicker of fear just below the surface. He leaned forward, their noses inches apart. Familiar anger surfaced, driving him to reach up and yank the information out of Mattie. Instead, Trey directed the ugly emotion into his hard tone. "Where is Ike Hayes?"

"Changing the subject, are you?" Her voice held none of her fear, only cold contempt.

"I paid you good money, and I want my answers."

Her gaze cleared, then hardened as she slid the successful madam into place, a woman who had seen and done it all. For a price. "You won't find Ike through me."

Though he was revolted, and so angry he could barely see straight, Trey still pulled his lips into a grin. "Make no mistake, Mattie, I will get my answers." He let go of the breath he'd been holding and dropped her hand. "But not like this."

He turned, leaving her breathless and glaring. Opening the small compartment in her desk, he retrieved his money.

"Have you no shame?" she said, rushing toward him.

Stopping her pursuit with a look, he dug into his vest pocket and then tossed a coin onto the bed. "For services rendered."

Her glare spat fire, and her voice dripped with ice. "You've crossed the line, Marshal Scott."

Pivoting on his heel, he threw her one last, disgusted look. "It's not the first time."

He turned his back on her and yanked open the door.

"You don't want to make an enemy of Mattie Silks, Marshal. It's a mistake." Her bitter warning shot through the cold silence that had entered the room.

Trey treated her to one final withering glare. "And *you* don't want to make an enemy of me, Miss Silks. It's a bigger mistake."

Chapter Ten

Hours after leaving Mattie's brothel, Trey couldn't stop thinking about the woman, her lies and the ugly business she ran. His gut twisted in anger as he considered the kind of men who frequented the establishment, violent, immoral men like Ike Hayes, who stole life for the sheer pleasure of it.

Anger surged through him, threatening to consume him, but Trey tamped it down with a hard swallow.

How many of Katherine's childhood years had been spent in a brothel like Mattie's? How many times had she observed women taking money in the place of love and respect? How many lonely nights had she worried her own life would become the same as her mother's—only to have her fears realized when a former customer of Sadie Taylor's stole her innocence?

In that moment, the line between vengeance for Laurette and restitution for Katherine blurred in Trey's mind. He couldn't understand why God would allow such kindhearted women to suffer brutality. Apparently, there was no mercy in this cruel world.

Leaning back in his chair, Trey propped his feet on

the desk in front of him and speared a hand through his hair. Mattie had made it clear that talk had already begun about him and Katherine, just as he knew it would.

Well, Trey might not be able to right the wrong done to Laurette, at least not specifically, but he could correct the mistake he'd made with Katherine. Then maybe, *maybe,* he could alleviate some of his guilt over failing Laurette.

And regardless of Trey's past defeats, Katherine deserved freedom from her fear of all men, including him. If only he understood how she could cling to an invisible God that had abandoned her to a childhood inside a filthy brothel, a childhood that had ultimately led to one night of unspeakable violence. In spite of her personal hardships, she still held strong to her faith.

In that moment, he realized it was that very faith that drew him to her. Before meeting her, he'd been consumed with anger, driven by his hate and blissfully ignorant of the need for peace in his life. Marriage to Katherine Taylor might be just what he needed to start a new life.

But if he did talk the woman into marriage, what would it mean for his love for Laurette? Already, thoughts of his wife were becoming hazier and harder to grasp. In fact, he hadn't even thought of Laurette the past few times he'd been in Katherine's presence. If he found Ike and personally served up justice to the outlaw, perhaps then Trey could come to terms with Laurette's murder at last and move on with his life.

He exhaled a ragged breath. Because of his growing feelings for Katherine, he had not only betrayed the memory of his wife, but he'd inadvertently added further ruin to a fine woman's shaky reputation.

Well, he couldn't change the past, but he could right the future. It wasn't until after hours of hard thought that an idea finally materialized, one that just might work to convince Katherine to marry him.

Lack of sleep, Trey discovered, made him very smart.

Katherine woke from a fitful, dream-ravaged sleep. Squinting through the shadows, she dragged in a shaky breath and studied the clock on the mantel. Midnight.

Sighing, she tossed to her left, turned to her right, then rolled back to her left again. Unable to find a comfortable position, she huffed, kicked at the sheets, then set to tossing back and forth again.

She turned to prayer, whispering aloud a portion of the thirty-second Psalm. "O Lord, You are my hiding place; You will protect me from trouble and surround me with songs of deliverance. You…"

Unable to remember the rest, she tried another from Matthew. "Come to me, all you who are weary and burdened, and I will give you rest."

No matter how hard she tried to quote Scripture, she couldn't dispel the image of Trey Scott's tender expression as he'd taken her hand into his to show her a moment of comfort. He'd been so kind to her, so gentle, and Katherine never knew she could feel such…confusion.

Before Trey had come along, she'd been completely satisfied with a future dedicated solely to Molly and the other Charity House children. Security, comfort, love—those came from her heavenly Father. There was no point in wondering what other blessings she might find in marriage.

Sleep. She needed the blissful escape of sleep. But even the familiar sounds of the Colorado night couldn't soothe her. The rustling of leaves grated on her nerves; the insects chattering with one another distracted and annoyed. Of course, the fact that Trey's parting words still echoed in her ears didn't help matters, either.

Make no mistake, Miss Taylor, I'll ask...when I'm ready.

Pounding her fist into her pillow, Katherine barely stifled the urge to scream out her frustration. Trey Scott certainly had more than his share of audacity.

There was something alluring about a man who took what he wanted and then guarded it with complete conviction once he had it in his possession. That sort of caring made a woman feel safe, cherished.

With that thought, Katherine threw off the bedcovers and pushed herself out of bed. Gritting her teeth, she began to pace. With each step, she struggled against the awful notion that she'd lost an important battle before it had truly begun. Trey Scott might be a lawman. He might still be in love with his dead wife. And he might carry a driving need for vengeance that could one day destroy him. But he was also handsome and charming and had a way with Molly that truly amazed Katherine.

With a soft thud, something landed at her feet, drawing her attention from her troubled thoughts. She looked down at the object on the floor, leaning over at the exact moment a virtual onslaught of various colors, shapes and sizes rained through her open window.

Reaching to the floor, she picked up one of the... *flowers?* Before she could grasp what was happening, more followed. And more still, accumulating into a soft rainbow of color at her feet. Studying the blossoms, she noted that a scrap of paper hung from each of the flowers' stems. Trying to read one of the scribbled messages, she bent forward. But another batch flew into the window, pelting her gently in the head and shoulders.

As the flower assault continued, a wave of girlish giggles slipped out of her lips. She fumbled to the nightstand and quickly lit a lantern.

Picking up a random stem, she read the scrawled, nearly illegible message aloud. "Marry me."

Half dreading, half hoping to read the same message again, she chose another flower. "Marry me." She picked up three more. "Marry me. Marry me. Oh, and what's this? Marry me."

The protective shield she'd wrapped around her heart started melting.

Another batch of flowers shot through the window, followed by a loud whisper. "Katherine."

With something perilously close to a smile on her lips, she headed toward the window. Only to be hit in the face with a red geranium.

"Katherine, come out here."

Afraid to move, to breathe—and not quite understanding why—she stood frozen in place, staring numbly at the window.

"Katherine."

Realizing Trey's whispers were getting louder with each demand, she dodged another rapid-fire round of blossoms and rushed to the window. Leaning her head into the crisp night air, she locked gazes with her favorite U.S. marshal one floor below.

Whipping off his hat, Trey bowed. "Fair maiden."

When he straightened, his expression looked a bit worried, as though he wasn't completely sure of himself. And for a brief moment, the loneliness Katherine had held at bay all her life disappeared inside a painful hope that Trey Scott would become the man she wanted him to be.

She didn't want to disturb the magnificent picture Trey made with his hat in hand, and his smile flashing, but curiosity got the best of her. "What do you want, Trey?"

He bent down on one knee. "Marry me. Take my name as your own."

Ridiculous as he looked, she'd never been more charmed by a man. "You're going to wake up the rest of the house."

With an uncharacteristic lack of grace, he shifted to a standing position. "Then come out here and let me ask you properly."

She had an insane urge to rush outside and fling herself into his arms. "I don't think that's a good idea."

He lifted on his toes and leaned forward. "Then I'm coming up there."

"You wouldn't. *You can't.*"

He started toward the trellis. "I can, especially when my woman is being unreasonable and stubborn."

My woman? Katherine's pulse picked up speed, but she knew better than to read too much into his words.

Trey Scott had an agenda, coming here at this indecent hour. And it certainly wasn't a godly one.

Looking around to make sure they were still alone, she leaned farther out the window and lowered her voice. "Go home, Trey. We'll talk in the morning."

He wrapped his fingers around the bottom rung in front of him. "Looks like I'm coming up."

"No, you're not. You're going home."

He started to climb, missed his footing then started again.

Panicked that he might follow through with his outrageous threat, she said, "Stop."

He continued, made it halfway up the wall, wobbled a bit on a faulty slat then fell to the ground, landing flat on his back.

"Trey?"

No response.

"Trey."

Nothing.

"*Trey,* talk to me."

"I'm...all right."

"Can you move?"

He waved a hand in the air.

"Stay there. I'm coming down."

He immediately jumped to his feet. "I knew you'd see things my way."

"You tricked me, you beast."

"I guess this means I have to come up there, after all." He had the brass to look pleased.

"Stay there. I'll only be a moment."

Pivoting back to the interior of her room, Katherine lowered her gaze to the collection of flowers on the floor. Tears of hope welled in her eyes, mocking her attempt to remain rational. As hard as she tried to harden her heart, a wisp of a sigh rose from her soul.

She wasn't accustomed to romantic displays of affection. And, with a woman's instincts, she knew Trey wasn't accustomed to giving them. Which made his ridiculous flower shower all the more special.

No. She would not be moved by his calculated attempts to win her. Trey was a U.S. marshal, a man not only angry at God, but one who would abandon her and Molly each time he went to seek vengeance for his dead wife.

With that last thought, renewed determination dug deep. No matter what happened here tonight, Katherine had to get Trey Scott out of their lives.

She jammed her arms into her robe and quickly headed out into the hallway. She padded along the back stairs as quickly as she could without making any noise.

Releasing the lock, she opened the back door leading off the kitchen and collided directly into Trey. "Oh."

With one hand, he reached out, steadied her. "Miss Taylor, always a pleasure."

She glared at him, told herself she was too angry to notice how his gray eyes glinted like silver fire in the moonlight. Or how his hair shone dark as onyx. Nor did she notice how tall and handsome he looked with that devilish grin on his face.

No, she didn't notice any of *that.*

"Are you drunk?" she asked, more out of an attempt to gain equal footing than genuine suspicion.

"I may be a man with my share of sin, but that's one vice you won't pin on me." There was steel, hard and immovable, in his voice.

She'd clearly insulted him.

"Of course. I'm sorry. It's just so late. And you're so…*different* tonight."

He opened his mouth to speak again, but she crooked her finger at him. "Not out here. Come with me to where the neighbors won't see us."

He gave her a two-finger salute.

She ignored his arrogant attitude, squared her shoulders and set out at a clipped pace.

He dutifully followed behind her. Which put her instantly on guard. Trey Scott was anything but accommodating.

Once inside the house, he proved true to form. Shouldering the door shut, he said, "Marry me."

"No."

Angling his head, he spoke in that arrogant tone of his. "Did you like the flowers?"

Her heart flipped in her chest at his eager, almost boyish expression. He really was ridiculous, and a dear, dear man. Her defenses were quickly melting under his sweet attempt to woo her. A bit too quickly.

She had to catch her breath.

"Of course I liked the flowers, you big fool." She motioned to a stool sitting next to the chopping block in the center of the kitchen. "Now sit down and lower your voice."

He reached out and knuckled a lock of hair away from her forehead. "It seems, Miss Taylor, you've driven me to sneaking around in the dark. Don't you think you should try harder at saving my soul?"

She would not laugh. She would not laugh. She would *not* laugh. "I'm not taking responsibility for your tumble from bad to worse." She steered him toward the stool. "Now, sit."

He obeyed, then lifted a single eyebrow at her. "Bet I can change your mind about us."

Fighting the urge to smile at him, she put her best teacher glare in place. "Nothing you say could possibly make a difference to me."

He cocked his head. "Who said anything about talking?"

"You wouldn't dare. Not with the children upstairs.

Must I remind you that any one of them could come in here and catch us, like they did this morning?"

"Of course not." He threw his palms in the air. "I came only to talk. Really. You see, I've been thinking—"

"Imagine that."

He talked right over her insult. "I've come up with a brilliant reason why you have to marry me." He tapped his temple. "Got it all figured out."

"I'm running over with anticipation."

"Notice how I'm ignoring your sarcasm?"

Intrigued in spite of herself, she was careful to keep her tone neutral. "Mmm. So what is this brilliant reason of yours?"

"Molly needs a father." He shot her a triumphant grin. "And I think it should be me."

Katherine could only stare at Trey. He wanted to become Molly's father? *That* was the reason for his latest proposal? A strange sense of disappointment hung heavy in her chest, stealing her ability to breathe. Yet, a hidden desire kicked into life.

Oh, to have the opportunity to provide Molly with a complete family, to give her the life Katherine had never had, was tempting. Very tempting.

Needing a moment to gather her thoughts, Katherine started pacing.

"Think about it." Trey scrubbed a hand down his face. "We could provide Molly with two parents, a mother and a father."

She stopped midstride. "Oh, Trey. I—"

His eyes softened. "You'd make a wonderful mother."

For a dreadful moment, as Trey stared at her with that tender expression on his face, Katherine wondered

what his child would look like. Black hair, gray eyes—
a hidden wild streak.

No. No, no, no. This was the exact kind of thinking
that would lead her to make a dreadful mistake. They
weren't evenly yoked. And even if Trey mended his
anger at God and became a practicing Christian again,
he didn't want *her* as a wife. He loved Laurette, sought
her killer with such passion, there could be no room in
his heart for more.

Yes, he wanted Molly as a daughter. She didn't doubt
that for a moment, but on his terms. In the end Trey was
a man who would always put revenge for his dead wife's
murder ahead of everything else. Katherine would do
well to remember that part of the equation.

"I'm predicting we'll have an early snow," she said.
"What do you think?"

He rose. "I didn't come here to discuss the weather."

She slid a glance over her shoulder, her breath catching in her throat again. The man looking at her now
knew what he wanted. And possibly even why he
wanted it.

Which made little sense. As far she could tell, the
only thing Trey Scott *wanted* was vengeance. Right?

"I was giving you a chance to get this insane notion
out of your head," she said at last.

"Marry me."

"Let's see if I can make this simple enough for you
to understand… *No.*"

"But Molly—"

"Is perfectly happy at Charity House. She's not alone
here. There are forty other children sharing this home
with her."

"You're forgetting the moral implications in the matter." He strode closer. "You're the schoolmarm."

"Yes." She dropped her gaze to her shaking hands. "For abandoned children of prostitutes."

His eyes narrowed, becoming more determined than ever. "All the more reason to keep your reputation clean of any more ugly talk. I find it necessary to remind you that not everyone in this neighborhood wants Charity House to thrive. They could use a scandal of this nature, as unfounded as it may be, to shut your school down."

Her heart skipped only a beat at his words, but the sensation was sharp and fierce. "I have to trust God will protect us from such an occurrence."

His mouth dropped open. "You can't possibly be that naive."

"Believing that God will provide does not make me naive. It makes me—" she poked him in the chest "faithful."

He simply stared at her, his eyes wide.

"It does," she insisted.

Still staring at her with unblinking eyes, he slowly shook his head. "You were caught cavorting with a man in the supply closet of your school. At best, people will merely talk. At worst, they could try to shut down your school."

"Oh, Trey. Laney and Marc would never let that happen."

His chin lifted at a stubborn angle. "People will say you did things you didn't do. I can't live with that."

Cupping her palm on his cheek, she gave him a patient smile. "I didn't know you were such a prude."

"Having a firm set of ethics and morals when it comes to how people treat you does not make me a prude." He pressed his forehead against hers for a moment, then pulled back and took two steps away from her. "Let me make you a respectable woman. Let me give you the honor you deserve."

The sincerity in his tone nearly had her relenting, but then she remembered his devotion to his dead wife, the passion in which he pursued her killer, and Katherine doubted his words. Besides which, marriage would solve nothing between them. "No."

"Don't you want to be a good example for the children? For Molly?"

"Of course, I do. But, Trey, it's not like we were, well…you know."

"That doesn't matter." He shook his head. "No, actually, it makes it that much more imperative that you do the right thing. You have to lead by example, Katherine, especially in the seemingly small matters."

If only it were that simple. "In case you have forgotten, I'm the daughter of a prostitute." This time she raised her hand to stop him from interrupting. "Though I attend church every Sunday, my faith is always in question. And I will always be Sadie Taylor's daughter."

He winced but continued staring at her for a long moment, measuring. Gauging. "You're afraid."

She swallowed back a gasp, wondered at his meaning for only a moment before denying the absurd accusation. "No, I'm realistic."

He stepped forward, stroked his hand down her hair in an affectionate gesture. "I won't intentionally hurt you, Katherine. Marry me, and let me show you that I know how to treat a woman like you, a woman who deserves nothing but kindness from a man."

"I… I can't. And you know why." She didn't want to

bring up his dead wife again—it would hurt them both too much—but she would if he continued pressing the issue of marriage.

As though hearing her thoughts, he placed his finger on her lips. "I won't give you words I don't have, but I promise I will take care of you and Molly."

Be on your guard; stand firm in the faith…. As the Scripture from 1 Corinthians came to her mind, tears threatened. "And if you die? How will you take care of us then?"

He reached out to her, dropped his hand when she shook her head at him.

"It always comes back to that, doesn't it? I might live for vengeance. But you live in fear. Where's your faith?"

"Don't turn this back on me," she said, quickly closing her mind to the possibility that fear, and not logic, fueled her resolve.

"I won't force you to do anything you don't want to do. And I mean anything. We can have a marriage in name only, if that's what you want."

His soft, understanding tone set her on edge. Why was he being so nice, so caring and thoughtful of her fears? Why couldn't she trust in his consideration for her feelings?

Because, deep down, in a place shattered by violence, she didn't believe she was deserving of any man's kindness, especially this man, who only meant to offer her compassion. She was tainted, ruined. And Trey Scott deserved better.

He deserved a woman who wouldn't shy away from his touch.

Without looking at him directly, she turned to go. "Goodbye, Trey."

"We're not through, Katherine," Trey said, his voice barely above a whisper. "Don't leave now that we've come this far. Stay and fight."

She took the coward's way out. "I…*can't*."

Pivoting, she released a sob and ran from the kitchen.

Chapter Eleven

One week after the incident with Katherine in the Charity House kitchen, Trey stood outside the jailhouse and eyed his surroundings. The buildings lining the street cast long shadows on the pocked mud, indicating the end of another day.

As he pondered his next move with the stubborn Miss Taylor, the only outward signs of Trey's irritation came in the fast, rhythmic ticking of his pulse and the white-knuckled grip he wrapped around the railing in front of him. Otherwise, he stood unmoving as he watched the sun sink into a long finger of reddened clouds in the distance.

A cool breeze whispered across his face but did little to soothe his frustration. The swift spasm in his gut warned him time was running out, and here he stood, contemplating the sun and the sky and the breeze. Yet as hard as he searched for possible options to the problem of Katherine Taylor, not a single solution materialized.

The stubborn, willful schoolmarm had successfully thwarted his efforts to court her this past week. How was he supposed to honor his promise to protect her from the repercussions of ugly gossip when he couldn't even speak to her? He certainly didn't want her to find out from anybody but him that he was leaving town again.

How he dreaded *that* conversation, especially since he knew his departure would work against him in his bid to win her hand in marriage. Why couldn't Katherine accept his need to settle the past in the only language Ike Hayes understood? Violence for violence.

The end was drawing near at last. Trey felt it deep in his bones. And he would rather have Katherine on his side than fighting him every step of the way. Resisting the urge to charge over to Charity House half-cocked, he concentrated on thinking up a new plan.

Unfortunately, nothing came immediately to mind. Going to Marc for help was out of the question. The man was Katherine's friend. And Laurette's brother.

Laurette. Trey sank into a chair behind him and spread his thumb and forefinger across his brow. After knowing what marriage to Katherine would mean to Laurette's memory, he'd been so consumed with devising a plan to get the schoolmarm to marry him, he hadn't thought of his wife nearly often enough.

Even now, when he tried to visualize her in his mind, the image blurred fuzzier than before, wavering further out of his reach.

He didn't want to forget Laurette. As though to torture him further, a vivid memory of her wrapped in his arms and bleeding to death emerged out of the previously foggy images. Would he always be haunted by the memory of the day he'd found her alone, shot and frightened?

Familiar guilt reared. If he could relive that last day,

he'd handle events differently. He would never have left her with only two hired hands to protect her. It was small comfort that he'd balked at leaving her, but she'd been eight months with child. He couldn't have taken her with him, and he couldn't have stayed. The snow was coming, and they'd needed supplies for the winter.

While Trey had been gone, Ike and his brother had come looking for horses or money to steal. They had found neither and had killed for the sport of it.

Blinding rage overwhelmed him. Trey rose and slammed his fist into the railing. Welcoming the shards of pain that spread up his arm, he tried to clear his mind of the painful images of that day four years ago, but the memory wouldn't let him go.

The moment Laurette had died, Trey had vowed to find Ike Hayes and make him pay. Four years had passed, and Trey still hadn't extracted justice. Nothing would change the fact that he had failed to protect his wife. For that, he would never forgive himself. Not until Ike Hayes paid with his life. And whether Katherine understood his quest, whether she married him or not, Trey would hunt the outlaw.

The pounding of footsteps yanked him brutally out of his thoughts. "Marshal Scott, you gotta come quick."

Trey dropped his gaze onto one of the older Charity House orphans. "What?" A dark, ugly fear knotted into a hard ball of panic. "Is it Katherine? Molly?"

"No." Bending at the waist, Johnny slapped his hands on his knees and sucked in gulps of air. "They're fine."

Trey exhaled. However, before he could fully settle into his relief, Johnny's next words sent soul-gripping dread through him. "It's Laney. She's having her baby."

"It's a month too early."

Johnny nodded. "I know. Dr. Shane told me to come get you right away."

"Is she—"

Apprehension filled the kid's expression. "It's Marc. Every time Laney screams, he goes for Doc's throat—" Johnny broke off, took several deep breaths, then stood upright. "We need you to help us hold him off."

Knowing how much Marc loved his wife, Trey could only imagine the battle waging at Charity House. "You were right to come get me."

As Trey started for the stable, Johnny sent him a quick, impatient look. "No time for saddling horses. We gotta go now."

"Right." Trey slammed his hat on his head and broke out in a run for the orphanage.

Johnny followed hard on his heels.

As his feet conquered the distance between the jail and the orphanage, Trey silently prepared himself for chaos at the end of his destination. Rounding the last corner, he nearly barreled over a woman walking her tiny dog. Muttering a quick "Pardon me," Trey rushed up the front steps and burst into the front parlor of Charity House.

The deadly stillness struck him first.

Afraid to consider what the silence meant, he counted almost forty boys and girls of various ages sitting throughout the room. Their unnatural calm knotted a greater sense of dread in his gut.

Was it over then?

Molly broke from the pack and rushed to him. "Mr. Trey, don't let Laney die like my momma did."

Her fear was palpable, glittering in her eyes and throbbing in her voice.

Quiet moans of agreement hummed from the rest of the kids.

Forcing assurance into his voice, Trey picked up Molly, kissed her tearstained cheek, then said, "Nothing's going to happen to her with Dr. Shane here."

"But it's taking too long," said Molly.

Trey hugged Molly tightly against him, then caught Johnny's gaze. "How long?"

"Hours."

The declaration seemed to shake the rest of the kids out of their grim silence. Forty voices rose with questions, their words coming fast and incomprehensible.

Hoisting Molly onto his hip, Trey attempted to speak over their clamor. "Everybody, calm yourselves. She's just having a baby."

One of the orphans poked at him. "But that's how my momma died."

Another one added, "Yeah, mine, too."

Trey wanted to alleviate their fears and tell them they were speaking nonsense, but death in childbirth was a reality even he couldn't deny.

Molly placed a palm on each side of his face and forced him to look at her. "Whattaya gonna do to stop it, Mr. Trey?"

Her unrelenting assurance that he could actually make a difference shook him into action. "Don't worry, kitten. Dr. Shane is the best in town. He'll take good care of our Laney."

A loud crash came from the upstairs, followed by a string of oaths that threatened to blister the wallpaper right off the walls.

Trey set Molly to the floor.

"I think I better make sure the doctor can do his job."

He planted an emphatic smile on his face, then looked at each of the children. "I'll find out what's happening. Then I'll be back."

Taking the stairs three at a time, Trey charged toward the back room where the swearing grew louder, more pronounced. Unsure what he would find, he swallowed his uneasiness, then rushed into the room without knocking.

The heat hit him first, followed by the smell of sweat and fear. Concern lay heavy and thick in the air, wrapping around his throat and squeezing like a noose. Gasping through a deep breath, Trey circled his gaze around the room until he found the doctor and Marc in a contest of wills. The young doctor, Shane Bartlett, had his sleeves rolled up and was trying to push Marc away from him.

Marc pushed back, his chest puffed out, his eyes wild and unfocused. "I'm warning you, Bartlett. Don't let her suffer anymore."

The doctor's tired, red-rimmed eyes flickered with frustration. "Then move aside and let me work without obstruction."

Marc settled into a wide, feet-planted stance. "You leave my woman alone."

"I'm trying to help her!"

Knowing far too well what that stubborn look on his friend's face meant, Trey raised his voice. "What can I do to help?"

Marc answered for them both. "Stay out of this, Trey. Unless you want a fight, too."

Ignoring the threat, Trey looked around the rest of the room. Careful to avoid glancing at the bed, he focused on Katherine as she stood off to one side, turning a wet cloth over and over in her hands.

Her hair had come loose from its braid, cascading in a black curtain around her face. Lines of fatigue rimmed her eyes, but she managed to smile at him. The simple gesture transformed her face, making her look as though she were actually happy to see him. His heart warmed at the thought, but then she angled her head toward Marc and mouthed the words, "Do something."

Trey took a step forward, but then his gaze landed on Laney, lying in the bed. He'd purposely avoided looking at her, and now he knew why. Sweat poured down her face, her eyes glazed over in pain. Instant fear rose in his throat, and he took a quick, reflexive step back.

Was God going to take another woman he loved today?

Until that moment, he hadn't realized how much he cared for Laney. She was like the sister he'd never had, and he didn't want her to die. Yet he knew there was nothing he could do to help her at this point.

He shot her an apologetic grimace.

Laney gave him a watery smile in return, then buckled over. "Give me one of your guns, Trey."

"I don't think that would be a good idea right now," he said, surprised his voice came out as steady as it did.

She panted through what looked like a spasm of pain. Grinding her teeth together, she leaned back into the pillows and growled, "I said give me a gun."

Diverted from his fight with the doctor, Marc rushed to his wife's side and knelt beside the bed. Brushing her hair away from her face, he tried to soothe her with words. "It's gonna be all right, honey."

"Take your hands off me, Dupree." She took a deep

breath, then angled a glare at Trey. "I mean it, Marshal. Give me your weapon. Now."

Marc shared a look with Trey, then turned back to the bed.

"What do you want it for, baby?" Marc's voice wavered with concern.

She sneered at her husband. "To shoot you, of course."

Marc visibly cringed. "I'm sorry, Laney. I'll never touch you again."

Doubling over in agony, she let out a pain-filled holler. "No, you won't."

She ground out more words of condemnation between pants and screeches.

Feeling utterly helpless, Trey turned to Katherine for guidance. But she wasn't looking at him anymore. Her eyes were on her friend as she moved forward, lowered her voice and began whispering instructions into the other woman's ear. "Come on, Laney," she urged. "You have to breathe. Slowly, now."

"Leave me alone," Laney moaned. "I don't want to breathe. *Arr.*"

Katherine shuddered, but her voice came low and even. "That's it. Breathe through the pain."

Laney screamed instead.

Katherine knelt beside the bed and began praying in a soft, convicted voice. Didn't she know her efforts were useless? God couldn't possibly be listening.

But a part of him, the part that still had a shred of hope left, wanted to join Katherine in prayer. Or at least believe her efforts weren't in vain.

Paralyzed into immobility by his conflicting thoughts, Trey could only admire Katherine's calm strength. With each of Laney's pants, she continued to soothe her friend while praying for peace and relief.

"Laney, let me help you," Marc said, his eyes glazed over with a panic Trey felt as well.

"You've done enough already," Laney yelled at him.

Letting out a hiss of frustration, Marc jumped up and gripped the doctor by the neck. "Make it stop, Bartlett."

Dr. Bartlett swung a pleading look to Trey. "Get him out of here, will ya?"

Laney chose that moment to scream again.

Marc released the doctor and whipped back around. But before he made it to the bed, Trey reached for him and physically yanked on his shirt collar. "Let's go, my friend. This isn't a place for either of us."

Dr. Bartlett let out a quick, agitated sigh. "Thanks, Marshal."

Just before Trey turned to go, Katherine looked up and gave him a grateful smile. Within her eyes resided all the words neither had been able to say to one another. He hadn't realized how much he needed this woman's smiles, her softness. How much he needed the comfort he always felt around her. Warming to the notion, he pushed his lips into an answering smile, and a moment of quiet understanding passed between them.

As though sensing Trey's lack of concentration, Marc twisted and broke free of his grip. He rushed back toward the bed, but Trey moved faster. He grabbed his friend by the arm and clenched him with the force of a man used to dragging unwilling criminals into custody. "You need a break, old man."

"I'm not leaving my wife," Marc growled.

"Yes. You are."

Marc struggled, using his strength against Trey's.

Normally, they'd be evenly matched, but Trey was fresher and less emotional. After only a moment of pushes and tugs, Trey won the battle and shoved his friend toward the door. Before he left the room, he caught a glimpse of Katherine and Dr. Bartlett leaning over a basin together. The two worked without speaking, but there was a silent accord between them, a meshing of movements that indicated years of working side by side in a sickroom.

Trey shut his mind to the sudden urge to slug the good doctor and focused on maneuvering Marc out of the room. This was not a time to remember Molly's suggestion—or rather, threat—that she would ask Dr. Bartlett to marry her sister if Trey would not. Nor was it a time for… Was that jealousy he was feeling? Or was it envy for the camaraderie the two shared?

Either way, Trey wasn't going to explore the shocking emotion any further. At least, not while he had an unreasonable, panicked father-to-be literally thrashing in his grip.

By the time he'd wrestled Marc to the bottom of the stairs, the fight had left the other man completely. Satisfied he'd won the war, Trey released his hold. But then Laney let out a scream, and Marc's muscles bunched. He made it up two steps before Trey caught him again and yanked him back down. Tired of the game, Trey slammed his friend against the wall and pinned him there, with a restraining hand against his chest.

"Calm down, Marc. You aren't helping anyone with this behavior. The kids are petrified."

Marc jerked forward, but Trey hurled him back into the wall. Shifting his gaze up the stairs, Marc sighed. "Yeah, well, I know the feeling."

Trey took his friend by the shoulders and shook him. "Get hold of yourself. The children need to see everything's going to be all right."

Marc stared at him with an empty expression but stopped fighting.

Trey blew out a hard breath, then called out over his shoulder. "Hey, Johnny, I need you to come out here."

Johnny sped around the corner, nearly clipping his shoulder on the wall.

"Take Marc into his study. I'll be right behind you."

With his face draining of all color, Johnny looked at Marc, then back to Trey. "Not a chance."

"Don't worry. He'll cooperate. If he doesn't—" Trey glared hard at his friend "—I'll knock him out."

Another scream from the second floor sliced through the air. With the strength of three men, Marc broke out of Trey's grip. Down to his last tactic, Trey wrapped his fingers around his friend's throat. "Take another step and I'll make sure you're out cold for the rest of the day."

Marc glared back at him. Trey kept his feet poised, prepared to stare down his friend for however long it took to communicate his message.

"I think you mean it," Marc grunted.

Curving his lips into a fixed smile, Trey nodded. "I do. And at this point, Laney would congratulate me for it."

Marc glanced up the stairs.

"She's in good hands," Trey reminded him. "Let Katherine and Bartlett take care of your wife."

Trey shut his mind against the fact that Katherine was in that room with the young, handsome doctor, the two working side by side, sharing the miracle of birth…

No, he was being absurd. He had to focus on his

friend, not some petty, selfish jealousy that didn't have any place here.

With his shoulders slumped, Marc bared his teeth. "When this is over, I'm taking you out."

Trey grinned. "You're welcome to try."

Mumbling that it would be his pleasure, Marc stomped off toward his study. With a nudge from Trey, Johnny followed at a good distance behind.

Chapter Twelve

Trey waited until Marc rounded the corner before letting out the breath he'd been holding. After taking several more gulps, he turned in the opposite direction and entered the large parlor. Forty pairs of eyes locked with his. The look of solemn despair he saw staring back at him cut through the thin fabric of his confidence.

These children recognized the yells coming from upstairs for what they were—the sounds of a woman in the grip of a dangerous, perhaps even deadly, situation.

Molly tore herself out of one of the other girls' laps. "Is she gonna live?"

Trey lifted the little girl into his arms. "She's doing just fine. A little tired, but she's tough."

A bloodcurdling scream nearly lifted the roof off its rafters. Molly buried her face in Trey's neck. "She don't sound so very tough."

Trey patted her on the back, smiled at the others. "The hollering is a good sign. Means the baby's healthy."

At least, he hoped so.

Realizing he had to get all of their minds off what

was happening upstairs, he looked to the oldest girl. "Megan, why don't you take everyone outside and organize a game of—"

"Baseball. That's Laney's favorite."

"Excellent idea. Choose up teams, and I'll see if I can get Marc to join you outside."

Trey tried to set Molly down, but she wrapped her spindly arms around his neck in a tight grip and sobbed. After a few seconds of prying, he gave up. "I'll just keep Molly with me for now."

One by one, the kids trooped outside, looking as though they were about to face a firing squad instead of heading out to play. Their calm acceptance tore at Trey. Like him, these children had learned that life was unfair, and that loved ones often died before their time.

How could he help anyone have faith when he had so little himself? Doubt filled him, and his breathing picked up speed. Trey knew about hate, he knew about vengeance and anger, but what did he know about being a parent?

As though he could physically protect Molly from the harsher realities of life, he hugged her hard against him, then looked up to find Mrs. Smythe watching him.

"What can I do to help?" she asked. Her voice sounded brave, but Trey knew from the look in her eyes that she was eaten alive with worry.

"Can you keep an eye on the children for us?"

She nodded. "Of course. And I'll make sure they eat something later. So, is Laney—" she cocked her head in the general direction of the stairs "—all right?"

Molly whimpered into his shoulder. Trey gently rubbed the little girl's back as he spoke. "I think so."

Making sure he spoke in generalities—for Molly's

sake—he gave the housekeeper details of what he'd seen in the room upstairs.

"Well, sounds like everything's right on schedule," she said, relief hunching her shoulders forward. "I'll handle the children from here."

Trey nodded, then went in search of Marc.

He found his friend standing by the window in his study, staring at nothing in particular. Johnny stood against the wall on the other side of the room, shifting from foot to foot and looking miserable.

"I've got it from here, kid," said Trey. "The rest are outside, starting up a game of baseball."

Johnny's eyes lit with satisfaction. "I'll be the umpire."

Trey nodded. "Good idea."

Once they were alone, Trey was unsure what to say to alleviate Marc's fears. They lived in a harsh world where good women sometimes died.

Struggling to find words of assurance he didn't have, Trey moved to the center of the room and sat down in one of the two wing-back chairs. He shifted Molly so she could sit more comfortably on his lap, then spoke softly to the little girl. "It's going to be all right, kitten."

Marc turned, focused his gaze on Trey, then dropped it to Molly. Grimacing, he trudged over and ruffled the little girl's hair. "You scared, too?"

Molly's lower lip trembled as tears rolled down her cheeks. "I don't want her to die."

Marc flinched. "Me neither."

Trey lowered a kiss to the top of Molly's head. "She'll be all right." He commanded Marc's stare. "Laney's strong."

Marc spun on his heel and started pacing through the room. "I should *never* have touched her."

Trey recognized the absurdity in his friend's remark. "It's the way of husband and wife. Regret now is useless."

With a sigh, Marc glanced out the window, turned on his heel and tossed his large frame into the chair next to Trey's. He shut his eyes a moment, crossed himself and then looked toward heaven. "Dear merciful God, please protect my wife. Bring her through this safely."

Trey wanted to say his own prayer, but it had been so long. Would God still hear him?

Please, God, don't take Laney, too. Not today. Not yet.

For a prayer, it wasn't much, but it was all he could manage.

Molly patted his hand and then settled back against him. Trey hugged her a little tighter than before.

After a while, the screams slowed, then eventually stopped altogether. Unfortunately, the ensuing silence was far more frightening than the previous confusion and chaos had been. As the time continued to tick forward, with no word from upstairs, Trey's mind drifted to the little girl who sat unmoving in his arms.

So much trauma for one so young. Too much death.

How could he be responsible for adding to her agony? And yet, how could he just walk away now?

Wouldn't that be just as bad?

Molly relaxed her head against his shoulder and eventually dozed off. The moment Trey shut his own eyes, she stirred. With the resilience of youth, she hopped off his lap and grinned. "I think I'll go play now."

Trey waved her on her way. "Have fun, kitten."

Just as Molly left through one door, Katherine burst through the other. She slanted Trey a quick, unreadable look, then turned to Marc.

The other man jumped out of his chair. "How is she?"

"Exhausted, but fine." Katherine glided over to him and patted his cheek with affection. "Now go meet your daughter."

Marc slapped his fist into his palm. "A daughter! Did you hear that, Trey?"

"I certainly did."

Grinning like a little boy, Marc darted out the door. Seconds later his footsteps pounded up the stairs.

Katherine sighed after him. "I never thought I'd see the day when that man panicked like he did this morning."

Trey rested his hand on her shoulder. "He loves his wife."

Katherine turned back to him, tears swimming in her eyes. "And she loves her husband."

Now that he was finally alone with her, Trey had much he wanted to say, but all he could think about was how beautiful she looked in the fading light of the day. A tender feeling clutched his heart as he took in Katherine's disheveled appearance.

Without thinking too hard about what he was doing, he pulled her into his arms and held her tightly against him. "You did good work today."

After a moment of hesitation, she sighed and relaxed into him. "God was in the room, guiding us all."

He didn't know how to respond to that, so he merely stroked her hair, reveling in her warmth, her strength. "You were amazing. So calm."

"Thank you, Trey. But let's not forget, you played an

important role as well." She rubbed her cheek against his shoulder. "Confusion ruled until you arrived."

"I'm glad I could help."

She chuckled. "I don't know how you managed to get Marc out of the room."

"Simple." He tightened his grip. "I used brute force."

She let out a long, happy sigh—one of those contented sounds that grabbed a man's heart and twisted. For a second time in a week, she hadn't shied away from him. Was she beginning to trust him?

Stepping back, she stared into his eyes. "Laney asked for you, too."

Knuckling a black, meandering curl off her cheek, he said, "First we should talk. Katherine—"

She pressed her fingertip against his lips. "No, Trey, not yet. Later. We'll talk later. This is Laney's moment, not ours."

He nodded and followed her up the stairs. Once they were back in the room, the tender mood of husband and wife immediately drew Trey's attention. They sat together on the bed, smiling down at the bundle between them.

Marc looked up first and motioned him forward. "Come on in, Trey."

Trey hesitated, struck impassive by the change in his friend. Cradling an armload of squirming blankets, the other man looked as contented as Trey had ever seen him. Marc Dupree had come a long way from the hardened man obsessed with making money, even at the expense of his own happiness.

The startling transformation gave Trey a glimmer of hope that he, too, could change in time.

"Take a look at my daughter, old friend." The pride shining in Marc's eyes was unmistakable.

Trey edged closer, but with each step, a strange feeling of loss and a sense of new beginnings wrestled against one another inside him. With heavy steps, he maneuvered around the side of the bed.

Laney smiled up at him then, her eyes radiating peace and joy. Even in her exhaustion, she looked lovely. It was hard to reconcile this new vision with the desperate woman who had wanted his gun a few hours earlier.

Still grinning, she nudged her husband with her shoulder. "Let Trey hold her."

Marc pulled his arm from behind his wife. Holding his child with both hands, he lifted her toward Trey. "You have to hold her like this."

He demonstrated by cradling the baby in one arm and cupping a palm beneath the impossibly tiny head.

Hands trembling, Trey stepped back. "She's too small. I'll hurt her."

Laney chuckled. "Any creature that can put me through that much torture is not as fragile as she looks."

Reluctantly, he took the child, careful to support her head just as Marc had shown him. At the feel of the gentle weight in his arms, a tangle of emotions locked together in his throat, then sank to his gut and churned.

He'd spent the past four years focusing on death. Now, as he held this perfect little creature, he knew he stared into the beautiful face of life.

"She's perfect," he said, noting the mahogany hair, upturned nose and long lashes. "Looks just like her mother."

He studied the infant further, taking in the stubborn tilt of the baby's chin. "*And* her father."

Marc peered over Trey's shoulder, placed a hand on the tiny head. "We're naming her Laurette."

Unprepared for the declaration, a pall of bleak silence trudged across Trey's soul. He couldn't stop the tears from pooling in his eyes, didn't want to stop them.

Blurry-eyed, he looked down into Laney's smiling face. "Are you sure?"

She nodded her head at him, answering tears falling quickly down her cheeks. "God has blessed us with this new life today, and because of His generosity, there's no other name I would want for her."

"Thank you," Trey whispered.

Marc clutched his shoulder. "This is for all of us, my friend. It's time we started looking ahead, instead of behind."

Trey swallowed, unable to wrap his brain around the notion. But then blue, unfocused eyes blinked up at him, and the pain in his chest slowly subsided, as though the grip of grief that had clutched his heart for too many years was finally loosening. Just a little.

The baby gurgled at that moment. Inside that tiny sound, the past separated from the future, leaving only the joy of the moment.

Was it truly time to let go and look ahead?

Drawn by a force he didn't quite understand, he turned and linked gazes with Katherine. She smiled at him, her beauty heightened by the tears and acceptance flickering in her eyes.

In that moment, Trey knew he had to try.

Chapter Thirteen

Katherine didn't belong here. This was a moment for family, and as much as she'd like to think she was part of this tight-knit clan, she didn't have their shared history.

Feeling like an intruder, she shifted her gaze around the room. She caught sight of Dr. Bartlett looking at her, staring at her, really. He quickly broke eye contact, turned to watch Trey holding the baby, and then, just as swiftly, looked back at Katherine with such curious intensity in his eyes she felt a sudden urge to run.

Dr. Bartlett had never made her feel uncomfortable before. She took it as her cue to leave the room.

With careful steps, she silently slipped out of the room and closed the door behind her. Knotted muscles caused her to wince as she staggered down the hallway. Drawing in a shuddering sigh, she stepped into her own room, calmly shut the door, then collapsed against it. Ugly, bleak loneliness dug deep, throbbing in a painful rhythm within her chest.

She knew she was being selfish. She should be helping Mrs. Smythe with the children, not wallowing in her sadness. Yet her feet wouldn't budge.

Leaning her head against the door, she squeezed her eyes shut. Unfortunately, there was no sanctuary to be found behind her lids.

She shouldn't be disturbed by the emotions she'd seen in Trey's eyes. Loss, acceptance and finally *love*. She'd witnessed a man beginning the process of letting go of the past. But now that he'd taken the first step, she was suddenly terrified about what the end result would mean to her.

Was she holding back from him because of his badge? Or was it a deeper fear? Was she afraid he'd compare her to his dead wife and find her unworthy? Did she fear his rejection more than his abandonment?

Faith is being sure of what we hope for and certain of what we do not see...

Panic climbed into her throat as the Scripture came to mind. Katherine had been lying to herself all these weeks. She wasn't a strong, believing Christian. In truth, she had no faith when it came to her own future.

And just as Trey had accused of her, she *was* afraid. Afraid of his rejection. Afraid one day he'd see her like the rest of the town did, as nothing more than the daughter of a whore, and as a woman forever tainted by one violent act.

No. She countered that absurd notion with a stamp of temper. "Trey doesn't deserve this kind of censure. I will not think like this."

Maybe it was time to walk by faith and not by sight. Maybe it was time to give Trey Scott a chance to be the man she knew he could be in time and with God's healing.

Shoving away from the door, she quickly washed and changed her clothes. Too tired to fool with her hair, she merely brushed out the tangles and let it hang loose down her back.

For a moment, she felt better, stronger, but as she jammed her feet into her boots and went to work on the laces, she thought back over the scene she'd witnessed in Laney's room.

Both Trey and Marc had received the birth of the tiny child as the blessing it was. They were such good men. Each destined to command his family with honor, integrity and deep, abiding love.

Why didn't she feel joy at the revelation?

Because Katherine wasn't convinced Trey would ever love her enough, not the way Marc loved Laney. Not the way Trey still loved his dead wife.

On shaky legs, she rose from the bed and dashed out of the room. Avoiding the other end of the hallway— and the people behind that closed door—she trekked downstairs. Needing to gather her thoughts into some semblance of order, she veered toward the front porch, then slipped out of the house.

And nearly collided into Trey.

She froze, afraid to disturb him, afraid to turn away.

Seemingly unaware of her presence, he stood with his back to her, tense and unmoving. His turmoil was palpable, and she wept inside for him. At the sight of him standing there, looking so alone and sad, a crack in her heart opened, allowing him to fill it for just a moment before she slammed it shut again with a sigh.

He turned at the sound. In one swift movement, he caught her against his chest. Without speaking, he dropped a kiss on the top of her head, the tender gesture breaking her heart a little more. Oh, yes, this man had so much love to give. If only she knew how to trust him with her heart.

She pulled away, then stared up at him. His gaze softened, his eyes communicating something she couldn't quite name—didn't dare name. Out of a perverse need to gain perspective, she lowered her eyes to the tin star on his chest. She tried reminding herself he was a lawman. But, tonight, the dangers of his chosen profession didn't matter so much.

Returning her gaze to his, she raised herself onto the tips of her toes and pressed a kiss to his chin. "Trey—"

"Take a walk with me."

Feeling suddenly vulnerable, she inched backward, shaking her head.

"Please."

The genuine appeal in his eyes called to the part of her that could deny this man nothing. She knew he was hurting, knew he needed her in a way she didn't quite understand. She could no more walk away from him now than cut off one of her limbs. And in that moment, Katherine accepted the truth. She was beginning to care deeply for Trey Scott—a man who would continually come and go from her life, one day never to return.

He would break her heart. And Molly's.

Yet Katherine still yearned for him to find peace above her own selfish fears. She wanted him to experience the freedom in Christ that she had. She wanted him free from pain. And whether he was in her life or not, she wanted him to find true happiness.

Oh, Lord, give me the courage to face these new, frightening feelings. I'm so vulnerable to him right now.

Silently, carefully, she placed her hand in his. Smiling, he drew her down the stairs with him. He smelled of a tangy blend of spice and wood, a scent that would always linger in her mind as his alone.

As they walked side by side, his nearness attacked the doubt clutching at her heart, making her believe—for one small second—that being with Trey was the best thing that would ever happen to her in this life.

Fearful she would blurt out her feelings, Katherine started to turn back, but the gentle touch to her arm stopped her.

"Mrs. Smythe can take care of the children," Trey said. "I need you to walk with me."

His eyes told her he needed much more than that from her.

Katherine's heart rolled around in her chest, pounded violently against her ribs. "I... Yes."

He waited until she drew back alongside him before striding again down the lane. Clasping his hands behind his back, he walked at a leisurely pace. Light from the other mansions illuminated their path. The slender beam of the waning moon glowed small but bright, the stars especially brilliant in the dark fabric of the sky.

They continued to walk in silence, and she reveled in the smooth camaraderie that arose between them. No arguing, no wheedling, just comfortable serenity.

They ambled past the mansions and on to the outskirts of town. Only the stars and moon provided light now, the mountains standing guard, as though protecting them against the fierce enemies of the world.

Trey looked to the heavens, took a deep breath, then turned back to her. "The quiet is nice."

"Quiet?" She chuckled and spread her arms to the sky, sniffing the refreshing, subtle fragrance of the spicy mountain air. "The pine trees are snapping and crackling in the wind. The crickets are singing. I can barely hear myself think."

"You know what I mean."

She turned to him, waited for his eyes to lower to hers again. "Yes, I do."

Pulling a strand of her hair away from her face, he twirled the dark curl around his forefinger. "You've had a long day."

She sighed, barely resisting the urge to lean into him. "It was terrifying, but exciting, too."

Studying her face with the same intensity she'd seen in him when he'd stared at the baby, he released her hair, then dragged a knuckle down her cheek. "You didn't look scared. You looked in complete control."

She let out a self-deprecating laugh. "Oh, I'm a master at exuding confidence when I least feel it. Comes from teaching eager minds with too many questions I can't always answer."

He lifted a brow, amusement replacing the sincerity. "You? At a loss for words?"

"Don't start, Trey. Tomorrow you can scold me several times to make up for it, but not tonight."

"I wasn't going to scold."

She lifted a brow in a gesture identical to his.

A grin played at the corners of his mouth, his white teeth gleaming against his tanned skin speckled with day-old beard. "All right, I was. But you're right. This isn't the time."

The lines around his eyes deepened, while the shadows in his gaze darkened. "I don't understand what happened to me in that room tonight."

He took her hand and pressed her palm against his chest. "It hurts here."

She was content just to stand there, silently counting each of his heartbeats as they slammed against her hand. But the look in his eyes demanded she respond to his pain.

"You had quite a night," she said. "It's understandable to feel a little shaken."

"It's more than that."

She nodded, dropped her hand. "Yes."

"I don't know much about divine plans or God's will, but the birth of this baby, no—" He broke off, swallowed. "The birth of Lau... *Laurette* seems important. I can't explain why."

His stricken, confused expression had her reaching out and placing her hand on his arm. "Oh, Trey, we can't always know God's ways, or why He puts us through trials. All we can do is believe that good will eventually come to those of us who are in Christ. Even when we suffer unspeakable tragedy."

He didn't argue with her or give her an angry denial, but his mouth curved into a frown. "It always comes down to trust, doesn't it? Blind trust."

"That's what faith is, Trey. Trusting in what we can't see or know for sure. And it's the hardest thing we do as Christians."

He placed a finger under her chin, applying pressure until she looked into his eyes. "Sort of like trusting me to be good to you in our marriage, and trusting that I'll keep my promise to take care of you and Molly."

She stiffened at his words. "We aren't talking about me. We're talking about you and your ongoing struggle with God over the loss of your wife. We're talking about forgiveness."

"Forgiveness. Trust in God. I don't know much of these things anymore." His brows drew together in a heavy frown. "But you do. *Trust* me, Katherine. Show me how it's done so I can learn how to do it, too."

"Oh, Trey, what a pair we make. You can't trust God, and…and apparently, I can't trust you enough, either."

She heard the disappointment in his unspoken sigh.

"Why do you continue to fight me so?"

He asked a legitimate question. Why *was* she fighting him? She cared for him, and although he didn't care for her in the same way, she knew he did care. She also knew he would eventually find his way back to God, perhaps sooner now with the birth of baby Laurette.

Why not marry him?

Because, ultimately, he would break her heart.

Trey pulled Katherine tight against him, deciding her silence meant she was coming around to his way of thinking. This time he wasn't going to let her walk away from him before they'd settled matters between them.

He didn't know why it was so important to him, only knew his desire to make her his wife had become more than merely accepting responsibility for her reputation.

Maybe this urgency came with the birth of Marc's daughter. Something had happened to him in that room tonight. As he'd held the tiny child, his thinking had shifted. For the first time in years, he wanted a life free of bitterness and anger and vengeance. He wanted a future. And he wanted it with Katherine and Molly.

But he had to settle the past first. He needed to free

all three of them from the violence that drove him still. "When I get back," he said, "we're getting married."

She pushed out of his arms. *"When you get back?"*

Shock registered in her eyes, but the pain he saw flickering underneath that stunned expression warned Trey to tread softly. He'd made a mistake waiting until now to tell her. "I'm leaving in the morning."

Her gasp sounded more like an accusation. "You're leaving in the morning."

"I got word—"

"You got word."

In an attempt to lighten the mood, he made a grand show of peering around her. "Did you bring Laney's talking bird with you?"

"You're leaving. Going after a specific criminal, I assume?"

"I have to finish it, Katherine."

A single sob slipped from her lips before she gathered her control. "How long have you known about this…trip?"

"A week," he said, bracing for her reaction.

"A week." The words came out just above a whisper. "And you just tell me now?"

Taking the defense, he puffed out his chest. "It's my job to hunt down outlaws and bring them to justice."

"It's your job."

"I'm getting real tired of you repeating everything I say."

She jammed her hands on her hips and jerked her chin at him. "And I'm getting real tired of having this same conversation over and over with you. God tells us that vengeance is His alone. Quit trying to turn justice into your own personal quest to rid yourself of false guilt."

Trey swallowed back an angry retort and focused solely on winning the argument. "This isn't about guilt, false or real. I've sworn an oath to the president of the United States to uphold justice in this part of the country. *I'm the good guy.*"

She pressed her fingertips to her temples and shook her head. "Right. Of course. How could I forget? You're a lawman, Trey. But you're not a husband. Not *mine* anyway."

"I can be both. One does not preclude the other."

Wanting to soothe her fears, he reached to her. She took a single step back, creating a chasm between them that felt as wide as a continent.

"Are you going after your wife's killer?" she asked in a defeated tone.

He sighed, deciding the truth was the best defense. "Yes. It's time justice was served once and for all."

She gasped. "Justice? This quest of yours isn't about justice. It's about revenge."

"It's the only thing I have left that I can give Laurette."

"It won't change anything."

Hardening his heart to the look of disappointment in her eyes, he shoved a hand through his hair. "Even if Ike Hayes hadn't murdered Laurette, he's killed others. It's my job to find him and bring him to justice. It's what I do. It's who I am."

"And what if you don't come back? What am I supposed to tell Molly? That you were killed seeking revenge?"

With his patience pushed to the snapping point, he glared down at her. "I *always* come back. And when

I do, we're getting married. Molly will have the family you want for her. It's no longer up for discussion."

Her only response was a tight-lipped grimace.

"Did you hear me?"

"I heard you."

"Good." He gave her a single nod. "Then it's settled."

"Not by half. Now you hear me, *Marshal*." She poked her finger at his chest. "You better make good on that promise of yours to return. Because if you hurt my little sister, I'll make you sorry you ever chose to mess with a Taylor woman."

With that, she spun on her heel and marched across the open field, her dignity wrapped around her like an iron cloak.

Trey stared at her retreating back, his heart clutching in his chest at her bold threat. "Oh, I don't doubt it, honey," he whispered after her, smiling in spite of himself. "I don't doubt it for a minute."

Chapter Fourteen

One month, two days and six hours after their heated argument, Trey had yet to return home. As the midday sun spread golden fingers of light through the kitchen window, Katherine tried to go about her daily chores as though nothing was bothering her. To little avail.

Sighing, she used her wrist to wipe her forehead and then began pressing freshly kneaded dough into a bread tin.

Perhaps today would be the day Trey returned home.

Did he miss her, she wondered, as much as she missed him? Or was he thinking about their last argument and the ultimatum she'd given him to return unharmed or else she'd make him sorry?

How she regretted those impetuous words. He'd needed her comfort that night, her understanding, as he dealt with the emotions of the past. But she'd offered only accusations and shrewish demands. That wasn't the way she wanted him to remember her while he was gone.

In a matter of seconds, her mind skipped from worry to dread to fear and back to worry again. Furious at herself, she pounded at the dough, kneading with vicious intent.

If only she had some news of him. Was he safe? Had he caught the outlaw? Was he on his way home at last? Or—the worst of them all—was he lying dead in some hidden valley, alone and forgotten?

"I will not give in to this paralyzing fear."

She stopped kneading, closed her eyes and quoted her favorite verse from the Gospel of John. "Jesus said, 'Peace I leave with you; my peace I give you. I do not give to you as the world gives. Do not let your hearts be troubled and do not be afraid.'"

Please, Lord, help me to have faith over my fears. Please, bring Trey home safely to Molly and me.

Her stomach clutched at the thought of never seeing him again. Stifling a moan, she flicked loose flour onto the cutting board and began kneading again.

If this sickening dread was what she had to look forward to every time Trey left to hunt an outlaw, how could she ever expect to survive marriage to him?

She squeezed her eyes shut and prayed, "Lord, give me clarity. Reveal to me what I should do."

A movement just outside the window caught her attention.

Katherine squinted into the sunlight, her eyes focusing on the town sheriff dragging a familiar child in tow. One child. Not three. Not even two. But *one!*

The last time Katherine had seen Molly, the five-year-old had asked to tag along with Johnny and Megan as they headed into town to run an errand for Laney. How on earth had her sister ended up in the lawman's care?

And where were the other children?

In an attempt to gather more information, Katherine studied her heel-scuffing, head-hanging little sister as she made her way toward the back door of the house—with her arm gripped by the sheriff's hand.

Battling a large dose of trepidation, Katherine wiped her hands on her apron, circled around the counter and then opened the door leading into the backyard.

She stood on the top step, waiting for an explanation.

When neither spoke, Katherine bobbed her gaze from her sister to the sheriff and back again. Both held themselves unnaturally stiff, each shifting from foot to foot in an erratic, guilty rhythm.

"What's happened?" When both continued in their silence, Katherine sighed. "Are either of you going to answer me?"

Molly squeaked out an "I'm sorry, Katherine," but kept her head lowered and her arms wrapped around her middle.

"Sorry? For what?" asked Katherine.

Molly dug her toe into the dirt and shrugged.

Katherine turned her attention to the lawman, who seemed surprisingly...contrite?

What on earth was going on here?

"Where are Megan and Johnny?"

Two bushy white eyebrows drew together, and the sheriff shifted his hat to the back of his head. "I don't know about any others. I only found this one in town."

Gasping, Katherine turned her full attention to Molly. "You were in Denver, alone?"

Still gazing at the ground, Molly shrugged again. "I sort of got separated from the others."

Something in the way her little sister refused to lift

her head put Katherine on instant alert. "Look at me, Molly. Right now."

The child slowly—very slowly—lifted her head.

"Oh, Molly." A thick, hot blast of air escaped from Katherine's lungs as she rushed forward and lowered herself to her knees. "Your eye. It's swollen shut."

Molly hunched her shoulders forward. "I kinda fell into Bobby Prescott's fist."

Katherine fought to keep her shock from taking control of her reason. "You *kinda* fell?"

The sheriff cleared his throat. "Don't fret over it, Miss Katherine."

"How can I not?" She shot him an exasperated glare.

His answering gaze turned direct, unwavering. The grizzled lawman was firmly in place now. "Turns out, your little sister has quite a right hook when provoked."

"Molly! You've been fighting?" exclaimed Katherine. Nausea nearly overtook her. What had possessed the child to indulge in fisticuffs?

"At least she gave it to that Prescott boy but good." Lassiter patted her on the head like a faithful pet. "She's a scrappy little thing, your sister."

A strong sense of chagrin left Katherine completely unsettled. "You hit a boy?"

Clearly insulted by Katherine's tone, the five-year-old jerked her chin at an angry angle. "He said you was my mommy. I said, 'Yeah, so?' 'Cause, well, I want you to be my mommy, but then he called you a tramp. He said that you was slinking in closets with men for money. I was just shuttin' him up, but good."

Understanding dawned, and with it came the pain. The humiliation. The bitter reality. The talk had begun, and it had already circled back to Katherine's innocent little sister. "Oh, Molly."

Trey had been right all along. People talked. Reasonable doubt was ignored. Guilt instantly assumed.

And Molly had been the one hurt today.

This was no longer a simple matter of word getting out about a slight indiscretion in the school's supply closet.

It was so much worse.

Katherine took a deep breath and accepted the reality of the situation. It was one thing to hear the whispers directed at her. At least those comments were unfounded. Something had to be done about the new rumors, rumors that were entrenched in a semblance of the truth.

Neither she nor Molly could continue to live in this state of indecision. First, however, Katherine had to attend to Molly's injuries—both the physical and mental ones—and explain the right and wrong way to respond to provocation.

But not in front of a stranger.

Rising to her full height, Katherine turned her attention to the sheriff and gave him a tight smile. "Thank you for bringing my sister home. I can handle matters from here."

Lassiter stabbed a quick glance at Molly; then his lips flattened into a determined line as he returned his stare to Katherine. "Don't you let them town folk and their talk get to you, Miss Katherine. Anyone with sense knows you're a fine Christian woman."

"Thank you, Sheriff," Katherine said, shoving a shaky hand through her hair. "But why defend me? You don't really know me."

"I know what I know. Marshal Scott is the most honorable man in the territory. If he says you're a good woman, well, then I say so, too."

Tears pricked her eyes, but she held them back with sheer force of will. "Trey said that about me?"

He patted her on the arm. "He'll be home soon, and he'll help you sort this all out."

Her heart began to trip at the burden that lay ahead of her. Yet the man's confidence in her was heartening. "Thank you, Sheriff, for everything."

Laney chose that moment to materialize in the door frame. "Sheriff? Is everything all right?"

"I was just leaving. Miss Taylor can give you the sordid details." He rustled Molly's hair. "See ya, kid."

He turned to go but stopped and cocked his head toward Molly. "She's been hiding her right paw under her wing ever since we left town. That Prescott kid's got a hard head. You might want to get the doc to check out her hand."

The words pushed Katherine to action. Ignoring the sheriff now that he was leaving, she dropped to her knees and wrestled Molly's hand out from under her arm. "Let me see what you've done to yourself."

At the sight of the bloody, swollen fingers, Katherine fought back a wave of hysteria. "Oh, Molly."

Laney darted out of the house and knelt down next to Katherine. "You might have broken it, baby," she declared, swiping her fingers across the child's knuckles as she spoke.

Katherine cringed as Molly whimpered. "That hurts, Laney."

"It's what comes of fighting." Laney clicked her tongue. "We'll have to get Dr. Shane."

Fear sprang into the child's eyes, and then the tears started flowing freely.

Katherine smoothed Molly's hair off her forehead. "Don't worry, Molly. We'll get you patched up."

"I'm sorry, Katherine." Sniffling hiccups came out of the little girl, and she wiped her good hand across her nose. "But Bobby was being really, really mean about you. He made it sound like you being my mommy was bad or something."

Even though Katherine wanted to pull Molly in her arms and tell her everything would work out just fine, she also knew she had to set her little sister straight while the incident was fresh in her mind. "You can't hit every boy who says bad things about me, or you, or anyone we care about. You need to turn the other cheek next time."

Two black brows drew together in obvious confusion. "Huh?"

Katherine shared a look with Laney. The other woman nodded encouragingly.

Shifting to her knees, Katherine took the child's face gently into her hands. "What I'm trying to say, Molly, is that when a boy like Bobby says something ugly to you, you have to ignore him and walk away."

"Even when he calls *you* names?" squeaked Molly.

Katherine dropped her hands. "Especially then."

Molly scrunched her face into a scowl and chewed on her lower lip. "That doesn't sound right."

"It is, baby. Forgiving isn't easy, but boys like Bobby need it most from us."

"But he was the one who wronged me."

"Nevertheless—"

Johnny came barreling around the corner, his winded

shouts cutting her off. "Katherine, Laney, we lost Mo—" He came to a halt at the sight of Molly. "Oh, you found her. Whoa! That's some shiner, kid."

Laney rose and instantly took charge. Placing her hands on the boy's shoulders, she spun him around toward town. "Johnny, go get Dr. Bartlett. Tell him it's an emergency."

His gaze dropped to her stomach. "Another one?"

"It's for Molly this time." Laney's voice held a stern, unrelenting note. "We think she broke her hand."

"Oh." His eyes widened. *"Oh!"*

Footsteps pelted the ground as Johnny rushed off and descended the hill back toward town.

"Katherine," Laney continued, "get that child inside, and try to wash her up as best you can before the doctor arrives." She raised her voice an entire octave. "And for goodness' sake, everybody try to stay calm."

Swallowing back her rising hysteria, Katherine scooped up her sister and started for the house. At least one good thing had come of the incident. God had given her the clarity she'd prayed for.

In the end, Katherine had a responsibility to her sister. There could be no more waffling on the matter of Trey's proposal, no more worries over her own fears.

Yes, Katherine knew exactly what she would say when she saw Trey again. Of course, the man had to come home in one piece first.

Trey rode at a clipped pace, Logan's horse easily matching the quick gait. With the cool air shrouding them in a watery mist, defeat hung heavy between them. Trey blew into his cupped palms and tried to ignore the condemnation that seemed to brood in every rock.

They'd failed. For over a month, they'd checked out every possible lead but still hadn't come close to finding Ike Hayes. And now, thanks to the wasted time searching for the man who'd turned into a phantom, Trey had to push Drew's trial back another two months.

What was he missing? The instinct that had kept him alive for years kicked in, warning Trey he'd forgotten something important.

Something simple.

Silence clung to the edges of the gray morning, and exhaustion etched across Trey's soul; bitter failure circled around his heart.

He wanted the hunt over, wanted relief from this consuming hatred. He wanted *freedom.*

Katherine had claimed God was the way to Trey's liberty. And with time, both healing and forgiveness would come. All Trey knew was the impossible had happened. Katherine and Molly had inched their way into his heart. And now he needed both in his life, more than he'd thought possible.

Trey scowled, not sure which bothered him more— shoving Drew's trial back or Ike's continued freedom. Every day his nemesis continued to run free, Trey's anger grew more pronounced, rooting deeper into his soul.

Would Trey be able to come back from the violence once the hunt was over? With Ike's death, would Trey find the freedom he now craved?

Or was it too late for him?

As though sensing his edginess, his horse snorted and shifted beneath him. Trey patted the beast's neck until he settled into a rhythmic gait again. Clearing his thoughts, he surveyed the open terrain with a watchful eye. Although the sun was just peeking over the horizon, the day felt crooked to him. Off balance.

"Now what do we do, Marshal?"

Trey's mind cut back to Logan. He was just agitated enough to take out his frustration on his deputy. "First, you're going to refigure last year's expenditures, column by column, month by month. Then you're going to head to Mattie's and find a girl more talkative than the madam. Then—"

Logan cut him off with a snort. "Am I being punished for something?"

With one quick slash of his hand, Trey dismissed Logan's question. "It's time we both got back to our assigned duties."

"But what about Ike?"

As soon as Logan's words were out of his mouth, the solution came to Trey. In truth, he couldn't believe it had taken him this long to realize the obvious.

He'd been so bent on chasing after the outlaw, he'd forgotten the simplest tactic of war—find the enemy's weakness, magnify it, then render it useless and ineffective. "We're going to wait and let him come to us."

"We're going to *what?*"

Trey ignored his deputy's shock and allowed his mind to work through the particulars. He remembered Mattie's evasion when he'd questioned her about Ike, her parting threat when he'd turned his back on her and, lastly, Ike's devotion to his little brother. "I'd stake my life on the fact that Ike Hayes is on his way to Denver, if he's not already there."

Logan's face scrunched into a look of deep concentration; he was obviously trying to work through Trey's logic. "How do you figure that?"

"He's got reasons."

Logan's eyes lit up. "Drew."

"And Mattie."

Logan grinned. "And we plan to be waiting for him."

Trey's lips curled into a smile that didn't reach his eyes. "Exactly."

Soon vengeance would be his to take.

Chapter Fifteen

Regardless of Molly's constant squirming on the kitchen counter, Dr. Bartlett examined her hand without hurting her. Once he finished, he gave Katherine a sad smile.

Apprehension trickled down her spine. "Is it broken?"

"No." He shook his head. "But it's badly bruised."

Relieved, Katherine released a breath and reached out to touch his sleeve. "That's good news."

"I'll say." Molly slid off the counter, and let out a squeal of joy. "Can I go play now?"

With surprising speed, the doctor caught her at the waist and hoisted her back in place. "Not so fast. We need to bandage your hand to keep you from injuring it any further."

With a flick of his wrist, he pulled out a roll of bandages and began wrapping the child's injury. Molly took the opportunity to yank on his hair with her free hand and giggled. "Your hair sticks out kind of funny all over, Dr. Shane."

He smiled at her, obviously used to the declaration. "I know."

"I like it," she declared.

"Well, of course, you do." He winked at her. "All the smart ladies know what's what."

Molly giggled.

Dr. Bartlett grinned.

"Molly's healthy otherwise?" Katherine asked.

"Very," he said, without looking at her. "But I'd like you to come to my office this afternoon, Miss Taylor, so we can discuss her, uh…specific needs."

Katherine's brows drew together. "I think I know what to do. This isn't the first injury at Charity House."

"Nevertheless. I—" He broke off, slanted a quick look at Molly, who was entertaining herself by using her good hand to empty the contents of his medical bag onto the counter beside her.

He lowered his voice to a whisper. "What I have to say is private."

Katherine felt his urgency but had no idea where it was coming from. Had he heard the talk about her, too? Was he going to condemn her for what she'd supposedly done in the school's supply closet? Or would he show her compassion, like he had on the night of her attack, when he'd tended her wounds?

There was one way to find out. And she certainly wasn't going to trek all the way into town when he was standing right next to her in Charity House.

As he continued working on Molly's hand, Katherine said, "I'll be right back."

She stepped into the hallway off the kitchen and motioned Laney to join them. "We're about finished."

"Is it broken?" Laney asked, her eyes filled with concern.

"No."

"Praise the Lord."

"Would you mind taking Molly upstairs to her room while Dr. Bartlett has a word with me about her care?"

Before Laney had a chance to respond, Katherine gripped her friend by the arm and directed her toward the counter. "I'll only be a moment behind you."

Laney's eyes widened; then she looked from Katherine to the doctor and back to Katherine again. With each pass, speculation glittered deeper in her eyes. "I...see."

Katherine waved her off. Her friend was reading signs that simply did not exist. "No, you don't."

Laney lifted an eyebrow but then shook her head and smiled down at Molly instead of pushing further. "Come on, little one. Let's get you settled in the bed."

Molly's expression turned defiant. "I don't want to take a nap."

"You've had a trauma, Molly," Katherine pointed out. "It's best if you rest for a while."

"But I feel fine," Molly whined.

Katherine would not allow the five-year-old to reel her into this argument again. "Then consider it punishment for fighting. If you can't fall asleep, then use the quiet time to think about what you've done and how you will handle Bobby Prescott next time he says something ugly to you."

At that, Molly's head dropped at a wayward angle. "Yes, Katherine. I'm really sorry, you know."

"I know," said Katherine. She swept a braid off Molly's shoulder and clutched her gently. "But you're still going to be punished."

Head hanging, Molly silently followed Laney out of the kitchen.

Once they were alone, Katherine looked at Dr. Bartlett, noting how his features were set and stern, matched only by the severity of his black coat and crisp white shirt.

Prepared for the worst, Katherine lowered herself in a chair near the counter where Molly had been sitting earlier. "What did you want to discuss with me, Dr. Bartlett?"

Unable to meet her gaze, he shifted from foot to foot. He'd seemed so sure of himself earlier, his hands and manner full of confidence when he'd bandaged Molly's injury. But now, it was as if he'd become a different man.

Katherine studied him while he silently struggled to put words together. She'd never really noticed how handsome he was. His rumpled dark brown hair, strong features and gentle hands made a woman feel safe in his presence, even a woman with a horrifying past like hers. He was big, like Trey and Marc, but had been blessed with the soothing touch of a healer.

It was a wonder she hadn't seen any of his finer qualities before now.

"Miss Taylor—" He broke off and set to pacing around the room.

Katherine tapped her foot on the floor, folded her hands in her lap and waited for him to continue.

She watched him move, his grace at odds with his size, his shoulders large enough for a woman to set all her cares upon. Why couldn't her heart have fallen for this man? Shane Bartlett was handsome, compassionate and...*safe*.

The antithesis of Trey Scott.

He stopped pacing, pivoted to face her. Speculation wavered in his gaze. He looked very much like the way he had when he'd watched her in the birthing room with Laney. "Miss Taylor."

A warning twisted in her stomach. "Yes?"

"All this resurgence of talk about you in town, well, I know it's not your fault. Does the man who cornered you in the closet know—"

"I wasn't cornered," she hastened to explain before he accused Trey of something he hadn't done. "Nor was I doing what they say I was doing."

"You weren't—" He broke off, swallowed, then began again. "You weren't…kissing a man in the school's supply closet?"

"Not kissing, no. Or anything else remotely sordid like that. We were just talking. About Molly and her future."

He gave her an odd look. "Well, whatever you were doing, word is all over town that it was a lot more than talk."

Katherine blew out a breath. Although Trey hadn't actually kissed her, in a matter of weeks the gossip had turned decidedly ugly.

"Miss Taylor?" Dr. Bartlett swallowed. "Will the man in question do what is needed to stop the talk?"

She thought of Trey's parting shot when she'd left him gaping at her in the open field. "Yes. As a matter of fact, he's asked me to marry him."

And thanks to the events of today, she'd decided to say yes. That is, if he came back alive, she thought, her heart aching over the terrible prospect.

Oh, Lord, please keep Trey safe. Bring him home so we can sort through this together.

"Well, if he doesn't—" he touched her sleeve "—I'd like to offer to marry you in his stead."

She stared at him in genuine confusion. "You're asking me to marry you?"

His gaze turned solemn. "You can trust that I am sincere."

Although his tired eyes held conviction, she saw none of the tenderness she'd witnessed so often in Trey's gaze when he'd discussed marriage. His motives were clearly not from love and caring. So what urged him forward? "Why would you offer such a thing?"

"Miss Taylor, I see you at church every Sunday, in the same seat each week. In spite of your upbringing and what others say, I *know* you are a good Christian woman."

She smiled at the compliment and then folded her hands in her lap. "What I am, and what others say I am, are obviously at odds with one another."

"You suffer enough shame because of your mother's...profession." He pulled his shoulders forward and broke eye contact as he spoke of her attack. But then he straightened and stared straight into her eyes. "You don't deserve more of the same, no matter the reason."

"You'd marry me simply to stop the talk?"

A sorrowful look flickered in his eyes, only to be replaced with a determination she'd never seen in him before. "If not for you, then let me do this for your sister."

She smiled up at him. "You are a good man."

He shot her a look that had her sitting straighter in her chair. "This isn't about simple kindness," he said.

"Or even Christian charity. It's about protecting an *innocent* child from the heat of scandal."

She couldn't help but wonder if there was more underneath Shane Bartlett's calm exterior than she had at first realized. His severe expression told her this was not a man to trifle with, especially on this subject. Which made it imperative that she set him straight. "This is sweet of you, but completely unnecessary."

"No child should bear this kind of shame. Nor should you," he added, almost as an afterthought.

Katherine studied his face for a long, long moment. "You needn't worry about what the good folk of Denver will think of me."

If anything, he set his shoulders at a more determined angle than before. "You're a schoolteacher. Your reputation must be above reproach."

"I will never be considered a decent woman." She ignored his flinch and continued. "Let's not pretend otherwise. I do know what they say behind my back."

Even now, she could hear the words of condemnation echoing in her head. Words whispered within earshot in her own neighborhood.

His gaze hardened. "What do they say?"

She pitched her voice up an octave. "Oh, that's Katherine Taylor, the daughter of that harlot, Sadie. Bet she's just like that no-good mother of hers."

He nodded, a sage look coming into his eyes. "Guilt by association."

Determined to let Dr. Bartlett know she wasn't living in a cocoon, that she knew exactly what was said about her by the "good" citizens of Denver, Katherine continued. "Exactly. They assume I'm just like my mother and all that that implies."

He winced, his face set and stern.

Katherine couldn't help but think there was more to the doctor's strong reaction besides concern for her. But now wasn't the time to ask. "Nevertheless, I'm condemned and shunned."

He paced two steps, then turned to face her, his gaze intense and inflexible. "Perhaps in the eyes of some, you're tainted forever. But if we were to marry, we could leave Denver, go someplace where no one knows you or your infamous connections. You would be the wife of a doctor, and Molly would never have to suffer the… whispers."

Why was he so adamant?

"Leave Denver? But Charity House is our home. Laney took me in when no one else would even look me in the eye. I could never leave—"

"You'd rather Molly suffer the shame of *your* actions instead?" Disapproval glared back at her.

Katherine's hands flew to her heart, knowing the ridicule that was bound to come to her sister if she didn't rectify the situation soon. Regardless of what she and Trey had done in that supply closet, word was out. And it wasn't kind.

The doctor's expression softened as he wrapped her hands in his and knelt before her again. "Will you at least consider my offer?"

"Thank you for asking, but—"

"I'd be a good husband and father."

"Yes. I know you would."

"Does that mean you'll marry me?"

Oh, what a wonderful, wonderful gesture, to *ask* her, instead of ordering her. It was the kind of consideration that deserved complete honesty in return. "I can't."

"But—"

She pulled one of her hands free, pressed it to his lips when he tried to speak again. "Please, don't ask me again. I do appreciate your offer, but I don't love you." She worked her other hand free and clasped his shoulders, ensuring he'd look her straight in the eye. "And you don't love me."

"Love?" He spat out the word. "This has nothing to do with something so trivial. This is about protecting a child from spiteful talk."

His intensity told its own story. Shane Bartlett had very strong beliefs on the matter.

The question, of course, was why.

"This has everything to do with love," she said. "And when you're captured by the emotion yourself, you'll understand why I'm doing both of us a favor by saying no to your offer."

"And I can't change your mind?" Though his tone was mild, his expression was grave.

"No."

He rose, began gathering his things, but stopped and looked at her again. "If the man who threw you into this scandal refuses to marry you, will you reconsider? For Molly, if not for yourself?"

She nodded, hoping for all their sakes it never came to that. "Yes, perhaps I'll reconsider if the situation warrants."

"That's all I ask." He turned his attention to the table once more and began rolling the remaining bandages.

As she watched him prepare to leave, tears pierced through her composure. In little over a month, two men had asked her to marry them. Two *good* men who knew the details of her horrible past, and *still* they wanted to marry her. Her. Katherine Taylor.

Oh, thank You, Lord. Thank You for showing me in such a substantial way that I'm worthy of a man's caring, and that I'm so much more than what happened to me that night two years ago.

Dr. Bartlett made it to the door, stopped, then turned back to her. "Marshal Scott returned late this morning with his deputy. Perhaps you'll want to talk with him right away."

Her hand flew to her mouth. "How did you know? Has talk been that specific?"

He shrugged. "I don't think so, but I see things."

If Shane Bartlett knew about her and Trey, did others as well? "Did I, I mean, was I...that easy to read?"

"No." He twisted the door handle, his lips descending into a sympathetic grimace. "He was."

Chapter Sixteen

An hour after Dr. Bartlett had proposed to Katherine, she left the jailhouse dejected and out of sorts. Normally, she didn't make the trip to town. Although used to the accusing stares and whispers, she didn't enjoy them. In fact, they hurt. They hurt a lot. Thus she avoided the experience as often as possible. Except, of course, on Sundays, when she went to church.

Today, however, she'd ignored the familiar nervousness as she'd left Charity House and gone in search of Trey in town. For Molly's sake, as well as her own, it was time to settle matters between them. But, according to Deputy Mitchell, she'd missed Trey by less than an hour.

Her first reaction was an excited quiver in the vicinity of her heart. Trey was home. He was safe. He was no longer chasing vengeance.

But as she realized that *she* was the one who had sought him out, trepidation of another sort replaced her joy. Perhaps he'd changed his mind about her, about them. Perhaps he'd decided she wasn't worthy enough to become his wife.

No. This false sense of shame, and constant lack of confidence in her own value as a woman, wasn't of God. By allowing the disgrace of her attack to continue festering in her soul, she wasn't living the abundant life promised to her as a child of God.

Well, no longer.

Trey wasn't like the others, who condemned her. It was cowardly and wrong to question Trey's motives, especially after all they'd been through together. She would believe that good came to those who trusted in the Lord.

Nevertheless, a vague sense of doubt still swam through her mind, thundered in her chest.

Scuffing her feet much like she'd seen Molly do, Katherine made her way along the wooden sidewalk. *One, two, three.* She began counting the seams between the planks in an attempt to clear her mind of her foolish uncertainty. A man bumped into her, hard, jerking Katherine's attention from her task and nearly sending her to the ground.

"Oh." Air whooshed out of her, and she flayed her hands in order to find her balance.

The man did nothing to help her. Instead, he scowled, with eyes that had turned gunmetal cold and unforgiving. "Watch where you're going."

A sound of dismay slipped from her lips. "I… Of course, I apologize."

He paused and shot a hard glare at her, looking much like the ladies from church had when she'd encountered them in her neighborhood weeks ago. And just like that last time, her hands started to shake.

"See that it doesn't happen again." He all but snarled the words at her.

Katherine pressed her palms together and tried desperately to keep her rising resentment from taking control of her tongue. They both knew he had bumped into her on purpose. But she was Sadie Taylor's daughter, and that put her firmly in the wrong. Every time. All the time.

Nevertheless, she would rise above this situation and take the godly way out. "Again, I apologize," she said, managing a tight smile.

With a look of disgust on his face, he shoved past her. "Your kind should stay on Market Street, where you belong."

Katherine stood frozen to the spot. Even through the blur of her shocked resentment, her instinct was to turn around and yell after him that she was a good, moral woman, a woman above reproach. A woman deserving of some kindness.

But people saw in her what they wanted to see. They saw a ruined woman whose virtue and innocence were gone. Stolen, yes, but gone all the same.

The pain of her humiliation throbbed thickly in her throat. She wanted to lash out, to scream at the unfairness of it all. In that moment she fully understood why Molly had answered Bobby Prescott's accusations with her fists.

Although the encounters were never easy, Katherine had come to terms with this type of prejudice. But Molly was still a child, and for Katherine's innocent little sister, the guilt by association ended today.

Of course, respectability would come at a price. Marriage to Trey could be the worst decision she ever made. Or the best. At that last thought, a tiny whisper of hope threaded through her doubts.

Trust. Where she and Trey were concerned, it all came down to trust. And just as Sheriff Lassiter had said when he'd brought Molly home this morning, Trey would come to her, and they would work everything out.

With renewed determination, Katherine made the trip home in record time. As she crossed the threshold, her senses were assaulted with the fresh smell of furniture polish and the sound of familiar voices.

Katherine stopped and listened.

Molly's excited chatter came from the vicinity of Marc's study. "Whattaya think of my new bandage, Mr. Trey? It's really big, huh?"

Katherine's breath hitched in her throat when she heard Trey's deep voice respond to the question. "Very impressive," he said.

A long pause followed, and the breath she'd been holding escaped past Katherine's lips. She stabbed a quick glance to her left and then her right, discovering she was alone in the hallway.

Perhaps she would listen a moment longer.

Trey cleared his throat. "Tell me again how you hurt your hand."

An even longer pause followed the question. A vague sense of hope filled Katherine, and she moved another step closer to Marc's study.

"Kitten?" he urged softly.

Knowing it was wrong to eavesdrop, Katherine couldn't find the courage to make her presence known just yet.

"Well," Molly began, clearly reluctant to tell the full tale. Katherine could almost hear her sister shifting from one foot to another, her young mind sorting through the various explanations. "Like I said, Bobby Prescott's head kinda ran into my hand."

"Just like your eye ran into his fist?" Trey's voice sounded more than a little ironic.

"Right. Just like that. I think he got it but good for saying those bad things about my sister, but Katherine says I'm supposed to forgive him anyway."

Katherine held her breath, waiting to see if Trey would contradict her efforts at teaching Molly good Christian values.

The silence seemed to stretch out, but then Trey let out a grim, impatient snort. "Your sister is right, kitten."

"But, Mr. Trey—"

"Don't argue, Molly. No good ever comes from fighting."

Relief flowed through Katherine, and she decided she'd heard enough. Whether or not Trey truly agreed with her didn't matter at this point. He'd backed her up with her little sister. Perhaps he was finally coming around to her way of thinking.

Oh, Lord, please let it be so.

Placing what she hoped was a confident expression on her face, she entered the study. "Molly was valiantly defending my good name," she began. "Even if we all agree she didn't choose the best avenue to do so."

Trey rose from his crouched position in front of the child. His gaze slammed into hers and held firm. "Hello, Katherine."

At the sight of his intense expression, she had to fight for air, nearly gulping the next breath into her lungs. How she wished she'd prepared herself better for this first glimpse of Trey after his month-long absence.

She cleared her throat. Sighed. Forced a smile. "Hello, Trey."

A muscle shifted in his jaw.

Her heart skipped a beat.

He took a step forward.

She took a small step back.

He stopped, blew out a breath, took another tentative step forward.

This time she held her ground.

"It's good to see you," he said at last.

Unable to find the words, she gave no response. In truth, they'd left off on such bad terms, she didn't know where to begin their conversation.

"Katherine?" Molly angled her head. "Are you feeling all right?"

"She's fine, kitten," Trey said, grinning like a fool as he spoke. "She's just so happy to see me, she's struck speechless."

At that remark, Katherine found her tongue. "Molly, would you mind leaving us alone for a moment?"

The child fixed Trey with a questioning stare.

"Go on, kitten," he said. "You can tell me the rest of your story after I have a word with your sister."

Looking unhappy, Molly nodded obediently and left the room without a word of protest.

Shocked, Katherine stared after the skipping child. "What did you do to my sister?"

"Let's just say we understand one another." His gaze turned concerned. "Now, about her fight with the Prescott boy. We need to discuss what we should do next."

The genuine worry in his eyes took her breath away all over again. Trey's obvious concern for Molly ran deep. As deep as her own caring was growing for him, a caring that was quickly turning into...

Oh, please, Lord, not...not...love.

Frightened of her own emotions, she focused on her little sister. "It's actually very simple," she said a bit too quickly. "We settle things between us and stop the talk for good. That's why I went looking for you at the jailhouse."

"You went looking for me?" The happy note in his voice made her heart beat harder in her chest. She didn't tell him about the confrontation on the sidewalk. He'd only go in search of the man and settle matters in the Old Testament way.

And because of that, knowing Trey would protect her against something as small as a snub in town, she fell a little harder for him.

"I did," she said. "But you had already left."

He closed the distance between them, drew her hand into his and smiled into her eyes. "It's embarrassing, truth be told, how much that pleases me."

The declaration was swift, uncalculated. And powerful.

In spite of her every effort to remain unmoved, her eyes drank in the sight of him. He was big and healthy and *safe.* "I see you made it back in one piece."

He dragged her farther into the study and shut the door behind them. "Is that your way of saying you missed me?"

She had to remember her little sister and the reason for Molly's fight with Bobby Prescott this morning. Or she'd blurt out her feelings for him too quickly, too completely. "*Molly* certainly missed you."

"But did you?" he persisted.

She looked away from him, unsure how to answer without revealing everything in her heart.

He arranged his face into a pitiful frown, the gesture making him appear more boy than man. "You're going to make me work for this, aren't you?"

She sniffed. "I don't know what you mean."

"Right." He sank into a nearby chair. Lifting his arms into the air, he clasped his hands behind his head and relaxed into his palms. "Go ahead. Proceed with your best scolding."

"Of all the… You are a mannerless brute, Trey Scott."

In response, he proceeded to look at her with lazy tolerance. And then he raised a single eyebrow.

"Oh, honestly." She threw her hands up. "Yes, I missed you. *Terribly.* There, I said it. Satisfied?"

"Completely." The smile he gave her made her think of love and futures and possibilities.

A feeling of doom buckled her knees. She reached out to the desk for support. "I think you should know what started Molly's fight."

"The kitten told me."

"And?"

"Let's just say I am resisting the urge to tell you 'I told you so.'"

"Yet you said it anyway."

He rose. "Katherine. I *hate* that I wasn't here to defend you and Molly against the vicious talk in town." His tone turned serious, heartfelt. "I should have known it would come to this. Because of me, and what happened in that supply closet, Molly suffered today. It's time the nasty town gossip moved away from my women. It's time I made it right for both of you, before matters get any worse."

Tears slipped around in her eyes. She blinked rapidly, hanging on to her emotions as best she could. But how could she not be touched by Trey's words? He understood. The big, gorgeous, heroic brute. He might still be locked in the past, but for now—today—he was right here with her. And in spite of her very real fears for his physical and spiritual safety, Katherine would trust that God would provide for them all.

Walk by faith, not by sight...

In that moment, Katherine was filled with certainty.

Trey narrowed his eyes. "You're not going to get all weepy and female on me?"

She hitched her chin high. "Maybe."

"I've a better idea." He pulled her carefully toward him. When she didn't resist, he wrapped his arms around her shoulders.

It quickly sank in that she was being held in the shelter of Trey Scott's arms, and there was no panic, no shuddering fear racing through her. Slowly, she roped her arms around his waist and rested her cheek against his chest.

"Quit battling me, Katherine," he said softly. "I may not be your first choice, or even your second. Marry me anyway, and make me a better man. I promise I'll defend your honor *and* Molly's with my life."

Of course, he would. "Oh, Trey. That's a much better proposal than before."

He tightened his hold. Just a little. And all she felt in response was comfort. Safety. A warm sense of homecoming.

Was she finally healed of her fear?

"I've missed you, Katherine." He sounded more amazed than shocked by the declaration.

"I missed you, too." She sighed against him, wanting only to focus on what she could control. "Dreadfully."

As the silence lengthened into a comfortable calm, Trey kissed the top of her head and then took several steps away from her. "Now that we've settled that, I have a gift for you."

"You bought a gift for me?" Her heart gave a happy twist at the notion.

"Don't sound so surprised." He tapped her on the nose. "I am capable of considering someone other than myself."

She closed her eyes, remembering all the times she'd watched him playing with Molly and the other Charity House children. For months, she'd refused to see Trey as he really was—a man who cared deeply for his own.

For better or worse, she and Molly were his now. She just had to tell him so.

Smiling down at her, he placed a black velvet box in her hand. "I found this in Colorado Springs and thought immediately of you."

An enchanting, albeit uncharacteristic, nervousness flickered in his eyes. "Take this as a token of my affection," he said. "And a promise of my loyalty to you and Molly forever."

Katherine found she could only stare at the tiny box. Other than Laney and Marc, no one had ever given her a gift.

"Go ahead. Open it."

Her fingers shook as she pulled back the lid. A gasp flew out of her lips the moment her gaze fell on the sparkling sapphire ring.

Trey edged toward her, with a tentative smile on his lips. "I picked the stone to match the color of your eyes."

The thoughtful way he'd chosen this gift sent her heart aching for the man Trey could become if he allowed himself to let go of the guilt of his past and his drive for vengeance.

She knew he was on the right path, but would she truly be at the end of it?

Yes. She had to believe in him, and in God's power to heal his heart.

"I… I don't know what to say," she said softly.

"Say you'll marry me. Let me make you a respectable woman, for all our sakes."

He plucked the ring out of its case, his eyes clouding over with a new emotion. He had a look about him that she'd seen once before, in the birthing room with Laney and Marc. Hope overwhelmed her as he slid the band onto her finger and commanded her gaze.

Something had changed in him. She wasn't fool enough to question the what or the why at this point. "Oh, Trey."

She lowered her gaze to the ring, rotated her wrist so the gem caught the light. As she stared into the sparkling stone, her decision became remarkably clear. Somewhere between Molly's need for a family and her own need for security, Katherine had lost hold of all the reasons why she had to refuse this man.

Trey fiddled with the hair that fell across her cheek. "We can make it work."

She sighed and thought of a verse from Ephesians. *Be completely humble and gentle; be patient, bearing with one another in love.*

She and Trey might not be evenly yoked spiritually.

Yet. But Katherine knew he'd once believed in God. Surely he could again.

Oh, Lord, soften his heart, she prayed. *Help him find his way back to You. And if it's in Your will, use me as Your vessel along that path.*

With one last swallow, the fight finally let her go. "Let's find out."

Trey's mouth hung open. He clamped his lips together, narrowed his eyes, then started sputtering. "What… What did you say?"

She lifted her gaze to his, discovering that she liked this man flustered, especially when she was the one doing the flustering. "I said, let's get married."

His eyes narrowed, suspicion coloring over his shock. "Are you doing this for Molly?"

Refusing to lie, she nodded. "And for other reasons."

His lips pulled into a lopsided grin. "That's enough for now."

She smiled at him in return.

With a careful tug he pulled her into his arms. Eyes full of intent, he lowered his head slowly. Very, very slowly.

He was going to kiss her. Right here. Anyone could walk into the study. But instead of feeling scared or even nervous, Katherine felt…excited.

Sighing, she settled deeper into his embrace and lifted her face to accept his kiss. Their first kiss.

"My sweet, sweet Katherine," he whispered.

And then he pressed his lips to hers at last. The connection was so soft, so gentle she wasn't sure whether to be relieved or disappointed. Before she could decide which, he set her away from him.

Spinning in a circle, he stabbed impatient fingers through his hair, then looked back to her. "I have to go."

"Go?" she asked. "Go where?"

"To make plans for our wedding, of course."

They laughed in unison, the sound linking them together in their own private world of understanding. Oh, how handsome Trey was when he laughed.

Katherine vowed to give him many reasons throughout the ensuing years to laugh more often.

Trey watched several emotions flit across Katherine's face. Thankfully, he didn't see any regret. "I'll be quick," he said. "I don't want to—"

A loud, insistent knocking interrupted the rest of his speech.

"Trey Scott," bellowed an angry voice from the other side of the door. "Open up. I know you're in there."

At the sound of Marc's voice, a sigh of dismay slipped from Katherine's lips. "What is he so upset about?"

Trey made a face. "He's obviously heard the talk."

"Oh, dear."

Wanting to protect Katherine from an ugly confrontation, Trey went to the door to head off his friend. But with a hard shove, Marc pushed into the room and grabbed Trey by the lapels.

"Is it true?" He shook Trey hard. "Did you and Katherine do what they—"

"*Calm down,* Marc." Trey yanked away from his friend. "You're out of control."

"Me? How can you say that after what you've done to Katherine!"

Trey shook his head. He should have known it would

come to this. "No matter what you think you've heard, it's misinformation."

Marc looked wildly around the study, his gaze seeking and finding Katherine with phenomenal speed. "Talk is all over town about you two. And it's ugly. I'm told some of the neighbors are already drawing up a formal complaint against you."

Katherine lifted her chin, but her eyes were filled with trepidation.

"Leave her alone, Marc." Trey would not allow his friend to accuse Katherine of something she hadn't done. "She didn't do anything wrong."

"Maybe *she* didn't." Spinning back to glare at Trey, Marc continued, "You, on the other hand, had no right to corner her in the school's supply closet."

Trey bristled as renewed guilt knotted around his heart. "I didn't even kiss her," he defended.

But he knew he'd wronged her simply by seeking her out when she was alone and unprotected.

"It doesn't matter what you did or didn't do, Trey. You *knew* her past. You also knew how the town treats her because of it. This time they have real ammunition against her. Charity House will weather the storm. We always do. But you shouldn't have put Katherine in a position to suffer again."

Trey froze at the accusation. Marc was right, of course. Although Trey had tried to rectify the situation since that auspicious day at the Charity House School, he'd been more consumed with finding Ike than pushing the matter with Katherine. In truth, Trey hadn't tried hard enough to set matters right.

"I've trusted you like a brother," Marc said, waving

his hand in an angry slash toward Katherine. "And this is what you do with that trust?"

Trey heard the unspoken words as loudly as the ones his friend said aloud. "You got something to say to me, say it plainly."

"All right. For four years, your quest for vengeance has consumed you. I've watched, helplessly, as the soothing of your own misplaced guilt turned you greedy and selfish. It didn't matter so much before, because you were only hurting yourself, but now you're hurting Katherine and Molly. You're going to make it right."

Trey scowled. Until Marc's outburst, he'd considered the other man a friend, a brother, the only one who understood his burning need to hunt down Ike Hayes and avenge Laurette's senseless murder.

Trey inched his gaze across Marc's features, arranging his own face into a look designed to start a fight. "And you're going to dole out the consequences if I don't, is that it?"

Marc nodded. "If it comes to that, yes. But, first, I want the facts so I can prepare for an official attack." As he glanced to Katherine, his expression softened with genuine concern. "Did Trey force you to do anything against your will?"

She looked at Trey as she answered the question. "No. Of course not."

Marc's eyes narrowed. "Did he tell you to say that?"

Friend or not, Trey wasn't about to let this man question Katherine's integrity. "You want a fight? You bring it to me. But I'm warning you now. Leave. Her. Alone."

Marc's lips formed into a sneer, disfiguring his features into a tangle of raw emotion. "A not-so-friendly threat. Is that it, Trey? Well, here's one of my own. You better be planning to marry her."

Trey's fists rose in response.

Katherine swiftly moved in front of Trey, placed her hands over his and pushed until he lowered them to his sides.

"Marc," she said, turning to look at him directly. In the process she shifted in front of Trey, as though she were shielding him. "I appreciate your gallant effort on my behalf, but it's already settled. Trey and I are getting married as soon as he can take care of the details."

Marc stared at her, with a look of disbelief on his face. "Are you telling me the truth, and or are you trying to protect him?"

"Oh, honestly. As if he needs my protection. Maybe this will make my point." She flashed her ring at him.

Marc looked at her hand, up to Katherine's face, then back to her hand. "When did all this happen?"

Trey gave his friend the kind of self-righteous sneer that was meant to make him see red. "That's none of your business. All you need to know is that we're getting married by the end of the week. You can either congratulate me on my good fortune or move aside."

A grin slipped onto Marc's lips. "Well, it's about time you came to your senses, old man." He reached out and smacked Trey on the back. "I couldn't be happier for either of you."

Trey nodded. "You're invited to the wedding, of course."

Looking nearly as happy as he had at the birth of his daughter, Marc's grin widened. "Oh, I'll be there. I plan to bring my shotgun, in case you get any ideas about begging off."

"Won't happen," said Trey.

Trey turned to Katherine, stared at her for a long, thoughtful moment. She was so beautiful. So kind.

And soon she would be his wife. His future.

His heart jumped in his chest at the possibility of real freedom. All along he'd told himself his desire to marry Katherine was to protect her from town gossip, and from the legal implications if a complaint was filed against the Charity House School. But he now realized, as he stared into her guileless eyes, there had been more motivating his offer of marriage. A desire for a fresh start, a chance to right a wrong for one woman when he'd failed another so miserably.

It was time to start taking action. And the sooner he married Katherine, the better. "Come to think of it, I should make the arrangements before *she* changes *her* mind."

A promise filled Katherine's eyes as she repeated his words back to him. "Won't happen."

Thank You, Lord, was his only clear thought after that.

Chapter Seventeen

A week later, Katherine lingered at the back of the church, shifting restlessly. Now that the time had come to pledge her life to Trey's, nerves threatened to consume her. With her agitation barely under control, she studied the group assembled around her. Marc stood like a sentry by her side. Laney and Molly were poised at the ready in front of her.

A riot of emotion tangled in her chest. Needing an encouraging word from a man who understood the situation better than the rest, she turned to Marc. But at the sight of his concentrated intensity, her heart dropped to her toes and stuck. This man wasn't going to let her walk out of the church until the nuptials were complete.

His fatherly concern of the past week would have been sweet if his fingerprints weren't all over the wedding. He'd been involved in every aspect of the planning, rushing decisions as though time was of the essence. Worse, he hadn't allowed her and Trey any time alone, claiming they might change their minds if they actually talked to one another.

If Katherine didn't know better, she'd think Marc

truly wanted this marriage to happen. And not just for Molly's sake.

She only wished she understood why.

The moment Mrs. Smythe began playing the music on the out-of-tune organ, Katherine shook away her confusion and inched forward. The pews were full of forty grinning faces. She caught sight of Sheriff Lassiter sitting next to a solemn Shane Bartlett. There was no one else from town.

She didn't need anyone else.

"Ready?" she whispered to her sister.

Molly lifted the basket in her good hand and gave a quick, solid nod. "Ready."

Katherine couldn't help but notice how lovely the little girl looked with her long black hair hanging loose down her back, flowers sprinkled throughout. Thankfully, her eye had healed. The only sign of her fight with Bobby Prescott was the bandage on her right hand.

"You look beautiful, Molly."

Molly's answering smile was as radiant as Katherine had ever seen it. "So do you."

Reveling in her sister's joy, she squeezed Molly's shoulder. Angling her head toward the other end of the aisle, she said, "Okay, you can start walking now. Laney will follow behind you, just like we practiced this morning."

"Let's go get married."

Her heart filled with Molly's contagious enthusiasm, and Katherine nodded. "Let's."

Molly started down the aisle, stopped in midstep, then swerved back. Lurching forward, she threw her arms around Katherine's waist and buried her face in the flowing skirts. "Thank you for marrying Mr. Trey."

Swiping the back of her wrist across her eyes, Katherine swallowed a shuddering sigh; then she eased Molly's chin up. She stared into eyes identical to those of the mother they'd shared and lost. A tug on her heart hitched her voice up an octave. "I love you, Molly. The best thing that ever happened to me was getting that letter from the mine's foreman."

"Me, too."

With a two-finger salute exactly like the one Trey always gave them, Molly started back down the aisle. Katherine's heart clutched in her chest as she watched her little sister tossing rose petals on the church floor. She couldn't remember ever seeing the little girl as contented as she had been these past few days. Trey's presence in Molly's life had turned her into a vivacious, happy child. Nothing like the silent, frightened creature Katherine had rescued from the mining camp.

Through championing the child, Trey Scott had worked a near miracle in Molly's life. For that alone, Katherine would adore him until the end of her days. She would trust him to care for her as well.

And though the issue of his vow to avenge his wife's murder wasn't settled, Katherine had confidence in God's providence and healing power. When the time came to seek vengeance—*if* the time came—she prayed God would lead Trey to make the right decision.

Molly skipped the last five steps, then vaulted into Trey's arms. Trey spun her around, kissed her on top of the head, then set her down next to him. He whispered something in the little girl's ear that had her giggling, then scooted her to his right.

As Katherine watched the two interact, the sincerity of their affection for one another spoke louder than any declaration. Trey had taken on the role of father. And it suited him.

Laney always said that God was a God of new beginnings and second chances. Well, Trey was Katherine's second chance, and she was his.

For a moment, just one, everything seemed to slow down and stop. Even her breathing. She loved Trey, really, truly loved him. It was that simple. And that complicated.

Laney cleared her throat, bringing Katherine's attention to the back of the church once more. "Are you sure this is what you want?"

Katherine glanced over her friend's shoulder, her gaze uniting with Trey's. His eyes were filled with promises, and an eternal vow. If she'd had any doubts before, they disappeared under his silent appeal.

There were no guarantees, but with God's help, Trey would heal in time, just as Katherine had. For now, Katherine would take what happiness she could while she had him with her. "Yes, I'm sure."

Laney tilted her head to the side and regarded her with a searching look.

"Truly," Katherine said.

Laney nodded, relief flickering along the edges of her eyes. "Then I wish you the same happiness I have with Marc."

She winked at her husband, then began her stroll toward the front of the church.

Watching Laney's willowy descent down the aisle, Katherine suddenly remembered what her mother used to say when times were rough. "Where there is life, my dear, there is still hope."

Yes. While Trey was alive, Katherine would concentrate on each day as it came. She would no longer chose loneliness simply because she was afraid of being left alone. She would become the sort of wife a man like Trey would hate to leave, one to whom he couldn't wait to return time and time again.

A still, small voice whispered through her mind. *My power is made perfect in your weakness.*

Resolved, she lifted her foot to begin the march into her future, but Marc held her back. "You're sure this is what you want to do?"

Katherine winced. "What is it with you and Laney? A person would think you weren't sure of the wisdom of this marriage."

"A person would be right."

She opened her mouth to argue, to remind him of his heavy-handed machinations in the planning of every detail, but didn't know where to begin.

Surveying his concerned expression, she lifted her eyebrows. When he merely returned her look with a questioning glare of his own, she sighed in frustration. "Marc, I can tell by your expression, you have more to say to me. Just say it and let's be done."

He shifted his gaze to the other end of the church, then back to her. "Katherine, I know I've pushed you this week, but I don't want to force you into something you don't want to do."

"This? From you? The man who brought his shotgun to my wedding?"

He slid her a sheepish grin. "It was a jest."

"Ha-ha."

Glancing to the heavens, he shook his head. "Marriage is permanent."

"So is raising a sister."

Failure flashed in his gaze before it turned hard and unwavering. "All the more reason to make sure. Your past makes no difference to Laney and me. Never has. You and Molly will always have a home at Charity House. No censure, no condemnation. Nothing would have to change."

"That's sweet, but—"

"Say the word and we walk out of this church. Charity House will face whatever scandal comes from this together, as a family."

"Oh, Marc—"

"I mean it."

"I know you do, and that's what makes it all the more special. But I *want* to marry Trey."

He gave her a sad smile. "You don't have to pretend with me. I know how you really feel about him."

"You do?"

Could Marc see how much she loved his brother-in-law? Did he pity her because he knew Trey would never love her the way he'd always loved Laurette?

The concerned parent slid into place as Marc gestured toward the opposite end of the church. "I know you're afraid of him."

A strange disappointment etched across her soul. Apparently, Marc didn't understand as much as she'd hoped he would. "I admit there was a time that was true, but not anymore. I trust him completely." She smiled, then decided to tell Marc the rest. "I love him."

"Oh, Katherine."

"Yes." She sighed. *"Oh, Katherine."*

"He… I don't want to build any false hope for you, not now, not ever. Although I don't doubt he'll try, Trey may not make you a good husband."

"I know that."

"I'm confident he won't hurt you physically, but he's stuck in his anger and drive for vengeance."

"I know that, too. But with help from our heavenly Father, I believe Trey will find peace and forgiveness one day."

"If that never happens—" Marc rested his hand on her shoulder "—would you still be willing to go through with this?"

"Yes."

Squeezing her hand gently, he studied her face for what felt like an eternity. "You really do love him, then."

She patted his sleeve, and he dropped his hand to his side. "I know what you're trying to say, Marc. You don't want me to foolishly build a hope for something that may never occur."

"Don't misunderstand me. I love Trey. He's my brother, and he needs you, Katherine. He might never be able to tell you that, but he does. That doesn't mean he'll make you happy. He isn't an easy man."

"You forget, I've seen him at his worst." *And his best.* The sudden thought washed through her, cleansing her fears, solidifying her resolve. "Let's stop this disturbing talk, shall we? I want to get married."

Marc nodded, but the concern only increased in his eyes. "All right then, if that's what you really want."

"It is."

He jutted his elbow toward her, and she settled her hand in the crook of his arm. As he started down the aisle, she fell into step beside him. "If he hurts you, Katherine, I'll kill him."

Now that did it. Katherine had had more than enough of Marc casting his "brother" in the role of outlaw.

"And what if *I* hurt him?" She didn't bother hiding the righteous anger in her tone.

Obviously shocked, Marc stopped walking. He turned his head to study her with a look suspiciously close to respect. "Then you answer to me."

"Good. Because it goes both ways. It's just like you said, Marc, Trey needs me. And *I* need him."

"Then make him happy."

"I will."

With his heart choking in his throat, Trey watched Katherine and Marc walking arm in arm down the aisle. As though hearing his silent call, Katherine lifted her eyes to his. Captured by her beauty, he felt an unfamiliar sense of peace fill him.

They *would* make a good life together.

He liked how she studied him in return, her gaze skimming along his face, down his nose, along the contour of his jaw, each sweep a soft caress.

This woman would soon be his wife.

Trey braced his shoulders for the guilt to assault him. But none came. His throat convulsed with a heavy swallow, his head no longer full of reminders of the woman he had lost but of the woman he'd found.

With one final blink, he shifted his mind to Katherine and let Laurette fade into the past. He knew that a part of his dead wife would always live in his heart, but Katherine was his today, his tomorrow—his future.

And he couldn't be more pleased.

Gliding toward him, she looked fragile, beautiful, the blue dress matching her eyes. She'd pulled her hair into a fancy hairstyle, sprinkling flowers identical to the ones in Molly's hair throughout her own. Compelled to compare the two, he looked down at the kid. She grinned up at him, her smile so much like the one her sister had just flashed—minus a front tooth or two—his heart clutched in his chest. In the past few months, this child had become more daughter than friend.

It felt right.

Returning his gaze back to Katherine, his throat convulsed through a heavy swallow. She looked like spring. New love. Forever. His breath tensed in his lungs, held firm. He knew his bitter soul didn't deserve this woman, but now that he'd received her caring, her generous spirit and her unbending devotion, he couldn't give her up.

He wondered what Marc had said to her before they'd started down the aisle. He was probably trying to talk her out of the marriage. Trey couldn't much blame his friend. Katherine had that way about her, made a man want to protect her.

Well, Trey might not be filled with youthful optimism. His heart might hold more bitterness than most. But he would do his best to keep her safe and honor her and never harm her. He would do everything in his power to make life for Katherine—and Molly—secure.

Marc drew to a stop and gave Trey a warning glare. Just to be ornery, Trey grinned at him, then planted a kiss on Katherine's mouth.

"You look beautiful," he told her, his voice quivering with emotions he couldn't name.

"Thank you."

"Are you ready to do this?"

She nodded, her eyes filling with tears.

He cupped her cheek. She leaned into his touch and gave him a watery smile filled with…love.

The truth sent blinding shards of pain and excitement through him. Katherine Taylor loved him.

His heart cracked opened, and with one final wave to the past, he allowed her inside. This woman was his future. He took a step forward, roped his arms around her and kissed her lips again. "I'll give you the best of me."

The minister began the ceremony. "We are here to join Ethan Wendell Scott III and Katherine Monica Taylor together in holy matrimony. Katherine has chosen the first Scripture to be read from Ecclesiastes.

"Two are better than one, because they have a good return for their work. If one falls down, his friend can help him up. But pity the man who falls and has no one to help him up…"

In that moment, with his eyes burning, Trey silently vowed to become the man he saw shining in Katherine's gaze.

Chapter Eighteen

"You did good today, Mr. Trey."

Trey smiled at the little girl sauntering toward him, the flowers in her hair bouncing with each step she took. Watching her approach, he felt his heart burst with the need to protect, to love. "Thank you, kitten. I couldn't have done it without you."

She looked over her shoulder, giggled. Trey sent his gaze in the same direction, caught sight of his wife in deep conversation with Laney. Emotion squeezed his chest. Would he ever tire of looking at Katherine? She was so beautiful, and not merely on the outside, where everyone could see. Sometimes it hurt, deep in his soul, to look at her.

She'd suffered so much torment in her young life. How he wanted to do right by her now, as he hadn't been able to do for Laurette.

"I can't believe you did it," Molly said, still looking at her sister, obviously unaware of his turbulent thoughts. "You really married Katherine."

"I did. She's officially my wife now. And as far as I'm concerned, that makes you my daughter."

Wife. Daughter. It felt good to know they were both pledged to him forever now.

With a swish and fancy, little-girl swaying, Molly turned back around. A look of deep concentration marred her brow. "Did you know, Mr. Trey, Katherine hasn't yelled at you all day? I think that's the only time ever."

He tried to keep his features blank, his mood as serious as the little girl's. "I know."

"That's really good."

Unable to hold back any longer, he let go of his grin and chuckled. How easy life was in the eyes of a five-year-old. For the rest of the day, he vowed to let Molly's world prevail over his.

"Want to know a secret?" He leaned over, lowered his voice to a whisper. "Although it's sometimes fun to fight with your sister, I really like it when she doesn't yell at me."

Molly gave him one solemn nod. "Me, too."

Raising her arms to him, she waited. Understanding her silent command, he lifted her into his embrace, settled her on his hip, then offered his cheek. She planted a big, wet kiss on the same spot as always. "I love you, Mr. Trey."

His response was immediate. "I love you, too, kitten."

Suddenly shy, she cocked her head at him. "So do I get to call you daddy now?"

She might as well have gripped his heart and squeezed. "Absolutely."

Flattening a palm against his cheek, she nodded again. *"Daddy."*

Trey's heart stopped beating completely, then kicked wildly back to life. "Promise me something, Molly."

"Sure, okay," she said, her expression serious, her eyes never leaving his face. "Anything, *Daddy*."

He was sure his heart was going to explode from the affection he felt for this child, his daughter. He had to blink to stop the burning in his eyes. "Be good tonight while your sister and I are at the hotel."

She hitched her chin at him, mutiny blazing in her eyes. "I'm always good."

He lowered her to the ground, dropped a kiss on her head. "Right. I forgot."

Shaking her head at him, she planted her left fist on her hip and swung her bandaged hand back and forth. "Daddy. Daddy. Daddy."

"I know. I forgot. How about you go run over there and tell your sister goodbye. We're leaving soon."

She angled her head, considered him for a moment. "Be nice to Katherine tonight."

He hitched his chin at her in a similar show of stubbornness. "I'm always nice."

Obviously unconvinced, she stared at him a while longer, then stamped her foot. "Promise," she demanded.

He looked past Molly, fixed his gaze on his wife. As though hearing his silent appeal, Katherine looked up and molded her lips into a ready smile. "All right, kitten, I promise I'll be nice to your sister tonight."

That was one vow he knew he'd have no trouble keeping.

Katherine allowed Trey to lead her away from the church, the guests following them to the carriage hired to take them to the Palace Hotel. The plush interior of the coach was finer than any Katherine had known. Another detail Marc had insisted he settle for them. She had no idea where he had found such an elaborate conveyance. But, as she slid across the seat and allowed the sheer luxury to wash over her, she decided not to ask questions.

Today was a day for joy.

She splayed her fingers along the red velvet cushions, which stood in stark relief against the dark mahogany of the inlaid ceiling. Sitting in so regal a carriage, Katherine felt like a queen—with a very attentive king by her side.

Trey's gaze hadn't left her face since she'd joined him at the altar, making her feel cherished, special. The ceremony had been short, lovely, sweeping her away into a world of hope and possibility. Not wanting her senses to return and ruin the moment, she shut her eyes and pressed her head against the plush cushions behind her.

Trey climbed inside, his weight slightly tilting the carriage toward him. He issued the order to the driver, then shut the door behind him.

As he settled in next to her, his voice drifted over her like a soft whisper. "Look at me."

She opened her eyes, and her heart hammered against her ribs at what she saw in his gaze. Trey Scott had the look of love in his eyes.

As he leaned closer, his lips curved into a beautiful smile. "No regrets?" he asked, with something oddly hesitant in his manner.

"Not yet." She'd thought to tease him, but her words came out stilted, earnest.

He sighed. "Not a very hopeful answer, but an honest one, I suppose."

He stroked her cheek, her jaw, and a low rumble sounded in his chest. "I'll be gentle with you tonight, my love. We'll go at your pace, and I'll do only what you want me to do."

Sudden fear clogged her throat. "What if…what if I can't go through with it?"

"Then we spend the night talking. Get to know each other better."

Her heart turned troubled, unsure. She knew enough about men from her mother's business to know what he offered was unusual. Heroic, even. "That would be enough for you?"

Trey leaned forward and kissed her lightly on the nose. "I can be a very patient man, Mrs. Scott. Resourceful, too. Even if it takes a lifetime, I plan to give you every reason to trust me to take care of you in our marriage bed."

"A lifetime?"

"Yes."

"Well, then." Her eyes glittered back at him, and his heart hitched in his chest. "Let's hope it doesn't take *that* long."

Trey laughed, the sound chasing away the remaining tension between them. "Beautiful Katherine, I'll do everything in my power to be a good husband to you."

She covered his mouth with her fingers. "I know, Trey. I believe you."

"Good." He took her hand and pressed her palm against his heart. *"Good."*

He closed his eyes a moment and just breathed in

her clean, fresh scent. His stomach felt a little funny all of a sudden, and then the sensation spread up to his chest. Once he could breathe again, he decided he liked the feeling.

Liked it very much.

Chapter Nineteen

The next morning Trey woke first. Settled comfortably in an overstuffed chair, he drank a second cup of coffee while his bride continued sleeping in the other room. At the sound of her soft, feminine snoring, a wave of contentment rippled through him.

He couldn't help but think God had blessed him with this new marriage. And for the first time in four years, the thought of the Lord's hand in any part of his life didn't bring anger and bitterness.

Only awe. And a large dose of gratitude.

The evening had been filled with firsts for them both. And as their wedding night had progressed, Trey had been able to show Katherine just how patient he could be with her. Together, they'd overcome the obstacle of her fear of physical intimacy.

With a large dose of satisfaction, Trey kicked his feet onto the ottoman and wondered if they'd made a baby when they'd consummated their marriage.

But as soon as the thought came, painful memories of what had happened to Laurette and their unborn child broke through his pleasure. Heart-pounding fear gripped him, nearly paralyzing his ability to breathe. He'd failed Laurette. Violence had won that round.

Could he keep his new family safe? Or would he fail them as well?

No, he would not. This time he would do what was necessary to protect what was his.

Until he found Ike, there were going to have to be rules, nonnegotiable rules. When he had to leave town, Katherine, Molly and any children that came along would stay with Marc and Laney at Charity House. Once the school year began, he'd appoint a deputy to watch the premises.

A muscle shifted in his jaw as gripping anxiety clogged his throat and stole his breath. The drive to finish the business of the past was suddenly obscene, like a sharp, fiery stake stabbing into his heart.

He heard Katherine stir. Shaking away his ugly thoughts, he set his cup on the table next to him and went to the doorway that led into the bedroom. Leaning against the jamb, he studied his wife as her eyes blinked slowly open.

With her gaze unfocused, sleepy, she looked youthful, beautiful. His momentary concern for the future faded, and Katherine Taylor Scott filled his world. "Good morning, Mrs. Scott."

A smile played at the tips of her mouth. "Good morning, Mr. Scott."

"Sleep well?"

She stretched, yawned. "Lovely."

Trey's heart dipped in his chest. "Hungry?"

"Ravenous."

Laughing, he shoved away from the door. "Me, too."

In the same moment he leaned down to kiss her lips, a pounding came at the door.

"Marshal, you in there?"

Logan. For a lawman, the deputy had rotten timing.

Katherine blew her hair out of her face and sighed. "Looks like breakfast will have to wait."

"If we don't answer," he whispered, "he'll go away."

Three more raps. "Marshal. It's important."

Katherine sat up, wrapped the covers around her and then slid him an annoyed look, as though she was as disappointed as he was by the interruption. Unfortunately, the underlying dread in her expression was impossible to miss.

They both knew Logan would interrupt them for only one reason.

"Answer the door," she said at last.

He wished he knew what to say to alleviate her worry, but his mind wrestled with two thoughts—it was time to serve up justice, and it was too soon to leave his wife.

Logan's plea turned urgent. *"Marshal."*

"I'm coming," Trey shouted back. "Give me a moment."

He waited until Katherine snuggled deeper under the covers before moving back into the sitting room. He gave her one last look over his shoulder, then padded barefoot through the room.

Yanking the door open, he growled at the other man. "This better be good."

Logan tried to enter the room, but Trey barred entrance with his body. "Well?"

Shrugging, Logan stepped back. "A telegraph came in from the marshal in Nebraska territory. He caught Ike Hayes."

He caught Ike Hayes.

The need for justice knotted in Trey's gut, and all he could do was stare at Logan as the news slowly sank in.

This was it, then. After all these years of searching, retribution was within his grasp. Laurette would receive justice at last. She would not have died in vain.

"Marshal Roberts wants us to meet him in Cheyenne," Logan continued, "so he can turn over the prisoner to you personally."

"I'll be ready to leave in an hour," Trey said. "Meet me at the stables."

Trey shut the door behind Logan's nod of agreement. No time for thought. Only action. With deliberate movements, he gathered his belongings. Against his best efforts to remain calm, his head filled with memories, and his heart exploded with anger and frustration.

Ike Hayes had preyed on the innocent and killed for sport for too long. Trey would not miss this opportunity to bring the man who'd killed his wife to trial.

If for no other reason, he owed it to Laurette.

So consumed with ending the violence, he'd nearly forgotten about Katherine until his glance fell on the bed. She sat there, unmoving, her knees wrapped in the covers and pulled to her chest. She didn't say anything, just quietly watched him.

Her eyes were big and round and worried, and in that moment, she looked only a few years older than Molly.

"I have to go," he said.

She nodded, her eyes never leaving his face. He understood the fear settling over her. Just as he recognized the strength it took her to hold the emotion at bay.

"I have to do this," he said, his tone more desperate than firm. "He's the man who killed my wife."

She jerked at his declaration, sighed and then dropped her gaze to her knees. "Of course."

"Try to understand, Katherine. Justice must be served."

He wanted to repeat the words over and over, until he made her accept how important this was to him. To them and their future together.

She lifted her gaze and simply stared at him. After a long, dead silence her eyes filled with a deep sadness, but she continued to hold his gaze, with an unwavering conviction that belied her emotions.

"You have to do what you think is best, Trey."

"I *have* to finish this." Even to his own ears, his voice sounded hesitant, uneasy. "Then I—*we*—can move on with our lives."

She simply nodded. "Of course."

Katherine's patient acceptance shattered him. Where was the fight in her? The yelling? The accusations? A battle he could handle? This calm understanding—it nearly broke him.

"I—"

"No. Don't say anything else." She rushed to him, reached for his hand and clutched it to her heart. "God-speed, my love. May you have the peace of Christ and the conviction of the Holy Spirit in your heart as you go."

He dropped his belongings and pulled her into his arms. "Once I... Once justice is finally served, we can start our new life together, Katherine. We'll be free from the past. I promise."

And as with every promise he'd made to her in the past, he would keep his word.

As weeks turned into months, and still no direct word from Trey, Katherine's worry increased, putting her on edge.

Oh, Lord, please bring him safely home to me, she prayed. *Let this capture of Ike Hayes be the end of Trey's need for revenge. Give him the freedom only You can give.*

But no matter how hard she focused on her husband, Trey's safety wasn't Katherine's only concern. A few weeks ago, her body had started changing, no longer feeling like her own. The morning the vomiting had begun, she'd realized she was carrying Trey's child. One night together—their beautiful, all-too-short wedding night—had been enough to create a baby.

Out of her healing, and Trey's gentleness, had come this new life. She couldn't have asked for a richer blessing.

Unfortunately, the morning sickness had gotten worse these past two days, throbbing with the tenacity of sharp little rat's teeth. She lay in her bed just as dawn broke, trying her best to control the spasms of pain gripping her stomach.

She prayed softly for strength.

Lifting her Bible off the nightstand, she flipped to the thirty-first chapter of Deuteronomy. "Be strong and courageous. Do not be afraid or terrified—"

Another spasm cut through her. Leaning over the chamber pot, she spilled the last of the contents of her stomach. She hadn't been able to keep food down for two days now. She was so tired, uncharacteristically weak, and her stomach ached miserably. Even now, the energy to get out of bed eluded her.

Her throat clutched again. Unable to bear another bout of nausea, she willed the pain away and began reading where she'd left off. "For the Lord your God goes with you; He will never leave you nor forsake you."

In spite of the chill in the room, she started sweating. Her legs ached through to the bones, and her heart swelled with fear. Something was wrong. This pain couldn't be normal.

But she'd wasted too much time in bed already. Attempting to lift her head, she collapsed back against the pillow, conquered by the rush of agony. The terror, both thick and huge, ripped a single moan from her lips.

Another spasm of pain clutched her stomach, and she dropped the Bible to the floor. Rolling herself into a ball, she prepared for the inevitable nausea, but instead another pain followed the first. The third one made her cry out.

She expelled three more shaky breaths, then managed to stand. A hot, sticky liquid slid along the inside of her legs. Looking to the floor, she saw the red stain on her nightgown, the blood creating a small puddle at her feet.

"Oh, Lord, no. *Please,* not this. Trey doesn't even know he's going to be a father."

Just as she cried out for Laney, the room spun, and Katherine's head filled with dizzying, life-altering fear.

"Trey," she whispered just before her vision turned black.

Katherine opened her eyes to find Dr. Bartlett standing over her, a concerned expression on his face. The pounding in her head made her squint against the sharp light piercing the room.

She tried to lift her head off the pillow—someone had obviously moved her to the bed—but the effort wore her out. "What happened?"

The fast clicking of heels to wood accompanied Laney's soft cry. "Praise God, you're awake."

Katherine opened her eyes just as her friend knelt beside the bed, placed her cool palm against her forehead.

"We've been so worried about you." The terror was there in the other woman's eyes, in her shaking fingers, her stilted voice.

Katherine tried to close her mind to what Laney's fear meant and focus only on the words spoken. "We?"

"Me, Molly, Marc, the Charity House children."

Giving up the fight, Katherine allowed her mind to concentrate on a memory, one that refused to let her go but wouldn't fully materialize. Her head pounded out a series of sketchy details, then went blank. But then one painful, heart-wrenching image came into focus—the blood at her feet. "My baby?"

Tears filled Laney's eyes. "I'm sorry, Katherine. You lost it."

Why couldn't she make her head understand what Laney was saying? Why did the terror embrace her heart?

Dr. Bartlett's melodious, soothing voice drifted over her. "I'm sorry I didn't get here soon enough."

What sort of cruel twist was this? She and Trey had made a baby together, but it was dead. How would he accept this new loss? How would she?

Overwhelmed by too many fierce emotions, she simply stared at Laney and Dr. Bartlett.

Oh, Trey, why aren't you home yet?

She needed his strength, his arms around her. She needed him to tell her it wasn't true. But it was true; she saw it in the concerned eyes that watched her. Her baby was dead, and Trey hadn't even known of its existence.

For weeks, she'd spent her days worrying about Trey, about the harm that could come to him both physically and spiritually if he didn't let go of his drive for vengeance.

It hadn't occurred to her that she might be the one in danger. Had her ignorance killed her baby? Had she neglected some detail? Had she been so consumed with worry that she'd killed her child?

Laney sighed, the sound cutting through Katherine's terrifying thoughts. "I'm so sorry."

Although she heard the words, knew them to be true, Katherine couldn't make her mind focus on the fact that she'd lost her child.

The doctor moved slowly into view. "We nearly lost you as well."

Laney gripped her hand and squeezed. "You've been very ill, unconscious for four days now. We've all been praying for you."

"Four days?" The headache gripping the inside of her brain twisted to her eyes. She reached up to rub her temple, shocked at the shake in her hands. "The last thing I remember is calling for you."

"I found you in a heap on the floor. Marc carried you to the bed, then sent Johnny for the doctor."

Making prayers out of her wordless sighs, Katherine tried to call up the details of the past few days. She got nothing. "I never woke?"

Dr. Bartlett shook his head.

Laney squeezed her hand again. "Katherine, I know you're weak right now, but Molly has been…in a state."

Molly. Oh, her poor little sister must have been petrified. "Go get her, Laney. *Hurry.*"

Laney looked to the doctor.

Dr. Bartlett nodded. "Go ahead."

Once she was alone with the doctor, Katherine's fears twined inside her sorrow and guilt. "What did I do wrong?"

Shaking his head, he looked more tired than usual, as though he'd lost a lot of sleep. Over her? Had she truly been that ill? "This wasn't your fault," Dr. Bartlett said.

Words backed up in her throat. "Then why did my baby die?"

"Sometimes these things happen." He brought a cup of water to her lips and lifted her head. As she drank, he continued. "I know that doesn't bring much comfort to you, but there are mysteries of the human body we just don't understand. As the Lord says, 'My ways aren't your ways.' But Jesus will give you comfort if you turn to Him."

Katherine shut her eyes. She was aware that Dr. Bartlett was watching her reaction to his words, but she ignored him. Comfort, it seemed, wouldn't come with a few well-placed prayers this time.

She spread her hand across her stomach, not quite able to believe that her baby—the one she'd only just started to get to know and love—was no longer living inside her.

Oh, how she'd wanted this baby, more than she'd understood until now. She couldn't help but feel that she'd lost a part of Trey with their child.

Would this loss haunt her always? Would she never be free of the ache?

Guilt ate at her. Was this the sort of pain Trey had suffered these past four years? She finally understood a part of what drove him, but at a far too painful cost.

The door swung open, and Molly inched into the

room. The terror on the little girl's face forced Katherine to push her own grief aside.

Reaching out a hand to her sister, she said, "Come here, Molly."

Molly tiptoed forward, looking once more like the little girl Katherine had met in the mining camp, instead of the vivacious child of the past few months. Where was the childlike energy, the infectious laughter Katherine had come to associate with the five-year-old?

Katherine swallowed past the pain in her head, the aching in her bones. "It's all right. You can come closer."

Molly's eyes widened, and she took a step backward.

Katherine called on every scrap of her strength, sat up and forced a smile on her lips. "See? I'm fine."

A sob burst from Molly's lips, and she vaulted across the divide between them, then halted abruptly at the foot of the bed. "You look so sick," she said, her voice barely more than a squeak.

Katherine wanted to soothe her sister's fears, but she couldn't lie to her. "I am sick. But I'm not going to die."

Molly's face scrunched into a frown. "But, Katherine, sick people die."

"Not always."

Blinking back tears, Molly scuffled around to the side of the bed. When she got closer, tears started spilling.

"I'm sorry I worried you." Katherine patted a spot on the bed. "Come. Sit with me."

Molly shook her head, her gaze darting to the doctor, over to Laney, to the doctor again, then finally back to Katherine.

"It's all right. You won't hurt me."

"Really?"

Katherine lifted her arms. "Absolutely."

Leading with a knee, Molly edged one leg onto the bed.

Ignoring her own pain, Katherine wrapped the little girl in her arms and tugged her tightly against her. "See? I'm completely alive."

Molly wiped her cheek on Katherine's shoulder. "You scared me, Katherine."

"I scared myself."

Sniffing, the little girl pushed away. "Promise you won't get sick again."

If only she could make such a vow. "I'll certainly try not to."

"I would have been a good big sister."

For a shocking moment, Katherine feared she was going to break down and sob, unable to stop for days. She hated that her innocent little sister had been subjected to the cruelty of another loss, hated that the loss had occurred. But she couldn't give in to the weakness of her grief now. With her chin trembling, she forced a bright smile on her face. "I know, Molly. The best."

"I miss Mr. Trey. I mean… *Daddy.*" Molly's crestfallen expression mirrored the emotions in Katherine's heart.

Katherine dragged her little sister back into her arms. "Oh, Molly, me, too." She allowed a single tear to fall before she blinked the rest into submission. "Me, too."

Chapter Twenty

Trey arrived in Denver hungry for blood. With leaden feet, he trudged up the back stairwell of Miss Martha's boarding house. The cracked paint on the barren walls did nothing to improve his mood. He'd intentionally chosen this place to live because it left him cold. At the time he'd only needed somewhere to rest his head at night. In truth, it had felt wrong to commit time and money to a house when Laurette could no longer help him turn the brick and mortar into a home.

Thoughts of his dead wife still plagued him, heightened by his recent defeat. Thus, when he reached the top step, white-hot anger swirled up so fast, so completely it clogged the air in his lungs.

He forced the emotion down, took a deep breath and entered his room. Deadly silence slammed into him. The space felt foreign. Unwelcoming.

Empty.

He hadn't realized how solitary and lonely his life had become in the years since Laurette's murder. All his goals, all his dreams had been reduced to the sole quest for revenge.

He was tired of the pain. Tired of the burning hatred.

Trey suddenly wanted Katherine and Molly. Just seeing them would lift his mood and make him forget, for a time, the defeat he felt so strongly now. But first he needed to clean off weeks of trail dust and defeat.

While he washed, his mind kept running through the infuriating events of the past two months. By the time he and Logan had arrived in Cheyenne, Ike Hayes had escaped custody. Although Marshal Roberts had wounded Ike in the scuffle, the outlaw still lived.

Trey's jaw clenched with the effort to hold back his fury.

Ike. Still. Lived.

Those three words had driven Trey in his ruthless pursuit of the outlaw. He'd tracked Ike all the way from Cheyenne to Nebraska City. At each town, Trey had been no more than a day or two behind the killer. A week ago, the trail had dried up completely. Trey had been forced to return to Denver and to his original plan of waiting for Ike to come to him.

Looking out the window, Trey noticed the bustling activity on the street below. How could everyone act so normal?

Absently, he mixed shaving cream in the bowl he cupped in his palm. Ticking off the past weeks, one by one, his mind returned to the morning after his wedding night. The last time he'd seen Katherine.

Until the moment when he'd stared into her frightened, dejected eyes, Trey hadn't truly understood how much his quest for vengeance hurt her. By allowing grief to rule his every move, he'd kept Laurette's memory alive in his heart—and prevented Katherine from truly becoming his wife.

But after four years of seeking vengeance, he'd become comfortable in his bitterness. He didn't know how else to live. Nevertheless, he couldn't continue on the same angry path. He owed it to Katherine and Molly to break the cycle of pain and hurt.

Trey swallowed. Hard. If he never brought Ike to justice, if he never took revenge, could he truly commit his life, his heart and his future to Katherine and Molly?

How could he just let go of Laurette without finishing the quest to avenge her murder? How could he continue hurting Katherine and Molly?

He hadn't counted on finding love again. Katherine, with her goodness, and Molly, with her childlike devotion, had broken through his defenses. And the more they took over his heart, the less he hated.

Trey didn't believe God's plan for his life had included losing Laurette and their unborn baby, but he couldn't deny that their deaths made finding Katherine and Molly that much more precious to him.

He had the strongest urge to take both woman and child into his arms and tell them how much he cared.

He'd figure out the rest later.

Impatient to get to Charity House, he quickly shaved and finished dressing. But the moment he slammed his hat on his head, a sick feeling of dread navigated along his spine.

Something wasn't right.

He knew it in his gut.

Trey left his room in a haze and rushed down the street, toward Charity House.

As he drew up to the front of the house, the lack of activity struck him first, convincing him to stand on his guard. At this hour, the children were usually at their loudest, with an adult voice or two raised over the chatter.

Looking around him, a dark premonition shot through him, sending a shiver across his soul. The deadly stillness enveloped him. In response, an ache started in his gut, wrapped around his heart and then turned into the same twisting agony he'd endured when he'd ridden onto the ranch four years ago and found Laurette dying.

Pushing through the front door, he tossed his hat to the nearest chair. He only had time for impressions as he searched for human life. The ticking of the clock. The lemon oil Laney used on the furniture. The candles and lanterns blazing, casting their light into the room.

Where was everyone?

Trey raised his voice, surprised at the shake in it. "Hello. Anyone here?" He glanced around him, then swallowed several times. *"Anyone?"*

Mrs. Smythe shuffled into the hallway. The look on her face confirmed his worst fears. "Oh, Marshal Scott, I'm so sorry. She just didn't have the strength."

"What do you mean?"

A myriad of emotions flickered across the woman's face. "It's Katherine."

A gut-wrenching fear twined into guilt and finally settled into self-recrimination for leaving his wife alone for so long.

"What about Katherine?" Trey didn't realize he'd shouted until he saw Mrs. Smythe step away from him.

She pointed over his shoulder. "Upstairs."

The way she said the word sent a shiver of terror racing along the back of his neck.

"The doctor is with her."

Doctor? Stifling the panic that rose in his throat,

Trey spun around and took the stairs three at a time. Katherine was in trouble, and just like with Laurette, he hadn't been here for her.

Guilt mingled with panic pushed him faster as he headed straight for her room and burst through the door.

His gaze sought and found his wife. Pale and small in her bed, she looked like a woman who had given up on life. Molly sat next to her, gripping her hands in hers while tears ran down her face.

Katherine was dying. And he was too late to save her. *Just like Laurette.*

He sensed others in the room, but Katherine and Molly were all that mattered to him now. Molly sprang from the bed and vaulted into his arms. "Daddy, you came home."

Trey hugged her tight against him, his eyes never leaving Katherine's blank stare.

"I always come back, kitten." *Just never in time.*

No, he wouldn't allow death to defeat him, not this time. This time he would fight harder.

He settled Molly on his hip and then made his way across the room. He kept his gaze centered on Katherine, forcing his own fears aside as he recognized the loss of will in her. He'd always thought of Katherine as a woman full of sparkle. But now she looked dull, lifeless.

Every part of his body went on alert.

"Katherine," he whispered.

She shut her eyes, swallowed. A shudder wracked through her body before she looked at him again. The blank stare she gave him confirmed his doubts. Whatever had happened to her, she'd allowed it to defeat her spirit.

A hand touched his shoulder. He turned, his gaze

landing on Laney's worried expression. "Don't worry, Trey. She's going to live."

He defied one of his own rules and allowed fear to overtake logic. "What…what happened?"

Molly tapped him on the shoulder. "She lost the baby," she whispered.

She lost the baby. Pain suffocated his ability to take a breath. Hoping he had misunderstood Molly, he looked to Laney. She nodded slowly, sadly, and then Shane Bartlett moved within his line of vision. "It's true."

"I didn't know," Trey said softly.

"She found out only a few weeks ago," Dr. Bartlett replied.

Katherine had learned of their child while Trey had been hunting Ike Hayes. As his new wife had started preparing for their future, Trey had been clinging to the past, instead of remaining home with his family, where he belonged. *Where. He. Belonged.* The realization hit him hard.

Molly's lower lip trembled. "I would have had a sister or brother."

He patted Molly's back, turned to look at Dr. Bartlett.

"Katherine? Is she going to—" He broke off, unable to say the words, afraid if he did, they would come true.

Dr. Bartlett sighed. "She's fine, healthwise. But…" He lifted a shoulder in helplessness. "She's been like this since yesterday."

Trey turned back to his wife. She looked only half-alive, and then he knew what Dr. Bartlett was trying to tell him. Katherine was in shock, caught inside her pain and unable to release herself from the grief…the guilt.

He knew about those feelings, had felt them for months—no, years—after Laurette had died in his arms. For the first time since that fateful day, his quest for vengeance seemed secondary, less significant. All that mattered now was helping Katherine come back from the black world in which she hid.

If anyone knew what she was suffering, it was Trey.

He lowered Molly to the ground and then knelt in front of the little girl. "I need to be with your sister, alone."

"I think that's a good idea," Laney said as she took Molly by the hand and led her out of the room.

Dr. Bartlett left as well, shutting the door behind him with a click. The silence hung thick and heavy in the room as Trey strode toward his wife. *His wife.* He knelt beside the bed, touched her cheek. He was home. He'd finally come home. But was he too late? Was he bound to fail his women when they needed him most?

Familiar guilt ripped through him all over again. This time the feeling was stronger, more real, than ever before. Katherine hadn't wanted him to go, but he'd put vengeance ahead of her and her fears.

And now her soul was dying.

He shut his eyes and prayed a second time since Katherine had come into his life.

Oh, Lord, give me the strength to help Katherine break free from her grief. Give me another chance to do right by her.

He brushed the hair away from her face.

She blinked but didn't respond to him otherwise.

"Come back to me, Katherine."

As though his request finally lifted the veil cloaking her soul, her eyes cleared, and she slowly, hesitantly, lifted her arms to him.

The invitation was unmistakable.

With a moan of sorrow, he pulled her into his embrace, cradled her against his chest. There could be no more holding back, no more pretending this woman didn't mean the world to him. "My Katherine. I love you."

He just hoped he hadn't waited too long to speak his heart aloud.

A huge shudder worked through her, followed by a giant gasp.

"Let it out, honey."

Her sobs came then, spiraling on top of one another. Big, heart-wrenching sobs that ripped through his body as sure as if he'd been the one crying instead of her.

He rocked her as her whimpers grew louder, more painful to bear. But for her sake, he accepted them as her due. He knew she needed to grieve, needed to cry over her loss, but with each of her gasps, his heart broke a little more.

"I wanted our baby," she said through tight, short breaths.

The silent sobs in his heart screamed for release, but he buried them. There would be time enough later for his own grieving. "Me, too."

She raised her guilt-ridden gaze. "It's all my fault, Trey."

How many times had he said those same words? How many times had friends told him they weren't true? In that moment, he finally understood what so many had tried to tell him. No man, or woman, could control life and death. That was God's territory alone. Why hadn't he seen the truth sooner?

Forgive me, Lord.

"No, baby, no. You aren't to blame. These things happen."

Pain flickered in her gaze, but she nodded. "Dr. Bartlett said that the Lord, in His infinite wisdom, has a plan bigger than me. Bigger than my understanding. Bigger than this tragedy."

"Shane is right." And Trey knew—he *finally* knew—the same was true for him.

She fell silent, her sobs turning to an occasional sigh of distress. Eventually, she turned limp in his arms, and he laid her gently back on the bed, pulled the sheet up to her chin.

"I want you to do something for me, my love," he said.

She blinked up at him, her gaze clear but unreadable.

"Concentrate on getting well."

"There's too much to do. Charity House, chores… the school."

He cupped her cheek. "Laney is a very resourceful woman. She'll manage until you're well again."

"Molly—"

"I'll take care of her. She's my family now, too." Katherine opened her mouth; he placed a finger over her lips. "Do this, please. For me."

Tears welled in her eyes. "I don't know how to be sick."

How he loved her strength, her independence, but not enough to relent on such an important matter. "Then now is as good a time as any to learn."

She shook her head, clearly preparing to argue with him.

He dropped a gentle kiss to her lips. "You're not going to be sensible about this, are you?"

An echo of a smile quivered at the corners of her mouth. "Those lessons in patience never took."

Relieved by the small glimpse of the Katherine he'd left weeks ago, Trey pressed his lips to her forehead. "Concentrate on getting some sleep."

He rose from the bed, but her hand shot out to still his progress. "Don't leave me."

"Never. I just have to take care of a few things. Then I'll come and sit with you."

She nodded. "I'd like that."

He kissed the top of her head, then caressed her cheek, stunned he could feel both joy and fear at the same time. "I'll be right back."

"Trey, I have a question for you," she said, her voice stopping him as he tried to turn and leave.

He strode back to the bed, knelt beside her and waited.

Shifting her gaze around the room, she sighed. "What…what happened with Ike Hayes?"

She spoke in a deceptively mild tone, but her eyes reflected her concern for him.

Even when she needed to focus on her own healing, she fretted over him. Part of Trey admired her ability to think of others before herself, but part of him wanted to shake her and order her to concentrate on Katherine for a change.

Nevertheless, he owed her the truth. "He escaped."

"You didn't kill him or bring him back with you?"

"No."

"Will you go back—"

"No." He pulled her hand to his lips, pressed a kiss to her palm. "I don't know whether I'll ever get the chance to serve up justice, or whether Ike will run free forever, but I'm going to let God handle the particulars from here on out."

He wanted to believe his own words—for Katherine's sake as well as his own—but Trey didn't know if he could hand over the control to God completely.

As much as he wanted to start his new life, he couldn't abandon the notion that until Ike Hayes was caught and brought to trial, Trey would stand poised between two women—one gone forever, the other within reach, yet still so far away.

Both women pulled at him, each with her own power over his future. And because he wasn't sure he could fully release one for the other, his heart broke for them all.

Chapter Twenty-One

A week later, Katherine stood in her room, staring out the window at the activity in the yard below. As she watched the children play, the sound of their laughter skipped through her heart and tugged a happy smile onto her lips. Ready to join the healthy again, she pivoted on her heel, picked up her skirt and finished dressing, making sure she moved slowly, patiently.

If she were honest with herself, she would admit that some good had come out of her loss and subsequent illness. Confined to her bed, she'd had a lot of time to pray, to mourn and to reassess what she wanted and needed from her husband.

As fearful as she'd been of falling in love with a lawman, her heart had defied her good sense. And now the prospect of a future with Trey Scott by her side didn't seem so terrifying.

All her life she'd felt like she was on the outside looking in, never truly belonging anywhere. She'd been judged and found lacking so many times, she'd lost hope that she would ever find genuine love and acceptance beyond the Lord's unshakable love. Craving certainty, she'd built her own orderly life in a world that didn't want *her kind*.

Then Trey had come along and had beaten down her defenses with his arrogance, masculine pride and mule-headed persistence.

In the end, he'd shown her trust, commitment. And love. He'd helped heal her shame. Now she wanted to help him find his way back to God.

If only she'd tried harder to protect the seed of their new love. Clutching her stomach, she resisted the urge to cry yet again. It still hurt to think of their child, their mutual loss. Perhaps with time, a lot of prayer and Trey's love, healing would come here as well. With that thought in mind, she went in search of her husband.

She found him in the parlor. He stood looking out the window, silently watching the children at play in the yard, as she had done in her room moments before. A heady blend of spices and wood filled her senses as she moved closer.

From his clenched jaw and rigid stance, she knew something was wrong. A storm was brewing in him, and he looked ready to do battle. Fear surged up in a primal haze, gripping her heart and twisting. On shaky legs, she moved closer, and immediately recognized the hint of longing in his unfocused gaze.

"Trey?"

He turned to her, his expression grave and serious. She waited, afraid to move. He didn't respond, just clenched his jaw harder and stared at her as though he were looking straight through her.

Angling her head, she ignored the panic gnawing at her and focused only on his silent turmoil. "What is it? What's happened?"

As he continued to stare at her, despair coursed through her blood. But then his expression cleared, and with one swoop, he tugged her against him, bending his head until his lips landed lightly against hers.

It felt so good to be in his arms again. So right. And when he deepened their kiss, Katherine relaxed against him. In that moment, she knew they could have a true marriage. A happy marriage. If only they both tried a little harder.

But as he drew his head away from her, she had a sudden urge to cling. Something wasn't right.

"How are you feeling?" He whispered the question, as though he was afraid if he raised his voice, he would cause her irreversible harm.

"Weak," she admitted as she toyed with the hair falling over the back of his collar. Dropping her hand, she sighed. "But stronger than yesterday."

He nodded. "Good."

Tucking her under his arm, he dropped a kiss on her forehead. The unpracticed intimacy of the gesture rendered her hopeful, in spite of the foreboding that filled her.

She knew with a woman's instinct that this man loved her deeply. The kind of love she'd given up hope of ever winning in this lifetime because of the taint of her past. If only it was enough to conquer the apprehension tripping along her spine now.

Oh, Lord, give me the strength to hear what he doesn't want to tell me.

"What's on your mind?" she asked.

He turned toward the window, pulling her with him. "Molly. I was thinking how much she's changed over the past few months. She's a different child than the one I first met."

Gratitude overcame her, nearly buckling her knees. "You had a lot to do with that."

He didn't answer right away. The echo of a smile wisped across his lips. "I love her like my own."

The declaration warmed her heart, but the weary resignation in his voice put her on guard. "What's wrong, Trey?"

Straightening to his full height, he lowered his gaze to hers. "We have to talk."

A burning sensation knotted behind her eyes, and she was suddenly so very cold. She could tell by his concerned expression that he wanted to alleviate her worries, but they both knew he wasn't enough of a liar to pull it off.

Sensing what was about to come, and hoping against hope she was wrong, Katherine kept her eyes locked with Trey's.

He brushed her hair away from her face. "I have to leave you again."

Air caught in her lungs, clogging just below her throat until she was gulping for it. Not trusting herself to speak without begging him to stay just a little longer, she swallowed her words behind a sniff.

"I don't know how long this will take."

She folded her arms across her chest, but she couldn't still the wave of doom surging through her soul. Her heart ached for him. For her. For them both.

Although he moved restlessly under her unwavering scrutiny, he regarded her with severe gray eyes. "I'll come back to you."

"Don't make promises."

With the turmoil of decisions already made mixing with the regret swimming in his eyes, he sighed. "Maybe I need to make promises. Maybe this time *I* need the words."

He shifted his gaze to a spot over her shoulder, shuddered, then squeezed her tightly against his chest. "Katherine, I almost lost you while I was away. I don't want to leave you again. Not even for a few hours."

"Then why go?"

His frustration seeped into her. "I have to."

"What aren't you telling me?"

"Ike Hayes was spotted in Colorado Springs yesterday. I believe he's heading for Denver. I have to get to him before he gets here."

Katherine pressed her cheek against his shoulder, stilling the cry of despair rising from her soul. "How do you know he's coming here?" She was only half-aware that her words came out shrill.

He stood with the posture of a man who refused to bend. Ever. "I know."

A shiver started at her knees, moved through her stomach and ended in a vicious tremble that rattled her pounding head. "I suppose asking you not to go is a waste of breath?"

The determination in his eyes seared her to the bone. "He killed my wife and child."

Katherine staggered out of his embrace. Pain exploded in her head, making her dizzy and knocking her off balance. Regardless of all he'd said, Trey still hadn't let go of the past. He hadn't let go of his love for his dead wife.

Just as she'd always feared, he would continually

leave her to avenge Laurette's death, even if he said otherwise.

And yet, Katherine still wanted him in her life. Enough to take whatever part of himself he could give her. She knew that made her pathetic, but there was no reasoning with a heart bound by love. "You have to do what you think is best."

He flinched as though she'd slapped him. "Katherine, don't do this."

"Do what?"

"Meekly accept what I have to tell you. Where's the fighter I married? The woman who challenged me at every turn?"

A bitter wind blew through her soul. "Is that what you want? Do you want me to tell you what a fool you are? Tell you your quest for justice has turned into a selfish drive to ease your own guilt?"

"No. Yes." He waved a hand between them. "I don't know. Is that what you really think?"

"Does it matter?"

"Yes. You're my wife. What you say is important to me."

"Then tell me what you want to hear, Trey, and I'll say it."

"I want to hear honesty."

"All right. Vengeance isn't ours to take. It's God's. Life is all about loss, Trey. No matter how many times you go after Ike, and even if you kill him with your own hands, you won't bring your wife back."

"Katherine, *you're* my wife."

She shook her head at him. "Not as long as you continue this self-appointed, one-man quest to avenge

Laurette's murder. What happened to letting God have the control? Why can't you at least try to show mercy?"

"Mercy?" He spat the word. "Ike Hayes kills without conscience. I can't and won't give mercy to a monster like that."

"Oh, Trey. None of us deserve mercy. That's the point of the cross. God sacrificed His Son for us, not because we deserved it, but out of His grace."

"It's not that simple." She could see the emotions waging a bitter battle in his eyes.

"Yes. Yes, it is."

"I have to do this for us, for our future together," he said, with a frustrated hiss. "I have to finish it."

"Don't lie to me, or to yourself, Trey. This isn't about us. Going after Ike Hayes is for you, only you."

His jaw flexed, but he didn't deny her words. "I can't change what I am."

She would not cry. Not this time, not in front of him. "You think I don't know that? No matter what I say, you're going after that man. You say you want honesty from me? Well, here it is."

She ignored the foreboding that refused to let her go, the feeling that if he left now, he'd never come back. "Part of you will always be locked in the grave with your wife. If going after Ike Hayes is what it takes to set you free, then go."

His expression hardened to an unforgiving glint. "Why can't you understand? This isn't about Laurette. Or even Ike Hayes. It's about justice."

"*Your* justice."

"A threat to justice anywhere is a threat to justice everywhere." The fury in his eyes cut deeper than his words. "I made a vow when I took this badge. I left ranching because this is what I'm supposed to do."

"God calls us to love our enemies."

His eyes hardened. "That's an impossible command."

She felt the blood drain from her face as the truth struck like a fist. Trey wasn't just a man who wore a badge. He was the badge. "Go catch the bad guy."

He wrenched her into his arms. "Katherine, stop worrying. I will come back to you. No matter how many times I leave, I'll *always* come back. One day you'll understand that."

She held herself rigid in his arms, daring not to relax into him for fear she'd start begging. "You seem to think highly of yourself. Didn't you tell me I couldn't control life and death when I wept over our baby's death? Since when did you become immortal, the master of destiny itself?"

He stepped back, glaring at her. "Katherine, I need you to understand."

Katherine dropped her gaze to the floor. "Just go."

"I want—"

She clapped her hands over her ears, blocking the rest of his declaration. "I said, *go.*"

He stalked to the door, tossed her one final frustrated glower, then turned and walked out of the house.

Nursing her fears, Katherine couldn't shake the notion that this was the last time she'd ever see her husband whole again.

Oh, Lord, how will I survive without him?

Chapter Twenty-Two

Trey charged down the front steps of Charity House, saddened that Katherine didn't understand why he had to stop Ike Hayes, personally—with his own hands if necessary. No matter how much he craved the freedom she spoke of, Trey couldn't turn vengeance over to God that easily.

How could offering mercy to the man who'd killed Laurette erase the bitterness and guilt that had driven Trey these past four years?

"Daddy. Daddy." Molly rushed across the yard, screaming his name repeatedly. Skidding to a stop, she favored him with a little-girl glare. "*Daddy,* didn't you hear me calling you?"

Trey forced aside thoughts of Ike Hayes, grinned down at Molly, then ruffled her hair. "Sorry, kitten. Guess I have a lot on my mind."

"You wanna come play baseball with me?"

At the eager look in her eyes, regret split Trey's heart. He hated to disappoint the child, but he needed to confront Ike, face-to-face. "I have to go to work today."

Her eyes widened. *"Oh."*

Although he'd expected this reaction, Trey felt trapped by Molly's accusing stare. The worry trembling on her lips didn't help, either. This agony was what came from caring again.

He hadn't wanted to love this little girl, or her sister, hadn't wanted to start a family. But what he'd wanted and what had happened were two different matters. This child had become his daughter. Her sister had become his wife. Both were now a part of him, in his heart forever.

For that alone, he had to serve up justice to Ike and finally put the past in the past.

As the silence lengthened, Molly's lips dropped into a frown. "You're heading out again, aren't you?"

Unwilling to leave on an unpleasant note, Trey pushed his growing impatience aside and crouched in front of her, knuckled a braid off her shoulder. "Yes, I am."

The look on her face made him sick. It was somewhere between accusation and acceptance. Why was he destined to hurt and disappoint the women he loved most? "Kitten, don't worry. I'll be back soon."

She nodded, her lower lip quivering harder. "I know."

"Do me a favor while I'm gone?"

Her eyes turned wary, and wisdom far exceeding her five years flickered into life. "Sure. I guess so."

Concerned he had to leave like this—without time to make the necessary preparations—he tugged her into a tight hug. "Be especially nice to your sister."

Squirming, she pushed against him. "You are holding me too tight."

Tiny fists beat against his shoulders.

He loosened his grip, blinked back the emotion

threatening to pull tears from his eyes. "It's 'cause I love you so much."

She sighed, patted him on the back. "Me, too. But I'm still angry at you for leaving again so soon."

"I know, baby." Kissing the top of her head, he eased her back to arm's length and faced the situation head-on. "But I have to catch the bad guy."

She stepped farther out of his reach, then slapped a hand against her chest. "The one you hate? The one that killed your wife?"

Trey hadn't realized Molly knew so much about his past. "Yes."

She looked at him with a confused expression on her face. "But Katherine says we have to forgive those who hurt us, even the mean ones we hate most."

A part of his soul shattered at the grown-up look on her face, the childlike stubbornness in her stance. But he'd tried Katherine's way already. For her sake, he'd really tried to let God administer justice to Ike Hayes, only to have the snake slither back into his life. Right here in Denver, where his new family lived.

"Say you'll come back soon," she said.

He forced a smile onto his lips. "I will."

"Okay." She bounced toward him again, kissed his cheek. "Bye, Daddy. Stay safe."

"Bye, Molly. I'll try."

In the next second, she was gone, back to her world of carefree play. Her desertion left Trey with an empty feeling in the pit of his stomach. Why couldn't he shake the notion that he was making a mistake by leaving this time?

Because he knew, in his heart, that Katherine was right. He *was* seeking vengeance for selfish reasons,

reasons that kept him from making Katherine and her little sister a real part of his life.

But he also knew he'd be stuck in the grave with Laurette forever if he didn't follow through with this perfect opportunity to dole out retribution at last.

Either way, someone would end up hurt today. He prayed it was Ike Hayes.

With that thought, he left the orphanage on full alert.

When Trey arrived at the jailhouse, Logan was waiting for him outside. Relief fell across the deputy's face. "I was just on my way to Charity House to get you."

The premonition he'd been trying to ignore all day settled over Trey. "You got news of Ike."

Logan nodded. "He's at Mattie's. I'm sure of it."

Trey's first instinct was to charge over to the brothel and shoot the man in cold blood. But too much was at stake, and there were too many unknowns yet. He had to deal only in the givens. Or risk making a mistake.

Swallowing his impatience, he focused on gathering the information he needed in order to make the smart move. "Did you see him?"

"No."

"So you're not sure." Relief warred with disappointment, making his temper flare, but he held his reaction under tight control.

"Oh, I'm sure. You see, I was doing what you told me, uh, that is, I was, uh—" He broke off, swallowed, shook his head. "Well, I was getting friendly with one of Mattie's girls, just like you told me…"

Trey didn't see the need to remark on unnecessary details. "Go on."

"Anyway, I heard a commotion in the parlor. By the time I got there, the room was empty."

"Then how do you know—"

"Because Mattie was missing, and so were all the other customers. Usually at this time of day, the brothel's real busy, and Mattie's in the parlor, surveying her domain like she's the reigning queen of the world."

"What does this have to do with Ike?" Trey barked.

The deputy scowled at him. "I was getting to that. From what Lizzie says, only three men can get Mattie alone in her room. And only one can clear out the entire brothel."

"Ike."

"Right." Logan gave him one solid nod. "At first, I thought I'd take him out myself, but then I remembered what you've always told me. 'Never go into an unknown situation alone.' So I was heading to get you, after I checked to make sure Drew was still behind bars."

Trey was impressed. The young deputy had acted on logic instead of emotion. He'd make a fine marshal one day. "You made the right decision," he said, then cocked his head toward the jail. "Is Lassiter keeping watch over our prisoner?"

"Yeah."

Satisfied he had all the information he needed, Trey said, "Let's go."

Tamping down the desire to let emotion rule, he untied his horse, mounted and rode off, barely giving Logan time to get out of his way.

The thundering of hooves followed hard behind him.

Trey pushed his horse faster.

Logan matched the pace.

Side by side, they made short work of the distance

between the jailhouse and Mattie's brothel. Turning onto Market Street, Trey slowed his horse to an easy walk. Logan did the same.

With a sweeping gaze, Trey studied the fringes of the district, then turned and focused on the center of the street. Shouts echoed across the street. A man called out to a woman waving from a window in one of the brothels. A horse whinnied in the distance. The smell of cheap perfume, trail dust and stale whiskey wafted together in the air, nearly choking him.

Resisting the urge to cover his nose, Trey counted eleven men on foot, moving in groups of various sizes along the sidewalks. A lone horse and rider meandered down the middle of the street. Trey waited, watched. Patience was his ally now.

A group of three men entered a brothel on Trey's right while two men spilled out of another one on his left. Slapping one another on the back, the new arrivals staggered past a horse and carriage and then entered a well-marked saloon three doors down. Five more men followed them in.

That left three men on foot, one man on horseback.

"We do this right," Trey said to his deputy while keeping his eyes on the horse and rider trotting out of sight.

"I'll follow your lead, Marshal."

"Good." Once the street was clear of the three remaining men, Trey turned his full attention back to Logan. "No heroics today. Shoot in self-defense only."

Logan nodded, his gaze centered on Mattie's brothel, ahead of them.

Trey dismounted, drew his gun and then checked the

load. "I'll go through the front door. You come in from the back. We'll work as a team."

Logan climbed off his own horse. "You can count on me."

While Logan moved into position, Trey focused his thoughts on Ike Hayes and what he'd done to Laurette and their unborn child.

Trey tested the handle on the front door, huffed out a breath when it wouldn't budge. The wood was too sturdy for an easy entry. Stepping back, he unloaded two shots into the lock. He gave the door a hard kick, and it flew inward. The force of the blow dragged Trey and a cold stream of air through the opening.

Charging forward, gun poised at the ready, Trey took quick inventory of his surroundings. The foyer and main parlor were full of flickering candlelight but empty of human activity.

The hurried footsteps and slamming of doors on the upper landing told Trey that Mattie's girls knew trouble was coming.

They were wrong.

It was already here.

As Trey slipped around the perimeter of the parlor, his eyes gauged, searched. Step by step, he inched in the direction of Mattie's room. White-hot rage heightened his senses.

The terror Ike Hayes had spread around the territory ended today.

Trey's breathing came fast and hard, in short, painful gasps. Creeping closer to his destination, he twisted the knob, then eased the door open a crack.

The sick smell of death hit him hard. But before he could enter the room, Mattie Silks materialized from the other side of the door. With a hard shove, she pushed Trey back into the hallway and pulled the door closed behind her, leaving a small slit.

"I'm busy with a customer, Marshal. You'll have to come back another time."

"I'm here to arrest Ike Hayes. Turn him over to me now and I'll ignore the fact that you are harboring a wanted criminal."

"Well, it ain't Ike in there." Mattie looked at Trey with disgust. "So you can just be on your way, now."

"Right." He began to walk away, then turned back and pushed past her.

"Now see here." She yanked on his arm hard enough to stop his pursuit.

Keeping his eyes locked with hers, Trey shrugged her off and slowly, very slowly, pointed his gun toward the doorway.

"You won't need that." Mattie sighed in defeat as she glanced at his drawn weapon. "He's too ill to fight back."

Ignoring her, Trey shoved into the room. And stopped dead in his tracks.

The pale, sickly man that lay propped in Mattie's bed was obviously fighting for his life. Unable to reconcile his mental image of Laurette's killer and the man before him now, Trey could only stare.

"Are you Ike Hayes?" he asked, aiming his gun at the center of the outlaw's chest.

The man's eyes remained closed, his breathing ragged.

Mattie rushed to the end of the bed, then turned back to glare at Trey.

"Move aside, Mattie."

She spread her arms out as though to shield the outlaw from Trey's wrath. "Can't you see this man is nearly dead from a gunshot wound already? It won't do you any good to shoot him again."

Even a madam was lecturing him now. "Just how close to death is he?"

Mattie took a step forward but kept her arms outstretched. "I don't know."

"Then go fetch Shane Bartlett, and he'll tell us for sure."

Mattie didn't respond, just stood rooted to the spot as she looked around the room, like she was searching for an answer out of the empty air.

Trey hissed out a warning. "I suggest you go now, before I lose my patience entirely."

Mattie's eyes widened at the threat. She dropped a quick glance to his gun, then whipped her gaze back to him. "Maybe I will go see if I can find the doctor."

"You do that."

"Right." She kept her unblinking stare locked on Trey's weapon as she edged out of the room.

Alone at last with his prey, Trey watched Ike struggle for every wheezing breath.

How could this sickly, thin shell of a man be the murdering criminal Trey had hunted for four long years?

Of course, evil came in many forms. Trey refused to be fooled by the pathetic picture the outlaw made.

"Wake up, Ike. It's judgment time."

Red-rimmed, faded blue eyes blinked slowly open.

Trey was instantly struck by the oddity of the gaze staring back at him. Had Laurette looked into the same wicked, empty eyes? Had she felt terror rather than the rage racing though Trey?

"Ike Hayes?" he asked, surprised his voice came out as steady as it did.

"Who wants to know?" The man had the stupidity to shift toward the bedside table, where a six-shooter lay just out of his reach.

Trey cocked his pistol. "Go for that gun and you're dead."

Ike froze, his hand hovering near the weapon. Trey could see the outlaw's mind working, eyes shifting, hand trembling as he calculated the time it would take him to reach his gun and shoot.

"We both know you won't make it. Not with my weapon already cocked and aimed."

"Maybe I want to go down fighting."

Trey disabused him of the notion with a single shot. The bullet hit the lamp on the bedside table and shattered glass over Ike's entire forearm.

Ike's gaze turned wild, frantic, but eventually he raised his hand in the air, palm facing forward.

"Wise decision," Trey said. "Now let me see your other hand." Before Ike could move, he added, "Nice and slow."

"You ain't got the guts to shoot me," Ike snorted, his chest rising and falling with every ragged breath he took.

The need to kill rode him hard, but Trey forced cool indifference into his heart. He had precious little time before Logan joined them. Trey could shoot the outlaw now, for Laurette and all the other innocent victims the man had killed. No one would doubt the why behind Trey's actions.

Liking the idea, he felt his finger quiver on the trigger, but he staved off the hunger for blood. Barely.

Poised between past and future, Trey narrowed his choices down to two: offer mercy or administer vigilante justice.

Which would bring freedom fastest? Which would bring the longest-lasting relief?

As though sensing Trey's predicament, Ike snarled, "Are you going to stand there pondering what you *want* to do, or you gonna have the guts to do it?"

Trey's hand began to shake from the control it took to remain impassive.

What was taking Logan so long?

Ike's hand shifted an inch closer to the table where his gun lay. Trey stepped toward the bed. The driving need for justice overwhelmed all other thought. This man had killed Laurette. Killed her with ruthless intent, uncaring of the shattered lives he'd left in the wake of her death.

"This situation presents an unparalleled opportunity." Trey lifted his gun, his vision going black from hatred. "I can end both of our pain with a single shot."

"I must say, there's not much to criticize about your performance." Lacking any signs of fear, Ike laughed, then broke into a fit of hacking coughs.

Once the coughing was under control, Trey aimed dead center of the man's head. As he stared into Ike's evil eyes, all hope of offering forgiveness and "turning the other cheek" washed out of Trey, leaving behind only the cold, hard need to seek vengeance with his own hands. For Laurette. For their unborn child.

For himself.

"I'm sending you straight to Satan's playground," Trey said.

"No need to rush things." A smile slid onto his lips

as he focused on the gun pointed at his head. "I'll be there soon enough."

Trey began to pull the trigger, but a soft, willowy thought of Katherine tugged his finger away from the metal.

Trey shut his eyes and tried to concentrate on his bride. But, still, his hand itched to finish the deed he'd waited four long years to accomplish.

It won't bring Laurette back....

Katherine's words echoed through his head, knifing through his white-hot anger.

Vengeance is mine, the Lord said...

The command stopped Trey cold. What was he doing? He was about to kill in the same manner as had the man lying in the bed before him.

In that moment Trey knew he'd *never* be free if he killed Ike in cold blood.

Freedom would only come from letting go of his hatred.

Trey finally understood the healing power of giving mercy where it wasn't deserved. And from now on, he would leave final justice up to God. But just as he lowered his weapon, a shot rang out.

A burning sting spread through Trey's right arm.

Pain exploded in his head.

He paused. Staggered backward. Lifted his gun.

Another shot rang out.

Trey's hand went limp, and his gun slipped from his fingers. Instinct had him dropping to the floor as another shot blew toward him.

This one hit Trey high on the shoulder.

Ike's laughter rang shrill and cold-blooded, and was

the first thing Trey heard as he swam out of the vicious black pain in his head.

Trey reached for his gun again, just as Logan burst into the room. With a split-second sweep, the deputy took in the situation, shifted left and jumped on Ike.

Before Trey could scold his deputy for rushing into open fire, a numbing blackness consumed him. This was it, then.

The end of the fight.

But was God taking him to heaven? Or sending him to hell?

Chapter Twenty-Three

From the moment Trey left Charity House, Katherine hadn't been able to shake the notion that he was in trouble. And this time it was more than a selfish fear based on lack of faith.

It was a certainty.

So when the news came that her husband had been shot in the process of capturing Ike Hayes, her greatest concern was that she wouldn't get to him in time. That she wouldn't be able to tell him how much she loved him, and how sorry she was that she'd sent him away angry.

Oh, Lord, I pray Trey's wounds aren't serious. Forgive me my insecurities and lack of faith in Your will for our lives together. Please, please, give me another chance to show Trey how much I love him.

As she waited on the front lawn of Charity House for Marc to bring the wagon around, she continued praying, silently, fervently, asking the Holy Spirit for the words when her mind went blank from her overwhelming fear.

Finally, the sound of horse hooves broke through her prayers, and Marc pulled to a stop right in front of her. His set expression showed the same concern and apprehension she felt in her own heart.

"Don't worry, Katherine." He hopped down and came around to her side. "Logan said it was just his arm."

Katherine nodded, petrified the deputy had skipped over the details of Trey's injury for fear she wouldn't be able to handle the truth. What if his injury was life threatening?

No. The Lord commanded her to "Fear Not." For Molly's sake, as well as her own, she put on a brave face and pretended all was well.

Kneeling in front of her little sister, she swept the hair away from a tearstained cheek. "Don't worry, Molly, I'll bring Trey home. We'll get him well, just like you two helped me."

Molly's face collapsed into a mutinous expression. "Don't want to stay," she whined, taking a shuddering breath after she spoke. "I want to go with you."

"We've been through this already. You have to stay with Laney."

"No." Molly stomped her foot, becoming the unruly child she'd been the day they'd argued over a bath. "I want to go with you."

Katherine held on to her temper. Barely. "Mattie's isn't a place for little girls. Marc and I are going to bring him home, as soon as Dr. Shane finishes stitching up his wounds."

Molly's face turned red with rage, and she opened her mouth and screamed. At the top of her lungs. Loudly. Uncontrollably. Barely taking breaths in between.

Katherine had seen her share of tantrums, but nothing quite like this one. She looked helplessly to Laney, then to Marc.

Laney sighed, lifted her shoulders. "I don't know what to tell you."

Molly raised her voice even louder. "I want to see my daddy."

Marc touched Katherine's sleeve. "You might as well let her come. She'll just make herself sick. And that won't do anybody any good, especially not Trey."

Realizing this was not a time to play the stern parent, Katherine nodded. "All right, Molly. You can come with us."

It took a moment for Katherine's words to sink in, but once they did, Molly sucked in a deep gulp of air. Blinked. Then grinned through her tears. "I get to see my daddy first."

"That, young lady, is out of the question," replied Katherine.

Molly opened her mouth to start screaming again, but Katherine wouldn't have it. "If you so much as make a squeak of protest again, you're not coming with us."

Molly's mouth gaped open, but mutiny soon rose in her gaze.

Little sister eyed big sister. "No," Katherine said.

Molly's eyes darted to Laney.

Laney shook her head. "Don't do it, Molly."

Molly shot a silent appeal to Marc.

"You're on your own if you scream again," he said.

Pursing her lips, Molly said, "I'll be second, after Katherine."

Katherine lifted the little girl into her arms, kissed her on the cheek. "Good choice, Molly." She hugged her tightly against her. "Now let's go get our Trey back."

* * *

Trey sank into the blessed softness of the pillow beneath his head, gritting his teeth as Dr. Bartlett sewed up the last wound on his shoulder.

"I'm almost done, Marshal."

Trey nodded through the agony, taking each sliver of pain as his due. Considering the situation, he was fortunate to be alive. According to the doctor, he'd been unconscious for over an hour. During that time Logan had dealt with Ike Hayes's arrest and subsequent journey to his new residence in the Denver jail. In the meantime, Dr. Bartlett had orchestrated Trey's transfer to this room in the back of the brothel.

Trey knew he owed his deputy his life. No amount of thanks would be enough. And no amount of apologizing could erase the agony he'd put Katherine and Molly through in his quest for vengeance.

Katherine had warned him that vengeance was God's alone. He'd even agreed with her, in theory. But when he'd had an opportunity to confront Hayes face-to-face, he'd taken it.

In the end, Katherine had been right to worry. Trey had been so consumed with hate, he hadn't taken the precautions to protect himself.

Now, as pain screamed through his body, he realized his mistake. He wasn't in charge of his own life. He'd never been. God was the only one who controlled a man's destiny. Trey just hoped it wasn't too late for atonement.

Lord, forgive my pride and arrogance. I've lived with a hard heart these past four years. Help me to change.

Dr. Bartlett tied off the last stitch. "Okay, Marshal, that should do it."

"Thanks."

"It's going to hurt like the dickens for the next week or two."

"Nothing I don't deserve."

Dr. Bartlett didn't respond. Instead, he gathered his things, dropped various instruments into a black leather bag. "Just make sure you keep the wounds clean and free of infection."

He turned, then pinned Trey with a glare.

"What?" Trey asked, knowing he didn't really want the answer.

Shaking his head, Dr. Bartlett sighed. "Just get well."

Trey squeezed his eyes shut a moment, flinching at the underlying warning. "I will. For Katherine and Molly."

Dr. Bartlett nodded, his eyes holding a solemn expression. "They deserve nothing less from you."

Before Trey could comment on *that* remark, Katherine rushed into the room, looking wildly around her. She appeared frantic, out of breath. And he'd done that to her.

Her gaze finally connected with his. *"Trey."*

She seemed to put all her love, worry, anger and affection in that one word.

Trey lifted his head to greet her, but in his hurry, he shifted his arm at the wrong angle, and pain exploded through him. Gulping through the agony, he collapsed back onto the bed. "I'm sorry, Katherine."

She hurried to his bedside, her eyes filling with tears. "Oh, Trey." She looked at his torn shirt and gasped. "There's so much blood."

"It's not as bad as it looks," said Trey.

Dr. Bartlett, brutally honest man that he was, had the

audacity to offer his professional opinion. "Actually, it *is* as bad as it looks. If he gets an infection, he'll lose the whole arm. Maybe even his life."

Worry flickered in her eyes but was instantly replaced with steely determination. She knelt beside Trey and brushed her fingers along his cheek, the tender gesture belying her heated tone. "I'll nurse him back to health myself."

As Trey touched her lips with his good hand, she captured his wrist and sighed. "I love you, Trey."

Pleased with her declaration, he gave her one of his rare smiles. "I love you back, Katherine."

Dr. Bartlett cleared his throat. "I'll just leave you two alone."

Trey waited until they were alone before speaking his heart. "Once I'm well, I want us to buy our own house and start our new life together. You, Molly and me."

A spark of hope welled into an inferno in her eyes. "I like that idea."

With his good arm, he pulled her onto the bed with him, winced, swallowed hard, then smoothed his fingers through her hair. "Walk in faith with me, Katherine. Let's take life day by day. Revel in what we have, and don't worry about what we could lose."

She shifted off the bed, knelt before him and took his hand in hers. "First, help me to understand why you went after Ike Hayes. And I won't ever bring it up again."

After all they'd been through, he needed to tell his wife the truth. Only then could they move forward. "You were right, Katherine. By seeking vengeance, I kept Laurette alive in my heart."

He saw how painful this was for her to hear, but she urged him on anyway. "Go on."

Katherine Taylor Scott was the bravest person he knew. He wanted to follow her lead. "Because I wasn't able to save her, I thought if I avenged her death, I could make it right."

Her warm fingers rubbed his palm. "Oh, Trey, what happened on your ranch wasn't your fault."

He blew out a long breath. "I thought God had abandoned me that day. I still don't think I've completely forgiven Him, or myself, for what happened. Change that drastic doesn't come quickly. But I want to find my way again."

Her gasp of hope tore through four years of well-laid defenses.

"I had the chance to shoot Ike, but I walked away."

"Oh, Trey. You gave him mercy, only to be shot for your efforts." Her eyes were glazed with worry.

"I got careless. If I had been less driven by my hunger for blood, I wouldn't have let my guard down."

She gave him a soft smile. "That's one mistake I'd like to ask you not to make again."

She looked so flustered and beautiful and full of love for him. How could he not love her with all his heart? He inhaled, exhaled slowly, until his breath became normal again.

"From this point forward, I'll leave vengeance to God," he said. "Even though I'm still an Old Testament man at heart, I'm working on the rest."

"Through Christ, all things are possible, my love."

"Yes. *Yes.*" He lifted her chin, commanded her gaze. What he had to say was too important for her to miss. "Every time I face a gun, I know I risk my life. More importantly, I now realize just how much my death would hurt you."

Her eyes filled with tenderness and love. "Yes, Trey, your death would hurt me, as much as Laurette's has hurt you."

Why had it taken him so long to see the truth? "I'm sorry, Katherine."

The sheen of tears in her eyes spoke of acceptance, forgiveness…trust.

Certainty filled him.

They'd come so far. But the next step was his alone. "I'm giving up my position as a U.S. marshal."

Her eyes widened. "You're what?"

He shifted uncomfortably under her glare. "You heard me. I won't risk dying and leaving you and Molly alone."

She smiled at him, but the silent accusation in her eyes told a different story. "So you would quit for Molly and me?"

How could he find the words to tell her she made him want to be a better man? The man he'd thought he'd buried with Laurette. "By resigning my position as marshal of this territory, I let go of Laurette. And I commit to you and Molly, once and for all."

She angled her head at him, blinking back tears. "You'd do that for us?"

Trey had no more defenses left. "Yes, and for our future together as a family."

She dragged in an uneven breath, swallowed and then gave him a nod. *"No."*

"You— What did you say?" He shot up in the bed, ignored the pain shooting through his arm. "But I… We…"

"Stop sputtering, Trey. As much as I appreciate the gesture, you can't resign. The territory needs you, and when you offered Ike mercy, you let the past go at last."

He released a short hiss. "What if I die?"

She threw his own words back at him, the ones he'd used on her that first time, in Marc's study. "One day, we all die."

"That's not what I meant."

"I know what you meant. And, if that awful event happens, then I'll mourn you for the rest of my life. But until that time, we must live every moment together. Fully. Completely. As a family. For however long our forever turns out to be. We must put our future in God's hands and live one day at a time."

"You're sure?"

"You wouldn't be the man I love if you weren't also a federal marshal."

He hooked a tendril of her hair around his finger. In spite of his sins, God had blessed him with a woman to love not once, but twice. The first had been the delight of youth and dreams, while the second was a strong, mature love that would last the rest of his life.

"I'm still an insufferable, mule-headed pig," he said, unwilling to leave anything unsaid.

"I love you anyway, *Marshal* Scott."

With his good arm, he pulled her into his embrace, then smiled into her hair. "You've made me a happy man, Mrs. Scott."

Molly sprinted into the room, skidded to a stop when her eyes landed on Trey. "Daddy?"

Trey kept Katherine clutched against his chest, but he gave Molly a huge smile. "Hi, kitten."

Molly tore around the side of the bed and peered at her sister. "What's Katherine doing to you?"

Trey chuckled, then turned his expression serious. "She's hugging me."

Two little eyebrows lifted over wide eyes. "Do you want her to hug you?"

"Oh, yes. Means she loves me."

Molly shifted from foot to foot, then peered around Katherine again. "You know, Daddy, I love you, too."

Trey opened his arm wider, his heart filling with joy. "Then you better join us in this hug."

Molly bounced into his embrace, wrapping her arms around him and her sister.

With a big smile on his face, Trey pulled his women close and accepted the first in a lifetime of hugs.

Epilogue

Six years later

Ethan Wendell Scott IV pressed his compact little body closer to his big sister. "You gotta save me, Moll. I don't wanna take no stinkin' bath again this week."

Those big round eyes and trembling lower lip reminded Molly of her own predicament six years ago. "Don't worry. I have a plan."

"That's what you said the last time."

"Well, this time it's a good one."

He nodded in satisfaction, grinning up at her with little-brother devotion. "I knew I could count on you."

Molly grinned back. Ethan was her favorite little brother, even if he was her only little brother.

But, really, what's not to love? she thought. The little boy could spit as far as any of the Charity House orphans and twice as far as she could. In her book, that made him pretty special.

Trying her best to look stern, she glowered at the big man looming closer and closer. She couldn't help but think her dad got bigger and handsomer and kinder every year. One day she wanted to marry a man exactly like Trey Scott.

Not that she'd admit it now, when he'd turned into the stinkin' enemy. She scooted her brother behind her, mutiny twisting in her heart. No one would stand in her way as she protected the boy.

"You can't have him," she warned. "I mean it."

Stopping inches in front of them, Trey widened his stance, then settled into the standoff as though he had all the time in the world. "Hand him over."

"Never."

As they continued to stare at one another, Molly allowed a rebellious smile to lift the corners of her lips. A swift glimpse to her left revealed an opening in the hedge. Mentally, she measured the dimensions. The hole was the perfect size for a forty-pound boy and his eleven-year-old big sister.

"We're getting out of here, Ethan," she whispered from the corner of her mouth. "Just follow me."

Inching across the grass, Molly tugged her little brother toward freedom.

The enemy matched them step for step.

Bending forward, Molly lowered her voice. "Looks like I'm going to have to take out Dad. You make a run for it on your own. 'Kay?"

"But what if Momma catches me?"

Molly winked at him. "Don't worry about her. Her belly is too big, what with the baby almost here. She'll never keep up with you if you pump your legs real fast."

Chuckling, Trey pulled around to the left, effectively closing off their escape. "Don't even think about it."

"Stay back," Molly ordered, pressing Ethan tighter against her. "I'm warning you…"

Trey glanced to his right, then let out what sounded like a regretful sigh. "Now you're in for it. Here she comes."

Molly threw her own gaze in the direction of their house. Her sister was bearing down fast.

Determined to remain focused, Molly leveled a look on Trey that she'd practiced in the mirror for nearly a year now. It was the same one Katherine gave the students at school when they wouldn't listen to her. Molly just hoped it worked on U.S. marshals turned dads.

"I'm taking Ethan to the Charity House baseball game, and that's the end of it," Molly declared.

"Oh, no, it's not," Katherine said, drawing to a stop next to her husband.

Shifting her attention, Molly snarled at the woman who had become the best mother a girl could have—when she wasn't trying to force the bath issue, of course. "I promise we'll be home before dark."

Katherine sighed, then shared a look with Trey.

He lifted a shoulder. "I tried to warn her," he said, as though that was the end of his responsibility in the matter.

Molly grinned. Sometimes her dad could be such a man.

Shaking her head, Katherine turned back to Molly. "You two can go to Charity House after his bath. Not before."

Ethan chose that moment to voice his opinion, by stomping his foot and declaring, "But I want to go now."

Katherine snorted and then turned to Trey. "This is your fault, you know."

He glanced to the heavens and sighed dramatically. "I know, I know." Wrapping his wife in his embrace, he shifted so the baby didn't get in the way, then smiled down at her, affection glittering in his eyes. "It's *all* my fault."

Katherine smiled in return. "You know I can't resist a man who admits when he's wrong."

"Oh, I was wrong." He dipped his head toward hers. "I was *very* wrong."

Molly snorted. "You two aren't going to kiss, are you?"

They answered in tandem. "We certainly are."

"Oh, honestly," said Molly.

Ethan mimicked her, adding five-year-old enthusiasm to the words. *"Oh, honestly."*

Molly ruffled his hair. "Our parents are so strange."

"Yeah, strange," echoed Ethan.

Katherine pulled out of her husband's arms and settled back into the fight. "Surrender, you two."

Cornered and nearly out of ideas, Molly appealed to the man who'd defied her sister six years ago on her behalf. "Do something, will ya?"

Trey gave her a pitiful look. "Sorry, kitten, I'm going to have to agree with my wife this time."

So be it.

"All right, Ethan," Molly whispered in the little boy's ear. "We're going to make a run for it."

A low whimper slipped from his lips. "But, Moll, they'll catch us. They always do."

Molly looked to the heavens, sighed. Little brothers were so unforgiving of a few big-sister mistakes. "Hold on tight, kid. I'll show you what I mean."

Balancing on the balls of her feet, Molly tucked Ethan firmly in the crook of her arm. Leading with her shoulder, she charged forward. With the element of surprise on her side, she made it five whole steps without incident. But then she slipped and fell to her knees.

Next thing Molly knew, both she and Ethan were lying flat on their backs, a parent holding each of them down.

"Should we attack?" Trey asked Katherine, a look of sheer joy on his face.

Katherine's answering chuckle floated through the afternoon breeze. *"Absolutely."* She grinned down at Molly. "And this time we're finishing them off."

In a blur, fingers poised, then went swiftly to work. Ethan squealed in delight, enjoying their defeat entirely too much—the little traitor.

Molly Taylor Scott was made of sterner stuff. She clamped her lips shut, controlling the urge to laugh. "How many times have I told you," she gritted through her teeth, "I'm not ticklish?"

Undaunted, hands worked quicker, fingers searched and jabbed unmercifully. And then, just like every other time, Ethan did the unthinkable. He joined the enemy.

"Surrender, Moll," he said and started tickling her feet.

Molly bit down on her lower lip, but then someone went for her bottom left rib, and she couldn't control herself any longer. Letting out a hoot of laughter, she said, "You got me. I surrender."

Ethan jumped up, bounced around the yard, with his hands waving in the air. "We won, we won."

Molly shook her head at him. "You are such a turncoat."

Her voice belied the harshness of her words, holding all the affection she felt for her little brother. Even if he didn't know the difference between the good guys and the bad guys, he was still a pretty good kid. Most of the time.

Just like Katherine always said, God had blessed them all. But especially Molly. Her heavenly Father had given her the perfect family for her—a loving sister-turned-mother, a devoted, hardworking father and a feisty little brother, with another sibling on the way.

A day didn't go by when she didn't offer up thanks. *Thank You, Lord. Oh, thank You!*

Her dad helped her stand, hugged her to him. "Cheer up, kitten. Even the best warriors lose a battle or two."

Joining the embrace, Katherine squeezed in from behind. Little Ethan wasn't to be left out. He hopped on his dad's back, then grinned down at Molly over his shoulder. "You know, Moll, you were right about what you said this mornin'."

Molly twisted so she could look into little-boy eyes. "I was?"

"Yeah." He eyed his mother, then his father, then turned back to her. "We have the best parents in the whole world."

She tightened her hold, secure in the midst of her family's love. "We do, baby brother. Oh, we do."

* * * * *

Jane Myers Perrine grew up in Kansas City, Missouri, has a BA from Kansas State University and an EdM in Spanish from the University of Louisville. She has taught high school Spanish in five states. Presently, she teaches in the beautiful Hill Country of Texas. Her husband is minister of a Christian church in central Texas, where Jane teaches an adult Sunday school class. Jane was a finalist in the Regency category of the Golden Heart® Awards. Her short pieces have appeared in the *Houston Chronicle*, *Woman's World* magazine and other publications. The Perrines share their home with two spoiled cats and an arthritic cocker spaniel. Readers can visit her website, www.janemyersperrine.com.

Books by Jane Myers Perrine

Love Inspired

Deep in the Heart
The Path to Love
Love's Healing Touch

Love Inspired Historical

Second Chance Bride

SECOND CHANCE BRIDE

Jane Myers Perrine

Brethren, I count not myself to have apprehended: but this one thing I do, forgetting those things which are behind, and reaching forth unto those things which are before, I press toward the mark for the prize of the high calling of God in Christ Jesus.

—*Philippians* 3:13–14

This book is dedicated to Betty Davis Lynn, who has been a friend for longer than I can remember. Thank you for all these years of friendship and your Christian example.

Also to two friends and critique partners: Ellen Watkins and Linda Kearney, who keep me headed in the right direction.

And, as always, to my husband, George, for his love and support, even when he hated hearing those three little words—*I'm on deadline*.

Prologue

Central Texas, 1885

Annie MacAllister's father had always told her she'd never amount to anything because she never thought anything through. Maybe he was right. Maybe that's how she'd ended up in this swaying stagecoach while a disapproving woman glared at her in disgust and a dumpy man across from Annie leered.

Only an hour after the stagecoach left Weaver City, she tried to disappear, to shrink back into the hard bench of the stagecoach. She heard the elderly woman mutter, "Common."

Annie knew why the woman said that. Annie wore a cheap dress, tight across the bodice and fraying at the cuffs. Her long hair curled over her shoulders, and she wore paint on her lips and cheeks.

The expression on the man's face showed that he knew exactly what Annie was—an immoral woman who'd worked in a brothel. What he didn't know was how much she'd hated every minute of it—how she'd been forced into it.

Next to Annie sat a young woman who wore an undecorated black straw hat and a plain, gray cotton skirt. Her matching basque was trimmed with what had been a crisp white collar when she got on the coach but was now limp and soiled from the dust of the trip.

"Is this your first trip in a stagecoach?" the young woman asked Annie in a soft, educated voice.

Well, if that wasn't a surprise. The woman actually spoke to her in a friendly way. "Yes," Annie answered, then added, "ma'am."

"Mine, too." She smiled. "My name is Matilda Susan Cunningham." Miss Cunningham spoke clearly, just like Annie's mother had, although that was so long ago it was hard for Annie to remember.

"Miss Cunningham." Annie nodded. "I'm Annie MacAllister."

"Where are you going, Miss MacAllister?" Miss Cunningham asked.

"Trail's End."

"I'm going there, too." Miss Cunningham nodded. "Will your family meet you?"

Annie shook her head.

"My employer will meet me," Miss Cunningham said.

"Not your family, Miss Cunningham?" Annie almost bit her tongue. She should know not to pry.

"Please, do call me Matilda, won't you?"

Annie nodded, delighted by the attention of this kind woman.

"No, my family won't meet me." Matilda sighed. "My parents died when I was thirteen. My brother, only two months ago. That's why I had to find employment."

As Matilda looked out the window, Annie realized

that they looked a little alike. They both had dark hair and dark eyes, and were tall and thin, although she'd noticed when they'd waited for the stage that Matilda carried herself proudly while Annie hunched over.

When the coach stopped at a home station, all the passengers got off and entered the small frame building. Annie gazed yearningly at the beans and greasy meat the cook stirred and slapped on a tin plate.

"One dollar," said the station agent.

She only had three dollars and fifty-one cents to last her until she found work. She was hungry but not hungry enough to spend a penny yet. She went out to the porch and washed her hands in the pewter basin.

"Would you share some of this meal with me?" Matilda stood on the porch with her plate. "I don't believe I can eat all of it. If you don't mind helping me, I would appreciate that."

Wasn't she the nicest lady? To make charity sound as if Annie were doing a good deed for her. "Thank you, Matilda."

"Let's say a prayer first." Matilda bowed her head. "Dear Lord, we thank You for Your bounty. We thank You for leading us into new lives and know You will be with us wherever our paths take us. Amen."

Annie had been so startled she hadn't had time to bow her head before Matilda began to pray. She hadn't heard a prayer since her mother's funeral. Matilda's prayers were probably answered. God hadn't bothered to grant any of Annie's.

As the afternoon wore on, the pitching and jolting of the coach changed to a rocking motion, and everyone slept. At a stop in Rotain, the leering man left. An hour after that, the disapproving woman got off with one more glare at Annie. Oh, how Annie wished people could see her for the person she was, not for the deeds she'd been forced to commit to survive.

Well, that was the very reason she was on this coach. When she couldn't stand her life for one more day, she'd pulled together every penny she'd saved. Most of it had gone to buy the ticket to Trail's End, a town the ticket agent said no one ever visited. Once there, she'd get a new job, maybe cleaning houses or even working in a shop. She'd live an upright and respectable life and wouldn't have to put up with slurs and lecherous glances.

Matilda and Annie were alone on the last leg of the journey. They chatted for a while until the warmth of the coach caused Annie to fall asleep. She dozed until the lurching of the vehicle woke her with a start.

The motion flung her against Matilda, then tossed them both against the door on the other side of the coach. Annie grabbed the leather curtain and held it tightly, but Matilda's flailing hands couldn't grasp anything to keep her from ricocheting around the interior. She was thrown hard against a window. Then she smashed into the door on the right side and it made a loud crack and opened wide. The young woman flew from the carriage, screaming in pain and terror.

For a few seconds, Matilda's screams continued.

Then the cries stopped. Completely.

The coach finally came down on the right side with a terrible crash. Annie's ankles twisted beneath her, and her head hit the door frame.

Dust billowed up and engulfed her. Tears ran down her face, mixing with Matilda's blood, as well as her own, as it streamed from a cut on her head. Silence shrouded the coach until a man shouted from above her, "Are you all right in there?"

"I'm—" Annie croaked. She swallowed and said in a shaking voice, "I'm alive but the other woman—" She sobbed, the words catching in her throat.

The driver opened the door above her, reached down and pulled her up. The pain in her arm was sharp.

Once she stood on the road, Annie looked at herself. She was covered in blood and grime, her pink dress smeared with splatters and splotches of red while blood stained her sleeve as it dripped from a gash on her arm.

"What happened?" she asked.

"Wheel came off. Spooked the horses," the driver said. "I'm going to have to ride to town to get a new one." He looked inside the coach again. "Where's the other passenger?"

"Back there," Annie said, and pointed fifty yards behind. Fresh tears rolled down her dirty, scraped cheeks. "She fell out."

In spite of the pain, Annie ran toward Matilda, who lay absolutely still. "Matilda," she whispered as she took one of her friend's limp hands.

"No use." The driver shook his head. "She's dead, ma'am. Looks like a broken neck."

Annie sobbed. Matilda had been nicer to Annie than anyone in years. She'd had a future. Someone would meet her in Trail's End and help her get settled. Someone expected her. She'd been on the way to a place where she'd begin a new position, where she'd be respected and admired.

How sad that a decent, upright woman with a future had died and left the woman who'd worked in a brothel behind. It should have been Annie. She had no future.

No one would miss her. No one cared about her. No one even knew where she was.

Annie should have been the one to die.

"Do you know her name, ma'am?"

As she stood there, Annie remembered the words of that haughty passenger, how people had called her terrible names for years, how men always tried to take advantage of her. Memories of all the slurs and beatings and sins that were her life assailed her. Annie would never be able to get away from that. Never. No matter what jobs she found or how far she traveled, people would always recognize Annie as the woman from the brothel, cheap and sinful and beneath them. Women would judge and men would leer.

She didn't want that following her for the rest of her life.

She took a deep breath and held it for a few seconds before she said, "Her name was Annie MacAllister."

Chapter One

"I am Matilda Susan Cunningham." Annie said clearly as she stood on the deserted street—the only street—of Trail's End and considered her words. Matilda had spoken like a woman of education, exactly the way Annie wished she spoke. Oh, not that she hadn't tried to improve her speech. She was a natural mimic. Her father used to say she put on airs. Then he'd hit her.

"I am Matilda Susan Cunningham," Annie repeated, enunciating clearly.

The wind blew dust in Annie's face, then swirled down the street and around the dry goods and grocer's store on her left. Behind her was a rickety building, maybe a hotel. It looked as if the wind could knock it over.

Across the street, the dust blew through the doors of a saloon flanked by a bank and a small building that looked like an office. The sheriff's, perhaps. Further down the street huddled a few more little white buildings, all nearly hidden in the approaching dusk of early evening.

At the end of town stood a church. At least she

thought the small white building with a squat tower was a church, but it might be a school or a home.

That was all.

If she lived here long enough, she'd learn what all the buildings were, but now she wanted nothing more than to go wherever that unknown employer was supposed to take her. Every part of her body ached. The scrapes on her legs and the bump on her head throbbed while the wound on her arm continued to bleed.

And she was afraid, deathly afraid. What would happen if no one came? If her masquerade were discovered? So many ifs and so few certainties.

In her hand, Annie carried Matilda's purse. Inside, she found two letters, a clean handkerchief, a comb, seven dollar bills, a few coins and some pennies. Including Matilda's meager savings, Annie now had a total of ten dollars and eighty-six cents. How long would that last?

The wind continued to blow down the rutted main street, pulling Annie's hair from its tight bun. It swirled around the prim blue skirt she'd taken from Matilda's satchel and tried to lift it above her now properly shod feet.

Trail's End really was the end of the trail.

As she searched the street for signs of her employer, Annie thought about the accident. After the driver left for the new wheel, she'd checked on the injured guard who lay unconscious by the coach. Then she'd changed into Matilda's clothing and picked up the woman's new valise. When the men returned, they loaded Annie and the guard into a wagon.

"What about...about Miss MacAllister?" Annie had asked.

"We'll come back and bury the woman out here. No room in the wagon," said the driver.

With that, the wagon took off. During the ride to town, the poor guard moaned with every bump in the rough road. Annie had tried to calm him, but her experience with men had been of an entirely different nature. She used to sing to her father before his drinking got bad, so she tried singing to the guard, softly, songs she had learned as a child from her beautiful but fragile mother. The guard quieted.

After leaving the injured man at the doctor's farm, the driver had brought Annie into town and abandoned her in the middle of the street. At her feet sat the small valise that contained everything Annie now owned. She'd stood clutching her purse and looking around for at least an hour, attempting to decide what to do.

While she waited, the sun dropped behind the horizon and the breeze grew cool. Had Matilda been mistaken when she said someone would meet her in Trail's End? Annie looked up and down the street, but it was still deserted. No sign of anyone.

When a light went on above the saloon, Annie glanced up where she saw shadows moving behind the windows. She knew who they belonged to and knew that the women in those rooms were looking down at her, wondering who she was. Annie straightened her back and lifted her chin.

"I am Matilda Susan Cunningham," she said.

She considered sitting in one of the chairs on the porch of the hotel but feared they were reserved for guests. If no one showed up, would her money buy her a bed for the night? Probably. However, with no idea of what her future held, she couldn't afford to spend even one penny.

But someone was coming for her. Matilda had said that.

Annie picked up her right foot to ease the pinching caused by the oxfords she'd taken from Matilda's body. She'd hated doing it, but she figured a generous woman like Matilda would have wanted her to. At least, she hoped so. The wind blew down the street again, colder after sunset.

When it was dark, a few men rode into Trail's End, tied their horses and entered the saloon. Without hesitation, Annie turned away from them and picked up her valise. She hurried as fast as her aching legs would take her toward the hotel and the comforting light that spilled out from the open door.

She decided she didn't care if someone from the hotel tried to run her off. She was staying. She dropped the valise and lowered herself onto a chair. Perhaps she would have to spend the night here. She shivered again.

"Miss Cunningham?"

She'd fallen asleep, she realized. With a shake of her head, Annie attempted to wake up. Who was this Miss Cunningham? She quickly realized that she was Miss Cunningham and she jumped to her feet, every joint in her body complaining.

"Yes, sir," she said, ignoring the pain.

In the light streaming through the open door of the hotel, she could see the man. Handsome but serious, tall and strong, clean shaven with thick black hair and a square chin. Concern showed in his blue eyes. Solemnly, he studied her face for a moment, which made her want to turn away, to escape his perusal. Then she remembered who she was and stood up, tall and proud.

"I'm sorry you have had such a wait," he said in a deep, commanding voice. "The stage was supposed to bring you to my ranch. I didn't hear about the accident until I arrived in town to look for you. I hope you haven't been too uncomfortable."

He reached for her, and she started to leap away out of habit until she realized that he was reacting to the blood on her sleeve.

"You've been hurt, Miss Cunningham."

"A few bruises and scrapes. This," she said, looking at her arm, "and a cut on my head." She leaned against the chair to steady herself.

He surveyed her, his eyes moving from what she thought must be a bruise on her cheek and to the blood on her sleeve and skirt. "Let's get you back to the ranch."

She started again when he leaned forward, but he'd only picked up her valise. Of course.

"Is this all your luggage?"

"Yes, sir." She looked at his back as he strode away toward a trim little surrey, then hurried after him. He carried nearly everything she had, and she didn't even know who he was or the location of the ranch where he was taking her.

"And you are?" She lifted her head and spoke in the tone that she thought Matilda would use in this situation, strong and certain, despite the hunger, exhaustion, fear and pain competing for her attention.

"I'm sorry." He turned back toward her. "I'm John Matthew Sullivan, a member of the school board and president of the bank. Certainly you know that from my letters."

He smiled at her, an expression that showed both confusion and concern, a smile that so changed his stern visage that it might have warmed her except that she knew how easily men's smiles could come and go. Instead she said, "Oh, yes. Your letters." She put her hand on her forehead. "It has been a difficult day."

"It must have been." He placed the valise on the floor of the vehicle. "Do you feel well enough to start school tomorrow?"

She stopped, one foot inside the surrey, the other on the ground. She couldn't move as she struggled to make sense of his words. "Start school tomorrow?" she repeated.

She didn't want to go to school. What kind of school would there be in such a tiny place? What would they expect her to study and why?

"I know it's soon, but the students are so glad you're here. Because it was so difficult to find a qualified teacher, they've been out since the term ended last April. They're eager to get started again."

Teacher? I'm a teacher?

Oh, dear. Annie bit her lip. Matilda had been a teacher.

"Are you all right, Miss Cunningham?" he said, studying her closely.

She placed her hand on her aching head. No, she was not all right, but she was not going to tell Mr. Sullivan that and destroy her chance to sleep in a bed tonight.

"It's obvious you're exhausted. We'll postpone class until Wednesday so you may rest."

"That would be nice."

He handed her into the surrey, touching her arm for a moment to steady her. Then, as she settled herself in the carriage, he smiled at her, a flash of warmth lighting his eyes. Annie quickly looked away. She did not like it when men smiled at her that way. It made her want to run.

"You may have noticed that Trail's End is not a large town, but the people are friendly." He got in on the other side of the surrey and snapped the reins over the horses. "This area is beautiful in the spring."

The carriage was splendid, new and shiny with leather seats. The matched bays trotted in time with each other. Obviously Mr. Sullivan was a wealthy man.

"Where are we going?" Here she sat, in a vehicle with a man she'd never met, heading off to who-knew-where. Curious and frightened, she wished she could have read those letters Matilda had carried in her purse. "Is the ranch far?"

He looked at her again with a puzzled glance. "As I told you in my letter, you'll live in a room that adjoins the schoolhouse. It's located just a few minutes from my home and about as far from town."

The bays frisked along the road. After only a few minutes, he slowed and turned between stone pillars. "This is my ranch, the J bar M." He pointed at a sign over the drive.

J bar M. Annie carefully studied the sign. "The J bar M," she said.

In silence, they rode down a smooth dirt drive and turned onto a rougher trace. They traveled only a minute or two before Mr. Sullivan halted the surrey.

"Here we are." He jumped from the vehicle.

Annie searched both sides of the road until she spotted a stone building on the edge of the clearing, partially hidden by trees.

"Miss Cunningham?"

His voice startled her, as did the way he addressed her. She must get used to her new name as quickly as possible. With a jerk, she looked to her right where he stood ready to hand her down from the carriage. What would Matilda do in this situation? No one had ever helped Annie from a surrey. In fact, she'd never been in a surrey, but she'd seen enough to know she shouldn't leap out on her own.

She suddenly remembered the mayor's wife in Weaver City getting out of their wagon. She'd put her hand in her husband's and let him steady her as she descended. So that's what Annie did. As soon as she was on the ground, he dropped her hand and stepped away, smiling at her again with that look in his eye.

She'd seen that expression flicker in men's eyes before, but those were rude men, men who frequented saloons or tried to take advantage of young women in the stagecoach. Mr. Sullivan seemed different, upright. She must have misunderstood his smile, his warm gaze.

Scolding herself, she lifted her gaze to study the building for a few seconds. "It's very pretty."

"Yes, it's made of gray limestone, quarried only a few miles from here." He picked up her valise. "My wife chose the material shortly before her death," he said matter-of-factly.

Along the side of the building were three windows with clear glass that reflected the light of a bright moonrise.

"I'll go inside and light a lamp." He headed toward the building, going up two steps before disappearing through a door. In no time, a glow from an oil lamp shone softly through the windows.

As Annie entered, she saw six rough benches, each with a narrow table in front of it, and a desk—oh, my, her desk—in the front of the room, on a little platform. Stacked on the desk were a pile of slates and another stack of books of various sizes. The sight alarmed her.

"This is the schoolroom," Mr. Sullivan said, "as, I am sure, you must have surmised."

Surmised. Annie rolled the word around in her mind. It had such a weighty feeling. "Yes, I'd surmised that." She nodded.

He motioned toward a narrow room at the other end of the building. "That's the kitchen. You'll warm the students' lunches there and may use it to prepare your own meals."

So that's how schools did things. "How many students are there?"

Even in the faint glow of the lamp, Annie could see his puzzled expression. He must have written Matilda about that, too. "Twelve. Not a terribly large group to teach, but they are in all the grades from one through seven."

"I'd forgotten." She nodded again, precisely, a gesture that seemed to belong to her new character.

"Your bed and drawers for your personal accoutrements are through this door," he said as he put the bag on the floor in front of it.

Accoutrements. Another word to remember. "I have few accoutrements."

"There is a door to the outside in your room." He pointed. "The facility is behind the building."

She nodded again.

"Several of the mothers cleaned the building to prepare for your arrival. You have a new mattress, several towels and clean bedclothes."

"How nice of them. I must thank them."

"I'll leave you now to settle in. The children will arrive at seven-thirty on Wednesday. I trust you will be ready for them?"

"Yes, Mr. Sullivan."

"A lamp is on your desk with a box of matches next to it." For a moment, he studied the bruise on her cheek and her arm. "Miss Cunningham, may I send our cook, a fine woman, to help you with your wounds?"

"Thank you, but I'll take care of them myself. I'm very tired."

He nodded. "Then I'll wish you good-night."

"Good night, Mr. Sullivan."

His hand brushed her arm as he moved to the door. At the contact, he stopped and glanced at her as if trying to decide whether he should apologize, and then he turned away quickly, opened the door and closed it behind him.

A woman could fall in love with a handsome, caring man like that without trying, but not Annie. No, she'd learned a great deal about handsome men and ugly ones, and she didn't trust either. With a shake of her head, she told herself to forget her past. It was over, and she was ready to start her new life, preferably without any men, handsome or ugly.

She surveyed the amazing place to which her deception had led her. For a moment, being in a schoolroom made her feel an utter lack of confidence until she reminded herself she was no longer Annie MacAllister and straightened her posture. She was Miss Matilda

Cunningham, the composed and educated schoolteacher of Trail's End.

Well, she would be for at least a few days, until someone discovered she was not Miss Matilda Cunningham. During that time, she'd be warm and fed and safe, which was enough for now. With that bit of comfort, she picked up the lamp in her left hand, pushed the valise ahead of her with her foot and entered her bedroom.

It was tiny, but it belonged to her, at least temporarily. Even as her muscles protested, she turned slowly around the small space and smiled. It was hers alone! The narrow bed had been pushed against the rough, wooden inside wall. Two hooks hung beside the window, and a dresser stood next to the door out to the privy. When she placed the oil lamp on the dresser, the light wavered. Was it low on oil? Slipping her shoes off, she thought a sensible young woman would go to bed before it got so dark she would need a lamp.

But a sensible young woman would not find herself in a position like this. Annie lowered herself onto the bed and contemplated the fix she'd landed herself in when she'd assumed Matilda's identity.

No, a sensible young woman would not find herself teaching school when she didn't know how to read or write.

Chapter Two

John Matthew Sullivan snapped the reins over the heads of his horses as they trotted down the short road between the schoolhouse and his home. He'd chosen the pair carefully—they had exactly the right stride to pull the surrey he'd had built to his specifications. Painstaking and cautious described him well, characteristics passed on to him by his father.

But for him, the value of the animals lay in their magnificence and spirit, the sheer beauty of their matched paces and movement.

Beauty. His thoughts came back to the new teacher. Although he'd investigated her references carefully and heartily recommended Miss Cunningham to the school board, tonight he hadn't felt completely confident about the young woman who was to teach his daughter and the children of the community. She'd written fine letters, had exceptional recommendations and excellent grades from the teachers' college. However, this evening she'd behaved oddly, seeming uncertain and confused.

Of course, she'd just been in an accident, one in

which another young woman had died. She had a wound on her arm. Bruises, cuts and blood covered her.

Small wonder she was distressed and flustered. She was understandably upset from her experience. So what flaw could she possess that now nagged at him?

He slowed to allow an armadillo to saunter across the road and considered the question.

She was too young and too pretty to be a teacher. Under the grime—in spite of it, actually—she was very attractive with thick, dark hair and what he thought to be rich, brown eyes. As a respectable widower and pillar of the community, he shouldn't have noticed that. As a man, how could he not?

Of course, Miss Cunningham wasn't as lovely as his dear wife, Celeste, had been, but even with the dark bruise on her cheek, he could see her features were regular and, well, appealing. But definitely not as fine as Celeste's had been. His wife, alas, had been a fragile woman. Miss Cunningham appeared to be the opposite.

Even with the stains on it, her dress had been modest and ladylike. Her speech had been clear and precise, the tone well modulated. Neat and clean and a good example for the girls in her class. That was strictly all that mattered about the exterior of a teacher.

But she seemed so very young. Although Miss Cunningham had written she was twenty-three, she didn't look over twenty. Of course, there are people like that, who look younger than they are in actual years.

Miss Cunningham seemed like a moral young woman, not the kind of young woman who flirted with men like the previous teacher. Twice when he'd approached Miss Cunningham, she'd pulled away. She'd seemed almost afraid of him, but that was to be expected from an honorable young woman.

And yet something bothered him, something besides her looks and age. He couldn't nail down what it was. It had something to do with her reaction when he mentioned that the students were eager to start class. Surprise, almost shock. Even her confusion after the accident couldn't explain that to his satisfaction.

He'd visit with her tomorrow and see if he could discover what troubled him. He'd allow her to teach for a few weeks. If she didn't measure up to the standards of the school board, well, actually, they could do nothing. It had taken months to find a teacher of quality like Miss Cunningham. No one wanted to come to Trail's End. The school board had been fortunate to find someone who needed a position as much as they needed a teacher. It would be impossible to find another this year.

"Buenas noches, Señor Sullivan," Ramon said as his boss drove into the stable.

"Ramon, what are you doing out here so late?" He stepped out of the surrey and tossed the reins to the man. "You should be home with your family."

"Gracias, señor. El viejo fell today. I made the old man rest."

"Duffy fell?" What was he going to do about Duffy? After he was thrown from a horse last year, John had given him the easiest job on the ranch to keep him safe. He might need to hire another man to take the load off Ramon and keep an eye on Duffy.

"Tried to put a bridle up on a hook. Lost his balance and fell off the bench he was standing on."

"I'll check on him," John said. "I still don't expect you to work these long hours. Understand?"

"Sí, señor."

"After you finish with the horses, go home to your family."

As he spoke, John started toward the small room in the back of the stable where Duffy Smith lived. He preferred the room in the stable to sharing the bunkhouse with the younger, rowdier hands.

The elderly man had taught him everything he knew about caring for animals. He'd always worked hard. Too proud to rest at seventy, he still expected to do his share. That caused John no end of trouble and worry, but also made him proud. He'd probably be exactly the same in thirty-five years.

The room was barely large enough for a narrow bed, small table and a dresser. A lamp glowed in the corner. Duffy's skinny body could barely be seen under the colorful quilt Celeste had made for him,

"All right, Duffy. What's this I hear about you?" John held up his hand as the older man struggled to get up. "Don't try to get out of bed. Stay there."

Duffy's expression was sheepish behind his full beard and thick mustache, both streaked with gray. "I'm fine." He shook his head. "Stupid bench threw me, boss."

Just like Duffy to blame it on the bench. He hated getting old as much as John hated watching it happen. "Do you have everything you need?"

"The boys took real good care of me. I'm going to have a good night's sleep, and then I'll be back to work in the morning."

John shook his head. "You are the most stubborn man I know. Would it hurt you to rest for a few more days?"

Duffy glared at him. "Yes, boss, it would. I'm tough."

"Stubborn old coot." John shook his head. "I give up." He turned toward the door and said over his shoulder, "Take care of yourself."

"Always do, boss," Duffy retorted.

Once out of the building, John headed across the stable yard to enter the house. He climbed the stairs and with a few strides down the hall, he entered his daughter's room. He knew that with the trip to town and helping the new teacher to settle in, he'd be home too late to see Elizabeth before bedtime, to tuck her in and hear her prayers. But he wanted to see her anyway.

Silently, he moved across the floor until he stood next to the bed and watched her sleep, the moonlight illuminating her innocent face. With a smile, he leaned down, kissed her cheek and smoothed the blanket over her shoulders.

Elizabeth had always been more his daughter than Celeste's. With her endless energy and constant chatter, she'd worn her mother out, but he'd loved riding with the child, reading to her and caring for her as she grew up.

How have I been so blessed to have this beautiful child?

As he readied himself for bed, he thought again of the new schoolteacher, unable to rid himself of the nagging doubt. How to handle the situation, to assure the community—and himself—that Miss Cunningham had been the correct choice, even though she'd also been the only choice?

He'd keep an eye on her until he felt comfortable. For his daughter's sake, for the sake of all the children in the community, he would make sure all was right with the new schoolteacher. After all, he'd accepted the challenge to find a teacher. He'd hired her. He was responsible.

He was a Sullivan.

Pain—excruciating pain—and the sensation of turning and twisting, of lurching and rocking racked Annie. She grabbed the side of the coach and reached out for Matilda.

But the young woman wasn't there. With a sob, Annie woke up and attempted to sort out where she was and what had happened, why her right arm, her head and both legs—in fact, her entire body—hurt so much.

It was early morning. She knew that by the tendril of sunlight breaking through darkness to illuminate a narrow strip of ceiling. In the distance, a rooster crowed. In the dim light, she could make out something dark that stiffened her right sleeve. When she rubbed the cloth between her fingers, it crinkled. Blood, she realized.

Her arm throbbed. The blue skirt had wrapped itself around her legs. She shrieked in pain as she tried to untangle herself.

Most amazingly, she was alone on a clean bed in a room with white walls, spotless white walls. No sound of raucous celebration came from the other side of the wall.

"Oh, Lord," she whispered when she realized where she was and why. If this wasn't a moment to pray, even if she didn't expect any response, she didn't know what was. "What should I do, Lord?"

Her stomach growled—not surprising since she'd last eaten with Matilda almost a day ago.

How could life change so quickly and completely? It felt peculiar to know that the driver of the coach had buried Annie MacAllister out there, but here Annie sat in Matilda's clothes, on her bed, in her schoolhouse and with her name. Annie couldn't change any of that.

She looked around and realized she'd slept exactly where she had fallen across the bed last night, fully clothed, not even pulling the sheet over her. Her stomach reminded her again that she hadn't eaten anything before she'd dropped into bed.

Shivering in the cool morning air, she stood and stretched before she padded into the kitchen barefoot. She hated the thought of having to shove her feet into those sturdy little shoes. Why couldn't Matilda's feet have been just a bit larger?

That thought sounded so ungrateful. "I truly am appreciative, Matilda," she whispered. "Thank you." Then she shuddered. Taking the shoes off the feet of a dead woman had been one of the worst things she'd ever had to do.

In the cupboard above the stove, she found a can of tomatoes and an empty cracker tin. The other cupboard was bare except for several dead crickets and a shriveled piece of something Annie couldn't identify but wasn't hungry enough to try.

She'd eaten less than tomatoes for breakfast before, but at least she'd had a can opener then. Now she didn't. Certainly no one expected her to go without food, although never having been a teacher before, she didn't know. She thought Matilda would have brought food with her if that had been a requirement. Perhaps she could find Mr. Sullivan's house and ask him.

She picked up the bucket by the door of her bedroom, carried it outside and filled it from the pump in the yard, moving carefully. She saw no firewood so went back inside, took off her clothing and washed in cold water. Nothing unusual there. When she finished scrubbing off the grime and carefully cleaning the wounds on her arm and head, she put her bloodstained clothing in the water to soak.

Then she turned toward the valise. She hadn't had time the previous day to do more than pull a skirt and basque from the suitcase. Today she needed to see what else was inside. She took a deep breath. She did not look forward to exploring Matilda's personal effects. Taking on the identity of a dead woman had been more difficult, complicated and emotional than she'd ever considered.

Inside were two dark skirts, simple and austere with a pleat down the back, like the one she wore. One was brown and the other black. She pulled out two matching basques, each with new white collars and worn but spotless cuffs, and hung them next to the skirts. Under them, Annie found a lovely white jersey with a short braided front and jet beads around the high neck. For special events, Annie decided as she stroked and savored the softness.

Then came a black shawl, a pair of knitted slippers, several pairs of black cotton stockings, five handkerchiefs, a few more hairpins, a sewing kit and a small box. Reluctantly, she opened the little package. Inside she found a silver watch to pin on the front of her basque. When Annie ran her finger over the engraved vines, tears began to slide down her cheeks. This must have been the teacher's prized possession.

She set the watch down and forced herself to continue. In the bottom of the bag were two books, a notebook filled with writing and many little pictures and another letter. Annie was completely overwhelmed. She'd never had so many nice things. She'd never owned cotton stockings or a cashmere jersey or any jewelry.

Annie put on the black skirt, buttoned the basque up the front and then pulled on the slippers. With no mirror in the little room, she smoothed her hair back into a bun as best she could.

Then she wandered into the empty schoolroom. She didn't want to be there—and yet she did, very much. She was curious and excited and more than a little afraid with absolutely no idea how she would teach twelve children what she herself did not know. But she felt safe here. She would soon have wood and coal and perhaps something to eat.

She touched the books on her desk and opened one. What did those black marks stand for? She ran her hand down the page as if she could absorb their meaning. The paper felt rough and cold. The circles and lines and odd curlicues printed there fascinated and confounded her. Here and there she recognized a J and an M.

A yearning filled Annie. She'd always wanted to go to school. She remembered her mother telling her she was smart when she was just a child.

But after her mother died, her father said educating a woman was a waste. After all, he'd said, what more does a woman need to know than how to clean and cook and sew? She didn't need to be able to read to take care of a man.

That was about all Annie needed to know. As her father drank and gambled more, she'd had to work to support them. Only seven years old, she started cleaning houses. If she didn't earn enough for his whiskey, he beat her until she learned to leave the money on the porch and sleep outside.

Then he'd killed a man in a drunken rage, was hanged and the house was sold to satisfy his debts. When no one would hire George MacAllister's daughter, she realized she had two choices: starve to death or become a prostitute. She chose to work at Ruby's, a brothel.

She brought her attention back to the book. Wouldn't it be marvelous to learn? To read books about distant places and exciting people and thrilling adventures, to be able to read aloud to children or silently to herself, to write letters or a story?

Oh, it sounded more wonderful than any fantasy... but that was all it was. Soon, very soon, the school board would find out she couldn't read or write and nothing would save her. From what she'd seen, she didn't believe Mr. Sullivan would be kind or forgiving when he found out about her deception.

"Excuse me," came a sweet voice from outside as the door opened.

"Yes?" Annie turned to look down on a tiny, fairy-like creature with a heavy basket. Behind the child stood a Mexican man. She straightened and walked toward the little girl.

Light hair curled from beneath the hood of the child's green plaid coat. She looked up at Annie with enormous, intelligent blue eyes and a smile that sparkled with humor.

"Good morning, Miss Cunningham. I'm Elizabeth Sullivan. This is Ramon Ortiz."

The child struggled across the threshold, carrying an enormous basket. Annie would have taken it from her, but Mr. Ortiz caught her eye and shook his head, smiling.

Elizabeth dropped her burden by the door to the kitchen. "My father sent us with some things for you. He thought you might be hungry. And we brought you a blanket because the nights are cold."

Annie hadn't noticed the cold the night before because she'd been exhausted. How lovely to have a blanket. "Thank you."

Mr. Ortiz followed Elizabeth and placed a bundle on one of the narrow tables.

"How old are you, Elizabeth?" Annie settled on a bench so she and Elizabeth would be face-to-face.

"I'm almost eight, Miss Cunningham."

"What do you like most about school?"

"Reading. I love to read. And to write."

Of course the daughter of the man who hired her would love to do the things Annie couldn't. "Do you like to do sums?"

Elizabeth grimaced. "No, ma'am, but I will try. My father says women should be able to add and subtract."

"Of course we should." That was one thing she could do, thanks to keeping track of how much the men who frequented the brothel owed. That and her piano playing had made her popular with the other women there.

The little girl marched into Annie's bedroom to spread the blanket on her bed, tugging on it to make sure it hung squarely. She stopped to brush a little dust from the dresser and pushed the outside door more firmly shut. The child acted with such grace and helpfulness, as if she were an adult, that Annie smiled.

"I asked Ramon to place the food in your cupboard." Elizabeth frowned as she looked around the tiny bedroom. "I don't know why you couldn't have curtains or a pretty quilt."

"Thank you, but please don't worry about it, Elizabeth. This is the nicest room I've ever had."

Elizabeth's eyes grew round, but she was too polite to ask Annie how that could be. "My father and I hope you'll enjoy Trail's End. All the students are excited to meet you tomorrow. Most of us like school a great deal."

"Thank you, Elizabeth. I look forward to meeting them." Annie walked into the classroom. "Would you tell me something about each student?" She congratulated herself on sounding so much like a teacher—or at least like her concept of a teacher.

The child stopped to think a moment before she started counting off the students on her fingers. "There are the Sundholm twins, Bertha and Clara. They're only six so just babies. This is their first year in school. Tommy Tripp and I are in the second grade. We can both read and are learning cursive. Do you have a nice hand, Miss Cunningham?"

Annie looked down at her fingers. They were long and thin but covered with calluses from hard work and cuts from the accident. Her palms were red and rough. Why had the child asked if she had a nice hand? And what was cursive? What did it have to do with her hands?

When Annie didn't answer, Elizabeth continued, "Rose Tripp and Samuel Johnson and Frederick Meyer are in fourth grade. The Bryan brothers are all much older but still in the fifth reader because they miss a lot of school to help their father on the farm. There are three of them, but you won't see much of Wilber because he's almost sixteen and really strong. Martha Norton and Ida Johnson are in seventh grade. They know everything." She stopped and thought, her head tilted. "I could make you a list if that would help."

"I can tell you'll be a great help to me."

"Doña Elizabeth, I've finished putting the food away." Mr. Ortiz came into the schoolroom, carrying the empty basket. His voice was soft and respectful with a lovely lilt to it.

"Thank you, Mr. Ortiz," Annie said.

"I'm Ramon, Señorita Cunningham." He bowed his head. "Mr. Sullivan said he told you in his letters that each family contributes a wagonload of wood once each term. They stack it in the shed behind the schoolhouse." He nodded his head in that direction. "Mr. Sullivan sent me with a load so you'll have some when you need it. And I put a small pile next to the stove."

"Thank you, again."

"The shed's where students who ride put their saddles. They tie their horses on the rail outside it," Elizabeth explained as she moved toward the door. "Please excuse me. My father expects me home right away." She started out before she turned to say, "Oh, and we'll bring you a loaf of bread every week from our cook." She smiled. "I'm so excited about school tomorrow. It's been a long time since we had a teacher."

"Thank you, Elizabeth. See you tomorrow."

When they left, Annie entered the kitchen, ravenous. On the table lay a can opener. She opened one cupboard to discover it filled with tins, dried meat and a loaf of bread. A lower cabinet held a sack of oatmeal and another of potatoes. In the other cabinet were two plates, three glasses, a cup, knife, fork and spoon plus some bowls. What luxury!

The crickets and dried fruit were gone.

She felt incredibly fortunate, blessed with an abundance of belongings and a feeling of freedom, even though she knew it would last only a short while—a few days at most.

For the first time in years, she possessed enough food to last for nearly a week. More, if she rationed it carefully.

She considered lighting the stove but doing it with only one arm would be difficult. Besides, she didn't want to waste any more time when she had so much to learn. With a tug, she opened the drawer, took out a knife and sliced a piece of bread. She was about to take a bite when she remembered Matilda's prayer at the coach stop. If she were to be Miss Matilda Cunningham, she should say grace, even though it didn't come easily. "Thank You, Lord, for this food and for this place. Amen." She nodded, pleased with her first effort.

Her meal finished, she pulled her desk over to the window and studied each book. Hours passed as she copied the letters from a primer. She had to use her left hand because her right was nearly useless. However, she covered the slate with crooked lines and uneven circles that improved as the afternoon advanced. She pressed hard on the pieces of soapstone, writing each letter again and again until the soapstone shattered and her hand cramped. After she finished copying all the letters over and over, she scrutinized them and wondered what she had written.

One of the books showed the letters attached together in a beautiful, flowing wave. Wouldn't it be wonderful to make such lovely lines? Well, she wasn't ready yet. She returned to her straight lines and circles, wondering how on earth she would get through her first day as a schoolteacher.

That evening as she fixed her dinner—her third meal in a row of bread and cold canned tomatoes—she heard a knock at the door. She looked down at her food. The knock came again, louder and more insistent.

"Miss Cunningham," Mr. Sullivan shouted, and knocked again.

"Yes, sir." She abandoned her meal and went to the door. There stood Mr. Sullivan and a beautiful young woman.

Annie had never seen anyone as lovely. She had golden curls that fell from a knot on the top of her head, her eyes were a deep blue and sparkled with fun and her smile showed dimples in both cheeks. She wore a blue robe that matched her eyes and, Annie could tell, was beautifully made and very expensive. She was someone's pampered darling, Annie guessed.

"Good evening, Miss Cunningham." He nodded as Annie motioned them in. "I came by in case you have questions before school begins." He turned toward the young woman who was wandering through the classroom. "May I introduce you to Miss Hanson? She's the daughter of our neighbor."

The young woman turned and gave Annie such a warm smile that she couldn't help but return it.

"Won't you call me Amanda? I shall call you Matilda, and I believe we will be great friends! You must forgive our rudeness for dropping in on you unannounced." Amanda took Annie's hand. Annie hardly knew how to respond to the beautiful whirlwind. "I accompanied

John because he's very proper. I'm acting as his chaperone tonight."

"Amanda, I don't believe—" Mr. Sullivan started to protest.

"But I wanted to come," Amanda continued. "I admire you so much. I've always believed education is important, but I'm afraid my poor brain is barely able to hold a single thought for any length of time."

"Do not allow Amanda to mislead you." He nodded as the beautiful young woman floated toward him and placed her hand on his arm. "She is an intelligent and sensible young woman."

"Sensible? Oh, John, you certainly know better than that." She patted his hand before turning toward Annie. "I truly do respect your education and your ability to work with children, Matilda. I wish I had some talent, any talent."

"Oh, I feel sure—"

"Alas, I fear I'm but a useless butterfly." Her sweet smile turned her statement into a shared joke. "But John said he needed to stop by here before we join my father for dinner. I will excuse myself so the two of you may discuss education and such." Her curls bounced as she flitted toward the teacher's desk.

"How are you feeling, Miss Cunningham?" Worry showed in his eyes. "I hope you've recovered from the accident."

"Yes, thank you. I'm much better." His sympathy warmed her a bit. "Although I fear I will not be able to write for a few days," she said, glancing at her right arm.

"I'm sure the children will understand." He cleared his throat and appeared slightly uncomfortable. Annie suddenly felt nervous. "Miss Cunningham, when we spoke upon your arrival, I felt that we may not have communicated well."

"Oh?" What did that mean? Surely he couldn't have found out what she'd done already, could he?

"When I found you at the hotel, you didn't seem to remember much of the information I had sent you."

"I am sorry I seemed confused. With the accident…" She motioned toward the bruise on her face.

"Of course, but I want to make sure you have no misunderstandings about the expectations of the school board. May I sit down?" He settled himself on a bench, leaning on the table before him. Annie had little choice but to sit with him, though it was the last thing she wanted to do. He pulled a paper from the leather case he carried.

"Do you remember all the requirements stated in your contract?" He handed it to her. "This is the agreement you signed last month."

As he leaned forward she could feel the warmth of his breath on her cheek and smell the scent of bay rum cologne. She took a deep breath as an unknown and confusing emotion filled her.

She swallowed, closing her eyes in an effort to regain her balance. When she opened them, the gaze that met hers was icy cold and hard. Chiding herself for allowing her thoughts to roam, she took the sheet from his hand and looked at it. She recognized that there were different sections and a signature at the bottom. Feeling that Mr. Sullivan wouldn't lie to her and having no recourse if he did, Annie nodded and handed the paper back.

"I would like to review the points with you, Mr. Sullivan. Would you read them one by one?" she asked. "So we can discuss them if necessary? Just to make sure I understand them all."

He glanced at her, puzzled, but began to read. "The agreement says that you will receive the sum of thirty-two dollars per month and lodging during the school term."

Thirty-two dollars a month! Oh, my, it's a fortune! She could save it to live on when she had to leave, if she lasted a month. She could buy a ticket to another destination, she could buy a good dinner and…oh, she could buy shoes that fit!

He continued. "You will teach for six months per year for three years, with four holidays each year. If you wish," he said, glancing up at her, as if gauging her understanding, "you may sponsor an extra term in the spring. When school is not in session, you may live in the building for the sum of three dollars a month if you clean the schoolhouse."

"All right."

"You agree to arrive by the fifteenth of October—well, you're already here, so that point is moot. Next, you will not associate with people of low degree, who drink alcohol, use tobacco or play cards."

She nodded again. She didn't plan to do any of those things or associate with anyone who did.

"You agree to go to meetings of the school committee when you are needed."

"Of course."

"You are not to marry while you are in the employ of the school."

"I have no intention of marrying." She had no need for a man, gentle or not.

"You are expected to be a member of and contribute your knowledge to the Trail's End Literary Society."

Oh, dear, what did that mean? Well, it was too late to balk now. "Yes, sir."

"You will attend church every Sunday, and prayer meetings, as well."

She couldn't do that. Although Matilda would go to church, Annie wasn't good enough—not nearly good enough—to frequent God's house.

"Miss Cunningham?"

She looked up to see him scrutinizing her, eyebrow raised. "Of course."

"Fine." He smiled. "You have met my daughter, Elizabeth?"

"Yes, she's a lovely child."

"She and I will pick you up Sunday morning." He glanced back at the papers he held. "Finally, the contract lists your duties. You will start the stove on cold mornings, you will help students with their lunches and have them clean up afterward, you will sweep and mop the classroom every evening and you will teach all classes to a level deemed acceptable to the school board at the end of each term."

"Yes, sir. Thank you." She nodded. "I'm glad you reminded me of those duties. Lighting the stove will be difficult with the injury to my arm. Could someone help me?"

"I'm sorry I didn't consider that. I'll send Ramon down in the morning to light it until you are able."

"What time does school start?"

"As I told you yesterday, at seven-thirty. Out at two-thirty. Many students help with chores on the farms in the morning and after school. They may arrive late or have to leave early."

"Of course." She nodded as if she remembered that.

He placed the paper back in his case as he stood, contemplating her solemnly. "You have come to us highly recommended. Your references state you are a woman of high moral character."

She nodded again and vowed to be exactly that kind of a woman, if God would just teach her to read and write overnight.

"We hope you will do better than the previous teacher. She was an incurably giddy young woman who ran off to marry a young farmer after teaching for only three months. I hope you don't anticipate doing that."

"No, sir. I'm not the least bit giddy," she answered truthfully.

"I'm sorry Amanda and I bothered you." His eyes rested on her face for a moment before he glanced away. "As I said, I feared you might have forgotten some of these points and wished to make sure that we were in agreement before school began."

"Thank you. That accident—" She pressed her hand against her temple, which still throbbed.

"John." Amanda approached them. "It's getting late. I'm sure my father's getting hungry. You know what a bear he can be when he doesn't eat on time."

Annie smiled at Amanda's description of her father.

"You are quite beautiful when you smile," Amanda said. "Oh, my, I've done it again." She lifted her shoulders and bit her lip. "It sounds as if I think you are not beautiful when you don't smile. I didn't mean that at all. Just that you are even prettier then." A dimple appeared in Amanda's lovely ivory cheek. "It was wonderful to meet you, Matilda. I shall see you again very soon, I'm sure." She moved toward the door with a rustling swirl of her skirt. "Come, John. I have no desire to face my father when he's hungry."

He glanced at Amanda with affection, then looked back at Annie. "I believe everything is in order for tomorrow. Ramon will come down to light the stove, and I'll ask his wife, Lucia, to help with the lunches until you are used to the routine and your wounds have healed."

"Thank you, Mr. Sullivan." She rose as he took the other woman's arm and turned to leave.

But Amanda hadn't finished. She pulled on Mr. Sullivan's arm. "John, I cannot agree with this 'Mr. Sullivan' and 'Miss Cunningham' nonsense. You're going to be working so closely together and the three of us are going to be such good friends." She turned to Annie. "You must call him John and he should call you Matilda." She nodded decisively, as if she had taken care of the entire problem.

"But that wouldn't be proper," Annie said.

Mr. Sullivan turned toward Annie with an amused smile. "You'll learn that Amanda is not at all proper."

"John!" Amanda protested.

"But she is headstrong and stubborn and won't let this go until we agree with her decision."

"Well, yes, that is true." Amanda nodded. "You might both as well do what I've asked."

"But I feel most uncomfortable…" Annie objected.

"Miss Cunningham," John began, then paused as he mentally changed her name. "Matilda, you might as well give in. Amanda will push until she gets her way. And she always gets her way."

Amanda smiled smugly.

"Yes, sir," Annie said, then forced herself to add, "John." Although the use of his first name seemed much too familiar, it didn't feel as odd as she'd thought.

"There." Amanda clapped her pretty little hands. "Now we are all friends." She waved and pulled John toward the door. "Excuse us. We must hurry or my father will have started to eat the furniture."

Annie stood in the doorway, watching through the rapidly falling dusk as John assisted Amanda into the surrey, holding her elbow as if she were precious porcelain. Amanda accepted his care as her due, then waved at Annie as the vehicle moved toward the ranch house.

Amanda was a lovely woman. Oh, Annie wished they could be friends, as Amanda seemed to think they could. She easily pictured Amanda having a friendship with Matilda, but not with Annie. Annie felt stuck between her two identities as she closed the door and walked between the tables in the schoolroom. She was no longer just Annie MacAllister, and she wasn't entirely Matilda Cunningham, either.

John had seemed solemn and judgmental—just a little—but he'd been concerned for her. An odd combination, but she hoped it meant he would give her a chance.

"Tomorrow," she murmured. Tomorrow evening, would she still be here? Would the children find out their teacher couldn't read or write? Would she be on a stagecoach out of Trail's End by evening?

Or would she have another day—perhaps another week—of food and warmth and safety?

Oh, please God. She offered up another prayer, still fairly sure it would make no difference. Please grant me at least a month, just long enough to get one check and find another place to live.

Chapter Three

Nine faces turned toward Annie, smiles on their lips, their eyes sparkling with excitement.

She'd never felt so guilty before. Had she known her deception would rebound on the nine eager students before her, she wouldn't have... Yes, she would have because she had to escape, to find a place to live. But she regretted the consequences and was sorry she didn't have the ability to give these children what they expected and needed.

She glanced down at the silver watch she'd pinned to the front of her basque. It made her feel like a teacher. Seven-thirty. Time to begin.

"Hello, class. My name is Miss Cunningham. I'm your new teacher." Annie stood on the platform and looked at each student. Every child's face glowed with happiness and anticipation.

Hers was the only one in the room that didn't. For a moment, she considered confessing her deficiencies and running from the schoolhouse. But where would she go?

The children kept their eyes on her, probably expecting her to do more than just stand on the platform in front of the classroom. Annie forced herself to say something. "Why don't you introduce yourselves?"

A slender girl with dark, tightly braided hair stood in the front row to Annie's left. Like all the girls, she wore a long-waisted dress with a lace flounce and black boots. A few covered their dresses with Mother Hubbard aprons.

"I'm Martha Norton. I'm in the seventh grade." Martha nodded at a plump young woman with her dark hair pulled into braids with far less perfection. "This is Ida Johnson. She's in the seventh grade also. We help the younger children," she added proudly with a lift of her chin.

"Thank you, Martha and Ida." In her mind, Annie repeated the names as she smiled at both girls.

Two boys stood in the second row on Annie's right. Boys on the right, girls on the left—they had arranged themselves that way as soon as they entered the classroom.

"I'm Frederick Meyer," said a boy with short blond hair. He wore what seemed to be the boys' uniform: a round-necked shirt in plaid or stripes with trousers that stopped just past the knees and boots. "This is Samuel Johnson," he said, introducing the boy next to him. "And that's Rose Tripp." He pointed at the red-headed girl.

After the other children introduced themselves, Annie said, "We're short three students this morning."

"The Bryan Brothers," Martha said. "You won't see much of them, Miss Cunningham. They have to help on the farm. When they come, they're usually late. Wilber misses a lot. He's almost sixteen and his father doesn't see any reason why—"

"Thank you for all that information, Martha. We'll welcome them back when they are able to return." She paused and looked around the class. "I need to tell you something else." Annie pointed at her right arm. "Children, you may have heard I was in an accident on the way here."

They all nodded.

"Because I hurt my arm, I'll be unable to write for several days. I've been practicing with my left hand and am not very good, so you'll all have to help me."

They nodded again.

An hour later, Annie was enjoying listening to the buzz of activity in the classroom as the students worked together.

"A, B, C, D," chanted the first and second graders while Martha and Ida held up slates with those letters written in strong, firm strokes.

Annie stood behind the group and studied the lesson with much more interest than any of the students, willing herself to pick up everything the older students taught the younger ones. She traced the letters on the palm of her hand, attaching sounds to the memory of the letters she'd practiced, hoping she would remember them that evening.

She looked over Martha's shoulder as the girl gave math problems to the fourth graders and watched the students write the numbers, studying how they formed them on their slates. She'd practice them that evening, as well. By the time Lucia came to help with lunch at noon, Annie had learned a great deal.

The children had brought their lunches to school in pails, and they sat outside in the warm October sun to eat with their friends.

Lucia brought plates for both Elizabeth and Annie. "I'll bring you lunch every day," she said. "And I'll wash your clothing as I have for all the teachers. I noticed when I put another blanket in your room that there is a dress soaking. Is that the one you were wearing when you were injured?"

Annie nodded.

"Then I'll clean and launder it, as well."

"Thank you." Annie felt so spoiled. To show her appreciation, she'd buy Lucia something when she was paid. If she was still here. If she got paid at all.

After lunch, the boys kicked a ball around while the girls tossed hoops to each other, laughing and shouting. Fascinated by their energy and joyful abandon, Annie watched from a bench by the clearing.

When the children came back into school at one o'clock, she glanced at the watch and wondered what she would do with them for another ninety minutes. How would she fill the time? She'd already taught them everything she knew. Almost everything.

"Children, do you want to sing?"

The girls nodded; the boys shook their heads. Annie laughed. She closed her eyes and tried to remember the songs her mother had taught her, deciding which ones the children would enjoy.

"White wings, they never grow weary," she began. When she finished the chorus, she opened her eyes to see rapt expressions on the students' faces—even the boys.

Elizabeth and Ida smiled and clapped, and Martha said, "Oh, Miss Cunningham, that was so beautiful. Please sing more."

"I'll sing again, but this time, you have to sing with me."

Although the boys grumbled, they joined in. She taught them all to sing the chorus and had begun to teach some harmony on the verses when she looked up to see John Sullivan at the door. He wore an odd expression, a mixture of admiration and surprise.

"Miss Cunningham." He nodded at her. "Children." They nodded back at him.

"I came by to pick up Elizabeth and to ask how your first day of teaching went. When I approached the school, I heard your wonderful music." He nodded. "I wasn't aware singing was one of your talents."

"Thank you. The children seemed to enjoy it."

"You didn't mention your musical ability in your letter of application."

"I didn't realize it would be of interest." She smiled and turned toward the students. "Children, you may go now. I'll see you tomorrow."

Eight of the students grabbed their lunch pails and dashed from the building while Elizabeth ran to her father and held her arms out. He reached down to pick her up and envelop her in a hug, his expression softening.

Annie titled her head to watch the two, the love between the often stern banker and his daughter obvious.

"Miss Cunningham is a wonderful teacher. She's really good at math," Elizabeth said, and grimaced, her lips turned down.

"Not your favorite subject," he said.

"No, but it was all right. And we helped her write because of her arm, you know."

"Yes, sweetheart, we're sorry about her arm." John gently placed her back on the ground. "Would you please go read for a few minutes? I need to talk with Miss Cunningham."

Oh, dear.

"Thank you for coming by," Annie said. "The day went well, I believe. We got to know each other, and I began to measure the levels of each child in mathematics and reading."

"After I heard you singing, I couldn't help but wonder—do you play the piano or organ?"

Annie looked around the schoolroom, in case she'd missed such an instrument in her post-accident fog, but there was none. "I play the piano and have played the organ, but I don't read music. If someone sings the melody for me, I can play anything."

"A most talented young woman. I'm sure Reverend Thompson would like to talk to you. We're in need of an organist at church."

At church? Annie playing the organ in a church? Oh, no. She didn't think so. She shouldn't even be inside a church let alone to help in the service. No, she wasn't fit for that.

"I don't think I should. Thank you, but I'd need to practice and wouldn't like to take time away from the children or from preparing their lessons."

"We have both a piano and a fine organ in our house. You may practice there. Perhaps you could even teach Elizabeth a few tunes. Of course, the church pays only a pittance. It may not be worth your time."

She glanced up at John. She wanted to tell him that money was not the problem, but she could hardly explain the real reason for her reluctance. "It's not the money at all. I just thought—the children. I'm so new, and I do have responsibilities here."

"I don't mean to push you, but you'll be at church every Sunday. And if you're there already…"

He smiled. The expression softened his features and distracted her. Might have even attracted her…if she were a different woman with a different past.

"You have no idea how much we need a musician." He shook his head.

"Well, yes, of course." She gave in. "I'll discuss this with Reverend Thompson on Sunday, but my arm—"

"Aah, yes. Perhaps not immediately."

After she'd completed cleaning the schoolhouse, Annie heated a can of vegetables and added jerky and cubed potatoes. With a slice of bread, it made a delicious meal. After she washed the dishes and wiped the small table, she took the lamp into the schoolroom and began her work.

How clever, she reflected as she studied the readers, for the publisher of the first level to have a letter next to a picture of something that starts with that letter "A, apple," she read, tracing the letters in the word as she said it. "B, bug." Soon she knew the entire alphabet and had practiced all her letters and many of the short words. Although the round letters she wrote slanted to the left and were a little oddly shaped, an unaccustomed pride filled her because she'd accomplished so much in one night.

Then exhaustion hit her. Tired and chilled but exhilarated at all she had learned, she carried the lamp into her bedroom, washed and got ready for bed.

If she worked all weekend, perhaps she could learn to read an easy story. Of course, putting the letters together into words was difficult. Would it be possible to have the older girls read a story? She could listen and learn, too.

Yes, tomorrow she'd have Martha do just that, Annie decided as she slipped into bed. She wrapped herself in the blanket and fell asleep, feeling warm and safe—and proud to be doing something important.

John sat up in his bed, unable to sleep. He threw the covers off, stood and moved to the window. Often the sight of the land that had belonged to his family for eighty years soothed him and he could fall asleep again. As he watched, poplar trees swayed, their branches teased by a gentle breeze while the light of the rising moon bathed their leaves in silver.

To his surprise, he could see a light coming from the schoolhouse. It had to be long after midnight—why would Matilda still have the lamp on? What could she being doing up so late? Working? She'd told him she wanted to prepare well.

But even knowing that she spent extra time in preparation didn't calm his concern about her. Several times over the past few days she'd seemed puzzled and uncertain when he talked to her. Had she been injured more seriously than he'd thought? Was she sick? Or had the people who'd written her references exaggerated her competency?

She'd blamed her confusion on the accident. What a terrible ordeal she'd gone through. After the death of her only relative, she'd set off to an unknown future only to suffer an awful accident and watch another person die. In addition, he'd seen the bump and bruises on her forehead, the cuts on her hands and the blood on her clothes from the wounds.

Yes, a most unfortunate incident, but that changed nothing. He was still responsible for the education of the Trail's End children. That was the Sullivan way. Whether her actions were due to the accident or mistakes or illness made no difference—if she wasn't teaching well, he'd have to take action. He'd keep an eye on her to assure himself that his daughter and the other children received a proper education.

Keeping an eye on her would not be a burden, given how pretty she was.

As he watched, the light in the schoolhouse moved from the schoolroom toward the room in the back. Then it was extinguished.

With a yawn, he returned to his bed and pulled the covers up. This time, he slept.

Saturday morning, after surviving three days as a teacher, Annie woke up early. She stretched and discovered she had fewer aches. She checked the wound on her arm and found it was healing quite well.

She felt much better. Although she'd slept only a few hours, she was ready to get up and get back to work, to start learning more. At least until she looked out the window.

The sun had barely begun to rise. The morning appeared only as a fiery glow across the horizon, just beginning to sketch pink rays across the dark sky. This was too beautiful a morning to spend at her desk. For a few hours, she'd reward herself for all the time she'd spent at work. She'd take a walk and enjoy the birds and the sun and whatever else she found. After washing and dressing quickly, she forced her feet into her shoes and raced to the door and outside.

Which way should she go? Straight ahead lay the Sullivan ranch, and she didn't feel comfortable heading that way. She might look as if she assumed a friendship that didn't exist, and she certainly didn't want to trespass on their privacy. Behind her lay the road and, on the other side, another ranch. To her left and right lay land that probably belonged to the Sullivans but surely they wouldn't mind if she explored a bit on the acres farther from their home. She'd walk toward the sun and enjoy the marvels revealed in its expanding light.

As more birds joined the morning chorus, she was surrounded by music. She followed a faint path—barely a trace, really—with tall prairie grass on each side. What might be hiding in there? Mice? Possibly snakes, but this morning she didn't care. She merely wanted to revel in the daylight, to feel the cool air on her face and the sun on her cheeks, to experience the solid crunch of the ground beneath her feet.

She moved through a thicket, dodging the branches that attempted to snag her skirt, touching the rough bark of the trees and noting the bare branches. She knew the sunlight would color her face, but that didn't matter. Real ladies would protect their complexions by wearing bonnets or never coming outside in the sunshine, but she'd always loved her walks, even as a sad child and, later, as a woman escaping the heat and terror of the brothel for a few minutes. She held out her arms to feel the joy around her, to draw it in and allow it to warm those cold places inside.

Once through the grove, she found a very inviting tree stump, seemingly placed there just for her. She sat on it and breathed in the beauty surrounding her.

Within moments, she heard hoofbeats coming hard

and fast. Her first reaction was to leap to her feet and hide in the trees, but the rider came into view before she could move. He didn't seem to notice her. He rode with such joy, such abandon, as if this were what he'd been created to do. He and the horse moved together, a picture of effortless perfection and absolute happiness.

The rider wore no hat, his short dark hair blowing a bit. She could hear the sound of deep laughter, and she almost laughed herself, enjoying the sight of this man and his horse, the pure splendor of the two together with the sunlight behind them. A shiver of delight filled her.

Her slight movement alerted the rider that he wasn't alone. He turned the horse and pulled it to a stop, facing her from nearly fifty yards away. Who was he? Putting her hand above her eyes to fight the glare, she still couldn't see his face. He snapped the reins and moved toward her.

Why was she sitting out here alone with an unknown man closing in? Immediately instinct took over. She leaped to her feet and ran toward the trees.

"Matilda?"

The voice belonged to John Sullivan. She stopped and turned, her heart pounding. He galloped up to her, and she realized that he looked like a completely different man out here at dawn, riding as if nothing else existed in the world.

"Hello. You're up early this morning." When he reached her, he dismounted with a fluid motion and smiled.

He wore denim trousers, scuffed boots and plaid shirt, which was quite a contrast to his usual attire. She sensed an ease she hadn't noticed when he wore his proper suit and polished shoes. He was, without a doubt, the handsomest man she'd ever seen. But, of course, handsome men could be the meanest, the roughest and most demanding—

She stopped her train of thought. John was not a customer, and she was no longer in a brothel. She studied his face, his usually stern features softer somehow, more open.

"I like to walk in the morning. And I love to be outdoors," she explained.

Holding the reins of his horse with one hand, he nodded his head. "I do, too. I don't get out nearly as much as I'd like."

"Why don't you spend more time riding?"

"I'm the town banker. Telling my depositors that I'd rather be with Orion—" he rubbed the horse's nose with one hand "—they're not going to be happy with me."

With a sliver of a smile that charmed Annie against her will, he added, "That's why I get up early and ride for an hour. The pleasure lasts me all day."

"It looks so easy for you. When did you start riding?"

"Since I could stay on a saddle. Anyone who lives on a ranch has to." After a moment he said, "If I remember correctly, you ride also."

Annie gulped and wished she could read the letters Matilda had written so she'd at least know what she should be able to do. "Oh, no. I hardly—"

"Surely you're too modest. You listed some competitions you'd participated in."

Before she could reply, the rising sun caught his eye, and he glanced up before turning away to put his foot in the stirrup. "Excuse me. It's time for me to go home for breakfast with Elizabeth. She expects me to be on time."

He mounted, then looked down at her. For a moment,

his gaze met hers and stayed there. Again, that trace of a smile emerged and delighted her, making her want to smile back, although she could not interpret the meaning hidden in his expression.

After a few seconds, she realized who and where she was and lowered her eyes to break their connection.

"Matilda, if you will excuse me?" He nodded at her and turned his horse, riding back down into the valley.

As soon as he was gone, she felt a little cooler in the morning breeze. Well, if that wasn't absolutely ridiculous. She shook her head and reminded herself she was the schoolteacher, not a foolish ninny. John was the banker, the member of the school board who supervised her, and the father of one of her students. If she were to let her barriers down, if she could truly believe that a man wouldn't hurt her—if, if, if. That would never happen. She couldn't allow it.

Nonetheless, she'd watched him ride toward his ranch until he'd disappeared into the trees. Still she stood there, long after he'd disappeared, stunned at how glorious the sight of him had been.

Chapter Four

"Good morning, Miss Cunningham!" Elizabeth shouted, and waved when her father stopped his surrey in front of the schoolhouse Sunday morning, a clear, slightly chilly day. Annie waved back as she walked toward them.

"Good morning," John said with a slight bow as he got out to help her into the backseat next to Elizabeth.

A perfectly normal action for a gentleman, Annie told herself. No reason to feel awkward when he was only steadying her to get in the surrey. On the one hand, she still fought the urge to pull away from him when he reached for her. On the other, she could not stop admiring him. She wanted to believe he wasn't like the men who'd taken advantage of her for years, many of whom were leaders in Weaver City, men of high standing. Was John different?

Forcing herself to relax, Annie said, "Good morning to you both. What a lovely morning. Such lovely sunshine." She settled on the soft leather seat and ran her hand across the smooth, cool surface, watching John's back as he clicked the reins. Although looking like a pillar of the community in his black suit and hat, Annie remembered the man she'd met on the meadow, the one who rode so hard and so fast, she thought no one in the county could beat him. Here now, he acted somber and upright. But she knew what he was like on his horse early in the morning. She'd wanted to laugh with that man, entranced by the joy that emanated from him, by the excitement that lit up his eyes.

It was his eyes that gave him away. When they were chilly and grayish, he was Mr. John Matthew Sullivan, banker and father. When they were blue and sparkled with laughter, he was John, a man who seemed to love life.

"It's nice today, Miss Cunningham, but it will get cold shortly. November is not a warm month here. Oh, have you seen the lazy S?" Elizabeth pointed to a gate on the south side of the road. "That's the Hanson Ranch. You've met Miss Hanson, haven't you?"

Annie nodded as she looked at the sign. How odd. The readers she'd studied showed the letter S standing straight up, but on the sign over the gate, the S lay on its side. Perhaps that was the way an S was made in Texas. Yes, that must be the reason. Did all states have slightly different alphabets? She'd have to practice the Texas S on its side this evening.

"That's why Mr. Hanson wants my father to marry his daughter."

Annie's head jerked up, and she looked at John's back. His shoulders became rigid. "Because Mr. Hanson owns the lazy S?" she asked.

"Yes, because their land and our land are so close that it could be just one big ranch," Elizabeth explained.

"I believe you have said enough about private matters, Elizabeth." His voice held a chilly note.

"But, Father, this isn't private. Everyone in Trail's End knows."

"Elizabeth Celeste Sullivan, please do not say anymore."

"Yes, Father. I'm sorry." She sat silently on the seat next to Annie, dejected.

"Why don't you tell me about the church, Elizabeth?" That seemed like a safe topic.

The little girl brightened. "Our minister, Reverend Thompson, rides the circuit, so he's in Trail's End only one Sunday a month. He's here today. The elders lead the service on the other Sundays. My father's an elder," she said proudly. She filled the few minutes it took to get into town with information about the church service and all the members but did not mention Miss Hanson again.

As they approached the small white building, Annie realized she'd correctly identified the church on her first evening in town. Once inside, she noticed five rows of pews on each side with a stove in the middle. A small table with a wooden cross graced the front of the building. Thirty people sat in the church, including her students and their families. They nodded at the Sullivans and Annie when they entered. She didn't recognize a family with three large boys but guessed that they must be the Bryans.

Elizabeth guided Annie to a pew in the front of the sanctuary and then stepped aside so Annie could precede her. John sat on the other side of his daughter. Shortly after their arrival, Amanda and a stout gray-haired man Annie guessed to be her father entered and sat across the aisle.

"Look, there's the sheriff," Elizabeth whispered when the door closed and a thin, dark man slipped into the back pew just as the minister came to the podium in the front.

"Because we have no organist, I will lead the singing this morning. Let us open the hymnal to number fifty-two."

John handed her an open hymnal. There was no music on the page, only words in very small letters. She attempted to read them but the congregation had finished the song—struggling with the pitch and timing—long before Annie could make out the first two or three words.

"Wasn't that terrible?" Elizabeth whispered. "We really do need an organist."

They certainly did. No one had been exactly sure what the tune was. Only Amanda's clear voice sounding above the stumbling efforts of the congregation brought a hint of the melody to the hymn.

When the service was over, Annie rehearsed in her head what she should say as she waited to meet the minister. When she finally reached him, he took her hand and smiled at her with warmth, as if she really were Miss Matilda Cunningham and a member of his flock.

"You must be the new schoolteacher. How happy I am to see you this morning. I've heard about your accident on your way here. I trust you have recovered?"

"Yes, Reverend Thompson. Thank you."

"I know the children are delighted with you. Martha Norton tells me you sing beautifully although I didn't hear you this morning."

"How nice of Martha." As he continued to watch her, Annie added, "I'm not familiar with most of the hymns, Reverend. When I learn them, I promise I'll sing."

"Our new teacher tells me she plays the organ," John said from behind her.

"Miss Cunningham, we are in desperate need of an organist."

What excuse could she give? "I play the organ only a little, but with my arm…" Annie held it out. Although it had healed some, she still protected it.

"Oh, but if you would just try for us, Miss Cunningham."

The pleading in his gentle eyes stirred her guilt. "I'd be happy to try, but I don't read music. If someone could sing a tune for me, I might be able to play it."

"Miss Hanson knows all the hymns we use. Perhaps she'd teach you some. The organ's just over there. Why don't you sit down and see if you can play it? I don't know when we last had a musician here."

Annie soon found herself on the hard wooden bench, running her fingers over the cool keys. The intricate carving on the high wooden music holder reminded her of her mother's tiny organ which Annie had played until the sheriff of Weaver City seized it to pay her father's gambling debts.

She spent a moment or two trying to remember the songs she knew. Obviously few of the ones she'd played in her previous life would be acceptable, so she attempted to remember "Amazing Grace." The notes came out a little screechy, and her pumping was uneven mostly due to the pain in her leg and the stiff pedals. But the sound improved the second time.

"Let me sing a hymn for you to try," Amanda suggested. In a pleasant voice, she sang "I Need Thee Every Hour" while Annie pressed the keys and pumped the pedals, attempting to follow along.

"That sounds wonderful," John said. "But we must go. Lucia expects us home for dinner shortly."

Annie looked at her watch, surprised to see it was nearly one o'clock. Time always passed quickly when she sat at the organ. She suddenly realized she was exhausted, and both her arm and legs hurt from the exertion.

"Reverend Thompson, I'll practice and hope to be able to play by the next time you come through."

"Thank you, Miss Cunningham. I will look forward to hearing you again."

"Amanda, I hope you and your father will join us at lunch," John said as Annie ran her fingers over the cool ivory of the keys once more. How lovely to play again, even on this ancient instrument.

"Of course we will, John." Farley Hanson pounded John on the back. "This time we're lucky to have the lovely new schoolteacher dine with us."

"Oh? I didn't realize I was to join you." Annie looked from one man to the other.

"We'd really like to have you. I should have mentioned it earlier." John inclined his head slightly and smiled. "I hope you can join us."

"Please come, Miss Cunningham. I want to show you my room and all my dolls and books."

"Yes, we'd love to have you." Amanda gave her the smile that Annie was sure no one refused. "We can work on some more hymns on the piano in John's parlor."

After accepting the invitation, Annie ended up in

the carriage driven by Mr. Hanson after he'd placed his daughter next to John. Amanda had laughed and teased her father about his matchmaking but accepted John's help into the surrey while Elizabeth hopped in the back.

"Where are you from, Miss Cunningham?" Mr. Hanson asked as they left town.

Annie felt relieved that the ride was short, and therefore, the conversation would be, as well. She was a terrible liar—clearly she hadn't inherited that skill from her father.

"East Texas," she replied. That sounded general enough. "Now tell me about your ranch and this town. How long have you lived here?"

"All my life. This is my family's ranch. I brought my bride here thirty years ago. She died last year." He turned toward Annie with a smile. "I've been a very lonely man since then." His gaze suggested she could alleviate that.

Oh, dear, not a lonely widower. She must not allow herself to drive with him again or he might believe she encouraged him. He launched into a lengthy description of his land, cattle and enormous worth, which lasted until they arrived at the Sullivan home.

The long, two-story stone house had a wraparound porch and large windows with dark green shutters. Green hills towered in the background, creating a magnificent setting for the lovely house that was far grander than any home she'd seen before.

John held the door open for them and Annie entered a front hall that opened to a parlor on each side. Tables filled with lovely bric-a-brac and cabinets displaying a wealth of beautiful possessions covered every inch of the parlor not already occupied by lovely, plump davenports and beautiful chairs upholstered in gold velvet.

"I don't believe I've ever seen such a beautiful home."

"Yes, it is nice," Amanda agreed. "John's wife, Celeste, helped design the house and furnish it."

"A very talented woman." Annie turned to look at John. "And a loving wife and mother," he said with a solemn expression. "Elizabeth, would you please take Amanda and Miss Cunningham to your room to wash their hands?"

As she followed Elizabeth through the house and upstairs across beautiful carpets, Annie became slightly overwhelmed by the Sullivans' wealth.

"John's wife ordered all the furniture in the house from Boston. It's the finest you'll see in the state," Amanda explained as they entered Elizabeth's bedroom.

Indeed, it was. There was a washstand with inlaid patterns on the drawers and a matching armoire. A delicate spread covered the intricately carved bed.

"Belgian lace," Amanda whispered.

The chamber looked more like a museum than a child's bedroom.

Against the wall stood a full-length mirror. Annie approached it hesitantly. She'd never seen her entire body before—only her face in a small, dull mirror the women in the brothel had shared.

The view surprised her. She looked thinner than she'd thought she would. Maybe a little pretty, although it was hard to think that while standing next to Amanda.

Annie turned all the way around, studying herself. The basque fit a little oddly—tight around her arms, which were apparently more muscular than Matilda's had been, and a bit loose around her waist. Nonetheless, it looked plain and neat and clean, all of which suited a teacher very well. She attempted to smooth an escaped curl back into her bun.

"Miss Cunningham, look at my toys." Elizabeth pulled her to the bed. Five beautifully painted china dolls leaned against the pillows, dressed fashionably in pastel dresses with large-brimmed hats.

"Elizabeth, aren't they lovely?" Annie longed to pick one up one but feared she would drop it or muss the lovely gown. "Do you play with them?"

"When I was younger, but now I prefer to read."

After Annie poured water from the china ewer into the matching basin, she washed her hands and dried them on a soft towel embroidered in flowers.

"Miss Cunningham, you may wish to go in here before we go to dinner." Elizabeth opened a door for Annie.

Inside was a porcelain fixture of some kind. The rounded bottom section and the part above were painted with brilliant flowers and gold accents. It was the prettiest piece of furniture Annie had ever seen, but she had no idea of its function.

"Let me talk to Miss Cunningham for a moment," Amanda said, and then explained the water closet to Annie.

Annie had never seen such a thing. She hadn't even known they existed. What luxury never to have to go outside at night or in the cold.

Seated at the dinner table a few minutes later, she studied the silver serving dishes and the lovely ivory china with silver rims. Mr. Sullivan's wealth exceeded anything she could imagine. Never had she felt more out of place than she did here.

During dinner, Mr. Hanson continued to treat Annie with special attention that embarrassed her terribly. He was at least twenty years older than she was and not at all attractive to her. She felt very uncomfortable with his flattery and gallantry. How could she stop him without being rude?

When the embarrassing meal finally ended, John said, "Farley, if you don't mind, I'd like to talk to Matilda about some school business. Also, she has expressed an interest in playing our piano."

"Thank you for the meal, John. I will go attend to some work I need to finish this afternoon. Miss Cunningham, it was a true pleasure."

"Thank you, Mr. Hanson," Annie said, grateful to John for the reprieve from Mr. Hanson's attentions.

When the Hansons left, John sent Elizabeth into the parlor and watched her seat herself at the piano before he turned to Annie. "Farley Hanson's wife died last year. As I'm sure you've guessed, he's looking for a new wife. I feel I must remind you of the terms of your contract."

She frowned, attempting to understand his words.

"If you came to Trail's End to find a rich husband, Matilda, I warn you I will oppose any such effort."

Annie stepped back. "I assure you I have no desire to marry. I only wish to teach school." Shaking, she turned to join Elizabeth in the parlor, unable to comprehend the tone of John's voice and the ice in his eyes.

John was completely baffled by his own behavior. Why had he spoken to Matilda so rudely? He watched her as she approached the piano and sat on the bench next to his daughter. As Elizabeth sang, Matilda followed, playing only with her left hand, which reminded him that she still had not recovered from the accident.

Why had he felt the need to warn her away from Farley, a good man and a friend? Seeing him flirt with Matilda had bothered John. He had to admit she had done nothing but politely discourage the old fool.

Perhaps he himself was the fool, struggling with an odd emotion that was so different from how he'd felt about any woman before. He was confused and uncertain around Matilda, both feelings he was not used to coping with.

What was it about her that drew both him and his friend? Men who had never acted foolish about a woman before?

Well, of course, there was the fact that men outnumbered women greatly out here. He'd gone to St. Louis to find Celeste, who had hated every moment of her life in Texas. A woman as lovely as Matilda with no family to guard her as Farley did his daughter—such a woman was sure to attract attention.

Yet she showed no flighty tendencies. She did not flirt. She had not encouraged Farley, nor had she showed any interest in John himself. He realized with a start that this was what probably bothered him most.

He sighed as he watched Elizabeth and Matilda in the parlor. He'd always found the ranch house stifling, a reminder of his overpowering, controlling father. He often didn't like the man he was in this house, much like his demanding parent. At times like this, he longed to be outside, training horses with Duffy or riding across the prairie or even mucking out a stall.

It was time and past for him to stop allowing his father to dominate his life from the grave. But habits formed over a lifetime bound him like a lasso. The lectures that a Sullivan behaved differently—was not guided by mere feelings—still echoed and shaped his behavior.

He watched the teacher with his daughter. Matilda played a chord, then placed Elizabeth's hand on the piano keys and told the child to do the same. She smiled up at her teacher, so sweetly, with so much trust, and followed the instructions. When Elizabeth picked out the tune after Matilda had showed her the correct keys, they both smiled.

This was a woman who obviously loved children and who was a good teacher. A woman who attracted him so much that he walked into the parlor to stand next to her, hoping that she would turn that beautiful smile on him.

And he'd done it even before he realized he'd moved an inch.

Annie glanced up to see John next to her. Which man was he now? The stern banker who lectured her? Or the daredevil who raced across the meadow with wild abandon? The banker intimidated her, but she actually feared the other man more. The man with the fleeting smile and the sincere blue eyes was far more dangerous to her because that man attracted her. That man she could fall in love with.

When she stood to leave after practicing a few more pieces, he looked down at her. "I must apologize for my earlier words, Matilda." He shook his head. "I meant them as a mere reminder, but they came out rude and judgmental. I'm sorry."

Yes, this was a man she could care about. But she dared not allow herself to.

Chapter Five

On Monday morning, Annie called the students to order. "Children, let us go over some of the last letters of the alphabet." Annie picked up a slate to show the Sundholm twins. "Here's a Q." Her circle was round and even. "Here's an R." Her strokes were strong and clear. "And here's an S." She made it just the way she'd seen it on the sign in front of the Hansons' ranch.

To her surprise, the older children became very quiet looking at each other as if they did not know what to do.

She looked at the S but could see nothing wrong with it. It lay flat on the line she had drawn below the letter.

"Miss Cunningham," Elizabeth said. "I think you want to tilt your slate like this." She took the slate and turned it so the S stood straight up. "The way you held it, the letter looked like a lazy S, like the Hanson brand."

"Thank you, Elizabeth. How clever of you to notice that." Annie put the slate down and bit her lip. "Children, why don't you run outside now for just a little bit."

"But, Miss Cunningham, it's not even time for lunch yet," Ida said.

"Yes, children, I know, but it's a lovely day. Run

around a little. I'll call you back for arithmetic in a few minutes."

When they left, Annie sat behind her desk and dropped her face into her hands. How could she ever have thought she could fool these children? A lazy S. She'd written a lazy S. Now they all knew she didn't know a real S from a lazy S. Eight-year-old children knew the difference, but she didn't. Tears spilled between her fingers.

"Miss Cunningham."

She looked up to see Rose and Samuel.

"We didn't mean to hurt your feelings by laughing. We're sorry," Samuel said. "The other children sent us in because we hurt your feelings."

"Miss Cunningham, you're the best teacher we've ever had. Please don't cry." Tears gathered in Rose's eyes.

"I'm the best teacher you ever had?" She wiped at her face with her hand.

"Oh, yes. You are so nice and so pretty. And you sing so well, and you know your numbers." Rose nodded. "We all really like you."

"The last teacher didn't want to teach us anything. Sometimes she was mean." Samuel looked at her with wide, sad eyes. "Please don't cry. We won't laugh anymore."

"Oh, children, I want you to laugh. I want you to enjoy school." She stood and waved her hand. "Go on outside, and play for a few more minutes. I'm fine. Just a little tired and shaken. From the accident, you know."

"Yes, Miss Cunningham." The two ran toward the door.

The best teacher they've ever had? Annie collapsed

in her chair, laughing so hard that tears of joy spilled down her face. For the first time in her life, she felt like the luckiest woman alive.

On Wednesday, Annie sat on a bench in the shade of the twisted post oak trees and watched the children play. The students ran and hopped, laughing with the delight of the young. The sun reflected on Rose's red braids and Frederick's blond hair seemed to set those colors on fire. The last blossom of a blue mist flower that shown purple against its ashy green leaves drew her attention while a goldfinch sang te-dee-di-de.

She smiled. She never thought she'd find herself in such a paradise. She'd lasted for six whole school days. She'd learned to print well and had just begun to work on cursive. Late at night, she'd puzzled through the stories in the first three readers, read several geography lessons and assigned poems for the upper levels to memorize. She was successfully teaching herself as she taught her students.

"Miss Cunningham!" A shout interrupted her reverie.

Annie leaped to her feet and ran in the direction of the voices where little Clara Sundholm lay on the ground. Annie kneeled next to the child.

"What happened, Clara?"

Tears rolled down the child's face. "I fell down." She pointed to a scrape on her knee.

"Oh, sweetheart." Annie wiped the child's face with her handkerchief. Clara held her arms out. Startled, Annie picked up the girl who threw herself against her teacher's neck and sobbed.

"There, there." She patted Clara on the back as the

child cuddled against her. Annie had to squeeze back tears herself. The softness of the child and her utter trust opened something inside Annie. The reaction felt like ice melting. She felt a warmth and tenderness she remembered from her own mother's hugs and she allowed the child's affection to curl around her heart and embrace it tightly.

She stood and carried Clara to the bench where she settled down with her. Little by little, the girl calmed down and with one last sob, fell asleep, her head against Annie's shoulder.

Annie looked down at the exhausted child. She gently rubbed Clara's cheek with the back of her hand and softly sang a lullaby as she rocked the little girl.

When the sound of hoofbeats intruded, she looked up to see a stranger approaching on a roan gelding.

"Good afternoon, Miss Cunningham." He pulled up his horse a few feet from her bench.

All she could see was a thin face with a long, jagged scar across his cheek. Startled and a little frightened to be alone in the clearing with this unknown man and her students, she clutched Clara more tightly to her chest and turned to look for the other children.

With slow grace, the man dismounted and stood beside her. "Who are you?" Annie demanded, fear making her forget her manners.

"Didn't mean to alarm you, ma'am. I'm Cole Bennett." He took off his hat to show dark hair tied back with a strip of leather. "Sheriff Cole Bennett."

Of course. She recognized him from church.

He nodded toward the bench. "May I sit down?"

With a nod, she relaxed—but only a little. Yes, sheriffs were lawmen, but many were retired gunfighters, nothing more than hired hands for crooked ranchers.

"Teacher." Clara squirmed. "You're holding me too tight."

"How are you, Clara?" He smiled at the child who lit up his gaunt face. He was a handsome man, despite the scar.

"Hello, Sheriff." The child looked down at her knee and then at the others playing in the grass. "I'm fine now. I want to play." She jumped from Annie's arms and dashed toward her friends.

"I came by to introduce myself, ma'am." He leaned forward on the bench. "To let you know that if you need anything for yourself or for the children, you only have to come to town or send Ramon to get me."

"Thank you, Sheriff. That's comforting to know. If I need you, where would I find you?" She cautioned herself not to relax too soon. She knew this type of man too well. Her father had once been handsome and charming, at least for long enough to court her mother.

"Most often I'm in my office in the jail, which is just down the street from the hotel."

"What are you doing here, Bennett?" John's voice interrupted.

Annie looked up in surprise. Although his horse stood only a few feet away, she hadn't heard his approach. Wary of the sheriff, she'd missed his arrival. From his words and glower, she could tell that John obviously did not approve of her conversation with the sheriff.

"I thought I should introduce myself to the new schoolteacher." He stood, nodded at her and put his hat back on. "A pleasure to meet you, ma'am."

"For me also, Sheriff." She got to her feet and watched as he mounted his horse and rode off.

"Matilda, I know you are innocent in the ways of the world, but you should not associate with that man." John shifted in the saddle as his black horse danced sideways.

"He merely stopped to introduce himself. He seemed nice."

"He's anything but nice. Bennett's a retired gunfighter. He's not the type of man a schoolteacher should associate with."

Although Annie was glad John considered her innocent in the ways of the world and hoped he would never find out differently, she wondered why he spoke so strongly. She did not plan to keep company with the sheriff. He'd only paid a polite call on a newcomer to town.

John wasn't jealous, was he? How absurd. He was just a man very concerned with appearance. She'd noticed that before. It was important to him that the teacher he'd hired would avoid anything that could be considered immoral.

"Please remember you agreed not to associate with people of low degree. That describes Sheriff Bennett exactly." He tugged on the reins to control the restless horse.

"I have no plan to associate with anyone of low degree," she said, irritated by his repeated lack of trust in her.

He nodded. "I only wished to clarify the matter."

"You need not clarify this issue. Be assured I understand my contract. If you remember, we went over it together." Afraid she would lose her temper, Annie turned toward where the students were playing. She kept an eye on Clara, telling herself she did that not because she didn't want to meet Mr. Sullivan's eyes but to assure herself the child had recovered.

After nearly a minute, she heard, "I've done it again, Matilda."

She turned back to see him shaking his head.

He smiled ruefully. "I jump to conclusions about you. Again, I apologize."

"Thank you." What else should she say?

"I came here to tell Lucia to return home. Her son is sick."

"Oh, dear. How ill is he?" Annie stood.

"I don't believe it's serious. Ramon just requested that Lucia come home to care for him."

"I didn't know she and Ramon had a son. How old is he?"

"Miguel must be almost eight by now."

"Eight? Why isn't he at school?"

"He works at the ranch."

"But he should be in school. Certainly Miguel will do much better in life if he can read and write."

"Unfortunately many young people in this area don't attend school because they are needed by their families. Others cannot afford school, even with the low tuition rate."

"How sad," she said, recognizing that he could have been talking about her as a child. What would John think of her if he knew her story? What would he say? More importantly, what would he do? Annie never wanted to find out.

"I also came to give you a message," he said. As Annie took a few steps toward him, he frowned in concern. "Are you limping?"

She looked down at her feet. Although she'd laced her shoes loosely, they pinched so much that she hobbled toward him. "I hurt my foot in the accident. My shoes rub, but I'm sure I'll be fine shortly."

"We cannot have you in pain, Matilda. Not even for a short time. Do you need new shoes?"

"I would like a new pair, but I don't have the money to buy them yet." And she had no idea when she would be paid—or if she would be paid when the children told their parents about the incident of the lazy S.

"Then I'll advance you part of your salary." He reached in his pocket, took out a bill and handed it to her. "You have, after all, taught for a week. Do you need anything else?"

Annie, astounded, almost couldn't think clearly. "A brush. I lost my brush in the wreck, and some soap."

"I'll have Lucia bring you soap tomorrow. Also I'll put some money on account for you at the general store, as well as the bank. You can draw it from either place for your necessities."

"Thank you, John." She smiled, delighted by the feel of money in her hand and the thought of wearing shoes that fit properly. "You said you had a message for me?"

He simply watched her for a moment, his eyes filled with an admiration that made her self-conscious. She shifted, ill at ease under his scrutiny.

He finally cleared his throat and said, "I've been asked to bring you to a meeting of the school board on Tuesday of next week in my office at the bank. We'll leave here shortly before seven." He turned, got into the surrey and had driven off before she could say anything or ask for more information.

What would they expect of her at such a meeting?

Would they test her? Would they expect her to read for them? Or to recite a poem?

She sighed. Well, there was nothing she could do about it now. She'd have to wait until Tuesday and hope she could show herself to be competent.

"Thank you, Mr. Sullivan. That sounds fine. I'll be ready," Annie yelled.

Two o'clock Friday, at almost the end of the school day, Elizabeth waved her hand, trying to get Annie's attention. "Miss Cunningham, Miss Cunningham."

Annie looked up from Clara's arithmetic. "Yes, Elizabeth?"

"Guess what I'm getting for my birthday?"

"When is your birthday, Elizabeth?"

"Today, today!" Her face glowed with excitement, then changed quickly to dismay. "I was supposed to tell you. Lucia is bringing a cake today, just before the end of school. So everyone can celebrate with me. I'm sorry. I forgot to tell you."

"That's all right." Annie smiled at the rest of the class. "Do you mind that Elizabeth forgot to tell us, or can we all agree to eat the cake Lucia brings to help Elizabeth celebrate?"

Everyone shouted their approval. "I think we'll all enjoy celebrating with you."

"Good." Elizabeth smiled again. "But can you guess what I'm getting for my birthday?"

"A new doll?" Clara asked. The boys made sounds of disgust about such a feminine gift, but Elizabeth shook her head.

The guessing continued: an apple, a hairbrush set, new shoes, a dress. No one found the correct answer.

"A pony!" Elizabeth finally said. "My father is giving me a pony. I'll ride it to school on Monday."

"A pony," Martha said. "What color?"

"I don't know yet. He'll have it for me when I get home."

Everyone told Elizabeth how excited they were about her present and wished her happy birthday. After they shared the delicious torte Lucia brought down, the other students left for the day.

With an impatient Elizabeth dancing around, anxious to get home to see her pony, Annie helped Lucia clean up and then saw them off, waving as the two headed to the ranch house in the wagon.

Finally alone, Annie went back into the schoolhouse and twirled around the room. She'd lasted another day. "Thank you, Lord," she whispered, the prayer feeling more natural.

The students had sung a lot and done sums orally, but she seemed to have them convinced she was a real teacher. Over the weekend, she'd have two days to work, to learn, to attempt to read several stories in the upper-level readers and understand them. Two days minus time for Sunday services, but that still left her plenty of time. Annie pulled a desk over to a window again and began to work.

The wind picked up at sundown, whipping around the corners of the sturdy schoolhouse. Surely, Annie thought as she looked out the window, a storm was coming to break the drought. But no sound of rain pattered on the roof.

Annie had finished reading several stories and sat up to stretch. Her shoulders hurt constantly from leaning over the desk, but the persistent work helped her feel more confident. As she leaned her head on her hands in an effort to relieve a headache that plagued her, she heard a persistent sound from the back of the building, loud enough to be audible above the roar of the wind. What in the world was it?

She shook her head and picked up the book again, but the odd sound continued, just loud enough to distract her. A glance at her watch told her it was only ten o'clock, which meant she had several more hours of work ahead.

But the noise didn't stop. It interrupted her concentration as she read the moral story about a little girl named Minnie who always complained. The author of the story held Minnie up as a good child who attempted to teach everyone to behave as perfectly as she did by her constant nagging. She seemed like a whiner to Annie. Happy to have a reason to stop reading this particular story, she stood and headed toward the sound.

When she walked past the kitchen, the sound grew louder. Entering the bedroom, she realized it came from outside her back door.

She stopped. Should she open it? If there were anyone outside who wished to do her harm, it would be easy enough for him to break in. Slowly she approached the door, opened it and peeked out through a narrow slit.

No one was there, but the sound continued. She looked down. On the top step stood a tiny ball of fur. In an instant, it tore past her feet and into the building as the wind grabbed the door and slammed it behind the creature.

Annie turned. In the middle of the room stood a small bit of black fluff with four white feet and a dot of white on its nose. From its mouth came the loudest caterwauling Annie had ever heard. And it didn't stop.

"Come here, kitty." Annie reached out her hand, but the little animal backed up and growled. Annie put her hands on her hips and looked at the cat. What should she do?

"Are you hungry?" It did not, of course, answer, but strutted out of the bedroom with its little black tail standing straight up like a scorpion's. And it kept up the loud, demanding meowing. How could such a small creature make so much noise?

Annie had no other choice but to follow it. She was, after all, in charge of the schoolhouse, responsible for its good order and cleanliness. Allowing the kitten to wander through didn't seem responsible. Of course, what harm could something so small do?

More than she would've thought. By the time Annie found the cat, it had pounced on a piece of soapstone and knocked it to the floor causing it to break and scatter dust and fragments all over; discovered a piece of paper that it tore up into small scraps with great delight; and scratched on the door jamb, leaving deep marks with its sharp little claws.

"No, kitty." When it didn't pay any attention to her, Annie took advantage of the animal's inspection of a bug to pick up the kitten.

"Meooooow," the tiny creature complained in a voice loud enough for one of the cougars Annie'd been told lurked in Texas, then wiggled away.

Annie went into the kitchen and opened a can of milk, poured it in a bowl and added a little water. She found the kitten exploring her desk and put the bowl next to it. In no time, the cat had lapped the bowl clean and began washing her face with her tiny white foot.

Before it finished, the cat blinked a few times, then curled up on the desk and fell asleep.

What was she going to do with it? She watched for a few minutes while it slept, its sides rising and falling. She placed a finger under the animal's chin and scratched. Loud purrs sounded through the schoolroom.

What was she going to do with it? Annie picked up the lamp in one hand and the cat in the other. The little creature pressed its soft, furry warmth against her chest and continued to purr. She suspected the schoolhouse wasn't the place for a kitten. Maybe a big mouser who lived outdoors, yes, but not this little speck of fur that was barely the size of a mouse.

Annie put the lamp on the dresser, then opened the door and leaned over to put the kitten back outside. It woke up and looked at her with wide, startled eyes, digging its claws into her basque and refusing to let go.

"All right." Annie stepped back inside and closed the door. "You can stay for tonight—just tonight. Tomorrow, when the wind lets up, you're going back outside." She lifted the kitten's chin and looked into its face. "Is that understood?"

It purred.

Annie folded a towel and placed it in the corner of her bedroom. "That's your bed for tonight." She placed the cat on the towel, then began to undress. Before she slipped on her nightgown, the little animal had scaled the blanket on the bed and curled up in the middle of it.

"All right." Annie laughed. "You can stay up here tonight. But tomorrow you're back outside," she repeated.

"Miss Cunningham, Miss Cunningham!"

Someone was knocking and calling her name at the

front door. Annie turned over and attempted to ignore the sounds. It was Saturday morning. Certainly she had the right to sleep late. Or was there something in her contract about getting up early on Saturday mornings?

Then the knocking began at the back door. She opened her eyes slowly and discovered a cat lying on her pillow. Oh, yes, the kitten. The sight reminded her that her exhaustion this morning was due to a small, furry tornado that had raced across the bed all night long.

Sunshine filled her room. What time was it?

"Just a minute!" she shouted with as much courtesy as she could find inside her sleep-deprived body. She slid off the bed, stumbled toward the dresser and picked up her watch. Nine o'clock. She should be up by now.

"Just a minute," she repeated but more politely. She'd glanced at the chemise she slept in and wondered how she could answer the door—she had no robe. When she moved the cat so she could use the blanket, it howled in protest. Annie wrapped the cover around her and opened the door to peek outside. "Oh, good morning, Lucia."

Lucia stood outside with a bundle in her hands. "Good morning, Miss Cunningham. I'm sorry to bother you, but Mr. Sullivan sent me."

Was the board meeting this morning? Annie shook her head. No, Tuesday evening. Had she forgotten an appointment John had scheduled for this morning? She opened the door and allowed Lucia inside.

"It will take me a moment to get dressed."

Lucia took another step inside, put the bundle on the bed and untied the twine. As she did, the kitten jumped across the covers and attacked the string. Lucia jumped back.

"Oh, Miss Cunningham, you have a kitten." She

scratched the cat's ears. "It's so cute. Does it have a name?"

Annie thought of the little creature's loud protests and remembered the story she'd been reading about the girl who always complained. "She's Minnie. She wandered in last night when it was so windy, but I'm not keeping her."

As if she understood, the kitten started her loud me-owing.

"Miss Cunningham, we have badgers, foxes, arma-dillos, bobcats and raccoons in this area. If you don't keep the cat, the scavengers will eat her."

Minnie wouldn't even make a mouthful for any of those animals. Perhaps she'd keep her a few more nights, or until she was big enough to defend herself.

"Mr. Sullivan sent me to ask if Elizabeth could come over to show you her new horse."

"Of course."

"I brought you some bacon and a few biscuits, so you wouldn't have to fix your breakfast this morning." She handed Annie the bag. "I reminded Mr. Sullivan you don't work on the weekends, but Miss Elizabeth was so insistent. He can't turn her down."

"I'm glad she wanted to share her excitement with me."

"And he's bringing over a horse for you to ride," Lucia said.

"He shouldn't do that." Annie clasped her hands in front of her. "I really don't ride."

"Well, Mr. Sullivan seems to think you ride and that you'd be happy to have the opportunity."

Matilda probably rode well. She'd looked like the type of woman who did everything capably. Annie was the type of woman who'd never been on a horse and wasn't all that fond of the large animals. They had a tendency to prance and to show their big teeth.

"Maybe he has me confused with one of the other applicants for this position."

Lucia shook her head. "You were the only applicant."

Oh, dear.

"Mr. Sullivan sent me over with a divided skirt, one of his wife's. It should fit you." Lucia held it up. "He didn't know if you had brought your riding clothes with you."

Annie shook her head as she took the garment from Lucia. What had she gotten into? "I didn't bring riding clothes," she said. She did not add "Because I've never ridden a horse, ever."

She'd have to ride. Clearly John expected it. It would make Elizabeth happy, but could she even stay on the horse's back, never mind actually ride it?

She'd have to. Suddenly, teaching herself to read didn't seem so hard after all.

Chapter Six

After Lucia left, Annie pulled on the divided skirt with her brown basque, combed her hair, then settled down to enjoy a biscuit and share the bacon with Minnie. With a few minutes remaining before ten o'clock, she went outside to await the Sullivans.

"Miss Cunningham!"

Annie looked up to see a pretty chestnut pony frisking along with Elizabeth on its back.

"This is my pony, Brownie." The child brought the horse next to Annie and stopped it after a few unsuccessful tugs on the reins.

"Soft hands, Elizabeth," John said from a few yards behind his daughter, astride Orion. He was wearing denim trousers, a plaid cotton shirt and a wide-brimmed hat. He looked quite handsome and approachable—the banker was nowhere to be seen today.

He nodded toward the pretty brown-and-white pinto mare he led. The animal looked calm which made Annie feel just slightly better.

"Good morning, Elizabeth. Good morning, Mr. Sullivan." Annie smiled and put her hand on the new pony's neck. "She's beautiful. Tell me all about her."

"My father bought her for me at an auction in Fredericksburg. They just delivered her yesterday." Elizabeth loosened her hold on the reins a bit, and the pony pranced sideways.

"She has a lot of spirit." Annie watched as the girl attempted again to rein in the pony.

"Maybe a little more than I realized." John moved his horse closer to his daughter with the protective affection he always showed toward her. "But I'm sure that with practice, Elizabeth will be able to control Brownie."

"She's a wonderful present. Thank you for bringing her to show me."

"As I'm sure Lucia told you, Elizabeth and I were hoping you could join us for a ride. We're going over to the high meadow so Elizabeth can spend some time getting used to Brownie there," John said.

"I haven't ridden in so long." She studied Elizabeth, who rode with her elbows in, lightly holding the reins, her feet resting comfortably in the stirrups. Could she do that? If the horse didn't start bucking or doing those other wild things she'd seen the animals do, probably so.

He frowned as if attempting to remember. "I thought you'd written that you rode daily."

"Well, yes, but I've never been a very good rider." Well, didn't that explanation sound foolish? She walked toward the gentle mare. The horse didn't seem intimidating. Annie feared she'd have to get on her back and attempt to ride, but how?

Again, she remembered the mayor's wife in Weaver City. She stood on a step and put one foot—the left foot?—in the stirrup and threw her right leg across the horse.

But even if she could get on the horse, she'd never fool anyone into believing she was an accomplished rider. And, although she'd healed greatly since the accident nearly two weeks earlier, her leg still ached.

"Oh, Miss Cunningham, we're going to have so much fun."

She turned back to see Elizabeth smiling in anticipation. With a sigh, she said to John, "If you could help me, I'd appreciate that," she said. "My leg is still a problem."

John quickly dismounted and tied his horse to a post. "I do apologize. Elizabeth wanted to show you Brownie so much that I didn't even consider that you may still be in pain."

The horse wasn't too big. As long as it stood patiently before Annie, she might as well try to get on. She put her hand on the nose of the mare, which nickered softly.

"She seems like a nice creature."

"Elizabeth learned to ride on Mercy."

If a child could ride this horse, certainly Annie could. She took the reins, stood on the step and placed her foot in the stirrup.

Mercy shuffled her feet and moved away, which almost caused Annie to fall on her face. She'd grabbed the saddle and held on, but it confirmed her belief that horses could not be trusted.

"I'll hold her still." John took the reins.

Reciting the points of mounting a horse to herself, Annie swung her leg over the saddle and found herself on Mercy's back.

"Well done," he said, looking at her closely for a

moment. With a much smoother motion, he mounted his horse.

Watching Elizabeth trot off ahead of her, Annie held the reins lightly, sat straight with her elbows in and gently pressed Mercy's sides with her legs. Fortunately, the mare followed Elizabeth's pony toward the meadow. As they broke through the grove of trees, Annie gasped in delight at the view. In the distance, she could see herds of cattle grazing. She pulled on the reins and, amazingly, Mercy stopped.

White-tailed deer—three or four does, several bucks and three fawns, slender, graceful and so fragile looking—grazed on the long grass and clover. When they heard the horses, the deer lifted their heads, then turned and disappeared into a thicket.

Twined around tree stumps were thick trumpet creepers, their orange blooms brilliant against the grass. Hummingbirds and butterflies flew from flower to flower in the warm sunshine.

"This is beautiful," she said, her voice conveying amazement. "You must love this place." She took in the beauty for a few more minutes before she asked, "How long have you lived here?"

"Forever, it seems." He smiled as he looked across the meadow. "My great-grandfather came to the area from Boston. He joined with Stephen F. Austin in 1823, when Mexico opened the area up to Americans. We have letters he wrote to my great-grandmother before she joined him. He said that hundreds of bison covered the land as far as a man could see." He stretched his arm out and waved it across the area ahead of them.

His pride in his family glowed on his face, and Annie was torn. On one hand, she felt drawn to him, in awe of his passion about the place of his family in history; on the other, she wondered what she was doing next to him, looking out over this land that had belonged to his family for generations when she didn't even know where her parents had come from.

"In 1835, my grandfather was at Gonzales. He stood by the canyon and waved the 'Come and Take It' flag with the 'Old Eighteen.' My great-uncle fought and died at the Alamo with Davy Crockett and Jim Bowie, and my father fought at San Jacinto."

"Your family has been part of Texas from the beginning."

He nodded. "The Sullivans have been on this land for over sixty years. I can't tell you how proud I am of my family and my name. We are Texans.

"But enough about me, Matilda." He turned and smiled at her. "Why don't we sit over there." He dismounted, tied his horse up and turned to her, his closeness warming the chilly morning. Holding his hand out, he waited for her to dismount.

Well, she had little choice. Reversing her method of mounting the horse, she attempted to turn in the saddle; but her aching right leg made her clumsy. Her foot slipped in the stirrup at the same time the mare took a step. If he hadn't caught her, she would've fallen in a heap at his feet.

Awareness of him shot through her. Embarrassed of both that odd feeling and her clumsiness, she shrugged from his grasp and turned toward him. "Thank you."

"We should have been more considerate about your injuries." He took her arm again and helped her sit down on a log. "Now we can talk about you."

Not what Annie wanted. She needed to change the

subject but couldn't think of a way to distract him. They were surrounded by the sounds of nature, held gently by the splendor of the high meadow, serenaded by the birds and all the melodies of God's world.

"Are you comfortable?" he asked once they were both settled, watching Elizabeth ride her pony around the meadow.

"Why don't you tell me about your background and interest in education?" Annie replied before he could ask any questions. "Did you attend Trail's End school?"

"Until sixth grade. At that time, my father decided I needed a better education, and he sent me to boarding school in Dallas."

"How old were you?"

"Ten or eleven." He shrugged. "It was expected."

He must have been lonely. She felt sad for the little boy he'd been.

"That's the reason I'm determined to raise the educational standards here." He rested his elbows on his thighs and clasped his hands together as he watched his daughter, love and pride evident on his face. "Her grandparents want her to go to St. Louis for school. I want to keep Elizabeth here with me as long as possible, but I also want her to have a good education."

As if Annie were the one to do that. A stab of guilt shot through her.

She thought he was about to ask her a question, so she hurried on. "What did you do after boarding school?"

The scent of flowers along with the occasional buzz of bees was hypnotic, so much so that Annie was worried she might slip up and say something she shouldn't to this man who believed she was who she said she was.

"I attended Waco College and studied business and finance."

As she watched him, she saw his expression change from his excitement about the school in Trail's End to a distinct lack of interest. Noting the change in his voice, as well, she asked, "Didn't you like it?"

"When I was young, I wanted to be a veterinarian." He gave a deprecating laugh. "I've always loved animals. I wanted to attend Iowa State College."

"Why didn't you?"

"My father expected me to be a banker and rancher, to take over his businesses." He turned toward her. "As you may know, ranchers don't respect the new science of veterinary medicine."

"They don't? Why not?"

"Ranchers have been caring for their animals for years, probably centuries. They won't put up with some new college graduate telling them what to do."

Thinking of the ranchers she'd known, she said, "I see your point."

"And Iowa, as you know from geography, is a long way from Texas. I probably would have hated Iowa. It gets cold there, and it isn't Texas."

Then he laughed, a true laugh. Annie joined him, even though she didn't know why they were laughing. But hearing the sound of their amusement soaring over the meadow felt wonderful and freeing.

"Someday," he said, "I'll tell you a few interesting stories about how we take care of animals on the ranch. Even better, I'll show you our veterinarian's office. Duffy, one of the ranch hands, taught me everything he knows. He's the one who made me want to be a veterinarian."

His gaze held hers. All she could think was how blue his eyes were, not cold at all as she'd thought earlier. His smile, even the tiny sliver he showed her, made her breathless. She didn't feel at all like Annie or Matilda but instead, like a new, very happy and slightly unsure young woman.

"Matilda, you have a wonderful laugh," he said in a soft voice that made Annie believe he'd felt the same way about their shared moment.

What was happening between the two of them? She was overcome by a feeling of breathlessness and wonder, and a need to know more about the man. He slowly reached out and took her hand, looking at her as if she were the most beautiful woman in the world.

Elizabeth's voice shattered the enchanting moment. "Father, I'm tired now, and Brownie wants to go home."

In an instant, he let go of her hand, stood and turned toward his daughter while Annie put her hands to her cheeks, certain they were pink with embarrassment. How could she have dared to look at John like that?

And yet, he'd returned her gaze and held her hand, filling her with pleasure and feelings she didn't recognize.

If she weren't so happy, she'd be completely terrified.

As he drove to pick up Matilda for the school board meeting, John thought about the conversation they'd had Saturday morning. He'd wanted to know her better and had attempted to learn about her life, but she had been reticent. No, more than reticent. She'd avoided talking about herself by asking him questions. Not that he didn't enjoy telling her about himself, but he'd wanted to see if she seemed less disoriented. Or perhaps he had just wanted to know the lovely young woman better.

The conversation had convinced him she'd suffered no ill effects from the accident, but his own state of mind confused him. Something had passed between them three days earlier that had turned his life inside out. Although she was his daughter's virtuous young teacher, he wanted more—more than he should. And now he had no idea of how to treat Matilda. Should he act like the school board member or the man who found her to be beautiful, charming and everything he desired in a woman?

There was no doubt what his father would say, if he were alive: act like a Sullivan and forget this absurd folly. But John no longer had to answer to his father, and he enjoyed this feeling of attraction too much to deny it.

He found her waiting for him when he arrived at the schoolhouse. He stopped the surrey and stepped out to help her, behaving like the man he was, the man he'd spent most of his life becoming: upright and honest and never foolish. But he feared his smile showed how he really felt.

"Good evening," he said as he took her hand to help her into the vehicle. "Do you have any questions about the meeting tonight?"

For an instant, her lovely skin went pale and her beautiful dark brown eyes opened wide, enormous in her face. He suddenly felt protective. What could be frightening her? "Don't worry. The school board is happy with your first two weeks. You won't have to do more than answer a few questions." He got into the surrey next to her.

"Thank you," she said. "I have worried."

The quiver in her voice helped him understand how much she had worried about the upcoming meeting, but he had no idea how to calm her. With a snap of the whip, the horses took off.

"Miss Cunningham, we are delighted to have you meet with the board," Mr. Johnson, the grocer, said. "The children seem very happy with your teaching. Ida and Samuel have expressed this often."

"Thank you, sir." She looked around at the members of the school board in the bank office. She knew Mr. Hanson, of course. She thought the tall woman with pale blond hair in the corner must be the grandmother of the Sundholm twins. In the corner sat Mr. Tripp, the carriage maker and the father of Tommy and Rose. John looked very much in charge, certain and sure in conducting the meeting. This was Mr. Sullivan she was seeing—he was no longer John, the man she'd spent time with Saturday morning.

"Miss Cunningham." He spoke in a serious but reassuring voice. "Some of the members would like to ask you questions."

Annie nodded.

"I wonder if you could tell us what techniques you use to teach," Mr. Hanson said. "I have heard that you use the older children to teach the younger ones to read."

Annie calmed the flutter in her stomach. "Well, yes, I do." What other choice did I have when she knew so little? "I believe that the older children review what they've learned when they teach the younger ones, and it allows me to work with another group on arithmetic."

"An interesting concept," Mr. Johnson said. "But

don't you find that the older ones need additional help with their reading and writing?"

"Of course, but right now we are reviewing. The children have been out of school for almost six months. I want to make sure they remember what they learned last year before we move on to new material." Oh, she spoke as if she knew what she was doing. She sounded like a real teacher. Confidence began to spread through her.

"How long will that take?" the elderly woman asked.

"A month, perhaps." Until she learned to read much better. "Although I expect to do this occasionally during the school year. I've seen how working with the younger children helps the older children retain information."

"Perhaps you can tell us some other methods you use." John opened the leather folder and inspected a paper inside. "How have you used what they taught you in school?"

She paused to give herself time to gather her thoughts to make something up. "I learned to use two subjects together, one to teach the other," she blurted out with no idea where the words had come from. In the back of her mind she could remember someone—had it been her mother?—teaching Annie her numbers while reading her stories. It had been so long ago, and she'd been so young.

"Could you give us an example?" the elderly woman asked.

"I use a song to teach the alphabet," she said, surprised at her own words.

"Would you sing it for us?" Mr. Johnson asked.

"Oh, yes," Mr. Johnson said. "We'd like to hear that, wouldn't we?"

All the members agreed.

Floundering, Annie wondered what to do. Everyone on the board sat in silence, waiting for her. She cleared her throat, then opened her mouth to sing the multiplication table, which she knew very well now, to a tune. She had no idea if the numbers would fit the tune, but she had to do something. Fortunately, the numbers and the notes came out almost even, with just a little flourish at the end. When she finished, Annie looked around the room. All the members looked at her with pleasure, even admiration.

"As I said before, you have a lovely voice, Miss Cunningham," John said. She glimpsed that half smile briefly, before he became serious again. "The children are fortunate to have you as their teacher."

"Thank you, sir." She lowered her eyes, pleased to have survived that question.

"If there is nothing more," John said, looking at each board member, "some of the mothers have prepared a small party to welcome you, Miss Cunningham."

Once the other members of the school board began to leave, John could think of no reason to put off the short drive to the ranch. After he'd helped Matilda into the surrey and started the horses toward the ranch, he reminded himself that, although there was clearly something between them, she was alone in a strange place with no male relatives to protect her.

He wasn't the kind of man who would take advantage of a vulnerable woman. Of any woman. But neither did he have any idea how to behave toward her in their situation.

"You did very well at the meeting tonight," he said.

"Thank you."

After that, conversation languished. He sensed that she was as uncomfortable and uncertain as he was.

When they reached the schoolhouse, he stopped the vehicle, walked around it and held out his hand to steady her. When their hands touched, he felt the attraction again, stronger now. Standing close to her as she turned to walk toward the schoolhouse, still steadying her with his hand under hers, he was drawn by her scent. He guessed it was only the soap Lucia had given her, but on Matilda it smelled like every marvelous fragrance in the world.

When she reached the steps of the schoolhouse, Annie looked up at him and removed her hand from his. "Thank you, John. I enjoyed meeting the other members of the school board. I believe the evening went well. Don't you?"

But his thoughts were elsewhere. Under the bright light of the moon, he could only think of how lovely she was: her oval face, her beautiful dark eyes, her long lashes, lovely arched brows and the thick, dark hair he longed to feel loose and curling through his fingers. "Matilda, you are very beautiful," he whispered, reaching for her hand again.

Her eyes opened wide in fear. She pushed his hand away as she attempted to escape from his touch, almost in a panic.

As soon as he realized his actions and words scared her, he stepped back. "I apologize. I don't know what I did, but I'm deeply sorry my words and actions frightened you."

How had he alarmed her? He had no idea. He hadn't thought he'd spoken or acted disrespectfully; yet she was terrified. What had he done?

Her shoulders shook and tears ran down her face. He reached out a hand in an effort to comfort her, but she moved away. With the steps behind her, there was little space for her to flee. He quickly took another step backward.

"Are you all right?" He looked into her terrified eyes as he attempted to hand her a handkerchief. She didn't take it. She didn't answer.

"What can I do?"

She shook her head. Without a word or a glance toward him, she stumbled up the steps, entered the schoolhouse and closed the door behind her.

"Good night, Matilda," he said to the door. He stood in the clearing for a moment and watched, wondering what to do. After several minutes, the lamp went on in the schoolroom and then moved toward her quarters. He strode to the surrey.

He had no idea how he'd upset her. He'd been raised to be a model of moral rectitude, to be a dutiful son with the added burden of living up to not just one but two biblical names. He'd been faithful to his wife and had never looked at another woman during their marriage or since—not until now.

Yet somehow he'd frightened Matilda beyond all understanding when he told her she was beautiful. Didn't women like that? Or was it holding her hand that scared her? Or both?

Had something happened in her life that made her skittish around men, or was her reaction due to her virtue? And what should he do about it?

He leaped onto the seat and clicked the reins. He had no idea what he should do, but knew better than to go back to the schoolhouse and ask her tonight.

* * *

Shaking, Annie closed the door to the schoolhouse and leaned against it.

Was it so obvious what she was? Was trash written across her face? Why did men believe they could touch her whenever they wanted? How did they know that she wasn't a lady? She'd tried to become one. The futility of all that effort caused tears to pour down her cheeks while loud sobs racked her.

"Meow?"

The cat was still inside. She hadn't been able to put the tiny thing back outside. It had become such good company in spite of its constant noise. Or perhaps because of it.

She took off her shoes and padded slowly across the classroom, lit the lamp and carried it to her bedroom with the kitten trotting behind her.

She noted the narrow bed where Minnie sat, the unsteady dresser where she'd placed the lamp and the dresses hanging on the nails. A shabby little place by the standards of some but beautiful to her. She'd felt safe here.

For a moment, she closed her eyes. Those times from the past, the terrible experiences that she'd tried so hard to forget, were shoving their way past the barricades she'd built, plunging into her thoughts. The terror and pain of the first time, the raised hands, the beatings, the brutality. The fear that caused her to shrink back still, to try to hide from men by escaping into herself.

With his touch and his whispered words, John had opened the doors, and the horror of all those years had come swirling out to overwhelm her. She fell onto the bed, longing to be free of memories. But of course that was impossible.

Back when she worked in the brothel, she spent most of her nights playing the piano, but every now and then, a man would buy her time. It was always the customers who knew she didn't want to be bought. Usually they were rough. She touched her lips and remembered they'd been cut and bleeding in the past.

Some part of her knew that John would not abuse her this way. And the whispered words and hand-holding was nothing compared to what she'd suffered before she arrived in Trail's End. But those actions had often been the beginning of the process. They announced what a man had on his mind. The forwardness made it clear that a man knew what kind of woman she was back in Weaver City. Back when she was Annie MacAllister, a woman who'd worked in a brothel.

But she wasn't Annie MacAllister anymore. She was Matilda Cunningham. At least that's who she was to John.

She sat up. Had she completely overreacted? Had standing alone in the darkness with a man awakened those nightmares? Perhaps her reaction wasn't his fault at all.

"He held my hand and whispered that I was beautiful," Annie said aloud. What was so bad about that?

Annie wiped her tears away. Yes, she'd overreacted. She'd leaped ahead in her mind to what had happened when she was a prostitute. John wasn't one of those men. He'd held her hand to help her across the ground, like a gentleman, and he'd told her she was beautiful, perhaps because he actually meant it. He hadn't forced her in any way. He'd moved away when she'd become frightened. Could it be John wasn't like the men from her past? Perhaps he'd only acted like a man attracted to a woman and she'd overreacted.

If that was the truth—and she now thought it was—how could she face him again?

The following afternoon, Rose approached the teacher's desk. "Miss Cunningham, I'd like to read a story to the twins. Would you listen to make sure I don't make any mistakes?"

Although she didn't know if she could read fast enough to tell if Rose made mistakes, Annie nodded. Rose sat on the bench with Bertha and Clara while Annie stood behind them and leaned over so she could see the book.

As Rose read, she put her finger under each word. How nice. Annie could easily follow the printed words as Rose read them, and she recognized almost all of them.

After Rose finished, Samuel asked if she would listen to him read a story. He read a more difficult story but in the same way, pointing at every word.

Annie was suddenly struck by a realization that nearly took her breath away. The students were not practicing their reading. They were teaching her.

She was mortified and moved. So much love for her students filled the slowly warming corners of her heart that she couldn't speak. She'd never tell them she knew but was incredibly happy that she had ended up in Trail's End with these students. Thank you, Matilda, she thought. And thank You, dear God.

That afternoon, after all the students but Elizabeth had left, Annie picked up one of the books she'd found in Matilda's valise, the one with the drawings. In what Annie guessed was Matilda's clear writing, she found plans and activities to use in class, but she didn't have any of the supplies to make a thaumatrope, or decorations for the holidays or a game of anagrams. She sighed. Perhaps she could ask the school board for supplies when they met next.

Several minutes later, she checked the watch on her collar. It was almost four o'clock.

"Perhaps I should walk home, Miss Cunningham."

"Your father wouldn't want you to walk home alone."

"Could you walk with me? Then Ramon could bring you back." She looked at Annie pleadingly.

"If no one comes within the next few minutes, we'll do that. Let's give them a little more time."

"They might have forgotten me." She stood to look out the window.

"Elizabeth, do you really believe your father would forget you?"

"No, Miss Cunningham." She smiled. "I know he'd never forget me."

"Why don't we go in the woods, to look for flowers and identify trees?" That, at least, was something Annie knew. She held out her hand, and Elizabeth skipped over to take it. "We'll be close to the schoolhouse so we can hear your father when he arrives."

They found a jasmine twined around a dead tree and listened for the song of a mockingbird and the tapping of a woodpecker. After a few minutes, they heard a surrey stop and a voice call for Elizabeth.

Elizabeth ran through the grove of trees. By the time Annie arrived, she had jumped into her father's arms and he hugged her.

"I'm sorry, Elizabeth," John said. "One of the traces broke and Ramon had to find another. Then, well, many little things happened." He put Elizabeth down and turned toward Annie. "Good afternoon, Miss Cunningham." He nodded at her.

"Good afternoon." She noticed he kept his distance.

"Elizabeth, would you please wait in the surrey? I need to talk to Miss Cunningham privately."

What did he want? Had he found out her background or that she couldn't read? She had so many secrets. It could be anything. She stepped back. They seemed to be playing a child's game with one of them constantly moving away.

"Please, don't be frightened, Matilda." He took off his hat. "I apologize for whatever I did last night that frightened you." He paused. "I don't know what I did exactly that scared you but promise you have nothing to fear from me."

She struggled to consider a response, but he continued.

"I meant no disrespect. I realize that an innocent young woman like you may be uncomfortable with a man expressing his..." John seemed to run out of words, and she could not help him. "I'll behave more circumspectly in the future."

He hadn't figured that she was a fallen woman. But while she felt great relief that he still thought she was an innocent, she couldn't help but be embarrassed that she had overreacted and had misunderstood him so completely.

"I'd like to give you this, as a show of my regret for having frightened you." He held out a book to her.

"Oh, no, I cannot take a gift." She shook her head.

"I believe you will like this. Please."

He stood in front of her, tall, strong and determined.

But when she noticed the pleading look in his eyes, Annie took the book he held out. She tried to make out the letters on the cover, but the printing was strange and she couldn't understand what they spelled.

"It's a book of poetry. The sonnets of Shakespeare."

The name sounded familiar, but she could not quite place it. She decided to keep her response simple. "Thank you."

"You're welcome." He smiled down at her, his eyes now filled with relief. She wanted to apologize to him in turn, but she still could not find the words. He stepped back and glanced toward his daughter in the surrey. "Good afternoon, Matilda."

"Good afternoon, John." She enjoyed saying his name almost as much as she enjoyed hearing him say hers.

She watched the surrey drive off. "Thank You again, God," she whispered. "You are truly generous and gracious."

She opened a page of the book and could make out the words Shall I and to a summer's day. The other words in the first line of the poem stumped her.

Well, she'd just have to keep practicing.

But this time she'd have something better than the children's readers to work on. This time she had a book of beautiful poetry. What had John called them? Sonnets, yes, that was it. She'd have to find out the difference between a poem and a sonnet.

But the best part was that these poems came from John. She rubbed her hand over the tooled cover of the book and smiled as she watched the last bit of dust disappear beyond his horse.

Yes, John had given her this book, and she'd treasure it forever.

Chapter Seven

"What fun to have your company for the meeting of the Literary Society," Amanda said to Annie as she snapped the reins and the cream-colored mare moved a little faster.

In a pale blue phaeton, Amanda sat up straight and held the reins firmly, obviously enjoying the display of her skill. She wore a fur-trimmed cape over a soft blue robe with a bustle that forced her to sit very straight.

Fingering her black skirt, matching basque and wool shawl, Annie felt a stab of envy before Amanda turned to her, tilted her head and smiled.

"You and I are going to have so much fun together, Matilda. Just the two of us going off on our own, even if it is just to town! I hope you'll forgive my silly chatter, but I'm so pleased to have a friend like you."

"Oh, I do not think you are silly. Being with you is a delight." How could she possibly envy Amanda for having so much when she shared so much with Annie?

They had just entered town when Amanda said, "I'm happy John asked me to take you. He usually attends these meetings and escorts the teacher. I do hope there is no emergency."

"I don't know why John could not attend, but I do thank you for carrying me with you."

"I know you'll have wonderful suggestions for the meetings." As Amanda stopped the phaeton in front of the church, several men approached the vehicle, except for the sheriff, who actually looked as if he were attempting to escape. Amanda stopped him in his tracks. "Sheriff," she called, "would you please help me down?" She tossed him the reins.

"At the first meeting, I will just listen and learn," Annie said.

"Probably wise, but I am so seldom wise." After the sheriff tied the reins to a post, Amanda put her hand on his arm. Annie could not help noticing how uncomfortable the sheriff looked.

Then Mr. Johnson appeared on Annie's side and helped her down. "My wife is the president of the Literary Society, Miss Cunningham," Mr. Johnson said with a proud smile. "As you must know from the other places you've lived and taught, this society is the cultural center of our little town. We're very proud of our group and the example of the women in our community."

"I know this meeting will be an uplifting experience," she said, hoping that nothing was expected of her yet.

When they entered the church, she saw Mrs. Johnson in the front of the room. She was a tall woman with ramrod-straight posture, a flinty glare and a firm command of the meeting.

"First," she said, "I want to introduce our new teacher, Miss Matilda Cunningham." Annie stood and smiled at the several dozen people assembled there. She knew her students and their parents, as well as the people who attended church, but there were some she hadn't met before.

"Miss Cunningham, we welcome your suggestions and hope you will make a presentation for us in the future," Mrs. Johnson said. "Perhaps a patriotic poem?"

Annie smiled and nodded.

After a business meeting, the program began. Ida recited a section of "The Prairie" with lovely hand motions. A very uncomfortable Samuel Johnson stumbled through "Concord Hymn" under the unyielding stare of his mother. Finally, with Amanda leading them, everyone stood and sang "Hail, Columbia" and "My Country 'Tis of Thee."

When the program was over, the ladies served refreshments. Annie found herself surrounded by the parents of her students, who told her how much their children enjoyed school. After a few minutes, Annie excused herself to look for Amanda. She found her in a quiet corner with the sheriff, one hand on his arm while she flirted, smiling brilliantly.

How could a man resist Amanda's beauty and charm? Well, the sheriff could. He glanced down at Amanda occasionally but kept his face expressionless. His lack of interest, however, did not deter Amanda. Finally, she took his arm and pulled him toward Annie.

"Isn't it delightful?" Amanda said. "The sheriff has consented to follow the phaeton home." She looked back up at the sheriff. "My father will appreciate your making sure I arrive home safely."

"That's what he paid me for, Miss Hanson."

Amanda's face fell. "He paid you? My father paid you to follow me home?"

"Yes, ma'am. He came to my office this morning. You just tell me when you're ready to leave and I'll follow."

"Well, I have to admit I was surprised to see you here. You usually don't attend these meetings."

"No, I don't."

"And you usually don't accede to my requests so readily."

"No, ma'am, I don't." He nodded. "I'll be waiting outside."

Amanda watched him saunter out. "Is he the most bothersome man you have ever met?"

"I think he's a very nice man," Annie said, trying to keep her amusement out of her voice.

"Yes, I imagine he would find you interesting and treat you courteously." Then she shrugged. "But he finds me to be a flibbertigibbet and can barely tolerate me," she said.

"Oh, I'm sure he thinks you're lovely."

Amanda sighed. "Well, I wish he did, but I have to admit that he doesn't. He ignores me or swats me away as if I were of no consequence, although he always does it very politely." She shrugged. "I guess I've lost my touch with men. Or at least with this one." She sighed again before asking, "Are you ready to go?"

"Yes." Annie said good-night to Mrs. Johnson and the other parents and then followed her friend to the door.

During the short drive between town and the schoolhouse, Amanda teased the sheriff mercilessly as he rode behind the phaeton on his horse. He answered each comment with a courteous, "Yes, ma'am," or "No, ma'am."

"The man is the most frustrating person," Amanda whispered as she stopped the vehicle in front of the schoolhouse. "I'm going to make him miserable on the way to our ranch." She kissed Annie on the cheek before the sheriff helped her down.

As they drove away, Annie put her hand on her cheek. No one had kissed her with affection since her mother had died. That Amanda Hanson was a darling.

She continued to watch the phaeton and the sheriff until they disappeared around a curve. Annie felt very sorry for the man under Amanda's continued assault. If Annie weren't an upright woman who scorned gambling, her money would be on Amanda.

"Miss Cunningham, Mr. Sullivan asked me to bring you these." It was almost three o'clock on Wednesday afternoon and all the children had left when Lucia arrived with a bundle. Annie left her desk where she worked to read a story from the fifth reader—she had fairly well conquered the other levels and their moral little tales—and took the parcel Lucia held out.

What could it be? "I shouldn't accept gifts from Mr. Sullivan."

Lucia lifted an eyebrow. "Don't think of this as a gift. Just open it."

Annie tore the paper from the bundle to find a pair of shoes inside. "Oh, Lucia, I can't. It wouldn't be proper."

"Miss Cunningham, I've watched you hobbling around as long as you've been here. Elizabeth has worried about you, too. Mr. Sullivan told me you injured your foot in that carriage accident. Is that right? Does it still hurt?"

Annie nodded. "I'd planned to buy myself another pair in town but my foot hurt too much to walk that far."

"I apologize if I speak out of turn, Miss Cunningham, but it seems to me that people who are as poor as you and me can hardly turn down something practical like this. They're just shoes, and there's no one else wearing them right now."

Annie looked at them. They were black and not as serviceable as Matilda's, mostly made up of little straps and a small heel. The leather was so soft that Annie could not help but rub it gently.

"I think if he was after your virtue, he'd give you something nicer than a pair of his wife's old shoes."

"His wife's shoes?"

"When he came to breakfast this morning and Elizabeth reminded him about your problem, he asked me to go through his wife's things. He said he had no idea if her shoes would fit you, but it was a waste to let them sit in a closet if you could wear them."

Annie tugged off Matilda's shoes and slipped Mrs. Sullivan's on. They were a little snug also, but the leather was soft enough that she could feel the shoes give. "I think they'll get more comfortable as I wear them."

"They're dusty. I wanted to clean them up but Mr. Sullivan thought you'd want them right away. Mrs. Sullivan died nearly four years ago, and they've just been sitting in her armoire."

"How did she die?" Annie asked as Lucia started to put cans away in the cupboard.

"She got sick and never got better. She wasn't a

happy woman, always wanted to go back home. She didn't like the heat or the sun or the wind in Texas. She missed the theater and libraries. She hated the fact that we don't have electricity or telephones."

"How could she not love Texas?"

Lucia laughed. "There are folks who don't." As Lucia closed the cupboard, the schoolhouse door opened and Amanda entered.

"Does Elizabeth look like her?" Annie asked.

"Elizabeth is prettier. She has a sparkle that her mother lacked."

"How delightful." Amanda entered the building with a swirl of her skirt and a laugh. "You're talking about the late Mrs. Sullivan. Or, as my father says, 'the first Mrs. Sullivan.'"

"Hello, Miss Hanson." Lucia picked up her basket. "I'm on my way out. Goodbye, Miss Cunningham." Lucia nodded at Annie and Amanda as she left.

"Goodbye, Lucia. Thank you for the food," Annie called after her. "'The first Mrs. Sullivan'?" Annie asked Amanda.

"Yes, my father hopes I will be the second Mrs. Sullivan. I don't know how to convince him that will never happen."

"Does John want to marry you?" Annie paused, realizing that her words sounded insulting. "Oh, not that any man wouldn't want to marry you."

"I used to believe that." She sighed. "It's a depressing thought that John is only lukewarm toward the idea of spending the rest of our lives together. And the sheriff runs whenever he sees me."

"I take that to mean the ride to your ranch did not turn out as you had hoped."

"Did the sheriff take me in his arms and vow his undying love? I fear not." Amanda sighed and looked so downcast that Annie had to smile. "You find that amusing? When I go into decline, you won't laugh."

"You're hardly likely to go into a decline." Annie motioned toward a bench and Amanda sat. "Tell me what happened."

"Well, after we left here, I slowed the phaeton down so Sheriff Bennett would have to ride next to me. Instead, the man sped up and rode ahead of the carriage. He told me that he was making sure I did not ride into an ambush." She laughed and shook her head. "I do not know why I bother with the man."

"Well, I do know why. The sheriff's the only man that does not come whenever you smile. He's a challenge."

"Of course."

"If he paid the slightest bit of attention to you, you'd get bored and have nothing to do with him."

"Well, that does sound like me, but only back when I was much younger."

"And how old are you now?"

"I'm almost twenty, and still not wed." Amanda smiled sadly. "I don't believe your statement about finding the sheriff a challenge is completely true. He's a man I admire and trust, which is unusual for me. I find most men foolish, except for John. And I find him boring. Sheriff Cole Bennett is neither."

"This isn't a game you are playing with him?"

"Oh, la, I don't know." She waved her hand. "Now, let's forget all about men. I am going to sing a solo in church Sunday and need to sing it for you so you can play."

"Of course, but first I want to ask you one thing. If

'the first Mrs. Sullivan' disliked Texas so much, why did she marry John?" What a nosy question. She opened her mouth to take it back, but Amanda had begun her answer.

"None of us really knows. But once Elizabeth was born, she just wasted away. It was awful to watch, and nothing could cure her." She slowly turned her gaze to Annie. "You aren't interested in John, are you?"

"Of course not. He's my employer," Annie replied.

"I wish you were." Amanda sighed. "If you were, my life would be so much easier. If John married you, I wouldn't have to marry him."

"Would marriage to John be so terrible?"

"Oh, no." Amanda sighed. "But it would be dull. I want more." She stood and twirled. "I want excitement and fun and— Oh, Annie, I want so very much more!"

"I hope you find it," Annie said.

"Now, listen," Amanda said, returning to the mundane. "Let me sing my solo for you and see if you can finger the melody."

The next day, Annie sat at her desk, correcting the twins' slates during the children's outdoor time when she heard a loud thumping on the roof of the schoolhouse. She leaped from her desk, frightened that one of the children had fallen. She ran outside, but couldn't see them. Where could they have gone?

Then she heard loud laughter and was almost run over as the boys ran around the building toward her.

"Children," she shouted. "What is it? Are you hurt?" Then she looked at their laughing faces and saw a ball in Frederick's hands.

"We're playing alle-over, Miss Cunningham."

"Are you going to throw the ball?" Martha asked the boys as she came around the building followed by the rest of the girls.

"Did we disturb you?" Ida asked. "I forgot. The ball bouncing on the roof probably startled you."

Annie nodded, then put her hand on her chest to calm her rapidly beating heart. "The game you're playing made the thump on the roof?"

"Oh, yes! It's so much fun." Elizabeth hopped and skipped. Her face was flushed, and her hair had escaped her big bow. "Have you ever played alle-over, Miss Cunningham?"

"No, I don't believe I have. How is it played?"

"Boys against the girls," Samuel said. "With a team on each side of the building. One team yells 'alle-over' and throws the ball over the building. When the other team gets the ball, they run around the schoolhouse before anyone on the first team can tag them."

"It's our favorite game," Tommy said. "Except most of the girls can't get the ball over the schoolhouse."

Ida studied Annie for a moment. "Are you a good thrower, Miss Cunningham?"

"I don't know. I've never played this game. I'm not sure a teacher should."

"All the other teachers have played," Rose said. "And we really need you."

"Yes, Miss Cunningham, please play," Frederick begged.

"All right. I'll try." From all the cleaning she'd done in Weaver City and now in the schoolhouse, she thought she'd become fairly strong, and the game did look like fun.

The children cheered and returned to their sides of the schoolhouse.

It surprised Annie to discover she was able to throw the ball over the building, an odd talent but useful in this situation. Before long, with the throwing and running and laughing and shouting, her hair had fallen from its bun and perspiration beaded her forehead.

Then, just as she shouted, "All right, boys, here comes the ball. You can't catch us," Annie looked up to see John staring at her.

"Oh, I'm sorry." She attempted in vain to straighten her hair. She did not look in the least bit like the responsible teacher she should, but she was having the most wonderful time.

"I was just admiring your skill," John said. "I didn't realize we'd hired such an excellent athlete to teach here."

Embarrassed at having been caught in such disarray, Annie said, "Children, I think it is time for us to go inside."

"No, no, please continue. It looks as if you had a great game of alle-over going on here."

"You know the game?"

"Of course. One of my favorites when I was a student here. Unfortunately, I never get to play it anymore."

Annie smiled at the image of the town leaders tossing the ball over and running around the bank building.

"Please play," Tommy begged. "Miss Cunningham's too good."

John said, "Why not?" He took his hat and coat off and placed them carefully on a bench. "Gentlemen, let's play."

By the time Annie called an end to the game fifteen minutes later, dirt covered John's expensive clothing, his dark hair curled against his sweat-covered forehead and he was smiling and laughing.

Again Annie was amazed at how handsome and happy John was. The way he looked reminded her of the time she'd seen John on his horse tearing across the prairie. Suddenly she felt a little breathless. Probably because she'd been running so hard. Probably because the game had worn her out.

More likely because John was here.

"We're so pleased you joined us, especially Elizabeth." She looked down at the child who leaned against her father's leg. "Is there anything you need to discuss with me?"

"No, nothing. I was on my way to the bank after lunch and heard the laughter. I had to track it down."

He gave Annie a smile that caused her stomach to drop out. She felt slightly weak.

"I'm glad I joined you, but now I'll have to go to the ranch and clean up so I can go back to work."

He hugged Elizabeth, then looked at Annie. His glance took in her hair, loose and curling around her face. He looked into her eyes and let his gaze linger for just a moment. "Good day, Miss Cunningham."

"Good day, Mr. Sullivan," she said in the voice of a teacher, trying to disguise her feelings. Little by little, every time she saw him, she trusted him more. And, yes, every time she saw him, she felt more and more attraction.

Yes, something had changed for her, but she didn't know exactly what. And she didn't think she wanted to know. She couldn't face that—not yet.

Chapter Eight

A month. Annie had lasted almost a month. During that time, she'd taught herself to read and print. Every Saturday, she wrote out assignments for the next week and made sure she knew how to complete every task. While the older children worked on cursive, she practiced with them.

By staying up late every night and working all day Saturday and most of Sunday, she'd become a teacher. Now she felt she earned every penny the school board paid her. Most importantly, the students were learning—all twelve of them.

The Bryan brothers, Philip, Travis and Wilber, had started attending school a week earlier, after their chores on the farm were finished. Although Wilber had immediately moved to the sixth reader, the two younger brothers had trouble with the fifth level.

"Children!" She stood up from her desk. "Attention please." When all the students had put down their slates and books, Annie said, "Thanksgiving is in ten days. We'll take part in the service on Wednesday evening preceding the national holiday."

The students clapped and could barely contain their excitement.

"We're not going to sing, are we?" Philip asked.

"Some of us will sing. Others will recite sections of President Lincoln's proclamation, about Thanksgiving." She held up the American history book in which she'd found the words. "I'll read the entire proclamation to you, then assign parts." She glanced at the class. "Listen carefully." She read, "The year that is drawing towards its close has been filled with the blessings of fruitful fields and healthful skies. To these bounties..."

The children listened attentively until the sounds of an approaching horse distracted them.

"Miss Cunningham, the stage brought you a package." John interrupted her reading as he opened the door. In his arms was a large box, almost half the size of her desk.

She took a step toward him as her stomach clenched. Who would send her a package, especially such a large one? No one knew where Annie was or cared about her, and Matilda said she had no family.

But she'd probably had friends. Of course she had. Why hadn't Annie considered that?

"Miss Cunningham, you have a package." Clara hopped up and down. "It's so big."

"I've never seen a package that came on the stage before," Frederick said.

Annie hadn't, either. She wished she could enjoy it, but it worried her—she could lose the position she loved because someone knew the real Matilda and had sent her a package, a large package.

"Open it!" The twins jumped up and down in excitement.

John placed the box on her desk. The address written on the top said very clearly, "Miss Matilda Susan Cunningham, Teacher, Trail's End, Texas."

There was no mistake. Annie put her hand on her chest and took a deep breath. Someone knew where Matilda was supposed to be and would expect to hear from her and probably wondered why she hadn't yet.

"Children, this box is personal." John's words stilled the excitement of the students. "It's Miss Cunningham's. She'll want to open it in privacy."

Disappointed, the students returned to their seats.

"Thank you, Mr. Sullivan." She turned toward the class. "Children, I'll open the box tonight. I don't know what my—" she paused to consider her words "—friends may have sent. Tomorrow, I promise I will show you everything that is not personal." She forced herself to smile. "That will give you something to look forward to. Do you want to guess what is in here?"

The students perked up.

"Each one of you can make a guess. Write your guesses up here, on the blackboard. Tomorrow we'll see who is correct." As the students rushed to the front, Annie added, "We'll start with the youngest. Bertha and Clara." When they came forward, she handed them the chalk. "Choose something you know how to spell."

"Very nicely done," John said quietly. "You changed their disappointment into a challenge." John gazed at the board where Clara wrote book in her clear printing.

He did not, Annie noted, look at her or step closer. The desk separated them, a comfortable barrier.

"I'll give a prize to those who guess correctly what is in the box." John reached into his pocket and pulled out a handful of coins. "A penny for each." He held one up.

While the students buzzed about the prize, he placed the money on her desk. Before Annie could move her hand away, his fingers touched hers. A response rushed through her, a feeling of warmth and...well, she still didn't know what it was, but the emotion was...pleasant. Yes, pleasant and maybe more than that. She pulled her hand away and glanced up to find herself looking into his eyes.

For a moment, his gaze held hers and she could not turn away. The linking of their eyes led to a deeper sharing on a level she couldn't understand. It felt as if, while they stood there, their eyes and fingers and emotions connected. An understanding flickered between them. She took a step closer to him.

"Miss Cunningham, did I spell pencil correctly?" Rose asked.

Annie snatched her hand from the desk and turned toward the board, mortified to be caught staring at John in such an oddly intimate manner. Fortunately none of the students seemed to have noticed the private moment the two of them had shared.

"Use a c instead of an s, Rose. P-e-n-c-i-l."

"I'll leave you with your class, Miss Cunningham." He smiled at her and a velvety warm yearning filled her. "Would you like me to take the package to your quarters?"

She returned his smile before dropping her gaze. "Please leave it here."

As he left, she watched him go. At the door, he turned and waved.

As difficult as it was, Annie pulled her concentration back to the excited children, each of whom wrote a word on the board. Candy, paper, pens and clothing were among the guesses listed. Annie herself had no idea what could be in there. In fact, she feared opening the box, but whether she did or not wouldn't make a bit of difference. Whoever sent it threatened her future.

After the students finished writing their guesses, Annie continued with President Lincoln's proclamation about Thanksgiving. She passed the book to the students so each could write down their lines to memorize, but the presence of the box distracted the students—and Annie, too.

After lunch, the students practiced singing "We Plow the Fields and Scatter," and worked on memorizing their presentations.

"Remember," Annie said as the students prepared to leave for the day, "everyone must come to the Thanksgiving service. It's one of the times we show the community what you've learned here."

And then she was left alone with the box. With anticipation and intense dread, she approached it and pulled off the string. As soon as the twine hit the floor, Minnie was on it, battling it with all her might. Minnie had grown since she'd catapulted into Annie's life, but she was still just a kitten. Annie was suddenly very grateful for her companionship as she tried to calm herself enough to deal with the box. Finally, she opened the container and looked inside. The contents filled the entire box and on top of it all lay a letter. She picked it up and took it to the window to read. It was written in cursive, the beautifully curved letters strung together in straight lines. She was glad that she had improved at reading cursive even if her efforts to write it were slow.

"Dear Tilda," she read aloud. So that's what her friends called her. Tilda. "We hope you arrived safely in Trail's End and have settled in. Please write and let us know how you are."

How could she do that? Her friend would certainly know Matilda's handwriting. Well, she'd consider that later.

"The church took up a collection for you and the school. Please find enclosed paper, books and other supplies."

How lovely. Weren't church people wonderful?

"My mother's health continues to…"

What was that next word? Annie went to the blackboard and printed the word to sound it out. "De-ter-i-or-ate," she said. "Deteriorate. My mother's health continues to deteriorate. I will not be able to visit you for Christmas as we had planned."

Thank goodness for that.

"I do hope you will come back home for a long visit when the spring term is finished. Your friend, Edith Palfrey."

Annie looked at the address at the top of the letter. The teacher had come from Houston, a long trip for a young woman alone.

Setting the letter aside, Annie began to unpack, placing each layer on a different table. First she pulled out a large jar of hard candy. The children would love that. Next were packages of paper and yards of fabric, as well as lace, beads and other trim. In a large envelope were scraps of material, the type women saved for quilts. Beneath that were embroidery frames with yarn, scissors and a pot of glue. Pencils, pens, a knife and bottles of ink followed and, on the bottom, ten books—a few readers and books on science and history.

Annie stood back and surveyed the bounty that

threatened to topple off some of the tables. Where should she put all this? What would she do with such a quantity of supplies?

And how would she use everything? The pens? She'd never used one before and guessed she'd need to practice. But first, she'd practice using a pencil. She held one up, admiring the wood grain.

She put the fabric and trim in the empty drawers of her dresser. Some of the books fit on top. The scissors, pencils and knife went in her desk drawer. The rest she stacked on the bookcase.

"Thank you, Edith Palfrey and everyone at the church," Annie whispered. Matilda certainly had wonderful friends. "Dear Lord, bless them all."

What was she going to do about Matilda's friend Edith?

She looked at the letter. She couldn't answer it, but she could learn from it. For an hour, using a newly sharpened pencil, she copied the letter over and over, now able to use her right hand. Despite her aching arm, her handwriting began to take shape. It flowed. Although it looked a great deal like Miss Palfrey's hand, the writing showed Annie's individual touches.

After her success reading Miss Palfrey's letters, she decided to attempt those from John to Matilda. She took them from her desk drawer. In his clear hand, they were easy to read and spelled out what he had told her before. Relieved that she already understood everything that was expected of her, she slid the letters into the desk and picked up her pencil again.

It wasn't until Annie moved the cat from the middle of the bed and crawled in after midnight that she allowed herself to consider what had happened that day with John. She allowed herself to savor that moment, when his touch hadn't frightened her at all—in fact, it had pleased her. In her mind, she could see the expression in his eyes. Could it have been true affection that had glowed there for an instant? Only a moment, but she'd seen it. At least, she thought she had. How and why would a man so handsome and rich and personable find Annie interesting?

Well, he wasn't exactly interested in Annie. It was the real teacher who attracted him.

And yet, wasn't she Matilda now? She'd become the teacher when she'd left her former life on the road to Trail's End. She'd become the teacher when she'd entered the schoolhouse, when she'd taught herself to read and write. Everything that was Annie, every single bit, had perished out on the prairie a month ago.

She was no longer the same person. No reason existed why John shouldn't find her attractive. Except, of course, that she was only the teacher and he was the banker who lived in a huge house with many beautiful furnishings and silver trays on the dinner table and a water closet so grand it looked as if it belonged in a palace.

And, no matter how much she tried to convince herself, she was not Matilda. She only wished she were. She pondered as she rubbed Minnie, who had curled up against her side, purring.

John had been courteous and respectful—he hadn't allowed himself to be alone with her since that other occasion. That showed esteem for her.

How did she feel about that? John was handsome, a Christian man who loved his daughter. He treated

Annie with respect. But she couldn't forget the warmth of his fingers against hers and the longing in his eyes.

If things were different, she could fall in love with him. If she were truly Matilda—if she didn't have Annie's terrible background, if she weren't living a lie—she could fall in love with him.

She had no idea how to behave around a respectable man like John. No knowledge of what the tender glances and affectionate smiles meant to a man, or how a lady—a real lady—responded. She was amazed to discover that she was no longer afraid of John Sullivan. In fact, she'd begun to feel she could she trust him.

The next day, Annie gave a penny to each child who had guessed an item in her package. Then they began to make a cornucopia from a length of yellow fabric Edith Palfrey had sent. They would stuff it with their pictures of the abundance from the land.

As the students worked on the art, Annie had an idea. "Would you please write a note to my friends?" she said to Ida, gesturing toward her arm. "I'd like to send a thank-you note, but my writing is so painful and slow."

She carefully dictated the letter to Ida, who wrote it in her nice hand. Exactly how to get a letter to Miss Palfrey wasn't clear to Annie. But she was certain Amanda would know.

Pumping the pedals of the organ, Annie played "Now That the Daylight Fills the Sky" while the congregation sang. This Sunday would only be Scripture reading, offering, prayers, and hymns because Reverend Thompson was on the circuit.

After the hymn was complete, John stood to read the

Scripture. "This reading is from the Gospel of John, chapter eight," he said.

"And early in the morning he came again into the temple, and all the people came unto him; and he sat down, and taught them. And the scribes and Pharisees brought unto him a woman taken in adultery; and when they had set her in the midst, They say unto him, Master, this woman was taken in adultery, in the very act. Now Moses in the law commanded us, that such should be stoned: but what sayest thou?... Jesus...said unto them, He that is without sin among you, let him first cast a stone at her.... And they which heard it, being convicted by their own conscience, went out one by one, beginning at the eldest, even unto the last: and Jesus was left alone, and the woman standing in the midst. When Jesus had lifted up himself, and saw none but the woman, he said unto her, Woman, where are those thine accusers? hath no man condemned thee? She said, No man, Lord. And Jesus said unto her, Neither do I condemn thee: go, and sin no more.

"May we all remember these words of our Savior. 'Go, and sin no more.'" He bowed his head. "Let us pray."

"Neither do I condemn thee," Annie whispered. Had Jesus really said those words? Well, John had read them from the Bible, so Jesus must have.

Jesus had forgiven the woman. Annie struggled to understand that. Jesus forgave the woman taken in adultery.

"Go, and sin no more," Annie whispered the words. Her hands shook so much that she had to fold them together. She'd decided she'd sin no more before she left Weaver City. That resolution had been reinforced when she'd assumed Matilda's identity, but she didn't realize that Jesus could forgive her—or that anyone could.

Thank goodness she didn't have to play a hymn right away. John's prayers always lasted so long that she'd have time to recover from her amazing discovery: she'd been forgiven and she wasn't the only sinner.

What wonderful news. There was hope for her. Jesus had spoken to and forgiven a sinful woman. Jesus reached out to her through the scripture, through His words, through His love, through His forgiveness.

In Weaver City, no one could partake of communion unless the elders and minister believed they were good enough and gave them a communion token. Annie had never been granted one because she was not good enough in their eyes.

But Jesus had decided she was. She couldn't stop smiling. Jesus forgave her. Jesus had given her a second chance.

So wrapped up was she in her joy that she didn't hear the end of the prayer until John cleared his throat and said a very loud, "Amen," which led her to believe she'd already missed several. With a start, she began to play the next hymn.

After that, she turned around on the organ bench and studied the congregation. Tall and solemn, John stood behind the pulpit to receive the offering. Her students and their families watched him, serious and devout.

Would they listen to and believe her? If she got to her feet now and confessed her sins and deception, would they forgive her as Jesus had?

They might, but she didn't think they would. Not all of them. Even though he'd read the words from the gospel, John probably wouldn't like his daughter being taught by a formerly illiterate ex-prostitute. Amanda would turn her back on an immoral woman. She could only guess the reactions of the others, especially that flinty stare of Mrs. Johnson. She thought they wouldn't be as forgiving as Jesus.

Feeling like a coward, she decided not to risk the life she'd stepped into, the life she loved so much.

Not yet.

Chapter Nine

The evening before Thanksgiving, Annie stood back to admire the cornucopia the students had created as Wilber hung it on the front wall of the church. The pictures of squash and wheat and apples poured from the opening in plentiful, interesting colors and shapes.

"Very lovely, Matilda."

She looked to her right, not surprised to see John there. She'd become aware of his presence in ways most unusual to her: his scent of bay rum, the sound of his confident stride, the feel of his warmth, although he wouldn't stand too close to her.

She was still amazed that his presence no longer frightened her as much as it confused her. He'd kept his word, and yet she still had no idea how to respond to him. How did a woman act around the town banker? Her ignorance made her feel stiff, nervous and uncomfortable.

"Everything is so pretty." Amanda danced into the room, her pale green skirt twirling with her. "You are so very talented." She put her hand on John's. "Aren't you proud you hired such a marvelous teacher?"

"Of course I am." He put his hand over Amanda's and patted it.

Amanda would fit the role of John's wife exactly. She had beauty, manners and charm. She knew how to talk to a man, to allow his hand on her arm without flinching. Of course, Amanda found John boring, but Annie knew marriages had been built on much less.

"And you." Amanda rushed to give Annie a hug. "You must be so proud of your students." She stepped back and smiled at Annie. "You're the best teacher the children have ever had."

"Oh, certainly not," Annie protested. If so, the children had put up with terribly ignorant teachers.

"I agree with Amanda." He stood next to his friend and nodded. "You have done a fine job."

"Thank you."

"And look at your new clothes." Amanda placed her hand on the sleeve of Annie's white jersey. "Cashmere. It's so soft."

"It's actually not new. I just haven't had an opportunity to wear it before."

"Isn't it beautiful, John? Doesn't our teacher look pretty tonight?"

Too embarrassed to listen for his reply, Annie glanced behind her and noticed the pews were filling. Her students stood at the back of the church, looking uncertain. "I need to help the performers. Will you excuse me?" She hurried toward the students, glad to have a reason to escape for a moment.

As people entered the church, Annie inspected the crowd and attempted to estimate the number in attendance. She noticed that the sheriff stood in the doorway. After that, Annie was too busy to notice anything.

The students recited President Lincoln's proclamation with only a few errors. Loud and enthusiastic applause followed. Then the older students staged a tableau of the landing of the Mayflower, followed by the girls singing hymns of thanksgiving. The program ended with Mr. Johnson declaiming about the blessings of Thanksgiving in the home, and a psalm sung by Amanda. After John's benediction, Annie checked the time. After days of work and preparation, the program had taken less than an hour.

"Beautifully done." Mr. and Mrs. Johnson shook her hand.

"I was proud of my boys," Mr. Bryan said, shuffling toward her. He looked so very ill and thin; she could understand why his sons had to help so much. "Didn't know Wilber could learn all those words." He shook his head. "Wish he could spend more time in school—" Before he could complete the sentence, his body was wracked with coughs.

"It's all right, Dad." Wilber led him to a chair. "I'll get you some punch."

In the small back parlor of the building, the church ladies provided refreshments. On this warm November evening, the crowd moved outside to socialize while Annie returned to the sanctuary to take down the decorations.

"Very well done, Miss Cunningham." The sheriff stood in the doorway to the parlor with a glass of punch in each hand. "I thought you might like something to drink after all that work."

"Thank you, Sheriff." She took the punch from him and sipped it.

"And maybe a little help with the decorations. All

your students have left you here to clean up while they eat. Some have even headed home."

When he reached to remove the cornucopia from the wall, she realized that it was handy to have someone taller and stronger do part of the work. "I appreciate your assistance, Sheriff, but I suspect you have another reason for not joining the group in the parlor."

"What?" He looked at her, uncertain of her meaning.

"I've seen your attempts to escape from Amanda Hanson."

His expression of surprise and—what else had she seen in his eyes? Sadness?—made Annie wish she could take back her words.

"I'm sorry," she hurried to say. "That was ill-mannered and interfering."

He smiled ruefully for an instant before he assumed his usual impassive expression. "Just startled me. I thought I'd hidden my efforts to stay away from Miss Hanson pretty well."

"Why would you want to do that? She's lovely."

"Yes, she is." He shook his head. "She is also a singularly persistent young woman who gets an idea in her head and won't let go, no matter how impractical and foolish that idea is."

"You believe her interest in you is foolish?" Annie considered his statement for a moment and realized its validity. In her experience with the upper class, they'd always made it obvious Annie wasn't one of them. However, in Trail's End, as the schoolteacher, she hadn't been aware of exactly where the line was drawn, especially not after Amanda's warm welcome and the kindness of the parents and students.

"I can't believe Mr. Hanson would be happy to see a

former gunfighter courting his little darling," the sheriff continued.

"But if Amanda wanted that...?"

"I don't have any money." He shrugged. "I didn't hold up stagecoaches or rob banks in my youth. I have a fairly honest streak in me and I live on what I earn. I don't have nearly enough money to keep her in handkerchiefs much less those fancy gowns she loves. And can you imagine her standing over a hot stove to prepare dinner?"

"I can't believe Amanda's going to give up."

"I don't allow myself to yearn for what I can't have." His eyes met Annie's. "The sheriffs and schoolteachers of the world don't get to marry into families like the Sullivans or the Hansons. I don't even think of it."

"Would you like to?" she put her hand over her mouth. "Oh, there I go again. I'm sorry."

"What I'd like doesn't matter. It's what I know. I figure Miss Hanson will get tired of chasing me, and life will be easier for both of us."

Annie saw Amanda glance in the sanctuary from the yard, her smile widening when she saw the sheriff.

The sheriff followed Annie's gaze to see Amanda heading inside. "Have a nice evening," he said to Annie as he grabbed his hat and dashed out the door.

"Drat the man," Amanda said as she entered the sanctuary at the exact moment his boots disappeared. "He seems absolutely determined to get away from me." She threw herself into a pew and sighed. "I do not understand why. Other men enjoy my company."

Annie settled next to her. "Then why don't you flirt with those other men?"

"Oh, la, I do, but I've know them forever. The good

ones are married and the others, well, the others are stuffy or ne'er-do-wells or gamblers or just not…interesting." She frowned. "Or they want to marry me for my father's money. You know," she sniffed, "it's difficult to be courted because Daddy has money."

"I'm sure."

Amanda waved her hand. "This discussion is much too gloomy. Tell me, where did you get the lovely fabric to make the cornucopia?"

"Didn't I tell you? I received a package from my friend Miss Palfrey. She sent papers and pens and yards of lovely fabric."

Amanda laughed. "Oh, Annie, did you ever think that she sent the material so you could make new clothes for yourself?"

"No, the students—"

"The students can use some of it. I'll come by and pick some lengths for Lucia to make you a few new basques." She stood. "Daddy's probably ready to go home. Why don't you come to our house after church Sunday for dinner?"

How should she answer the invitation? Annie didn't want to spend time with Mr. Hanson, concerned that she'd encourage his attentions.

"Don't worry about my father." Amanda laughed. "He's courting a very nice widow in Fredericksburg who's much closer to his age."

When she walked into the Hanson house on Sunday, Annie noticed immediately that it was more expensively furnished and impressive than the Sullivans'. The parlors were larger and more cluttered, the dinner table groaned under the number of dishes and the walls of Amanda's bedroom were covered with pink velvet.

"Let's look at the stereopticon," Amanda said after they'd eaten. "We ordered some new slides I know you'll love. Come over to the sofa and I'll show you."

Amanda pulled a tall metal stand across the table and placed a piece of cardboard on it.

"I've never seen one of these," Annie said, inspecting the object.

"Oh, you'll love it. Look through there." She pointed at an oddly shaped oval opening. "This one is of the pyramids in Egypt."

A wonder took place before Annie's eyes. She felt as if she were there, in this place called Egypt, as if she could reach out and touch the oddly shaped structure even though she knew it was merely a picture on the card Amanda had placed in the stereopticon. Although she felt sure a pyramid was the triangular building in the foreground, she had no idea what it was or where Egypt was or why anyone had built such a thing.

"Here's a picture of an abbey close to Yorkshire."

Amanda continued to put in more slides. Something the French were building called the Panama Canal, the countrysides of England and France, views of New York and Chicago and San Francisco. As she watched them, Annie realized how ignorant she was. Oh, she'd worked so hard, but she had so much more to learn, so very much more.

She'd come across a few of these places in her reading, but she'd had no idea the cities were so much bigger than Weaver City, which was the largest place she'd ever been. She'd learned from the picture in the stereopticon that New York had lots of tall buildings and crowds of people—more people than Annie had ever seen in one place at one time.

What was the Panama Canal? Where were these other places and why were they important? She suspected she should know most of them in order to teach history, but she didn't.

Her mind in a swirl, she leaned back against the sofa. She'd worked so hard and she still didn't know enough, not nearly enough. Amanda knew all this because she'd lived in an educated household and had gone to school. For years.

How would she ever learn it all? It would take the rest of her life. But she only had a few weeks.

"Matilda, are you all right?" Concern wrinkled Amanda's forehead.

No, she was not all right but she couldn't confess that now. "A little overwhelmed," she said. "I've never imagined these places looked like this." She sat up. "Do you have more slides? I'd like to see them all."

Because Annie had shown so much interest in the stereopticon, Amanda sent it home with her. She spent the rest of the day looking up the places in the history book and making notes. By midnight, she'd learned a great deal about Egypt and Greece, but so much remained for her to study. Tomorrow, she decided, she'd show some of the slides to the class and then assign a place to every child to report on, using the books Miss Palfrey had sent. She would learn as the students did for as long as she could.

With Minnie in her lap, Annie settled on the front step of the schoolhouse and leaned against the door. It was nearly dusk. The students had left hours earlier and she'd been reading the seventh-level history book ever since. Dates and names flitted hither and yon in her brain but refused to organize themselves there. Her head ached as if she'd hit it several times with the book. That probably would have been easier than reading the volume and nearly as effective.

Leaning forward, she dropped her head into her hands and tried hard not to cry. She'd believed she'd made it, that she'd learned enough, that she'd become a teacher. How stupid and pretentious of her. She'd listened and read enough to learn words like pretentious but the real facts—what the older students had to know—still eluded her no matter how much time she spent trying to stuff the knowledge in. Each new fact raised more questions which made her realize how much more there was to learn. On top of that, history seemed interconnected. To understand the American Revolution, she had to understand the Magna Carta, the history of England and much more.

As she considered the situation, the wind swept through the grove of trees around the schoolhouse. The branches waved noisily and the leaves shook, whispering secrets to each other.

Weary, she felt so weary and old and…foolish. Heedless, as her father had always said. She took a deep breath. She hadn't thought of him for months, not since she'd become Matilda Cunningham. Now he came back to mock her, to tell her that he'd been right, she never planned ahead.

She hated that.

Dear God, please help me. I know I've sinned by telling this lie, but now I want to be the best teacher I can. Please help me. As she prayed, she let her pain pour out wordlessly, knowing that God heard her. Finally she whispered, "Amen," but kept her head bent.

Hearing something in the breeze, Minnie leaped from Annie's lap and ran inside the schoolhouse.

"Matilda?"

She lifted her head from her hands. In the fading light, she could make out John on his flashy black horse, the right mount for a successful rancher.

"Yes," she answered.

He dismounted, and tied the horse to the stair rail, only a few feet from her. "I wanted to check your windows and see if everything's tied down. We're supposed to have a storm tonight, although it may be all wind." He surveyed the sky with a frown while the wind blew and the leaves crackled.

"Do you believe we'll finally get rain?" she asked. They hadn't received a drop since she'd arrived, and everyone discussed the possibility of drought. She turned her eyes away as if studying the darker sky in the east, but she could still feel his presence, the warmth of his closeness.

"I don't know, but I hope so. I'm going to check the schoolhouse."

"Thank you."

She heard him outside the building, checking the windows. Then he entered through the back door and, from the rattling she heard, seemed to be making sure that all the doors and windows fit tightly.

Within five minutes he was back. "Everything seems all right. You should weather the storm with no problem." He placed his hand on the stone wall. "The walls of this building can withstand anything, but the windows and the doors aren't as strong."

For a few seconds, she studied him, then smiled. "John, why are you here? Since I arrived, this building had held up in other windstorms and you didn't come to check on things." She touched the wall. "It's made of stone."

After studying the schoolhouse seriously for a few seconds, he turned toward her and grinned sheepishly. "All right, it was an excuse. I wanted to see you. I want to see more of you, but I don't know how. If I spend time alone with you here, gossip could ruin your reputation. So I decided to come down to check the windows."

She wanted to spend time with him, too, but how? "I'd like to see more of you, too."

As they looked at each other, a "meow" came from beneath the steps.

"What do we have here?" John leaned down to peer beneath the steps and picked up Minnie.

"That's Minnie." She glanced up at him. "Is it all right to have her in the schoolhouse?"

He held the tiny animal in the palm of one hand and gently rubbed her ears. A loud purr emerged from the little body. Annie was amazed by how gentle his large hands were. Finally, he gave Minnie to Annie and said, "She seems healthy. I'm sure she'll be a great mouser when she grows several inches."

He continued to watch Annie, the now familiar expression of yearning in his eyes that touched the longing within her. "We haven't solved anything," she whispered.

He took a step toward Annie and she didn't move away. Then he lifted a finger and ran it down her cheek, slowly, tenderly, the warmth of his caress pouring into those cold and barren places within her.

"No," he whispered. "No, but we'll keep trying. If it's all right with you, we'll keep trying. There has to be a way."

She nodded, putting her hand on his for a moment before he stepped away. "Goodbye," he whispered. "You stay inside where it's safe."

As she watched him ride off, she wished she could call him back. She wished he would lean toward her again and run his finger down her cheek.

He cared for her. At least, she thought he did. John was gentle and concerned for her. How would a kiss from him feel?

Chapter Ten

❧

"Miss Cunningham, you want to know what I'd really like to do?" Wilber Bryan asked.

She stood outside, watching the children play duck duck goose. The weather had become colder each day in December, but the students still liked to run around outside after a morning of work. Pulling her shawl more tightly around her, she asked, "What is that?"

"I'd like to take the eighth-grade examination."

She turned from the children to study Wilber's face. "The test students take to get into high school?"

He nodded. "I can't go to high school, but it would feel good to know that I'm smart enough, that I know enough, too."

Annie could almost hear the words Wilber hadn't said. His sentence might have ended with, "If I didn't have to take care of the farm." No, with his family situation, he couldn't go beyond eighth grade, but if taking the examination was his dream, Annie would do whatever was possible to help him.

"How are we going to do that, Wilber?"

"I wondered." He dropped his gaze to the bare

ground. "Would you teach me? I don't have to do much at the farm right now, not until we start planting. I can stay late after school maybe, if you could teach me then. And maybe I could come on Saturday afternoons?"

"Wilber, you know we can't be alone together in the schoolhouse, don't you?"

He nodded. "I know." With a shrug, he added, "That's okay." Shoulders bent, he began to shuffle back to where the other students were playing.

"But I have an idea, Wilber. Let me check on something. I'll let you know if we can work it out."

He turned to smile at her. "Thank you, ma'am. I could pay you a little for your time. My parents know this is important to me. They'll help."

Annie knew the Bryans had nothing extra—not a penny—and the more she taught, the more she learned. "Don't worry about that."

When Lucia arrived to help with lunch, Annie asked, "Would you like Miguel to be able to read and write and do sums?"

Lucia looked around her quickly. "Shh, Miss Cunningham. There are people here who do not think Mexican children should be in school."

"But would you like him to?" Annie whispered.

"So much. He could have a better life. Mr. Sullivan is very good to us, but who knows what will happen tomorrow? Only God knows where Miguel will end up working in twenty years, but if he could read and write... Oh, that would be a wonderful thing. He'd have a future."

"Wilber Bryan asked me to tutor him but I can't do that alone. If you came to the schoolhouse after two-thirty and perhaps on Saturdays to chaperone, you could bring Miguel. I can work with him while he's here. No one would know but the four of us."

Tears gathered in Lucia's eyes. "Oh, Miss, yes. We can come. Thank you."

The next afternoon, Annie explained Lucia's agreement to Wilber and suggested he stay late the next day.

"Thank you." Eagerly, he opened the math book to the section on algebra and started working on his slate.

The next afternoon, Annie said, "Miguel, I have some books here you may enjoy," Annie said. She put a primary reader on his desk. "You can see pictures of different objects. The letters that make up the objects' names are below the picture." She pointed at the page.

"I see that, Miss Cunningham."

She handed him a slate. "Write the list of words over and over, until your letters look just like the ones in the book."

After an hour with Wilber and Miguel, Lucia had to leave to help with dinner. Annie gave each student a book to study and bring back the next day. When she closed the door behind them, she felt a sense of purpose. The intelligence God had given her might change the lives of these two young people and, if she wasn't mistaken, also of Lucia, who'd carefully watched everything her son was doing and used her finger to copy the letters on the tabletop. Tomorrow Annie would give her a slate to practice with.

Amanda nudged the door of the sheriff's office open, slowly and silently, in the hope of seeing his initial response when she entered. "Hello, Sheriff Bennett."

He glanced up at her, exasperated and not a bit pleased. Never one to back down in the face of disappointment, Amanda walked right in, showing a confidence she wasn't quite feeling.

Like a gentleman, he stood.

"Because it's almost Christmas, I've brought you some cookies." She placed a plate of decadent chocolate fudge, several lemon scones and pulled cream candy on his desk. "The lemon ones taste especially good."

"Thank you." He nodded. "And thank your cook, please."

"You don't believe I made them myself?" She smiled at him, showing every dimple.

He didn't respond. Instead, his eyes returned to the paper he'd been reading. His lack of interest was enough to make even the most determined flirt give up. When she didn't leave, he fixed his gaze on her. "Do you wish to report a crime?"

"Sheriff, I swan. You ignore everything I do. Don't you recognize it when a young woman flirts with you?" She glanced up at him and fluttered her lashes.

"Miss Hanson, I've been a lawman for years. I recognize clues. It's not that I can't identify them. Sometimes I'm just not interested in pursuing them."

She almost staggered when the meaning of his words hit her. Not interested. She touched the charming blue bonnet, which brought out the color of her eyes, to make sure it sat correctly on her curls. He hadn't even noticed how stunningly attractive it was. With a sigh, she said, "I made the cookies myself. I hope you enjoy them." Then she hurried out of the office.

As she turned to close the door behind her, she was startled to see the sheriff studying her as if she were one of the tempting delicacies she'd brought him. Almost immediately, his expression became neutral, but she'd seen that bit of…of some emotion she hadn't seen in him before. She could read clues, too, and he'd been lying—he was interested. In fact, she could say that for a second, she'd seen desire on his face.

"Goodbye, Sheriff," she called. With a smile of determination and delight, Amanda climbed into the phaeton, flicked the reins and started home to prepare a new strategy.

Annie's first Christmas in Trail's End would arrive in a little over a week. If she weren't a mature, professional teacher, she would have skipped down the road in anticipation of the holiday. She forced herself to walk slowly and primly from the schoolhouse toward town. Coins jingled in her purse and a few dollars were folded inside. On this cold, bright Tuesday afternoon, she planned to buy presents. A bottle of soothing balm for Lucia whose hands were raw from washing clothes, something frivolous for Amanda and a bag of candy for the students.

As she walked, she noticed the grass along the verge had died, and dust rose from the road to cover her shoes. The children said this had been the driest year they could remember—no rain for five months. She studied the clear, cloudless sky. No chance of showers today, either.

Only a few feet from the dry-goods door, she paused and opened her purse to count her change. When she'd reached fifty-seven cents, she heard the door of the store open and she glanced up to see a man walk out. She recognized his face. In horror, she turned away, allowing him to see only her back.

Although he'd stopped only a few feet away from

her, she didn't think he'd seen her face. Hadn't he been looking down the street in the other direction when he'd left the store? She stood there trembling, her head bent, praying. Please, Lord, don't let him recognize me.

After what seemed like forever, she heard him walk away, his boots clomping against the boards of the sidewalk until he mounted a horse and rode off.

When the sound of hoofbeats died away, Annie allowed herself to breathe again, but she couldn't stop shaking.

What had brought Willie Preston from Weaver City to Trail's End?

Had he recognized her? She thought not. Preston had frequented Miss Ruby's enough to recognize Annie, prostitute and daughter of the drunken murderer George MacAllister. But she didn't think he'd seen her well enough to identify her. Besides, she looked very different now.

More than anything, she wanted to go back to the schoolhouse and hide, but she would not allow Willie Preston to change her plans. With a quick glance down the street to make sure he'd left, she turned and entered the store. As she studied a bolt of fabric she couldn't afford, she asked Mr. Johnson, "Was that a newcomer to town? The man who just left?" Her voice quivered a little, but other than that, she sounded fairly normal.

"Him? No, just passing through." Mr. Johnson finished straightening the cans on a shelf. "Had a lot of questions, but said he had to head back to Weaver City."

"Questions?" She realized she was clenching the fabric. She forced herself to let go of it before she set wrinkles in it.

"Wanted to know a few things, like where the Sullivan ranch was."

"Did you tell him?"

"Told him I didn't know anyone named Sullivan," he said. "Can't trust strangers, that's what I think."

Preston had asked about the Sullivan ranch? Did that mean he knew where Annie lived? Had he tracked her down? If he had, why?

Oh, no reason for that. Annie was no one. She'd never done anything important enough for someone to look for her. His being here had nothing to do with her. Must be pure coincidence that she lived in the place he'd asked about.

But why had Willie Preston come to Trail's End? Why had he asked questions about the Sullivans? Preston would work for anyone, doing whatever his employer paid him for. Did his questions mean the Sullivans were in danger? Oh, surely not. What connection could there be between Trail's End and Weaver City? Between Willie Preston and the Sullivans?

After she got home and put the gifts away, she paced through the confines of the schoolhouse. If she weren't so worried, the sight of Minnie racing behind her and attacking her hem would have made Annie smile, but she couldn't find anything amusing at this moment. She went outside and settled on the bench to think. However, she found all of her thoughts in such a jumble, she couldn't stay still. Why was he here? What would he do about her? Would he hurt the Sullivans? Did she need to tell John?

After twenty minutes with no answers, she went back inside. All the worrying in the world wouldn't solve the problem. She'd have to wait until Preston did something. It could have been mere coincidence.

But she didn't think so.

To distract her thoughts, she pulled the fifth-level mathematics book out and opened it. Numbers always calmed her.

When Annie opened the book, she saw something near the back of the book that she'd never seen before: math problems that used letters, as well as numbers. She read, "$25 + x = 39$." What did that mean? A few pages later, she discovered something called an equation, which used brackets and parentheses.

How did those letters and signs end up in arithmetic? What did one do with them?

She turned back a few pages to see the chapter heading: "Algebra." Algebra? What was algebra? Obviously it had something to do with x and y and other signs.

She hadn't bothered to study mathematics ahead of the children because she was good with numbers. She understood and could teach arithmetic with no trouble.

How could she possibly have guessed there was more to it than numbers? She closed the book and shut her eyes. This was worse than she'd ever considered. With the addition of geography and history, she had to work every night and all weekend to stay ahead of the students now. How could she possibly find time to learn algebra? And she figured there were probably more things she'd never heard of lurking in the book.

But she refused to consider that now.

How could a person possibly learn all this? It seemed as if every time she felt comfortable and confident, she discovered she didn't know a thing.

Perhaps she should leave at Christmas. She'd lasted

one semester—far longer than she'd expected to. Now all this new work faced her.

And Willie Preston had come to town.

But she loved this place. She looked around at the snug little schoolroom and the warm stove. She loved the children and they were learning. If she left, there wouldn't be another teacher until the next October. The delay would be worse than having a teacher who didn't know everything.

No, she wouldn't leave. She wouldn't allow Willie Preston to take this from her. She wouldn't allow algebra and the Panama Canal to frighten her. She'd learn it all, even if she never slept again.

"Dear God," she whispered. "Please be with me. Give me the strength and ability to learn everything I must." She paused. "And one other thing, God. I thought I was safe here, but I'm not. I can't ask You to help me with a lie, but please, please, let me finish the school year, and I'll never lie again. I promise." Leaving her thoughts with God for a few minutes, she finally added, "Amen."

Calm filled her as she listened to the sound of the wind swirling around the small building. Even with Miss Cunningham's past coming back in the form of the letter and package and Annie's seeing her own past in Willie Preston's visit to town, she knew God would guide her and grant her strength and courage.

She also knew God would expect her to confess and reveal her identity, but she couldn't do that yet. In a while she would. Sometime, but not with Christmas coming and the children depending on her so much.

Of course she had to tell the truth.

But not yet.

* * *

With the exception of taking her to church, John hadn't seen Matilda for three weeks. He had trouble thinking of reasons to stop by the schoolhouse when the students were there and even more trouble when they weren't, especially since he worried about doing something that frightened her.

He wouldn't be here now if his daughter hadn't given him a reason. Matilda had set up a spelling bee for today, part of several events she'd scheduled before the Christmas holiday. He'd promised five shiny pennies to the winner of the bee, and his daughter had decreed he must be there to present it. Not that he minded. He would do almost anything Elizabeth asked.

So there he sat on his horse, watching the students play alle-over. Although it was December, the temperature was mild. He'd arrived early, which left him nothing to do but watch the children—and their teacher.

He tried not to focus on Matilda because he feared his expression gave away his feelings. And yet he could see her well enough to notice the curly wisps of beautiful dark hair that had come loose from her tight bun and curled around her neck.

"Father!"

His daughter was jumping up and down, waving to him. "Hello, Elizabeth."

"Mr. Sullivan, how nice to see you." Matilda smoothed her hair back before she took the ball from one of the Bryan boys. "I'm glad Elizabeth talked you into attending."

"Good afternoon, Miss Cunningham. Have I arrived too early?" He got down from the horse and tied the reins to the rail.

She glanced at the watch she had pinned to her dress. "Oh, no." She smiled, breathless, her cheeks red from playing alle-over. She was truly lovely.

"We're finished here, Mr. Sullivan. Please come into the schoolroom and we'll get settled."

He watched as she effortlessly corralled the students and marched them inside. Each sat quietly and pulled out a few papers to study. Once the teacher reached the platform, she divided the students into teams and had them stand on either side of the room.

"Clara, please spell ocean," she said.

He couldn't take his eyes off Matilda. Her hair would not stay put, continuing to spill from its tight bun and curl around her lovely face. He couldn't think of anything else he'd rather be doing than sitting here at the Trail's End School Spelling Bee and admiring the teacher.

After two rounds, only a few of the students had dropped out. Matilda had comforted each, telling them what a fine job they'd done with difficult words. No wonder they all loved her. When Ida's turn came again, she said, "Miss Cunningham, give me a hard word."

The teacher smiled. Had he ever noticed her pretty smile?

Of course he had.

"Conscience," Matilda said.

When the bee ended six rounds later, Ida had won and accepted the prize with the confidence of one who knew all along she'd receive the pennies. After the award presentation, John nodded to the class and left, though he wanted to stay for the rest of the day. Duffy would laugh if he knew the teacher had John acting like such an idiot.

* * *

From the front of the classroom, Annie watched Amanda slip through the door, her arms filled with boxes. Immediately Wilber leaped to his feet to help her.

"Children," Annie said. "The evening of Tuesday, December twenty-second, there will be a holiday presentation here in the schoolroom, and we need to start decorating for that."

The students cheered, knowing her words meant an end to studying for the day.

"Miss Hanson is going to help the girls. Boys, I need you to take the saws from the shed and go out to cut evergreen boughs." She laughed at the speed with which they jumped up, grabbed their coats and ran outside.

Amanda opened a box of sliced apples and oranges that she'd baked for hours. The girls got to work decorating them with ribbons.

"Miss Hanson also brought Christmas cards." Annie held one up. "You can cut out the pictures and the verses and make an ornament for the tree by hanging them from a ribbon."

After an hour, the boys returned, their arms full of branches. After decorating outside, the boys brought boughs inside and hung them on the classroom walls while Amanda and the girls placed ornaments on them.

Annie took a deep breath, inhaling the scent of Christmas. "Doesn't it smell wonderful?" she asked.

After the excited children left, she gave Amanda a hug and thanked her.

Now she had to sit down and learn algebra, and more about geography, history and science. She opened the mathematics book and saw a chapter toward the back with the title "Calculus." She didn't even want to think about how much time that would take to master.

With a sigh, she lifted Minnie off her desk where the kitten had been batting an ornament, placed her on a bench and began to work again.

Never before had she joined a congregation in welcoming the Savior. Never before had she realized what the birth of the Holy Child meant to the world and to her. The fact that He had been born because He loved everyone, even sinful Annie MacAllister, amazed her. She was special. She was a beloved child of God.

She closed her book and stood to walk to the window where the sky darkened and the first stars shone. As she watched, she drew in a deep breath and thought about the shepherds in the field and how they must have felt when the Heavenly Host appeared to them on the plain: fear and glory and wonder.

This evening, joy and wonder filled her.

And a depth of love for her Savior so overwhelmed her that she wrapped her arms around her body as if attempting to hold it tightly within her.

"Thank You, dear Lord," she whispered. "Oh, thank You."

After a few hours of work, anticipation and joy washed over Annie. This was the first Christmas that she would truly welcome the newborn Savior. The feeling of joy was almost too much for her to contain.

Chapter Eleven

"Sheriff Bennett, you're looking very festive tonight." Amanda gripped the poor man's arm with determination and pulled him toward the steps into the schoolroom for the Christmas program. "Is that a new shirt?"

As she stood at the door watching the two, Annie felt sorry for Amanda, who was experiencing her first rejection—and a very decisive one at that. She probably shouldn't have asked both of them to help her prepare, but she'd needed assistance.

She wore a new basque Lucia had made her from the fabric Miss Palfrey had sent. She'd chosen lovely blue cashmere. Earlier, she'd attempted to catch her reflection in the windows, and if she wasn't mistaken, she looked nice.

"Sheriff Bennett, would you please put that big wreath over the desk?"

"Matilda, I pray for patience every day," Amanda whispered to Annie as they watched him put the wreath up. "But that man is trying what little I have left."

"Why don't you pray for God to help you win the sheriff?"

"I don't think God works that way. I believe God has given me the tools." She gestured toward her lovely dark green gown. "It is up to me to use them." She sighed. "Perhaps it is just not meant to be."

"How does this look, Miss Cunningham?" the sheriff asked.

"Down a little on the left side."

"Good evening, Miss Cunningham." Elizabeth walked in with Lucia. "Lucia and I felt you needed something to brighten your room because people will walk all over the schoolhouse tonight." She held up a lovely quilt with a lone star design.

"How lovely," Annie said. "Come, help me put this on the bed."

The cover brightened the room and made it look less shabby. "Thank you, Elizabeth. I'll be so warm. It's lovely."

"Elizabeth? Have you arrived yet?" John's voice came from the schoolroom.

"Oh, there he is." Elizabeth skipped toward the door. "My father had to come from town. That's why Lucia and I were early."

Before she left, Annie looked around her small chambers. Little by little, it had become hers. Using a length of fabric, she'd covered the area where she'd hung her clothes, Wilber had placed a piece of wood under the dresser to level its leg and now the new quilt. It felt like home.

Hearing the buzz of conversation in the schoolroom, Annie hurried from her bedroom and began to greet the parents and other guests.

"Grandmother, this is what I made." Bertha pointed

to her ornament on the decorated bough behind Annie's desk.

"Miss Hanson helped the children so much with their ornaments," Annie told Bertha's grandmother.

"I didn't realize Miss Hanson taught young children, as well as all her other praiseworthy activities," the sheriff said, shaking his head.

"You have no idea how talented I am." Amanda smiled and took his arm. "Why don't we find a nice place to enjoy the program, and I'll tell you all about it."

The man was doomed, at least for this evening.

"Very nicely done." John stood next to Annie, admiring the decorations. "I look forward to the program."

For a moment, she savored being near John and wished she could lean closer or put her hand on his arm. Then she glanced at her watch. Time to start. With a clap of her hands, she walked toward the front and the crowd quieted. "Welcome to the Christmas program of Trail's End School." First she led the group in Christmas songs interspersed with tableaux: playing in the snow and throwing snowballs, a family singing and reading the Bible and a stable scene. After several students recited and others sang, everyone joined in to sing "Oh, Come, All Ye Faithful."

With the program over, Annie watched the students and their guests as they wandered around the classroom looking at the displays, chatting and enjoying the cookies and lemonade.

"Is Mr. Sullivan courting you?" The sheriff seemed to have escaped from Amanda and stood at Annie's elbow.

"What?" Annie whirled to face him. "Why would you think that?"

"I'm a man."

"And what, exactly, does that mean?"

"I know how a man looks at a woman he's attracted to."

Annie looked around the schoolroom. John stood talking to Mrs. Johnson. As he listened to her, his gaze found Annie. That warmth she'd seen before glowed in his eyes.

"Like that," the sheriff said. "Most teachers would love to be courted by John Matthew Sullivan. He's wealthy. What more could you want?"

"I… I'm not interested. At all."

"You plan to be a teacher all your life? Die unmarried?"

"Until they have to drag me out of the schoolroom." She laughed, but it wasn't a joke. She would love to marry and have dozens of children, but beneath the facade lay her real self, and no man would want to marry Annie. And Annie, well, she wasn't sure she could love a man enough to have his children, despite what she'd been feeling for John.

The sheriff studied her face. "I've wondered if you have a secret in your past."

"What do you mean?" Annie asked, startled.

"I've learned to read people pretty well. But don't worry—I won't ask you about it. Maybe you'll tell me one day."

She wouldn't.

"And your secrets?" she asked.

He shrugged. "I have a few. They aren't all bad. It's just better that no one know what they are." He grinned for a moment, then became serious again. "I believe we're two of a kind, Miss Cunningham. We've worked hard to get where we are and might prefer no one investigate very closely how we did it. Maybe we have pasts that are better left hidden." He headed toward the refreshments.

Two of a kind, the sheriff and Annie. Perhaps so, but she refused to let him know how close he'd come to the truth.

By eight-thirty, most of the crowd had cleared out. She'd told the sheriff that Wilber would help clean up the next morning and watched Mr. Hanson assist his daughter into their carriage. Elizabeth and Lucia had left earlier. After everyone had departed, she looked outside and saw one horse remained. Orion. Had John waited for her outside the schoolhouse after everyone else had left?

"Matilda, could you please bring me a lamp?" he called.

That sounded innocent enough. She nodded and went back into the schoolroom.

When she brought the lamp, he said, "Can you hold it for me? Right here?" He pointed close to the horse's front left foot. "Orion's got a rock caught under his hoof and I can't see it. I can feel it, but it's not coming out." He held up a short knife to show her. "I don't want to hurt him." He held the hoof closer to the lamp. "I could walk him home, where I've got a better tool, but I don't want him to be in pain."

She watched him attempt to remove the rock, his hands tender and careful with the big animal. Then a cool breeze hit her and she shivered.

"I'm sorry. I forgot how cold it is. You should go back inside."

"No, this is interesting." And it was, seeing the trust

of the animal as John hunted for a way to pull the rock out. "And you need me to hold the light."

With a final pull, the pebble popped out. John placed the animal's foot back on the ground and stood to put his hand on the horse's neck. "Good boy. It's out and you're fine." Then he turned toward her. "Thank you. We're fine to go now."

In the shadowy solitude, Annie felt that familiar breathlessness she experienced when alone with John— only with John. He glanced at her, and in the dim glow of the lamp, she saw a vulnerability in his expression, a fierce longing that amazed her.

Odd that vulnerability and longing should cause her to take a step back. But it did.

"I've frightened you again. I'm sorry." He straightened. "But I don't know how I did that. Matilda, you must know I'd do nothing to hurt you."

She nodded. She did know that.

"Do you know…" he began to say, then stopped as if he were reconsidering his words. "I'm very attracted to you."

For a moment the impulse to run came over her but he didn't move toward her or reach in her direction. And, for some reason, she wanted to hear what he had to say.

Because the lamp had grown heavier with each second, she put it on the ground. The light pooled around their feet but left their expressions in shadows.

"Please don't be frightened," he said. "I have thought about this for weeks, about what I want to say to you." He paused and cleared his throat. "This is not easy for me, but I want to tell you how I feel, and I wonder if there is any chance you return my feelings."

"I don't know."

"Do you find me repulsive?"

"Of course not." How could he think such a thing? Had her behavior caused him to think this?

"But I scare you."

"Not much, not anymore." She paused. How to explain it? "Any fear I feel is no longer because of you. I've had…some frightening experiences in my life."

"Then I'm willing to wait, but I would like to know if that is a realistic thing for me to do." Suddenly, he laughed. "I'm so relieved to know you don't find me repulsive."

With a courage she didn't know she possessed, Annie took a step forward. She could see his smile.

"I'd like you to consider my words. I know you are a virtuous young woman. I won't push you or alarm you in any way, but I would like to court you."

She stifled a gasp. "But you cannot. I cannot keep company with a man. My contract."

"Your contract states you won't keep company with people of low character. I don't believe that describes me."

She watched him, feeling his intense gaze on her.

"I'm willing to wait until you feel comfortable," he repeated. "I would like to court you."

She could think of nothing more to say but realized he expected an answer. "Thank you." As soon as the words left her mouth, she knew they sounded ridiculous.

He took a step toward her. Annie didn't move away.

She could almost feel the air between them vibrating with emotion. He cared for her, she knew that. Her feelings weren't as easily categorized. He was a handsome man. He behaved carefully with her, which meant he was kind and considerate. And yet there must be more than that or the very air wouldn't be throbbing. Perhaps she couldn't recognize her feelings because they were so buried beneath the experiences of the past years. But there was something very real going on between the two of them.

The fact that she both recognized and accepted the powerful attraction made her wish to flee, but she didn't. He deserved more.

"'Thank you'?" he repeated. "What does that mean?" When she couldn't answer, he continued, "My request cannot come as a surprise to you. Surely you've noticed the amount of time I've spent at the school just to see you. Can't you read the interest in my face? Can't you tell how I feel when I look at you?"

"Yes, a little, but I didn't… I didn't understand. Not completely. I didn't realize…" She stopped, unable to think of words to complete her thoughts. She couldn't explain that, as much as he attracted her, in the end she would disappoint him. Who would want to court a former prostitute? And he would leave her when he found out.

He studied her, his expression uncertain. "How do you feel about my wish to court you?"

He was asking about how Annie felt? No, he wondered how Matilda felt. At the moment, neither woman could think of an answer.

"I find you very attractive, but…" She shook her head. "My past, those experiences I mentioned…they make it hard for me."

"No?" He sounded surprised, obviously not expecting such a response.

"I'm sorry."

He stood very still. She picked up the lamp and could see that his eyes were that flat, icy blue. "Then I shall wish you good evening, Matilda." He bowed stiffly before he turned and mounted his horse.

She watched him ride off. Had she done the right thing? He was handsome and rich and personable. She could easily fall in love with him, if she allowed herself to. If he courted her, if he asked her to marry him, Annie would become Mrs. John Matthew Sullivan, the wife of a rich man who would take care of her. Matilda might have welcomed his question and been able to assume that role, but Annie could not. Annie's life was a lie. She could not compound the lie by hiding it from a husband.

Awkward.

No, that word barely fit the emotions John felt. Embarrassed? Mortified? Maybe those fit better. Humiliated described the feeling best. He'd hoped he'd found a woman he could care for, a first in his life. He had cared for his wife, but what he felt now was so different.

He'd believed she hadn't been averse to him. He almost laughed when he realized what he meant was that she hadn't run away from him, that she had allowed herself to stand alone with him a few minutes in the dark. Obviously he had misunderstood everything she'd said and done, and had fooled himself into thinking there was or could be something between them.

He gave Orion a gentle nudge with his heels and the horse sped up. What he needed was a long, hard run to clear his head, but it would be too dangerous to do at night.

Her remarks were all that was proper but everything

he hadn't wanted to hear. He didn't wish for her to throw herself at him as Amanda flirted so outrageously with the sheriff. He had hoped she'd answer his question with feminine deference, which would indicate she returned his interest and would be flattered to be courted.

He drove into the stable yard and dismounted.

"Good evenin', boss." Duffy held the reins. "You look as sad as a cow that lost her heifer."

Exactly what he wanted—for Duffy to identify his feelings. Now he felt like an old fool, acting as ridiculously about Matilda as Farley Hanson had. He straightened, said, "Evening, Duffy" and headed toward the house.

After he kissed Elizabeth good-night, he went toward his bedroom, took off his coat and hung it on a chair.

At least Hanson had found a woman in Fredericksburg. Maybe John should look for a mature widow.

But he couldn't do that. He felt too strong an emotion for Matilda. He'd always supposed that if he found the right woman, she would return his feelings. He'd never expected to be turned down. The rejection—perhaps lack of enthusiasm was more accurate—had cut him deeply. He leaned his forehead against the glass. He considered praying, but the God he worshipped didn't expect John to come to Him with every little thing. His God expected John to take care of things himself, so he would.

He could not have meant what he said.

In an attempt to turn her thoughts from John, Annie had thrown herself into cleaning the schoolhouse. With the help of Minnie chasing after dust bunnies and scraps of paper, she'd swept the entire floor until not a speck of dirt or the tiniest bit of paper remained. Then she wet a cloth and scrubbed the surfaces of the desks and tables.

By that time, she'd worn herself out. Yet his statement still echoed in her brain. He would like to court her.

No, he would like to court Miss Matilda Cunningham.

No man wanted to court Annie.

What difference did that make? Everyone thought she was Matilda. She had thought of herself as Matilda for two months now and felt very comfortable in the role. She taught the children. She played the organ and attended church. She had discovered her faith and prayed.

And Jesus had forgiven her.

"Dear loving God." She knelt next to her desk. "Please help me. I know what I did was wrong, but it's turned out so well. The students are learning—Miguel and Wilber are speeding along with their lessons—and people like me. They respect me. Is that wrong? I'm warm and happy and have food and I don't have to—" she shuddered "—do those other things, those terrible things. Please guide me, dear Lord. Amen."

But she received no immediate answer.

Chapter Twelve

Annie had dreaded attending the Christmas Eve service with John. But when Duffy arrived with Elizabeth to drive her to church, she felt a stab of disappointment at John's absence. Elizabeth announced that her father would be riding his horse down later.

"Oh, Miss Cunningham, I hope my father bought me some books for Christmas and maybe pretty new clothes. A large parcel arrived yesterday." The excited child held her arms out to show the dimensions. She chattered on during the short ride to town, speculating about what that package might contain.

The women who decorated the church had placed candles in each window to guide the Christ child. Inside, tapers flickered in the wreaths and evergreen boughs, which decorated the plain pews and the pulpit. Annie had never seen anything so beautiful. She took her place at the organ and, as the congregation entered, she played the favorite songs of the season. She listened to the Christmas story from the Gospel of Matthew—oh, she'd read it herself last week, but to hear it in church, surrounded by the faithful, well, it was all so new, so marvelous. Her heart leaped when the minister proclaimed, "Christ is born," and the congregation answered, "He is born this night."

For a moment she sat on the bench and watched the smiling congregation leaving, chatting and making plans, while she just wanted to take in the glory of this moment. Her Savior had been born. She was so absorbed in this realization that she didn't notice when someone approached her.

"Happy Christmas," John said from a few feet away.

"Oh, it is a very happy Christmas," she agreed.

"You look lovely tonight, Miss Cunningham." He smiled at her. "You seem to be glowing."

"It is Christmas, sir." She smiled. "Has there ever been a more wonderful day?" Then she stood to hug Elizabeth, who was almost asleep on her father's shoulder. "Happy Christmas to you, Elizabeth."

The child gave her a drowsy nod. "Happy Christmas to my favorite teacher," she said.

Oh, yes. What a truly joyous night.

The next day, Annie dressed in her brown skirt with the gold basque. She wore a new black-wool cape she'd bought as a Christmas gift for herself. It was plain with no fur trim, but it kept her warm. Then she put on her new bonnet—black with black and white lace ruffles around her face. She attempted to see herself in the glass but couldn't quite make out her reflection. She could only hope she looked pretty. Oh, the bonnet wasn't as dashing as the leghorn shade hat she'd seen in the catalog, but this one cost less and suited a serious teacher.

She scratched Minnie under the chin, picked up the present she'd made for Amanda and started her walk to the Hansons' ranch for Christmas dinner.

Amanda had told her to ask John for a ride, but Annie hadn't. She felt uncomfortable around him after what had happened between them. She'd tried to imagine a life with John, but she could see no way around telling him the truth. No matter how much she tried to pretend she was someone else, to believe that the good life she'd built here was real and true, she still knew her secret would have to come out. Even as kind as he was with Minnie and his horses and his daughter, he'd never forgive her for her past and her lies.

So she would walk. It wasn't a long distance and she'd be comfortable in her new, warm cape. Besides, with dinner at two, it would still be light and not too cold by the time she started home.

When she arrived, carriages were being taken around to the stable by stable boys. She didn't see John's surrey. After she knocked, a maid opened the door, took her bonnet and cape, and Annie entered the front parlor.

In a corner stood a Christmas tree, at least seven feet tall, covered with candles and a star on top. She moved slowly through the crowd, nodding at the other guests until she arrived at the tree. The ornaments were miniatures of animals, musical instruments and toys—a tiny wooden doll, a small intricately carved cat, a bugle. There were red and green glass balls, metal ornaments and cardboard pictures. Strings of berries wound through the branches.

"Do you like it?" Amanda grasped Annie's hand.

"It is absolutely lovely, Amanda! Did you do this?"

"You know I'm a useless creature." Amanda laughed. "I pointed and told the servants what to do."

"Is the sheriff coming?" Annie whispered.

"No." She shook her head mournfully. "He said

someone robbed the bank in Derth. He had to investigate it today. And maybe tomorrow. He wasn't at all sure when he'd be back." She frowned. "You don't think he's trying to get away from me, do you?"

Annie paused and said, "Thank you for inviting me to dinner. I'm going to enjoy spending Christmas with you."

Amanda laughed. "You don't want to answer, do you? Probably wise."

When the twenty guests took their places at the long table a few minutes later, Annie found herself between Mr. Tripp and Mr. Norton. Amanda sat at one end of the table, facing her father with John on her right. Elizabeth sat with the other children at a table in another room.

As she took a sip of water, Annie glanced toward John. He looked so handsome in formal wear, his black coat a perfect fit on his solid shoulders, highlighting the darkness of his hair and the blue of his eyes. He'd nodded at her earlier in the evening but they'd not spoken.

After Mr. Hanson prayed, the servants began serving. The table almost shook with the weight of ham, mashed potatoes, sweet potatoes, corn, squash and many other treats that covered it.

Games followed the delicious meal, the last being the cobweb game. Ribbons of different colors hung from the ceiling, making a brilliant design. The end of each ribbon disappeared into the other parlor or down the hallway. Some went upstairs while others wound under furniture and doors.

"Take that one," Amanda whispered. "The red one with the white lace."

Startled, Annie did as she was told, taking the ribbon and attempting to untangle it—not easy with everyone else concentrating on the same task. A few minutes later, she found herself following her ribbon up the stairs and down the hall. It led to a closed door. She knocked, received no response and she stepped inside. The ribbon went under the bed so she knelt down and reached under the ruffles of the bed skirt where, after much searching, she felt a small box. Inside, she found a pair of earrings, each a graceful spiral of dark gold.

"What do you think?" Annie looked up to see Amanda at the door.

"They are lovely, but I can't accept them."

Amanda waved her hand. "Of course you can. You found them in the game."

"But you told me which ribbon—"

"Can you imagine how Mr. Johnson would look in those earrings?"

Annie laughed. When Amanda had her mind made up, no one could change it.

"Let me put them on you." Amanda assisted her and said, "Now, look in the mirror. Don't they look nice?"

Annie examined her reflection. Who was the woman who stared back at her? She was much prettier than she remembered, with her hair so full and shiny, set off by the dangling earrings and the warm golden color of her basque. "Thank you." With a laugh, she turned toward her friend. "I have a present for you." Annie pulled Amanda to the parlor and opened her purse. "Not nearly as grand."

Amanda pulled the paper off to reveal a handkerchief that Annie had embroidered with her friend's initials. She'd sewed lace around the edges using the tiniest stitches she could.

"You made this for me." Amanda hugged Annie. "It means so much to me. Thank you."

After all the guests had found their gifts, they gathered in the parlor to show them off. Annie glanced at her watch. Almost five o'clock. It would be dark before six. She started toward Amanda to tell her she needed to leave when Mr. Hanson said, "Let's sing some Christmas songs. Miss Cunningham," he said, bowing toward her, "would you play for us?"

Annie sat at the beautiful square piano with intricately carved legs. "I don't know very many."

"I'll stand right here and sing," Amanda said.

After singing "Jingle Bells" and attempting to remember the words of "The Twelve Days of Christmas," Annie pushed the bench back and stood.

"I have to leave," she whispered to Amanda. "I walked."

"Matilda, you cannot walk home now." Amanda looked out the window. "It's too dark and too cold. John," she said, turning to the group of guests, "would you drive Matilda back to the schoolhouse? She walked and it's far too late for her to walk back."

Everyone in the parlor looked up at John, who showed no reaction to the request. "Of course." He inclined his head a bit. "I wouldn't want our schoolteacher to get lost or ill." He turned toward his daughter. "Elizabeth?"

"May I stay here?" Elizabeth waved toward a girl of the same age. "Agatha is visiting for a few days. She wants me to spend the night with her."

John blinked. Annie guessed he was considering the discomfort of driving alone with the woman who had been so unenthusiastic about his request to court her. No one else seemed to realize his reluctance.

"I'll be fine. I walked here. It isn't far. Please don't leave early. Stay and enjoy the party." Annie hastened to the hall and took her cape from the servant there, scrambling toward the door. Not a very ladylike action, but she wanted to leave quickly. She did not want to be alone with John, not when her attraction for him warred with reality, leaving her so nervous and bewildered.

"Matilda, I must insist," he said from the hall. He wore his solemn expression and his eyes—although not icy—were certainly not warm. "It has become much colder over the hours we spent inside."

Annie opened the door. A gust of icy wind hit her, tugging at her hat and swirling her cape around her. Immediately, her eyes began to water and she shivered. She pulled her hood over her head in an attempt to keep her new hat in place and tried to hold the cape closed with her other hand.

"Amanda has already sent someone to the stable for my carriage. It will be around shortly. Why don't we wait inside in the warmth?"

Annie couldn't see to the end of the drive in the dark, and the cold wind cut to the bone. As much as she hated to do it, she said, "Yes, thank you, John."

Once inside the house again, Annie settled on a bench beside a window while John stood in the entry area and, after taking his coat from the maid, watched for the carriage.

"Why didn't you ask me for a ride to the party?" he said. "Certainly you knew I'd have been happy to stop for you."

"I didn't know if…if it would be comfortable."

"Certainly more comfortable than attempting to walk home on such a cold, windy evening."

"Sometimes I don't plan well." She realized she probably shouldn't have said that. His idea of a teacher probably included the ability to plan well.

"Aah. Exactly the kind of person I like. People who make plans often end up boring, but people who run off in the cold and dark often end up...frozen."

She glanced at him. Had he made a joke? She rather thought he had. She smiled.

For a few seconds, he watched her with the gaze he had turned on her before—warm, but showing as much puzzlement as she felt.

"I believe our transportation has arrived." He opened the door, followed her out and held out his arm to hand her into a covered carriage. Although open in the front, the roof and sides kept the wind off. Once she had settled on the seat, she discovered a warm brick under her feet. What luxury.

After he got in on the other side and accepted the reins from the stable boy, they rode in silence.

"John." She paused in an effort to gather her thoughts. He deserved an explanation for her odd behavior. "John, I'm sorry for my ungracious answer when you asked what...what you asked. You see, I have no experience with this sort of thing." She paused. "I've never received a request to be courted."

"The men from Houston must be very slow."

She heard a note of laughter in his voice.

"Nor have I ever met a man like you."

"What does that mean?" He turned to look at her intently.

"So very upright at times, but so different, so considerate with your daughter, and with animals…and very often with me."

The carriage had reached the road. He didn't say anything while he turned into the drive to the schoolhouse. As they drove again in silence, the carriage felt warm and cozy with just the two of them inside.

"I don't know why you would ask to court me," she said to finally break the silence. "Your question surprised me."

"Did I frighten you again?"

"I wasn't frightened."

"Does it scare you to be alone with me in this carriage?"

She paused to consider that. "Not at all."

No longer was the problem between them fear of him, but fear of what might be between them. How would she react to a deeper relationship with a man—one as good as John? How would she handle the damage from her past? How would he?

He smiled. "I'm glad because I need to ask you something, and this seems like the perfect time." Instead of taking the road to the schoolhouse, he headed toward the ranch. "It's an issue of trust."

"You missed the turn to the schoolhouse," Annie said.

"No, I meant to go this way. As I said, I have a request, a favor to ask you."

Within a few minutes, he pulled up to the stable, handed the reins to Duffy and swung out of the carriage.

"Good evenin', teacher." Duffy nodded at her.

"Good evening, Duffy."

"You going to help that pretty filly out of the carriage or do you want me to?" he asked John.

"I can do this, viejo. You just take care of the horses and keep them ready to go. I'll be back to take Matilda home in a few minutes."

When John put his arm out, Annie placed her hand on it and stepped carefully from the carriage.

"My favor isn't difficult," he said as they walked to the house. Once there, they entered the hallway where Lucia took his coat, gloves and hat, and Annie's cape.

"Please sit down." He waved at a chair as he sat behind the desk. "I believe Elizabeth has told you we'll be leaving Trail's End in mid-January, a few days before the end of the term. We're going to St. Louis to visit my wife's parents, Elizabeth's grandparents."

"A long trip."

"We'll be gone for nearly two weeks." He looked down at his desk, then back at Annie, as if judging her in some way. "Matilda, I don't have an accountant or manager for my ranch. It's not a large spread. I employ only Ramon, Lucia, Miguel and Duffy for the house, and have fifteen cowboys and their foreman in the bunkhouse to take care of the land and cattle."

It sounded like a huge place to her.

"Usually when I go out of town, Farley Hanson takes care of emergencies, especially if they involve money, but Farley plans to spend time in Fredericksburg." He smiled at her. "I wonder if I could prevail upon you to handle any emergency financial issues that come up."

"John, I don't have that much money."

He laughed, a deep, rich sound that pulled her into its warm embrace. "No, I don't expect you to pay. I need to be able to entrust the key to my safe drawer to someone in case there is a need for more money than I'm leaving with Lucia."

"Couldn't Lucia handle this?"

He shook his head. "I wish she could, but I need someone who can write down the withdrawal. None of the people here have that ability." He smiled at her. "I don't believe there's an urgent need for this precaution, but I'll feel better if someone I trust is here to take care of any money required for an emergency."

Someone he could trust? Not a word that had been used to describe Annie often.

"Of course."

He stood and turned to the bookshelves behind him. "I keep one key with me at all times, but the other key is here, in this book." He pulled a massive tome from the shelf, put it on the desk and opened it. "I glued an envelope in the front."

She watched him take the key out and noted the place on the shelf the book had come from. The name of the book was Moby-Dick; or the Whale—an odd title. She hadn't realized people wrote entire books on whales, but then she'd read so little.

He closed the book and handed her the key. "Come around to this side of the desk and let me show you the drawer."

As Annie moved around the desk, he took a few steps back to allow her room. "Put the key in."

When Annie did as requested, the drawer opened. She pulled it out and flipped open a lid to find stacks of money inside. "Oh, my. I've never seen so much. How much is here?"

"More than a thousand. The exact amount is in the account book there." He picked up a book on the corner of his desk. "Precisely two-thousand fifty-three dollars. If you need to withdraw any, please write it here," he said, placing his finger on a column. "And give the reason."

"Why do you need so much money?"

"A rancher can have large, unexpected expenditures. If the boys needed to move the cattle, they have to have expense money. Or if they need to purchase cattle, or if Lucia runs out of food or Ramon needs more feed." He closed the drawer and locked it. "I don't expect any of that. We have an account at the general store and the cattle should be fine. But if there were an emergency, I'd feel better knowing you'd take care of it."

She nodded. "Thank you for trusting me."

He slipped the key back into the book and put it on the shelf. "Now, shall I take you home?"

When he turned, they stood only inches from each other, so close together in that small space behind his desk. For a moment, his gaze tenderly stroked her face. He took her hand.

"You look very lovely tonight," he said in a warm, soft voice. "Are your earrings new?"

She nodded. "Amanda gave them to me."

As she smiled a little self-consciously, he studied her face. "Very pretty." He looked as if he wanted to say more, but then he lifted his eyes and glanced toward the door.

Aah, yes. It was open. She stepped back and broke the connection that had entranced them for a few seconds.

"It's time for me to take you home." He held her hand for a few more seconds before he dropped it. "Lucia," he called. "We'll need our wraps again."

By the time they'd reached the hall, Lucia held up Annie's cape for her to slip inside. Once swathed in their winter garments, he led her toward the stable where Duffy stood with the horses.

"Here they are, boss. I stuck a new hot brick in there, Miss Cunningham."

"Thank you, Duffy."

After carefully assisting Annie into the carriage, John got in on his side and took the reins from the older man. Without a word, he flicked the reins and the horses took off.

They approached the schoolhouse in a comfortable silence. Once there, he pulled the vehicle next to a stand of trees, which sheltered it from the wind and the road. The moonlight shining through the leaves of the live oak trees covered them with lacy shadows. She breathed in the pungency of evergreens, the smell of the leather of the carriage and John's scent of bay rum. An owl called from a tree on the other side of the schoolhouse. Only a second later, an answering hoot came from the meadow.

Warmth radiated from where her arm touched his— only a small area, but the slight heat filled her. It was a perfect moment.

She looked up at him, surprised to see his head bent toward her, so close while they sat in this secluded haven of peace and security.

When he placed his hand over hers, she didn't pull away. They were alone, just the two of them, with the rest of the world far away. Her past, her fear held at bay by the kindness and strength of the man who bent toward her as if all he wanted was to keep her safe, to protect her, to be with her.

"Matilda, it can be no secret how I feel about you. I believe I'm falling in love with you. I would like to know what you think about the two of us together. If you truly don't welcome my attentions, I'll leave you alone, but I've felt this evening a change in you, as if my attention may be appreciated."

She could tell by the ragged edge of his voice, in the yearning she heard, that he didn't want to leave her alone. She said, "I have so little to offer."

He took her hand. "You are beautiful."

"Oh, no. Amanda is. I'm not." She held her hand up when he started to interrupt. "Your wife came from St. Louis, from a good family, I've heard. The Hansons are a good family, and Amanda's rich and beautiful. She's perfect for you." She shook her head. "I'm a mere schoolteacher."

"You should not disagree with a man who tells you you're beautiful." Laughter echoed in his voice. "Besides being beautiful, you're intelligent and a fine teacher. You care about the children, you sing wonderfully, you play the organ and share your gifts with everyone. You're good and innocent and generous." He stopped and studied her face. "Have I left anything out?"

She wanted to move away from him, to escape his compliments, but she couldn't create any space between them in the tiny enclosure. "Oh, no. I'm not all that. I'm not good, not a bit."

"That's what I see, and you are beautiful."

For another minute, they sat next to each other. He slid his arm across her shoulders and kept his hand on hers while the shadow of the moonlight played across his features. Then he lifted her chin with the other hand and whispered, "Now I'm going to kiss you."

Fear stopped up her throat while tears gathered in her eyes.

"I've done it again, haven't I? I've moved too fast." He withdrew his hand from hers. "You're such an innocent. I promise to remember that."

He sounded so sad. "Perhaps a kiss on the cheek?" she whispered. She would like that, she believed. She hoped.

"That would be nice." She heard a smile in his voice. He leaned his head closer to hers until she felt his breath feather across her cheek. Then he placed his lips there for a few seconds.

When he pulled away from her, she placed the palm of her hand over the place that he had kissed.

"Now," he said briskly, "if you don't want another kiss, let me escort you inside before you freeze out here."

She paused for a moment, wondering if another kiss might not be exactly what she'd like, but John had already turned and opened his door. "I can—"

"Of course you can get out of the carriage and walk to the door by yourself, but I enjoy playing the part of a gentleman." He leaped down from the seat and strode to her side, assisting her down, his touch filling her with a glow on this cold evening. He kept hold of her hand and ambled slowly toward the schoolhouse. He stopped at the bottom step and leaned toward her so she could feel his cheek close to hers. "Good night," he whispered in her ear, his words tickling a little.

Dazed, she climbed the steps and let herself inside. As she turned to close the door, she saw him get in the carriage. In a few seconds, it disappeared. Again Annie put her hand against her cheek as if she could feel his kiss there.

The wonder of it all—she had not been frightened by

his nearness or his kiss, not a bit. And he trusted her, enough to show her where he kept that money, all that money, more than she'd ever seen before. He trusted her, which made her want to trust him in return.

After a minute, the world rushed back. No matter what he said or felt, she was not good and beautiful. And she hadn't been an innocent for years. No, she was only Annie. No amount of moonlight or sweet words or kisses would change that, no matter how much she wanted it to. No matter how much she yearned to be good enough for John, she had to remember who she was and what she'd been. Otherwise, she could lose absolutely everything she'd come to love so dearly in Trail's End.

Chapter Thirteen

On January eighth of the new year, Annie watched
the students leave on the last day of fall-term classes.
She had ten days to study before the spring term began.

Elizabeth and John had left a few days earlier to visit
her mother's family in St. Louis. They'd taken a train to
Corsicana, then changed to another headed for St. Louis.
The trip, Elizabeth had explained, would take over three
days each way. "Which," she had added, "leaves us less
than a week to visit with my grandparents but my father
says that is more than enough time to spend with people
he doesn't like anyway."

Probably one of those bits of information John
wished his daughter hadn't shared.

Over two weeks had passed since John had brought
her home from the Christmas party. Other than the few
times he'd come by to collect Elizabeth, she hadn't seen
him. With a sigh, she picked up Minnie, who was me-
owing at her feet for attention. "You are such good company," she said to the cat. Minnie had grown so much
in the months since Annie had found her on the door-
step—she was no longer a little ball of fur.

She settled at the desk with Minnie purring in her lap and turned to the geometry section of the math book. Wilber would be ready to start on it soon. He ate up lessons as if he were starved and, indeed, she believed he was. Staying ahead of him taxed her, but she would use this section when Ida and Martha came back next term.

If Annie were still here next term.

A few hours later, she heard a vehicle stop in the yard. Moments later, Amanda called out to her.

"What do you have planned for this week?" Amanda said as she closed the door behind her. "Anything fun?"

"Studying, as usual." She pushed the book away.

"How do you plan to celebrate Valentine's Day with the students?"

"Valentine's Day? What is that? When is it?" Annie frowned.

"February fourteenth. How could you not know?"

"We didn't celebrate it where I'm from. I don't even know what it is."

"It's the day when we tell people how much we love them. I always give my father a present."

"Like Christmas?"

"Not as grand and not at all religious. It's really just for fun. Let me show you something." Amanda reached in her purse and handed a piece of paper to Annie.

On the front of a folded page were two layers of paper lace with flowers around the edges. "This is lovely," Annie said. "What is it?" She turned the page over. "Where did you get it?"

"It's a Valentine's Day card. They're very popular in the East. A friend sent it to me." She opened it up. "She wrote a verse inside."

"Friends are life's greatest gift," Annie read. "That's so true."

"Do you want me to come and help the students make cards with you?"

"They'd really enjoy that. You made decorating so much fun at Christmas." Annie studied the card and ran her hand over the lace. "Do you have plans for this Valentine's Day?"

"I'll make my last attempt on the sheriff."

"Your last attempt? You're giving up?"

"I can't tell you what I'm going to do, but if my plan doesn't win the man, I am going to give up." She looked at an unconvinced Annie. "Really, I am. Truly. The spectacle of my chasing the sheriff while he runs the other direction has become entirely too mortifying. My failures have completely destroyed my confidence."

"Miss Cunningham, you have a letter."

Annie was in the mercantile, her work for the day finished. After completing a few purchases, she was admiring a piece of fabric.

A letter? Probably from Miss Palfrey, which was not good news. She hated deceiving Miss Cunningham's friend.

"I recognize the handwriting. It's from John Sullivan," Mr. Johnson said.

The grocer's words made her heart beat faster. She took the letter from his hand and noted John's clear handwriting. Why would he do such an improper thing as to write her a letter? "Must be something about school," Annie said.

"Must be."

Even if Mr. Johnson didn't seem the least bit con-

cerned about the scandal of a single man writing an
unmarried woman, Annie was. But she had to read the
letter. It came from John, after all.

Once outside the store, Annie tore the envelope open
and scanned the words.

> My Dear Matilda,
> Although I know it is not proper to write you, I
> can't stop myself. I have not been able to talk to
> you since Christmas and have missed you. Please
> know that I hold you in my deepest affection and
> will see you when we return home.
> Yours, John

When she reached the schoolhouse, Annie settled
on a chair and read the epistle again and again, touching the thick strokes of the pen, running her finger over
his signature. "I hold you in my deepest affection," she
read aloud, and smiled.

"What do you hear from your friend Miss Hanson?"
The sheriff sat on the bench outside the schoolhouse
and watched the children playing with battledores and
shuttlecocks on a sunny and unusually warm afternoon
in late January.

Annie pulled her gaze away from the students to
glance at him. "Why do you ask, Sheriff?"

He studied the children more intently. "I haven't seen
her in a few weeks. That concerns me.

"Who knows what she might get into that pretty
head?" He stretched his legs. "She hasn't approached
me lately. I don't sleep at night, wondering what she
might be planning."

"Why, Sheriff Bennett. I believe you pine for Miss Hanson's attention."

He didn't look at her, but a muscle in his cheek tensed.

"You do find her attractive."

He shook his head. "Doesn't matter if I do. Her father wouldn't allow me to court her. Some things in life you just have to accept."

"But you do find her attractive."

He leaned forward on the bench and smiled at her. "Miss Cunningham, if there's a man in Texas who doesn't find Miss Hanson beautiful, he must either be dead, blind or too stupid to survive out here. She's one of nature's finest works." He stood. "And you'd better not tell your pretty friend anything I said because I'll deny it and that would make her unhappy."

Annie grinned as he stood and ambled toward his horse. She'd love to see the final showdown between Amanda and Sheriff Bennett. No doubt existed in her mind who would win—Amanda was determined and the sheriff wasn't dead, blind or stupid.

He turned back to Annie and shook his head. "I'm too old to play games like this. That's what you can tell her."

"You can tell her yourself, but I don't think you will. It seems she's finally breaking down your resistance."

"I'm hardly any young woman's dream man. I'm old and used up and ugly." He touched the scar for an instant.

"Sheriff, you are far from ugly. Clearly Amanda thinks you are the handsomest man in Trail's End."

He grinned for a second at her reply. "Certainly you

have to admit I'm hardly the stuff a young woman's dreams are made of."

"One young woman seems to believe you are, Sheriff."

He stared at Annie for a moment, and then mounted his horse and left without a reply. Annie could hardly wait for Valentine's Day.

Annie awakened to knocking on the door of the schoolhouse and shook her head. She must have fallen asleep at her desk. It was late at night and the sound startled her. Who on earth could it be?

"Matilda?"

It sounded like Mr. Sullivan. Why would he be here? She stood and started toward the door in the flickering light of the oil lamp.

"It's John Sullivan."

She opened the door. "Hello, John." She smiled at the sight of him. "Welcome back. Is everything all right? Is there an emergency?"

"I'm sorry to bother you." He looked at her, taking in her hair, which she knew must be standing up at odd angles, and her face, which probably had deep marks on her cheek from the edges of her books.

She put her hands up in an effort to tidy the mess, but he took them in his grasp and held them.

"I shouldn't be here, but I've missed you." He smiled.

She couldn't help but smile back. Then she yawned.

"Were you studying?"

"Until I fell asleep. Where have you been? Elizabeth has been back in school for days."

"I've been away on business. When we returned from St. Louis, I received a telegram that I was needed in Austin to deal with a legal matter about the boundaries of the ranch." He stopped and studied her face. After half a minute, he continued. "I brought Elizabeth home, then took a coach that was leaving for the capital immediately. It all happened so quickly, I didn't have a chance to tell you. I feared writing another letter would cause gossip and speculation."

"Boss, you ready to go?" Duffy called from the shadows. "I'm an old man and getting cold."

"Duffy picked me up in town. The stage arrived late."

She nodded. "Are you all right? Is someone sick?"

"No." He continued to scrutinize her. "I wanted to see you. That's all. It's been so long."

She could hear the affection in his voice. As usual, she didn't know how to respond.

"I'm attempting to guard your reputation, although it would be done better if I hadn't come by." He laughed softly. "El viejo has never been a chaperone before. But if anyone finds out I've visited you this late, he can say that nothing improper happened."

"But he might tell—"

"No, Duffy knows better than that." He gazed at her for a few moments more without speaking. "I just wanted to see you," he whispered. "Only for a minute, but I had to see you. I've missed you." He touched her cheek softly. "Good night, my dear."

"Good night, John."

"Boss, I'm really…"

He reluctantly dropped her hand before he headed down the steps and toward the surrey on the other side of the grove of trees.

What had just happened? And where had the usually solemn, upright John Matthew Sullivan gone? She smiled. She liked the lighthearted John she'd met before. Perhaps, she'd find a way to spend more time with him.

On Thursday afternoon, both Miguel and Wilber worked in the schoolroom.

"Very well done," Annie told Miguel as he copied his spelling words. Lucia smiled. She was learning a great deal while she watched her son.

"Miss Cunningham." Wilber closed his science book and put it on the desk. "I'm going to have to leave now. My brothers and I won't be back the rest of the week." He stood, carried the book to the shelf and paused by her desk, his large frame towering over her.

"Why not, Wilber?" She got to her feet.

Wilber shrugged. "We have to dig a new well for the livestock. The old one dried up." He shook his head. "If we don't get some rain soon, we're going to lose crops and livestock. But what really scares us is the possibility of prairie fires."

"But it's only February, Wilber. Surely we'll have some rain soon."

"The drought started in May, ma'am. It's going to take a lot of rain to make any difference." He turned and headed toward the back door.

"Do you want to take a book with you?" she asked.

"No, but thank you. I won't have time. I'll miss being here."

"We'll miss you, too, Wilber." After Wilber left, Lucia rose. "We need to go, mi hijo, my son."

"Please, no, Mamá. I'm in the middle of answering questions about a story." He kept his eyes on the book.

"This drought," Annie said. "It's really bad?"

Lucia nodded. "We had another like it six years ago. Mr. Sullivan worries. Up north, they're getting some rain so the streams are running fairly well. As long as that keeps up, the cattle will be fine. But the crops suffer, and the grass and shrubs that feed the cattle, and the dry trees—all that could go up in flames any minute."

"Hello?" John stood in the door of the school. "A word, please?" His gaze settled on Miguel and Lucia.

"Mr. Sullivan," Lucia said, curtsying. "Come along, Miguel." She took her son's hand and hurried him away.

With the exception of church and evening meetings, Annie hadn't seen John since he'd come by that late evening in January. She didn't understand his inconsistent courting—was this how it was done?

Annie stood next to her desk. "Hello, John." He had obviously assumed his identity as member of the school board, serious and solemn. His expression worried her.

He frowned and said, "I have something serious I need to talk to you about."

She nodded.

"I'd heard something but I didn't know if it were true. But now...you're teaching Miguel?"

"Yes. Lucia comes to chaperone while Wilber is getting his extra lessons. Miguel comes with her."

"Matilda, you were not hired by the school board to give Wilber extra work or to teach Miguel."

"I don't mind. Wilber's making up lessons he's missed because he helps his father. He's so smart. I wish he could go to high school. He'd be a wonderful teacher."

"As you know, such a future is not possible, but Wilber is not the problem we need to discuss."

"What is the problem?" She thought for a moment.

"Certainly you can't mean Miguel? You believe I shouldn't teach Miguel?"

"Not at all. I wish every child in the county could afford to come to school. I'd like to have to build a bigger school and hire another teacher. My dream is to have this school overrun with the children of the community—all the children."

"John, that's wonderful. That's my dream, too."

"Farley and I are concerned about the children who can't afford tuition, or who have to work to help their families. We're discussing solutions."

"I should have known you would do all that," she said.

"I support your teaching Miguel, but I have to pass on some concerns of the community. There are those who believe Miguel should not be in school."

"Why not? Because he's Mexican?"

"A few people have complained."

"I'm paid to teach from seven-thirty to two-thirty for two terms of three months each. Isn't that correct?"

He nodded.

"Who I teach the other hours of the day is nobody else's business."

"You don't have to argue with me." He held his hand up as if deflecting her barely concealed anger. "But some members of the community would argue that you teach in a building owned by the board. As such it is the concern of the school board."

She sat down, so sickened by the reminder of the prejudice she'd fought all her life that her stomach churned. She did not want Miguel to go through that. "Does the school board want me to stop teaching Miguel?" she asked calmly, wanting to avoid a confrontation if possible. "Do you expect me to stop teaching Miguel?" she asked, her voice soft as she reminded herself that she needed John's support to keep her position.

"No. I'm just telling you what a few people have told me."

She stood, leaning on the desk to steady herself. "John, I'm a teacher. I'm supposed to teach. It's very much like a call from God." She stopped, amazed at her words. She'd never considered that before, but it felt right and true. "It truly is a call from God. If I continue to teach Miguel, will I be fired?"

"No, I just felt you needed to know that there has been discussion."

"Will the school board support me?"

"I'm not sure. But I do, after all, have some influence."

"I must teach him, even if the school board threatens to fire me." Those were the hardest words she'd ever spoken.

"Matilda, I will try to make sure the school board supports you. If there are consequences, I'll do my best to shield you."

"Thank you." She put her hand on her chest and felt her heart beating. "I was so frightened," she whispered.

"And yet you fought for Miguel."

Yes, she had, and the fact astonished her. She'd never stood up for herself before, but she'd found the strength to stand up for Miguel. Where had it come from?

But she knew. The courage came from God, who wanted her to teach. How she'd arrived here at this school, she didn't understand. She didn't believe God killed one woman so another would become a teacher. She just knew that she'd found God and been able to use the twists and turns of life to discover where she could and should serve.

She sat down, her legs no longer able to support her after the confrontation.

"Matilda, are you ill?" John knelt next to her chair.

Although she felt cold all over, when she put her hand on her cheek, it was hot. The physical reaction overwhelmed her because conflict scared her, and yet she had done it. Thank You, God. After several deep breaths, her head had stopped spinning and her heart had calmed down.

"I'm fine." And she was. "Discussing this with you wasn't easy for me."

"May I tell you how much I respect you for taking that stand?" He took her hand. "I can see that it was not easy for you."

For a moment, his eyes caressed her face. "May I also explain why I have not come to see you?" He settled on a bench. "An emergency came up, one I thought I'd settled before. I had to go out of town again." He shook his head. "There's something strange going on with that parcel of land. A question of ownership. That's why I had to go to Austin again."

"Did it turn out as you wanted?"

"It took longer than I would have expected, but I hope this time it has been resolved." He smiled. "And now I'm home."

His voice and his words suggested she was an important part of his pleasure in being home.

"When I'm away, I miss you." He shook his head. "I've never understood men who could not control their emotions, but now I do. I didn't mean to care for you, Matilda—in fact, I fought it." He gave an odd little laugh. "Now I find myself in an uncomfortable situation by wishing to spend time with you but not wanting to place your reputation in peril."

She tilted her head in an effort to understand where his thoughts had taken him.

"If I come down to the schoolhouse too often, even as isolated as it is, people will notice and talk." He shook his head. "I need to consider your circumstances, both how to court you and how to protect you."

"Can that be done?"

"I don't know, but I'll think about it. Please be assured that your reputation is safe with me, that I'll do nothing—like that foolish visit the other evening when I could not stay away from you—without due consideration."

He strode toward the door but turned when he got there. For a moment, he gazed at her as if he held her face tenderly in his hands and caressed it, as if he kissed her gently, as if he softly touched her lips with his finger.

And then he left, closing the door behind him. She heard him descend the steps, mount his horse and ride off, but even when she no longer heard the sound of hoofbeats, she still felt the phantom touch of his hand lightly stroking her face and the whisper of his breath against her cheek.

Chapter Fourteen

Amanda stood outside the door to the sheriff's office feeling a little foolish.

If the sheriff did not fall at her feet, if he didn't swear undying love—although she couldn't imagine in a hundred years that he would—she'd stop chasing him. Taking a deep breath, Amanda opened the door and walked inside. The sheriff sat at his desk working on some papers. Although he barely even glanced up at her, his scowl showed he wasn't pleased to see her.

Nevertheless, she squared her shoulders. "Good morning, Sheriff Bennett."

"Mornin', Miss Hanson." He nodded.

Why was she doing this when she knew he'd reject her? For a moment, she considered turning around, going home and giving up. But he looked up at her and that rugged face and level stare made her heart flutter.

"How can I help you, Miss Hanson?" His voice was polite but disinterested.

"Happy Valentine's Day." She took off her cape to reveal a lacy white dress trimmed in pink feather hearts.

For a moment, his grim expression softened as he

drank in the sight before him. His eyes moved from the pink roses twined in her hair all the way down the frilly dress to her white shoes tied with pink ribbons.

"Very, very pretty, Miss Hanson. I guess you're looking to flirt with some handsome young man. Don't have any here."

"No, Sheriff, I'm here to charm you."

He laughed and went back to reading the papers on the desk.

That's exactly what she'd predicted he'd do, but if the man thought he could get away from her so easily, he didn't know Amanda Hanson at all. As fast as dry lightning could start a blaze on the prairie, Amanda opened his desk drawer and pulled out his keys. Once she had her prize, she ran into a cell and slammed the door behind her. She put her hand through the bars and locked the door before she pranced to the hard bench next to the wall and sat down. Victory!

Stunned, the sheriff didn't move at first. Then he stood and ambled toward the cell. "What do you think you're doing, Miss Hanson?"

"Sheriff Bennett, you have ignored me since you came here a year ago." She stood and walked to the cell door. "I have tried every flirtatious trick I know to get you to notice me. You refused."

"You're wrong. I noticed every one. I just didn't fall for any of them."

She stamped her foot. "Oh, you're such a difficult man." She threw herself on the bench again. "I decided to lock myself up in your jail until you give in and court me."

"Is this the most romantic scheme you could come up with?" A smile tickled his lips.

"I've used up all the romantic schemes. I'm desperate now."

"Because you have found the one man in Texas who refuses to fall in love with you."

"You make me sound silly."

He raised an eyebrow in response.

"I…" She turned away. "I'm not playing now. This started as a game, but I discover I like you, very much."

"Why? Because I'm such a handsome man? Valiant and courageous."

She stood, closed the space between them and placed each hand on a bar. "As sheriff, of course you are valiant and courageous, as well as tough and rugged, which I find—much to my surprise, I must tell you—very attractive."

"I'm older than you, Miss Hanson, years older. I've lived a hard life and have nothing to offer a spoiled little girl."

"Now, see, if you didn't care about me, you wouldn't call me a spoiled little girl. You use that to discourage me." She smiled. "I don't discourage easily, and, although my father has given me everything I want, that does not make me spoiled."

"I'm forty years old. Double your age. More than twenty years of my life were spent as a hired gun. Not the kind of background a loving father would choose for his darling daughter's husband."

"Sheriff." She held his glance in hers. "Your attempts to reason your way out of this tête-à-tête convince me even more that you do care about me."

With that, he reached into his pocket and pulled out his key ring.

She blinked. "What is that?"

"This would be a pretty poor jail if we had only one set of keys, wouldn't it?" He stuck the key in the lock and opened the door. "Miss Hanson, why don't you go home so I can work?"

"No." Haughtily, she sat down on the bench. "I don't need to lock myself up. I'll stay in here even with the door wide-open."

"No, you cannot. This is my jail." The sheriff strode into the cell, picked her up and attempted to carry her out. He had not considered the vast petticoats under her dress or her strength. Every time he started through the cell door, she used her hands or her legs to stay inside while her ruffles covered his face so he couldn't see where he was going.

After a few minutes, sweat rolled down his body and pink feathers stuck to his neck and face. "You are harder to rope than an angry heifer and more trouble than an unbroken colt."

He tried a few more times before admitting defeat. "All right," he finally said. "You can stay here." He dumped her on the bench, picked up both sets of keys, left the cell and locked it behind him.

"You're locking me in?"

"Just until you father gets here."

"My father." She closed her eyes and leaned against the wall. "Why do you have to bring my father into this?"

"Isn't speaking to your father the proper action?" He wiped his face and hands with a towel.

With that, he left the office, leaving her locked inside the cell in her Valentine's Day dress, feathers floating around and roses tumbling from her rumpled locks.

She sincerely hoped no hardened criminals wandered in.

Half an hour later, she heard horses pull up in front of the jail, followed by the opening of the door.

"You have a dangerous felon in your cell?" her father said. "What do you want me to do?"

"I believe when you see who that felon is, you'll understand."

She buried her face in the froth of white lace.

"Amanda, is that you?"

She looked up.

"My daughter is a felon?"

"Well, Mr. Hanson, one definition of a felony is breaking and entering. I don't know if that covers stealing a set of keys from the sheriff's desk and locking herself in a cell."

Amanda's father looked at the sheriff. "My daughter took your keys and locked herself in a cell?" He slowly turned to study Amanda, shaking his head. "I spoiled you. I gave you too much. Bennett," he said, and turned back toward the sheriff, "on her deathbed, her mother made me promise to take care of Amanda." He shook his head again. "I tried. I cannot account for this."

"Father," Amanda began, "I can explain." But the more she thought about it, the more she decided she really couldn't. She buried her head in her dress again.

"Sounds as if she may need another man to take over, one who is not daunted by the difficulties and dangers that life with her seems to promise."

Amanda stood up and marched to the bars. "Another man to take over?"

"Miss Hanson has stated that she'd like to marry me."

Her father fell onto a chair. "I never thought she'd be so forward. I do apologize."

"What would your response be if I were to ask you permission to marry your daughter?"

Her father clutched his chest and seemed to be having a heart attack.

"Father, are you all right?"

After he took a few deep, shuddering breaths, he said, "You'd do that? You'd take my daughter off my hands? I warn you, as much as I love her, she's a bothersome filly. She gets something in her mind and no one can change it."

"Father!"

"Yes, sir. I'm aware she's a bothersome, stubborn filly."

"Sheriff!"

"But, Mr. Hanson, I have become one of those ideas that she won't change her mind about." He shrugged. "She's made my life hard, but if she's determined to marry me, we should probably just go ahead."

Fanning himself with his handkerchief, her father stood and walked to the cell. "Is the sheriff right? Do you want to marry him?"

She flounced toward the bench and threw herself on it. "I don't have the least desire to marry someone who says I am bothersome and stubborn." Tears began to seep from her eyes.

"Mr. Hanson, before I attempt to persuade your daughter to marry me, would you be agreeable to such a match?" the sheriff asked.

"Sheriff, I've waited years to find a man to marry her. She's turned down every single one. My daughter is my only family. There's no one to inherit the ranch.

As long as I've known you, I've been impressed by your hard work and honesty. I'd be very happy if you would marry her and take over the ranch when I'm gone. Hold it in trust for your children."

She reached her hand through the bars. "Father, you're not dying soon."

"No, but it's going to happen someday." He extended his hand to the sheriff and glanced at his daughter. "She doesn't look happy with you now, but if you can persuade her, she's yours and so is the ranch."

Amanda watched in amazement as they sealed the deal. A handshake between men, that's what she'd become. She wiped the tears from her cheeks with the hem of her dress, only to discover lace did not absorb tears well at all.

"Good day and good luck, Sheriff Bennett." Her father closed the door behind him, leaving her in the cell while the sheriff watched from a few feet away.

"Please let me out," she said in a small voice. "I'm sorry I've bothered you. I'll never bother you again. I promise."

"Does that mean we won't be getting married?"

"That's exactly what it means." Suddenly angry at his teasing, she leaped to her feet, took two steps to the door and grasped the bars. "Let me out of here now," she shouted.

He unlocked the door but pushed her back inside and then locked the cell behind him, and tossed both sets of keys out between the bars.

"Why did you do that?" Her head snapped up to study his face.

"I thought you might need a few minutes to cool off,

and I didn't want you getting away before we came to an agreement."

She took a few steps back until she ran into the bars on the other side of the cell. "An agreement about what?"

"Our wedding."

"But you don't want to marry me."

"I've wanted to marry you ever since the first time we met, but I told myself I didn't have the right." He took a step closer to her.

"I never..." She couldn't move any farther.

He took another step.

"What changed your mind?" she asked in a breathy voice.

"Well, you seem absolutely determined to marry me, and I would hate to disappoint you."

She wanted to argue with him, but she couldn't. Instead, she allowed him to lean closer, dizzy with the nearness of him.

"That kind of determination deserves a reward. Besides, I've always had a weakness for a forward little flirt. I just never thought your father would agree to my courting you. When you locked yourself in my jail, I decided that would show him the peril my life was in and he'd agree, if only to avoid the scandal." He put his arms around her and searched her face. "Do you truly love me or has this all been a game?"

"I love you," she whispered. "I've never said that before, to any man."

He nodded. "Will you marry me?"

She narrowed her eyes. "So that you can have the ranch?"

"Now that you mention it—"

She kicked him in the shin. He smiled at her.

"Because I love you more than I thought possible," he whispered.

"Oh."

"I don't want the ranch for myself. Your father wants it held in trust for our—" he paused to clear his throat "—for our children, Amanda." He studied her face for a moment, his eyes full of yearning. "Will you please marry me?"

She nodded and he finally kissed her. Kissing was something the sheriff did very well, which didn't surprise her one bit.

Then he pulled out another key ring and opened the door.

"Where did you get that?"

"You don't think I'd enter a cell with a very angry woman and not have a means of escape, did you?"

"Well." She took his arm and held it firmly. "I'd hoped, perhaps, we could spend a little more time here." She gave him the smile she'd learned he could not resist. "To discuss the wedding, you know."

"Hello, hello!" Amanda shouted from outside. Annie heard her phaeton stop and the jingle of the harness as her friend tossed the reins onto the seat.

It was Saturday morning. Did Amanda have more to tell her about her campaign to win the sheriff?

"Matilda?" Amanda called from the door.

"I'm right here." Annie stacked the slates and stood, wondering what had sparked such excitement in her friend's eyes. Indeed, Amanda almost flew around the classroom with the grace and splendor of a butterfly.

"Tell me. What is it?"

Amanda stopped and put her hands to her mouth for a moment as tears came to her eyes. "I'm getting married."

"What?" Annie stared. "The sheriff?" Annie nodded her head. "But I can't imagine he'd ask you to marry him or that your father would approve."

"He did and he did. In fact, they both did." Amanda threw her arms in the air and laughed.

"Isn't it wonderful?"

Annie gave her friend a hug. "Tell me everything!"

Amanda settled on a bench and regaled Annie with one of the funniest tales she'd ever heard. She was amazed by Amanda's boldness and wished she could have seen the sheriff's reaction.

"Oh, my." Annie shook her head in disbelief. "How is the sheriff? Has he recovered?"

"He's very happy." Amanda laughed.

"You're exactly the right woman for him. I'm glad he finally figured that out." As she'd predicted, the man had never stood a chance against a force of nature like Amanda.

"I'm not sure he even realizes what happened, but I don't care." Amanda wiggled on the bench. "Now let me tell you all the plans. We'll be getting married the next time Reverend Thompson is here."

"So soon?"

Amanda sighed and squeezed her friend's hand. "Oh, yes. That soon."

Chapter Fifteen

Annie brushed down the new gray skirt Lucia had made her and tugged the collar of the white basque. The earrings Amanda had given her swung merrily. With a twist, she wound her thick hair into a bun on top of her head, stuck in several hairpins and smoothed the sides back. Her hair had grown in the nearly five months she'd been in Trail's End, as had her wardrobe. Now the owner of four skirts and seven tops, she felt very stylish. With stockings to go with her two pairs of shoes, a new petticoat, two plain cotton nightgowns and a pretty shawl, she had nearly filled her dresser. And she had a nice amount of money in the bank.

She hadn't seen John in a week, not since Amanda's wedding. But he'd sent a note with Ramon telling her he'd be by early this evening.

But she was ready early, had planned that because she needed some time in prayer. She patted her hair once again, then entered the schoolroom and sat on the bench next to the large window overlooking the grove of trees behind the building.

"Loving and forgiving God," she began. She paused,

studying the scene outside. The trees were beginning to bud with that pale, sweet greenness that announced the coming of spring and birds flitted through the branches. "Dear God, You have give me so much. Please help me find one more thing—the wisdom to know what to do next." She dropped her face in her hands to listen. If she'd learned anything besides what she'd picked up from all the books she'd studied, it was how little patience she possessed, how difficult she found it to listen for the leading of her Lord and her Savior. She slowed her breathing and bowed her head, waiting.

"Matilda?"

Feeling quieted and filled, she turned toward John.

"I knocked and called but no one answered so I came in." He looked down at her for a moment with a hint of a frown.

"I'm sorry." Should she explain? She hated to discuss her faith. Of course, she couldn't discuss it with most people. They wouldn't understand how God had changed her. With John, she worried that saying she'd been praying might sound...well, pretentious, but how else could she account for her behavior? "I didn't hear you because I was praying."

He sat on the bench in front of her and looked into her eyes. "You were praying? Do you pray a lot?"

She smiled. "I don't know what a lot means. I pray when I feel the need, when I am overwhelmed or happy or worried or... I don't know. I pray whenever I need to."

John considered that. "Does God always answer you?"

"I don't know yet."

"Well, if you don't know if God answers you," he said, "why do it?"

"I've learned God's response may not be immediate. And because God has given me courage and strength and hope and forgiveness every time I pray." She looked into his eyes. "Doesn't that happen when you pray?"

"I don't pray a lot."

"But you go to church every Sunday."

"Yes, but I go to be an example. Faith," he said, "hasn't been that important to me."

"I'm sorry," she said, surprised by his admission.

"But I'm not here to discuss faith," John said decisively as he took her hand and stood. "Why don't we go outside?" He led her to the spot where she often watched the children at play.

Once he sat down next to her, his voice and his expression became serious. "Matilda, do you know how much I care about you?"

She nodded.

"When I can work in a few minutes to see you, I feel as if I'm sneaking around."

That would be hard on a man as principled as John.

"I can think of only one way to be together." He stood and walked a few feet away before turning back, his hands behind his back and his expression even more solemn. "Farley tells me Amanda and the sheriff will be having an 'at home' on Saturday. I'd like to escort you."

"What?" The idea astonished her. "But, if you do that, if we go together, people will think we're courting. They'll know how we feel."

He laughed. "Yes, that's what I hope."

"But this is so…so personal." Could she express this more clearly without hurting his feelings? How could she explain the fact that she did want him to court her and her reluctance to tell the world? "I've always been a private person."

He sat beside her and seemed to think about his words before he spoke. "I'm tired of seeing you only now and then. I want to be with you more, and I want everyone to know that we're together."

She'd both feared and hoped this would happen. Because John had such strong principles, hiding their relationship would eat away at him, deception would wound him.

She'd been through so much. After such a life, didn't she deserve happiness finally? After going through such horror and turmoil, didn't she finally deserve to be loved and cared for?

Looking into John's eyes, she saw that his solemn facade only disguised his vulnerability and yearning. She couldn't turn him down. She'd deal with the problems her response might bring later, but not now.

"I'd like that."

The joy on John's face convinced her she'd made the right decision. He let out a deep breath, smiling broadly.

"You've made me a happy man." He leaned forward and put his cheek next to hers. "I'll be by tomorrow evening at eight." As he spoke, his words tickled her ear. Reluctantly, he stood and looked at her, love shining in his eyes. "Goodbye, my love," he said.

She watched him leave, noticing a lightheartedness in his step as he ran toward Orion and mounted. After she could no longer see him, she closed the door.

She smiled again. She now understood what love meant, and she realized that she had been in love with him for some time. Why John cared for her she couldn't guess, but he did and she wouldn't argue with him about that.

* * *

The sheriff never stopped smiling. He looked like a different man during the visit he and Amanda made on Friday, the day after their return from their wedding trip.

"I don't intimidate anyone anymore," he said as he sat beside his wife outside the schoolhouse. "This town's going to be overrun by thieves and killers, vicious men, heartless criminals and the dregs of humanity, all cheering because Sheriff Cole Bennett has fallen in love."

"And you don't mind at all." After patting the sheriff on the arm, Amanda turned to speak to Annie. "Cole bought the sweetest little house for us. Daddy had moved us in while we were gone."

"Little is the important word. There's barely enough room for two—not much space for her huge wardrobe or all those shoes and wraps and hats and gewgaws."

"Who needs all that when I have you?" Amanda teased. He smiled at her. "We stopped by to make sure you know about the at home we're having at my father's house tomorrow."

"Yes, I do." It was, Annie realized with not a little trepidation, time to tell Amanda. "John will take me."

"John?" Amanda tilted her head. "John Sullivan?" Her eyes brows shot up. "John will take you?" When Annie nodded, then she leaned forward. "Are you and John courting?"

Annie nodded.

"Well, my, my, my." Amanda leaned back against her husband's arm. "When did this happen?"

"Little by little, over a few weeks. I'm not sure I realized it."

"I swan! Are you happy? Well, of course you are." She turned toward her husband. "Cole, would you please go check on the horses? I need to talk to Annie."

"Bossiest woman in Texas," he said with a grin as he moved toward the carriage.

"Tell me everything," Amanda said.

"John and I felt an attraction for each other, and he asked to court me." She leaned closer to Amanda. "Now, you tell me all about marriage. Is it marvelous?"

"Oh, Annie." Amanda sighed. "It's the most magnificent thing in the world. I'm so happy and so in love and Cole is amazing and he loves me." A giddy smile covered her face. "There's a lot it wouldn't be proper for me to tell an unmarried woman, but being married is wonderful if you're married to a man who really loves you."

With that Amanda leaped to her feet, pulled Annie up and gave her a quick hug. "We'll see you—and John—tomorrow," she said as she ran to join her husband.

Annie watched her friends drive off. She'd never known two people who truly loved each other and made each other happy. She'd thought her parents had been happy once, but she didn't remember exactly. Could a happy marriage have disappeared so quickly and left behind a person as miserable as her father?

Annie believed it was possible for a marriage to work. Perhaps love could be enough to bring two different people together. Maybe love could build a bridge between them.

She could only hope it did.

Saturday night when Annie and John arrived at the Hanson home, luminarias lined the drive crowded with carriages and horses. Candles sparkled in every window and guests ambled around the front porch and the side garden, the sound of their voices mingling with the music coming through the open windows.

She put her hand on her skirt to smooth out wrinkles that she knew were not there. Although Lucia had made sure her white cashmere basque and blue skirt looked perfect, Annie knew the other women were dressed much more formally and grandly in satin and lace with bustles and jewelry and other fashionable accessories.

"You're the most beautiful woman in the county," John whispered to her as he helped her from the surrey, seemingly reading her thoughts.

Annie put her hand to the top of the high-necked basque. Out of place, that was how she would look, the schoolteacher on the arm of John Matthew Sullivan. If a groom hadn't already taken the carriage away, she would've climbed right back on it and gone home.

Perhaps she could escape before anyone noticed she was there.

He took her hand and placed it on his arm. "Shall we?"

Clinging to him, Annie realized it was very good to be courted by a man so strong, a man whose arm felt sturdy and protective and comforting beneath her hand.

"John and Matilda," Amanda said as they approached the receiving line. "It's my good friend, Matilda Cunningham, the schoolteacher." Amanda spoke the words clearly and in a voice loud enough for guests in the farthest garden to hear.

When her friend leaned down and whispered, "You'll be fine," Annie realized she must have looked as frightened as she felt. She lifted her chin, straightened her back and vowed not to embarrass John, although she'd much prefer to run or hide. After all, hadn't Amanda just told everyone there that they were friends? That she belonged at the party?

"Miss Cunningham, how nice to see you and John." A very courtly Farley Hanson bowed over her hand. "I don't believe you have met my friend Sara Harper from Fredericksburg."

John continued to escort her around the room, greeting people and keeping her hand on his arm to show everyone that Annie was with him. Little by little, she relaxed and chatted with friends. When they returned from a walk in the gardens, a small orchestra had begun to play again in the large parlor and couples were beginning to gather.

"If you would join me for the first dance," Mr. Hanson said with another bow.

"I don't know how to dance," Annie whispered. The girls in the brothel had had to learn dances to entertain the gentlemen, but she was quite sure those were not the dances polite society performed.

"The first dance will be a turning waltz. I'll show you exactly what to do." He took her hand and led her into the parlor. "We'll allow the happy couple to start the dance. When you and I join them, that will signal for the others to follow."

"Mr. Hanson, you do me such an honor. Thank you."

"Nonsense," he said. "John is my friend."

Mr. Hanson did exactly as he'd said he would. With his hand resting on her back, he lightly guided her. Mistakes were not obvious in the crowd of dancers, fortunately.

When they finished the waltz, John claimed her for a

schottische. Although she realized she knew this dance, she allowed him to show her the slides, hops and turns because she enjoyed his attention. After that, Mr. Johnson invited her to polka, and she joined a visiting Hanson relative from San Antonio in a reel. By then, Annie had lost her reticence and enjoyed every dance.

John appeared next to her and offered his arm. "I'm a fortunate man," he whispered to her. "Every man here is jealous that I arrived with the loveliest woman on my arm."

Annie grabbed his arm and held on to it, grateful he'd found her.

"May I suggest a cooling walk in the garden?" John asked. "You've been dancing for hours."

"Thank you, John. I've had the most wonderful time."

Many of the guests had begun to leave and the garden was nearly deserted. As they walked past a trellis in the far corner, John pulled Annie behind it.

"Now that I have you alone," he said, "I'd like to kiss you."

Annie closed her eyes. She didn't want to kiss him. She'd be crushed if she discovered she didn't like it. But surely she could do it to make him happy. It was so little to ask.

"Matilda, may I kiss you?"

Taking a deep breath, she nodded. John lifted her chin gently and rested his lips on hers for only a few seconds. His kiss was sweet and loving. It warmed her and she melted against him.

When he lifted his head, she whispered, "That was the first time." The first time she'd enjoyed a kiss and wanted another. The first time a man hadn't frightened her with his touch.

They left the party soon after. She fell asleep with her head on John's shoulder and laughed when he woke her by carrying her to the door.

"Matilda, I have something more I would like to ask you," he said, his voice sounding rough and uncertain. He cleared his throat as they stood in the doorway.

Reaching up to touch his face, she could feel tension in his jaw.

"Would you marry me?" He held his hand up. "I know I should ask a male relative for permission first, but I don't believe you have any. Is that correct?"

She nodded, not that she'd have wanted John to meet her father even if he had still been alive.

Marry him? Being close to him filled her with breathless joy and made her feel sparkly inside, as if she'd swallowed a star. She opened her mouth to answer but had no idea what to say. She wanted to say yes. Didn't she have a right to be happy? Didn't John? She'd make him happy—she'd do everything in her power to make him happy. He was her rock, her strength. The answer seemed very simple.

"Yes, I'll marry you." She beamed at him.

He leaned down and kissed her again, which made her shiver with pleasure. There could be no happier person in the entire world than Annie.

"I have something for you." He reached in his pocket and took out something small. "It's a claddagh ring that's been in my family for a hundred years."

She rubbed her finger along the gold and felt a heart and a crown.

"My great-great grandfather gave it to his intended." He slipped it on her finger. "The message of the ring is, 'Let love reign.'"

"Thank you, John," she whispered. "It's lovely."

"I have one more request." He paused. "I haven't talked to Elizabeth about this yet. If you don't mind, would you wait until Monday to wear the ring? I know she'll be happy, but I need to…well, let her know."

"Of course." What did one more day matter? She and John would be together forever.

On Monday morning, Annie gazed at her ring, studying the symbol John had slipped on her finger and smiling at the promise they'd made. The engraving was so worn she could barely make out the heart after years and years of wear. With this ring, she joined the line of women who'd become part of the Sullivan family.

As soon as Annie entered the classroom, she saw Elizabeth waiting at her desk. The child hurried to Annie and reached up to hug her.

"Are you going to be my new mother?" she asked.

Annie took her hand and led her to a bench where they both settled. "I'm going to marry your father, Elizabeth. Do you want me to be your mother?"

Without a pause, Elizabeth said, "Oh, yes, Miss Cunningham, I'd really like you to be my mother." She hugged Annie again. "What should I call you?"

"You could call me Matilda or Mother. What do you think?"

"Mother." Elizabeth nodded. "That's what I want to call you, but not at school when other children are around. Here in school, you're still Miss Cunningham, at least until you marry my father, when you'll be Mrs. Sullivan." She nodded confidently after she reasoned this out.

When they heard more children crossing the lawn,

Elizabeth stood. "I'm very happy." She paused before she smiled and added, "Mother."

The spring term passed quickly. Annie learned geometry but that forbidding calculus would take more time than she had to master.

She and John had set the date for their wedding for June sixth, when the preacher came through. This gave her time to complete the spring term in mid-April and prepare for the ceremony.

Easter had come and gone, but she was still filled with the joy of what she'd learned: in the midst of darkness, resurrection lies ahead.

Annie had never felt so loved, so cared for, so pampered. Wherever they went, John introduced her proudly as his bride-to-be. They'd taken Elizabeth to shop in Austin and gone to Fredericksburg for dinner. She'd never believed she would have a fiancé—certainly not a fiancé like John Sullivan.

Only the continuation of the drought dampened their happiness. As the weather warmed, and February and March passed, every morning Annie looked out the window for clouds or signs of moisture. There were none. The usually glorious wildflowers bloomed in tattered patches and dried up quickly in the blazing sun.

Even the rain in areas north of Trail's End had ended and the creeks and streams had narrowed to trickles of water and barren arroyos. The Bryan boys came to school more often because there was nothing to do on the rain-starved farm. No cattle had died yet, but if this drought went on longer, they would—herds of them that none of the ranchers could afford to lose. Annie noticed Wilber's troubled expression. Of the three boys, he knew best what was at stake.

John worried, too. The level in the stock ponds had become so low the cattle crowded to share the small amount of water remaining. Duffy had taken crews out to dig for underground water but whenever they found a well, it lasted only a few days.

Prayers were lifted in church, but still the sun shone in the cloudless sky and temperatures soared. No rain came. A hot wind blew unrelentingly across the parched, baked land.

They heard reports of dry lightning starting fires in neighboring towns and watched the sky, praying that would not happen here, not in Trail's End.

Late one afternoon, Annie headed out across the meadows surrounding the Sullivan ranch for a walk. The grass was pale tan and high, scorched by the sun and scoured by the wind. On the broad, open plain, the meadow looked like a field of dry wheat waving in the strong gusts. For a moment, she stood watching the sunset while dust billowed around her. Then she settled under a tree to watch the orange and yellow and scarlet rays of the setting sun play across the rustling grass.

She gasped—for a moment, the colors of the sky and the rays of the sun shimmered on the grass as if the prairie had caught fire. Flames of gold and crimson seem to surround her while the wind blew flickering waves of heat over her.

Remembering the stories about fires destroying neighboring towns, the illusion terrified her. She leaped to her feet and dashed toward the schoolhouse. After running forty yards, she turned around. Her imagination was acting up—all she saw now was tall, dry grass and the last glow of the sunset.

Her vision of the fire was the scariest thing to happen to Annie that spring—at least until she saw Willie Preston in town again on a warm, clear morning in early May.

Chapter Sixteen

Rocking back and forth on scuffed boots, Willie Preston stood in the middle of the road and watched Annie with a smile that showed a missing front tooth. An ugly, scruffy man with a patchy beard and mean eyes, he was her past personified.

He took a step toward her. "Well, if it ain't Annie MacAllister, and lookin' real pretty." He shook his head. "Me and the boys missed you when you left Weaver City."

Afraid of what he might say or do, she longed to turn toward the schoolhouse and run, but what good would come of that? He'd catch her easily. She lifted her head and continued to walk. With calm determination, she strode around him toward town, which was only around the next bend in the road. Certainly he wouldn't hurt her with people around.

"Don't act so high and mighty, Annie," he shouted as he swaggered next to her. "You ain't nothing but a common prostitute. Your father was a drunk and murderer."

"I'm not like that anymore. I'm respectable."

He grabbed her arm and stopped her. "Don't care."

He snorted. "More like you changed names. Didn't know you was a schoolteacher, Matilda," he said, spitting out her new name with disgust.

She felt as if icy water was trickling down her neck. How could he know? Forcing herself not to shake, she turned toward him. "What do you mean?"

He laughed. "I saw you the other time I was through. Didn't think I did, did you? I come back and asked about you. They told me there wasn't no Annie MacAllister around, but the woman I described sure sounded like the new schoolteacher."

She took a deep breath and held it, forcing herself to remain on her feet, but she couldn't say a word.

"Yeah, you look pretty. Nice clothes." He grinned. "Hear you're getting married. To a rich man."

She nodded. Foolish to deny what anyone in town could tell him, what he already knew.

"Well, well. Seems like you wouldn't want that man, Mr. John Matthew Sullivan—" he drew the syllables of the name out "—to know who you really are." He nodded his head, as if he were thinking. "Seems like you'd do anything to make sure he didn't find out who his sweet little bride really was."

What did he want? She looked around and considered running again, but she wouldn't get far, only a few feet before he'd catch up and knock her into the dust covering the hard, dry road.

"Money, that's what I want."

He dropped her arm and took a step closer to her. She forced herself to stay in place, to look straight into his eyes.

"I don't have money. I'm a schoolteacher."

"Let me see your hands."

When she reluctantly held them out, he said, "That ring ain't worth a thing, but I know Sullivan has money." She could feel his spittle on her face and smell his putrid breath. "If you don't want him to know, you'll give me five hundred dollars."

She gasped. "I don't have that much."

"Bet your fancy fiancé has more than that just lying around his house. Get it for me tomorrow or I tell him everything." He stepped back. "Meet me in the meadow behind the schoolhouse at nine in the morning. Bring the money." He swaggered past her and toward town.

How much money did she have? She'd worked for six months for thirty-two dollars a month. Even if she hadn't spent a penny, that made only one hundred ninety-two dollars. A grand sum for her, but nowhere near what Preston wanted. Subtract the cost of her expenses and purchases, and she probably had one hundred fifty left, at the most. Would he settle for that amount?

John had thousands of dollars. She knew exactly where he kept the money and how to get to it. He wouldn't miss five hundred dollars—not right away. She could go to the house, slip into the study and borrow what she needed. Somehow she'd pay it back, little by little, after they were married.

She'd gone into town this morning to buy some ribbons, happy in the thought that her wedding was less than three weeks away. Now dread filled her and uncertainty about where she'd be in three weeks. As she considered this, she found herself walking in the direction of the schoolhouse. But she knew one thing. She wouldn't steal the money from John. No matter what, she couldn't rob him. He loved and trusted her.

So how could she get so much money? She suddenly stopped and stood absolutely still with the dust billowing around her and filling her shoes. What was she thinking? She'd known—always known—that she had to tell John about her past. She'd made excuses not to: the time wasn't right, she was tired from a day of teaching, there were people around, she didn't have enough time and on and on.

The real reason? She didn't want to. As much as John said he loved her, he hated liars. He was moral and upright. No matter how much she'd changed, she knew John. Her former life would shock and disgust him. He would not be able to accept her if he knew she was a soiled dove. And he'd never forgive the fact that she'd deceived him.

Tears slid down her face. When she took her handkerchief out and wiped her cheeks, the white cloth came away filthy. But still the tears came and streaked her face with grime.

Not wanting anyone to see her, Annie hurried down the road and turned toward the schoolhouse, taking a shorter way through brambles, which tore at her dress. She didn't care. She had to be alone to think, to reason this out, to decide.

Loving Savior, please give me strength and guidance.

Once at the schoolhouse, she ran up the steps, tore the door open and slammed it behind her. She dashed into the bedroom and threw herself on the bed and sobbed. Worried, Minnie rubbed against her and patted Annie's cheek with her paw.

When the initial storm had passed, Annie lay there hurting so much inside she could hardly breathe. She prayed again but heard no answer.

Because, she realized as she sat up, the answer lay within her. She'd always known that. She should have told John long ago, before she'd fallen so deeply in love with him, back when she'd thought and hoped no one would ever find out about her past.

But if she had confessed, not only would she have lost the man she loved and the daughter she'd found, she'd never be able to teach again. With Minnie behind her, Annie stood and entered the schoolroom. She ran her hand along the desktops and thought of the sounds of the children learning and playing. She loved this place and this life and these people. These had been the most wonderful months of her entire existence.

She forced her thoughts back to the past, back to the day she'd assumed the identity of Miss Matilda Cunningham. At that time, she'd prayed for a few days, then for a week and finally for a month of warmth and food. She'd been given over six months filled with joy and love. That should be enough to last her forever, but she was greedy, so greedy she wanted more. She wanted a life like everyone else's, happiness like Amanda's. She didn't care about the money or the big house, she only wanted what she could no longer have: John, Elizabeth, her students and her friend.

She'd built her new life on a lie. She had to face that and accept the consequences. She had to tell John. Turning back to the bedroom, she picked up Matilda's valise and packed it so she could collect it and leave after she told John. She had no idea what she'd do or where she'd go, but she knew she had to leave.

On the bed, she left what didn't fit inside the suitcase: the clothes she'd worn when she first became Matilda. She no longer was Matilda, but neither was she suddenly Annie MacAllister again. In fact, she had no idea who she was.

But she knew who she wasn't. She could no longer pretend to be Matilda. She sat down and wrote a letter to Miss Palfrey, to tell her what had happened to Matilda and beg forgiveness for her lies. Finished, she folded it, slipped it inside an envelope she'd addressed and left it on the desk.

Now, she had to go tell John. She couldn't put it off any longer.

She pushed herself to her feet and stood, drawing herself as straight as possible. After a deep breath, she left the building and headed toward the ranch with steps as reluctant as a woman making her way to the guillotine during the French Revolution.

John studied numbers on the balance sheet in front of him and made a few corrections. From the front hall, he heard Lucia's voice, followed by a knock on the door.

"Come in," he called.

When Matilda entered, he stood. "What a nice surprise."

Then he saw that her beautiful eyes were red and swollen. Her hands clenched her purse so tightly that her knuckles were white.

"What is it?" He started around the desk, but she held up a hand.

"Please sit down."

He wanted to hold her as she swayed in front of the desk, but the clear determination on her face convinced him to obey her request. What was the matter? Why did she look so ill?

"Lucia," he shouted, "bring—"

"No," she said, shaking her head.

"Sit down, my love."

She squeezed her eyes shut and continued to shake her head. "I need to stand." She placed her purse on the desk and said what sounded like, "I'm not Matilda Susan Cunningham."

She couldn't have said that.

"I am not Matilda Susan Cunningham," she repeated, each word clearly enunciated.

He frowned. "What? Of course you are."

"No." She fell onto a chair as if her legs would no longer hold her. "You have to listen to me. Be patient. This is hard to tell and hard to understand." She took a deep breath. "My name is Annie MacAllister. Matilda Cunningham died in the accident. I assumed her identity."

"What?" John leaned back in his chair and shook his head, attempting to make sense of her words. "Why?"

She took a deep breath and swallowed hard. "Because I'm not a person you'd want to know."

He shook his head. "Matilda—"

"My name is Annie MacAllister. I'm not a schoolteacher. I've never even been to school." She swallowed hard and closed her eyes before speaking. "I wasn't a moral woman."

"What are you saying?"

"John." She looked at him, her face pale. "I used to be a prostitute in Weaver City. I got on the stagecoach that day in October to escape that life."

It took a few seconds for her words to sink in. When he finally understood what she'd said, he felt as if he were being squeezed by a giant fist. His head hurt and his stomach clenched. Before he realized what he was doing, he stood and asked in tones of shock and bewilderment, "You're a prostitute?"

She continued to look at him. "I was."

He walked around the desk and glared down at her. "I brought a prostitute here to teach the children?" Then he whispered, "I fell in love with a prostitute?"

He crossed to the fireplace and leaned against the mantel, his head on his hand. He couldn't think, couldn't take in what she'd told him. After almost a minute, he heard her stand.

He turned around and studied her, not sure if he was angry or wounded, or which hurt more, the deception or the facts. Her lovely face suddenly appeared mottled to him, and her lips curved down in what looked like a death mask. Pity stabbed at him, but he forced it away, thinking of her past and her lies. She stood.

She put the ring on his desk, then turned and ran from the room. When he heard the front door slam after her, he lurched heavily into the desk chair. He put his face in his hands and felt tears, except that John Matthew Sullivan would never cry over a woman like…

He didn't even remember what she called herself—Annie something—but he knew he'd never cry over whoever she said she was. He couldn't allow himself to grieve for a prostitute.

When she ran out of the house, Duffy waited for her outside the front door. "Miss Cunningham," he said as he took off his hat. "Let me take you home."

"I don't have a home," she whispered, stunned to realize that truth.

He took a step toward her and reached to support her but she pulled away.

"I'll have the wagon hitched up in a few minutes. Come down to the stable and wait. I'll give you a ride back to the schoolhouse."

"Did you hear what happened? What he said?" she asked.

He nodded. "I was workin' next to the window. I'm real sorry. You've had a rough time. Now you come down here and sit down while I get the wagon ready," he said, attempting to take her arm again. "Mr. Sullivan doesn't mean those things. He's upset now."

She pushed his hand away. "Thank you, Duffy, but you know he does. And you'll get in trouble if you help me."

"You think I care about that?"

"But I do, Duffy. I don't want anyone to get in trouble because of me." She attempted to smile at him but couldn't. "I have to…" She stopped. She really had no idea what she had to do because a tiny part of her had hoped John would forgive her, accept her. What now?

"Thank you," she said, and started to walk back toward the schoolhouse.

Halfway there, Annie heard a vehicle coming up the road. She looked around, ready to run toward the trees and hide. She didn't want to see anyone. But before she could move, Amanda called out to her. Oh, she didn't want to see Amanda. Annie could only guess how she would recoil when she heard the story.

"Matilda, where are you going? Do you want to go to town with me?" The phaeton stopped. After a pause, Amanda said, "What's wrong?" She jumped from the carriage and took her friend's shoulders. "What happened? Are you hurt?" Amanda took out her handkerchief and wiped Annie's face.

"No." Annie shook her head. "Go away. Leave me alone. You don't want to be near me," she croaked. "You don't want to know me."

"Of course I do." Amanda embraced Annie. "You're my dear friend."

"No." Annie took a deep breath and pushed her away. Telling Amanda would be nearly as difficult as telling John. "I'm not Matilda Cunningham."

"Of course you are, dear." Amanda took Annie's hand and helped her into the phaeton. "Let's get you home." Before Annie could protest, Amanda had cracked the reins and the horse took off.

"Matilda Cunningham died in the stagecoach accident. Annie MacAllister survived."

Amanda frowned as if trying to understand.

"I'm not Matilda. I'm Annie MacAllister." She looked at Amanda and could tell her friend still didn't understand. Gently, she put her hand on Amanda's. "Please listen to me." When her friend pulled the phaeton to a stop in front of the schoolhouse, Annie said, "Before I came here, when I lived in Weaver City, I was a prostitute."

Her eyes round, Amanda titled her head to study her friend. Annie had known she'd be upset. Blinking tears back, she turned in her seat to get down from the carriage.

"You poor dear." Amanda hugged her again. "That must have been terrible."

Annie sat back and gazed at her friend. Tears ran down Amanda's face. Where was the condemnation she'd expected? "Did you hear what I said?"

"Yes. Life must have been very difficult for you. You

must have suffered and hated every minute of it. Let's go inside and you can tell me about it, if you want to."

"I can't go back to the schoolhouse."

"Did you tell John?" At Annie's nod, she said, "He didn't take it at all well, did he?" She sighed. "John is a proud man, too proud of his family and reputation. I'd hoped you'd soften that." She shook her head. "This would be hard for him to accept."

Annie didn't know how to respond. "I need to pick up my valise and Minnie, and I have a letter to mail." She looked down at her clenched hands. "I don't know where I'll go after that. Probably to the hotel so I can wait for the stage."

"No, you won't. You'll come live with Cole and me until you decide what to do."

"The sheriff won't want me there."

"Of course he will. Matilda, you're our friend."

"And there's no room." Annie knew the small house well from her many visits. "The other bedroom is filled with your—" she paused to try to remember what the sheriff had called them "—with your gewgaws."

"My friend, you are much more important to me than all the gewgaws in the world. Don't you know that?"

Once they had picked up her belongings, Amanda drove Annie to the tiny white cottage with dark blue trim. In front was a trellis, which Amanda planned to fill with roses in a few weeks, whenever it finally rained.

Amanda helped Annie from the phaeton and supported her up the steps as if she were an invalid. Once inside, Amanda settled her in the sheriff's comfortable chair. "I have to take the horse to the stable boy," she said. "I'll be right back. We'll talk when Cole gets home," Amanda said. Before she left, she fixed Annie a cup of tea.

Annie didn't know how long it would be before Amanda came back and the sheriff arrived home. While the tea cooled on the table, she sat quietly with Minnie curled on her lap and looked out the window. A few clouds drifted in the sky, more than she'd seen for months. As she watched, the sun sank lower and lower. She reminded herself about the message of Easter. It didn't help with the pain much now, but it would eventually.

When the sheriff walked into the house, Amanda took him aside for a few minutes. Then she served dinner, but Annie only pushed the food around on her plate and nibbled on a biscuit. After dinner, they settled around the cleared table.

"Annie, if you can, will you please tell us what happened?" Amanda put her hand on Annie's.

She looked at her friends. Concern showed on both faces. She swallowed and began her story. "My father was a weak man. He married my mother and changed because he loved her." Annie looked down at her hands. "She died when I was five, and he couldn't handle her death. He started drinking and gambling. In the end, he lost everything. I started working when I was seven, cleaning houses to support us."

"Did he ever hurt you?" Amanda asked gently.

Annie nodded. "When I didn't bring enough money home, he'd beat me. Finally I started sleeping outside, when the weather was good enough." She stopped to calm herself. She'd wished for years she could forget the terror of those days but never had. "The drinking and the fighting got worse. When I was fourteen, he killed a man in the bar and was strung up right there."

"Hung?" the sheriff asked.

Annie nodded. "After that, the good women of the community didn't want the daughter of a killer in their houses." She shrugged. "I couldn't read or write. No one would hire me. I didn't have any money. I couldn't even leave town. So I became a prostitute." She shivered and couldn't look at her friends. "I hated every minute of it. I saved my money for five years and finally bought a ticket to Trail's End. You know everything else except that my real name is Annie MacAllister. The woman who died on the stagecoach was the real teacher, Matilda Susan Cunningham. I took her place because...because I knew that was the only way to escape my past." She gave a forced laugh. "All that effort, and it didn't work. Didn't make a bit of difference."

"You couldn't read or write?" the sheriff asked.

She shook her head. "I taught myself to. I studied every night and taught myself what I needed to know to teach the students the next day."

"You are an amazing woman." Amanda shook her head. "You are courageous and remarkable. I can't believe you taught yourself all that."

She shrugged. "I had to."

"Why did you decide to tell John?" the sheriff asked. "You didn't have to."

"I did. I always knew I had to, but I couldn't find the courage to do it until yesterday. A man from Weaver City saw me and threatened to tell John if I didn't pay him five hundred dollars."

"What's his name?" The sheriff leaned forward.

"Willie Preston."

"Preston knew you from Weaver City?"

"Yes, he works for one of the ranchers there, Roy Martin."

The sheriff nodded. "I know Roy Martin. Mean as a snake and greedy."

Suddenly she began to shiver. She'd stayed calm for hours, but the hopelessness of her future and the loss of John hit her again, hard. And what would people think when they found out who she was? She had to leave town before that happened. She couldn't face the Johnsons or her students once they found out what she'd been.

Where would she go?

Amanda held her. "Matilda or Annie, I don't care who you are. We're your friends."

The sheriff took her hand. "Stay here until you know what's ahead for you and where you want to go."

Overwhelmed by their kindness and unable to speak, Annie nodded and allowed Amanda to take her to the spare bedroom. All of Amanda's gewgaws had been shoved in a corner and a small bed had been made up for her. Annie knew she'd never fit.

Not that it mattered. She doubted if she would sleep anyway. She sat next to Minnie on the side of the bed and clasped her hands. From the parlor, she heard voices, then the sound of the sheriff walking across the room and out the door. From outside on the prairie came the howling of a coyote who sounded as lonely as she felt.

She tried to sleep but couldn't stop thinking about how happy she'd been here, and how much she'd loved her students. And then John's angry face appeared, his furious shouts ringing in her ears over and over.

"Dear Lord…." She didn't know what more to say. He knew her sorrow. He shared her grief.

And He had forgiven her. When she turned her life over to Him, He'd given her a second chance. She clung to that as sleep finally claimed her.

Chapter Seventeen

"Father?" Elizabeth knocked on the door. "May I come in?"

John turned to look out the window of his study. Dark already. How much time had he spent pacing from one side of the room to the other? Rubbing his hand across his eyes, he moved slowly to the door, feeling as if he'd been very sick, as stiff as if he'd grown old. "What is it?"

Elizabeth stood before him, her hair braided neatly and wearing her long cotton nightgown. "My prayers. It's bedtime but you haven't heard my prayers."

"Not tonight." He didn't think he could bear to listen to prayers tonight, not when God had deserted him. "Go on to bed. I'll be up later." He started to close the door but Elizabeth put her hand up to stop it.

"Lucia told me Miss Cunningham was here earlier." She paused. "I didn't get to see her."

What should he tell his daughter? Probably at least part of the truth. "Miss Cunningham had to leave. She came to say goodbye."

"Why didn't she tell me in person? Why is she leaving?"

"An emergency." Not a complete lie. "Of course, she wanted to see you, but she didn't have time."

Elizabeth came into the study and sat in one of the chairs. As he watched, he realized how tiny she was, so little she took up less than half of the chair. How could he tell his daughter exactly what had happened? Of course he couldn't. She'd never understand. He barely did.

"When will she be back?"

"She won't come back."

She looked at him in surprise before her chin trembled. "She won't come back? She won't be my mother?"

He shook his head.

Elizabeth leaned forward and pointed at the desk. "It's the ring. She left the ring. She won't be back." Her body trembled and tears began. "Doesn't she love me?"

"Of course she does." He kneeled before her. "Sometimes things happen. She didn't want to leave, but she had to."

"Why? If she loved us, she wouldn't leave us." She gazed at him, her eyes filled with grief. "Did I do something to make her leave?"

"No, no. You didn't do anything wrong." He took her hand but didn't know how to comfort her. "She... she just had to go away."

"Where did she go? Can I visit her?" she sobbed.

John stood. He couldn't answer. He couldn't talk about this anymore. Selfish, he knew, but it hurt too much to respond to the child's questions. He picked Elizabeth up and cradled her in his arms, holding and rocking her until she fell asleep, worn out from crying.

"Lucia," he called. When the woman appeared at the door, he said, "Please take Elizabeth to her room and put her to bed." He handed his tiny, sleeping daughter to Lucia, then fell back into his chair. If he were a drinking man, he'd probably attempt to lose himself in a bottle, but he wasn't and knew that indulgence wouldn't solve the problem or alleviate the pain.

"How could she have lied to me?" he whispered.

He would have been happier never knowing, to live with Matilda—or whatever her name was—in happiness and ignorance. He wished she hadn't told him. But she had. If only he hadn't been brought up in a family that expected so much from him. Perhaps then he could've married a former prostitute without feeling as if he'd betrayed his name.

For a moment he clasped his hands, closed his eyes and attempted to pray, but he and God had never been all that close. His God was a moral being, not one John could go to in sorrow. In fact, he and God were barely on speaking terms. How could he confess or feel close to a distant God? He'd never been the type of man who told God about his problems and expected God to listen or solve them.

And yet she had.

Reaching out his hand, he picked up the ring and clenched it until the crown cut into his finger.

"I'd like to see Mr. Sullivan, please," a man's voice came from the front hall.

Who would come by so late? Before he could move, the study door was thrown open and the sheriff entered.

"Sullivan," he said, and settled in a chair in front of the desk as if he'd been invited.

"Sheriff." John nodded politely. "How are you and your wife?"

"Very well."

But the smile that usually covered the sheriff's face when he thought of his new wife didn't appear. "I came to talk to you about something. Actually, two things. First, I hear someone has shown interest in that parcel of land over northwest."

"Yes, I've been in and out of Austin because a lien was placed on it and questions have been raised about its ownership. How did you know that, Sheriff?"

He answered that query with another question. "Do you know a rancher up in Weaver City named Roy Martin?"

"Only by name. He's the man who's challenging my right to the title."

"Seems there's a man named Willie Preston in town, a man who works for Martin. Preston's come to Trail's End a couple of times for his boss. Don't know much more than that, but thought I should drop by and mention it."

"I don't know a Willie Preston, either." He glanced up at the sheriff, wondering. "Again, how do you know this?"

"Preston knew Matilda—or rather, Annie—in Weaver City. He recognized her in town and attempted to blackmail her. Said if she gave him five hundred dollars, he wouldn't tell you who she was." The sheriff nodded. "Guess you know the rest of that story."

The fact that Annie—he must think of her that way from now on—had come forward herself made no difference. She was who she was, and he didn't want to talk about her. "I still don't understand. Why is Preston here?"

"Might be that Martin sent him down to see if he could do a little mischief, figure out a way to get that piece of land cheap. Don't know. I'm going to talk to the man tomorrow."

"You think my land is safe?"

"Don't know." He sat in silence for a moment before he looked into John's eyes and said, in a soft voice with an edge of anger, "I hear you tossed her out."

"Men like Roy Martin and his man Preston are what a sheriff should deal with." John stood. "But this woman? She's none of your business, Bennett."

"Yes, she is. You see, she's a friend of mine and a friend of my wife, and that makes it my business. They're both over at my place, crying. A man can take only so much of that."

John leaned his palms on the desk and glared at the other man. "Your wife shouldn't be around that woman."

"I guess you mean Annie when you call her 'that woman.' Well, Sullivan, if you wouldn't mind sitting down, I'd like to tell you something about her." When John continued to stand, the sheriff said, "Have it your way. I'm going to tell you no matter what."

As the sheriff talked, John had to sit down to listen. The details of her life horrified him.

"Just seven years old," the sheriff said. "Younger than your daughter, beaten every day, sleeping outside and working to support her drunken father."

John's stomach churned. He stood and went to the open window to take a deep breath and gain control of himself. "She didn't need to become a prostitute."

"Not many choices for an illiterate fourteen-year-old out here that don't include a man."

John turned. "Illiterate?"

"Amazing, isn't she? She couldn't read or write when she got here. She taught herself and worked hard to stay ahead of the students."

"Sheriff, I appreciate your coming by, but—"

"Lucia told me that your daughter is upset and crying." The sheriff stood. "Think about what you're doing, Sullivan. Your daughter already lost one mother. Now she's lost another because you can't accept the love of a good woman." He turned toward the door. "Doesn't make sense to me."

"What you said sickens me, Sheriff, but what kind of man could forgive and accept that woman's lies and her past?"

The sheriff looked back at him. "Only a good Christian could, John."

He watched the sheriff leave and soon heard the front door shut behind him. For a moment, he considered what Bennett had said about Annie. It didn't change the fact that he'd had fallen in love with a prostitute. He'd been deceived and he couldn't forgive that. Guess he wasn't that much of a Christian. The idea of forgiveness had never sat well with him.

When Annie heard Amanda in the kitchen the next morning, relief filled her. Now she could stop pretending to be asleep.

She'd barely been able to sleep, all night, she'd looked out the window. She'd sat on the edge of the bed, thinking and praying. She knew God had heard, and felt the comfort of His presence holding her in love. Whatever happened, she wouldn't face it alone.

She rolled out of the tiny bed, washed up and straightened her clothing before she went out to the kitchen. In the early light, she checked her watch. Only six-thirty.

"Breakfast?" Amanda asked, then she gasped when she saw Annie. "Didn't you get any sleep?"

"A bit. Do I look that bad?" Annie tried to smile. "I'll sleep later, after I see Willie Preston. I'm not hungry, but thank you." She looked at her friend. "You're really becoming a homemaker, aren't you? Cooking and cleaning house?"

Amanda nodded, refusing to be distracted. "Coffee?"

Annie shook her head and walked to the window. Dark clouds roiled across the sky and the wind blew so hard the trees bent before its strength. "Do you think it will rain?"

"Probably not." The sheriff entered the room and sat at the table. "Looks like perfect conditions for dry lightning. Hope we don't get any."

After Amanda made a few attempts at conversation, they all finished breakfast in silence. Then the sheriff took a gulp of coffee and pulled Amanda to him.

"Goodbye." He kissed her, then turned toward the door. "Annie, don't you forget we're your friends."

Annie watched him ride out, holding onto his hat as the wind tried to tear it from his fingers. Once he'd left, she turned to Amanda. "I'm going out now."

"You can't." Amanda dipped a plate in the dishpan and picked up a towel. "The weather is terrible." She gestured toward the window. "You can't go out there."

"I have to meet Willie Preston. I want to know why he came to Trail's End, and I have to stand up to him."

She hugged her friend. "I'll be fine. I'll be back as soon as I talk to him."

"But you're almost ninety minutes early."

"I'll be fine," Annie repeated.

When she opened the door, the blast of wind hit her, almost pushing her back into the house. Leaning forward, she forced her way through the gusts that tore at her hair and clothing. Above her, dark storm clouds scuttled across the sky.

With the struggle against the searing, dusky blast, the walk took over an hour, nearly three times longer than usual. Upon her arrival, she looked around the plain but saw only the blowing grass that looked like a dry ocean.

Almost nine o'clock. He would be here soon.

After a few minutes of being buffeted by the wind, she sought shelter under a live oak, sitting against the rough bark of its trunk. Time passed, but there was still no sign of Preston. With an exhausted sigh, she rested her head on the tree trunk and closed her eyes, just for a moment.

Annie awoke with a start. How long had she slept? She blinked and covered her eyes as dust blew into her face. The clouds churned, dark and ugly, but no rain fell from them. In the distance she saw a flash of lightning.

Dry lightning, the plague of a parched prairie.

It took a moment for her to wake up enough to become aware of her surroundings. She leaned forward and took a deep breath. Thick smoke filled her lungs. Annie took a deeper breath. Yes, smoke. A roar reverberated across the meadow. She leaped to her feet and looked around her.

The fire must have started from a stroke of dry lightning while she slept. Or perhaps Willie Preston had started it. Not that it mattered.

From the east she saw smoke and flames, blown by the storm and headed directly toward her and the Sullivan ranch. With no thought for her own safety, she began to run. She had to get there before the fire did. She had to warn them.

As she sprinted across the rapidly closing space, she realized how quickly the wind raced and swirled across the plain. Flames leapt and spun and sowed more fires all over the prairie. The new conflagrations were fed by the maelstrom and moving much faster than Annie could. In no time, the blaze surrounded her, a huge roaring circle closing in.

To the south, she saw an opening. Could she reach it before it closed?

Hot air scorched her lungs and she gasped for air in short pants as she ran. She pushed herself, coming nearer and nearer to the quickly disappearing space.

Intent on reaching the gap, she almost didn't hear the distant call for help. Stopping, she turned west. When she'd run twenty yards and could see the top of the ranch house, she heard people yelling on the other side of the blaze, their words indistinguishable but their panic unmistakable.

After a few more feet, she saw the reason. Elizabeth stood perhaps fifty feet from her, and a glowing, crackling wall of fire separated the child from the house.

With a burst of speed, she dashed toward her and shouted, "Elizabeth!"

"Miss Cunningham!" Elizabeth ran toward Annie

and launched herself into her teacher's arms. "My father said you were gone," she sobbed.

"I'm here now." Annie clenched the child to her chest. "We have to get out of here." She put the child down and tore off part of her own skirt. "Put this over your nose and breathe through it." She placed another piece over her own mouth and nose, picked Elizabeth up and ran toward the narrowing passage on the south end of the blaze. "Hold on tight."

"I was just playing next to the stock tank. I didn't notice the fire until I couldn't get out."

"I'm here. You'll be fine." But Annie knew she couldn't run fast enough holding Elizabeth, even as tiny as she was.

"I'm going to put you down now," Annie said, and pointed. "See that opening down there? We're going to run to it together. Hold my hand. I know you can run really fast."

Elizabeth clung more tightly to Annie's neck. "No, don't put me down," she sobbed. "I'm scared. Don't leave me."

Annie looked up in time to see the gap to the south close as two fires met in an astounding blaze. She had to find a way to save the terrified child. "Let's go back to where you were."

"But there's fire, Miss Cunningham. Father and Duffy tried to save me, but they couldn't get through."

"I'll think of something." Dear Lord, please help me think of something.

As they ran toward the stock tank, Annie studied the fire. Six-feet high and collapsing in on them. She looked around her. She could put Elizabeth in the tank until the blaze passed but thought there wasn't nearly enough water to cover her, and the child would be so frightened alone.

"Look, Miss Cunningham! The fire's almost as high as the roof!" Elizabeth began to sob.

"Elizabeth!" someone called from the other side of the fire.

"I'm here with her!" Annie shouted.

Of course being together only meant that she and Elizabeth would both die in the blaze if she didn't think of something. If the flames didn't kill them, the smoke would.

"Elizabeth, get in the water." She took her to the stock tank. Obediently, the child followed her direction. "Throw me a blanket!" she shouted to the group on the other side.

She waited for the blanket as the flames raced closer. It finally arrived, tied in a ball and soaring over the fire.

"What now, Miss Cunningham?" Elizabeth was coughing so much Annie could barely understand her words.

"Stand up and wring your skirt to get as much of the water out as you can. I'm going to dip the blanket in there."

"Won't the water make me safer?"

"Yes, but I'm going to wrap you in the blanket and throw you over the flame. You'll be too heavy with too much water in your clothing."

"Throw me?" Tears mixed with soot on Elizabeth's face.

Annie knelt beside the child. "Pretend you're the alle-over ball. I'm going to toss you over the flame and into your father's arms."

A smile glimmered. "Pretend I'm the alle-over ball? I can do that."

Annie nodded and grabbed the wet blanket, wrung it out and wrapped Elizabeth in it. She closed the blanket tightly, took the four corners and tied them together, then shouted as she approached the narrowest section of flames. "I'm going to toss Elizabeth to you! Get ready! You'll have to catch her!"

Elizabeth was a lot heavier than the ball they used for alle-over but Annie hoped she'd be able to do it. It was her only idea, her only option. If this didn't work, if she tossed the child into the flames, it meant death. But if she could gather all her strength to make this throw, at least the child would survive.

"Hold still, Elizabeth." She stood sideways, held the knot on the blanket tightly with both hands. Using every bit of muscle she could muster, she swung the blanket back, then forward and let it go at the highest arc.

"Here she comes!" she shouted as the blanket cleared the flames. Within a second she heard a cheer. "We got her!"

"Thank You, God," she whispered.

The flame crackled, close and hot. She had only a few more seconds to breathe. Hurrying to the tank, she stood in it to dampen her skirt and then ripped her wet petticoat off and wound it around her hands and covered her head. Could she make it through? If she didn't try, death was certain.

"Annie!" she heard John cry.

"I'm coming." Taking a breath through the wet cotton, she located a place in the flame that looked narrow and began to run through the fire, her sodden skirt ensnaring her legs.

Flames licked at her, catching her sleeves on fire and swirling around her body. It felt as if the heat were melting her bones and flesh. Finally, she couldn't move any farther, couldn't stand up any longer. As she began to sink into the inferno, hands caught her and pulled her out while someone poured water on her.

She didn't remember anything after that for a long time.

When she awoke in a dark room, Lucia was kneeling on the floor beside her, praying. Annie's lips were parched and her throat and lungs hurt when she attempted to speak.

"Water," she croaked.

"Oh, Miss Cunningham, you woke up!" Lucia held the glass out and slowly trickled the liquid down Annie's throat and on her dry lips.

Waves of pain swept over Annie's body. Her arms were wrapped in something, as were her feet and legs. Her hands were slathered with balm.

"How long?" she whispered, after painfully swallowing the water.

"Two days. The doctor gave you medicine for the pain, to help you sleep."

"The fire?" she whispered.

"It rained. Only minutes after you came through the blaze, the clouds opened and it rained and put the fire out."

Rain. That was good. She fell asleep again.

The fifth day after the fire, she awakened to see John and Elizabeth by her side. Elizabeth leaned over, careful not to touch Annie. "I'm fine, Miss Cunningham. Only a few burns. Thank you."

Annie tried to smile.

"Thank you for saving my daughter," John said.

Were there tears on his cheek? Probably tears of joy for his daughter. Then she noticed his hands, both heavily bandaged.

"That was you?" she asked. "You pulled me through the fire?"

"Yes."

"Thank you." Of course. He was a good man. He'd have helped anyone caught in the fire. She closed her eyes and fell back to sleep.

The next day, Annie examined her injuries as Amanda changed the wrappings.

"I trimmed a little of your hair that was burned, but the petticoat protected your head and hands well." She moved down to unwind the bandages on Annie's legs. "The doctor said we can leave these off today. Your legs weren't burned too badly and the shoes protected your feet. But your ankles." She shook her head.

Then Amanda leaned back. "The worst burns are on your arms and your lungs."

Annie bit her lip as Amanda attempted to remove the wrappings slowly and gently. "I'll have scars."

Amanda nodded.

"Will I be able to write?" She looked at her hands, which were puffy and blackened.

"The doctor believes you'll heal completely, except for the scars." Amanda attempted to blink back tears. "You were so brave. You saved Elizabeth."

"When can I leave here?"

"John says you may stay for as long as you wish."

"How long does the doctor say?" she whispered, having trouble catching her breath.

"No one knows. You have to heal."

She nodded and closed her eyes again, remembering the hands that had reached out to save her.

A week later, Annie stood at the window. The rain had lasted two days, she'd been told. She could see the scarred section of the prairie where the fire had raged, but the rest was thick and green. Pink flox and orange-red standing cypress poked their heads up through the luxurious grass. Here and there she saw the fragile purple petals of the wine cup.

"Annie."

She turned to see John in the doorway. It was strange to hear him use her real name.

"You're leaving now?" No affection showed in his eyes.

"Yes. Amanda has asked me to spend a few days with her before I decide where to go."

He nodded again. "I'd like you to know that I've reconsidered my earlier words and actions."

"Oh?"

"Yes, I'd like for you to stay here. Because my daughter loves you and you saved her life, I'm grateful and willing to forgive you. Therefore, I'm asking you again to marry me."

Her gaze flew to his face but still no emotion showed there. He stood stiffly, his weight balanced on both feet, his healing hands at his sides. Annie didn't feel a proposal that started with *therefore* came with a promise of eternal love.

"Why would you do that?"

"It's what a Christian would do."

She blinked. He'd asked her because it was his duty.

"No, thank you." She picked up her purse and headed toward the door. Although her legs still hurt, she refused to allow him to see that.

He started to take her arm, but she pulled away. She refused to lean on him again. He dropped his hand.

"But you must marry me. Certainly you know you cannot go back into the world alone again. Here you'll be cared for."

"Thank you, John, but no." She moved past him and, holding on to the rail, slowly descended the stairs.

"You're not well enough," he said. "You still need to rest."

Even though she heard the pleading in his voice, his words didn't stop her. "Thank you for your hospitality and care." And she walked out the door without a backward glance.

Once outside the house, she refused Duffy's hand and pulled herself into the phaeton. The ride was not comfortable, but she sat up proudly.

For the first time in many years, she'd stood up for herself. She'd said "no" to a man. Although John may not realize it, she was a blessed and beloved child of God, a person of value, worthy of love and deserving of forgiveness.

Chapter Eighteen

Out of all the choices that had been forced on him, John knew he'd made one correct decision. He just wasn't sure which one it was.

At first, he'd believed he was right to break the engagement. After all, he'd spent his whole life as a moral leader of the community, an elder of the church, an example to all of the decent, ethical ways to live. He'd asked a fallen woman to marry him not once but twice. Showing no gratitude at all, she'd refused the second time, an action he now admired greatly considering the manner in which he'd presented it.

But the more time that passed, the less certain he became about his decisions, about which was the right one.

When he thought about her, he had to remind himself of the grievous sin she'd committed so he wouldn't soften his opinion of her. But now he wondered, why didn't judging immoral behavior feel right to him anymore? Why wasn't it enough to be both right and righteous?

Three days after Annie's departure from his home, he spent the evening with Farley Hanson and several bankers and cattlemen from Llano County, discussing the rumors about the railroad. If it came through, what route would it take? What land would be bought? Who'd make money and who wouldn't?

Once the men left, John felt alone, very much alone. Because he hadn't convinced Annie to stay, Elizabeth was angry with him. He hoped she would forgive him but for now she was in her bedroom, refusing to talk to him. Lucia and Ramon were polite to him as usual, but not warm.

Duffy told him right out to his face that he was a fool. Duffy pretty much described the whole problem only he didn't go far enough. A stiff-necked fool who didn't know how to change. Oh, he bet Duffy could add even more to that picture, but John preferred not to give him another chance.

He didn't like who he was and apparently no one else did, either.

Before he headed upstairs, John looked out across the scorched strip of land between the ranch and the schoolhouse. For a moment he remembered Annie, how she looked playing alle-over with the children, her hair spilling down, her face flushed and happy. She had glowed with pride for her students at the Christmas program. He thought of the sheriff's words, of her terrible childhood and her remarkable transformation after she arrived in Trail's End.

No wonder he'd detected a little panic when he first met her, after he'd told her she was the schoolteacher. How desperate she must have felt. She'd looked as if she wanted to turn and run, but she hadn't. Instead, she'd taught herself to read and write. She'd found a way to survive and had lived a moral life since her arrival. Annie MacAllister was a survivor and a remarkable woman. He admired her greatly.

In fact, he still loved her, but he had no idea what to do about it. At the moment, his high standards were of very little comfort and wouldn't bring him warmth and love, not like Annie would.

A few hours after midnight, he climbed the stairs but didn't go to the bed. He knew he wouldn't sleep because he didn't sleep at all anymore. He looked again at the charred swatch in the land and at the graveyard where Celeste and his parents lay. Finally, he allowed his eyes to move toward the schoolhouse.

The building was dark. Not a flicker of light shone through the windows. Of course not. She wasn't there. The longer he stood looking out at the dark, empty schoolhouse, the more obvious it was that Annie would never return to his life again.

In spite of her deception, in spite of her past, he couldn't forget her warmth and her love and her laughter and all the things that had made her the woman he cherished, in spite of everything.

Or maybe, because of all that. The woman who escaped from her terrible past and had built a respectful life and gave back to the community was a far stronger, braver woman than he'd realized—far more courageous than he.

What would she do if he went to her? If he were a different man, he could do that, but he was the upstanding son of Joshua Matthew Sullivan, heir to over sixty years of Texas history.

As he thought of the rest of his life without her, his soul groaned in anguish, a torment that continued to grow worse with each passing day.

What was he going to do?

A sob escaped his lips. Almost before he knew it, his legs collapsed beneath him, and he fell to the floor on his knees with his hands clenched in prayer. It was like nothing he'd ever done before, but never had his soul been in such agony. In fact, he'd never quite realized he had a soul until the pain began.

"Dear God, what should I do?" Tears ran down his face. He couldn't think of anything else to say. "What should I do?"

As he knelt, he felt a presence around him and within. The assurance of God's closeness filled him. It was as if God knelt beside him and shared his agony. Overwhelmed by the knowledge that he couldn't face the shambles of his life alone, he attempted to accept his utter dependence on God, to place his life in God's hands.

Giving up his self-reliance was not comfortable for John. For nearly an hour he struggled, until he realized the peace that flooded him felt so much better than his constant resistance and his efforts to control his life. Finally he whispered, "I turn my life over to You, Lord. Please help me."

He was not a man who poured out his feelings to anyone, but he'd never felt such serenity, comfort and understanding before. Letting down the last barrier, he prayed, "I still love her, Lord. What should I do?"

The answer came to him—so clear, so easy—as he remembered the words of the Scripture he himself had read at church. "Jesus said unto her, 'Neither do I condemn thee: go, and sin no more.'" He repeated the words aloud. "Neither do I condemn thee: go, and sin no more."

From what she'd said, Annie knew Jesus had forgiven her. Wasn't he incredibly presumptuous not to?

Filled with peace and assured of God's leading, he stood and looked out the window again. The darkness didn't seem as bleak to him. He fell into bed and slept immediately, finally certain of God's guidance and the calm acceptance that had eluded him for so long.

"I wish you'd stay longer." Amanda folded Annie's blue basque and placed it in the valise. "I'm going to cook something new tonight, a pineapple upside-down cake. I'd love to have your help."

"Sounds good." Annie studied herself in the mirror. Amanda had arranged her hair so the burns on her neck were covered. Most of the redness on her face had disappeared in the weeks since the fire. Her hands showed only a few patches of red against the pink skin. The long sleeves of her basque covered the dressings on her arms. Although the pain hadn't disappeared completely and she still struggled to breathe occasionally, she'd regained most of her strength. "It's time for me to go."

"Everyone will miss you."

Over the weeks of Annie's recuperation, people had dropped by, bringing food and small gifts for her, asking her to stay. As far as she could tell, no one had heard about her past.

She'd decided to remain Matilda Susan Cunningham until she left because explanations seemed foolish and hurtful now. Let the students and their parents remember her as a fine teacher.

"You have the recommendation I wrote for you?"

Annie nodded.

"You know you don't have to worry about Willie Preston. Cole tossed him out of town and told him never to come back. He told Preston to tell Roy Martin the same."

"That's good to know."

"I hope you'll teach again." Amanda sat on the bed.

She shook her head. "I'm through with that. I'll go to a big city, use my new name, and be a shop girl." She smiled at Amanda to comfort her. "That was what I'd always dreamed of doing. I'll be fine."

"Why don't you lie down and rest? The stage doesn't leave for two hours."

Annie nodded. The preparation to leave had exhausted her. "Thank you for taking care of Minnie." She picked up the cat and scratched her ears. "I'll miss her."

"Mr. Sullivan?" Lucia tapped on the door. "Breakfast is ready."

He sat up. The sun streamed through his window. "What time is it?"

"It's nearly ten o'clock."

He never slept that late, but he couldn't be angry with Lucia. She had firm instructions never to wake him.

However, he had things to do this morning. Leaping out of bed and feeling better than he had in a long time, he got ready to start the day, a day he hoped would end far more happily than it had begun.

The first thing he did after he washed and dressed was to find Elizabeth, and apologize to her. Next he grabbed a bit of breakfast while Ramon hitched the horses to the surrey. By ten-thirty, he'd left the ranch and tooled along the road to the sheriff's new house where he'd heard she was staying.

No one was home.

He knocked on every door and window. He looked inside, going all the way around the house twice. Both times, Minnie sat in the parlor window and meowed.

That was good, right? Annie wouldn't leave Minnie behind, would she?

John checked on the horses in the stable and found only the stable boy. All the boy knew was that everyone had left nearly an hour earlier, including the pretty schoolteacher with her suitcase.

John couldn't be too late. He couldn't.

It took only minutes to get to town. The stagecoach didn't leave until eleven. She couldn't be gone, not yet. Certainly he had time. Thoughts, worries and reproaches echoed through his brain.

When he reached town, he saw Amanda's phaeton next to the hotel. Annie was with her. Carefully, she swung out of the carriage. Once on the road, she picked up her valise and placed it next to her.

She was leaving town today.

He'd known she would at some point. She'd told him. The sheriff had told him. He'd just never considered that she really would, not until he could make some sense out of what had happened between them. Had he dithered too long? Had he left his apology until too late? Still he couldn't move as he drank in the sight of her.

Her hair was different, swooped low over her ears and in a braid on the nape of her neck. She was thinner, almost willowy now. When she smiled at Amanda, he felt as if he'd been kicked in the stomach. She was so lovely.

And she was leaving.

What was he going to do? He knew what he should do. He knew what he and God had decided together only a few hours ago, but he couldn't move.

Then he heard the sound of the stagecoach coming into town. In a few minutes, Annie would get onto the stage and disappear from his life. He couldn't allow that.

* * *

"Annie."

Annie turned when she heard John's voice and saw him driving his carriage toward the hotel. She turned away to lift her valise off the street.

"John, what are you doing here?" Amanda said from the seat of the phaeton.

He ignored her, got out of his surrey, twisted the reins around a post and crossed to Annie. Taking the valise from her hands, he said, "Please don't go."

Annie attempted to wrestle the bag away from him. "Mr. Sullivan—"

"Please, you used to call me John."

"I called you John when I was Matilda Susan Cunningham, your fiancée." Anger so consumed her that, with a strong tug, she pulled the satchel from his hand and turned away.

"I don't care who you are, Annie or Matilda or Miss Cunningham or Miss MacAllister. I only know I love you and want to marry you."

"John, there's quite a crowd gathering," Amanda said.

Annie looked around to see faces peering from all the stores while people spilled out of the buildings.

"I don't care," he repeated.

"You don't care?" Annie said.

"All I care about is you." He paused and cleared his throat. "I'm sorry for everything I said and did. I can't tell you how sorry I am."

"Mr. Sullivan," Annie whispered. "I'm Annie Mac-Allister. I always will be. You can't pretend I'm not. If you can't accept who I was and what I did, I can understand that." She turned away. "Please leave me alone. I'm getting on the stagecoach in a few minutes."

"Annie, I love you and accept everything you did to survive." When she didn't answer, he said loudly and clearly, "I love you."

The watching crowd murmured and laughed.

"John, we're in the middle of town." She looked around. More people had joined the crowd. "There are dozens of people watching. You can't say that out here."

"I prayed about this. I asked God to forgive me for being so stiff-necked."

"You did?" Annie asked.

John took her hands. "I don't care about the past. I want us to be together. I want you to be my wife."

"Why? Because that's what a Christian does?"

"No." He shook his head. "No, because I love you. Please forgive me."

She looked at him, at the pleading in his eyes. "I can't," she whispered.

"I hurt you too much. Please forgive me." He gazed at her. "Will you marry me? I beg you."

He begged her to marry him? John Matthew Sullivan begged her to forgive him? "I can't," she whispered. "I have a past. Men like Willie Preston could appear at any time. They could hurt you and Elizabeth."

"I don't care who you are," he said in a low voice. "As Matilda or Annie, whichever you choose, you would be my wife. No one would dare to threaten my wife."

"I can't," she whispered again. "I'm afraid of disappointing you again, of failing." With as much strength as she could muster, she took a step toward the stage but glanced back. She had to see John again before she left.

She could read both love and pain in his eyes. He wouldn't be easy to live with. He struggled for balance between his past and who he'd become, just as she did.

But he'd asked her forgiveness. As a Christian, how could she turn her back on him?

Seeing her indecision, he hurried toward her and took her hand, careful not to hurt her. "Please."

"I forgive you, but how can you forgive me? You know what I've done, you know how I lied to you."

"We'll work this out together, but God will be with us."

"God will be with us," she repeated. Did she have the courage to try?

"Will you please stay and marry me?"

She watched him and considered his expression, which looked stripped of all pride. In its place she found warmth and love. Warm blue eyes pleaded with her.

She nodded. "I'll stay." She dropped the valise.

"And marry me?" he persisted.

She nodded. "I love you, John."

"Thank you, God!" he shouted, then he put his hands around Annie's waist and lifted her in the air, turning round and round. Then, to the delight of the cheering crowd, he carried her to his surrey and gently settled her in the seat before he climbed in beside her.

"Let's go tell Elizabeth." He pulled her next to him and whispered, "I'll love you forever, Annie."

In that moment, surrounded by people who cared about them, with puffy clouds floating across a clear blue Texas sky and the cactus blossoms blooming yellow and purple, Annie knew she wasn't the only one blessed.

John Matthew Sullivan had received a second chance, as well.

* * * * *

SPECIAL EXCERPT FROM

*When a guide-dog trainer becomes a target of a
dangerous crime ring, a K-9 cop and his loyal
partner will work together to keep her safe.*

Read on for a sneak preview of
Blind Trust *by Laura Scott,*
the next exciting installment in the
True Blue K-9 Unit *miniseries, available*
June 2019 from Love Inspired Suspense.

Eva Kendall slowed her pace as she approached the training facility where she worked training guide dogs.

Using her key, she entered the training center, thinking about the male chocolate Lab named Cocoa that she would work with this morning. Cocoa was a ten-week-old puppy born to Stella, a gift from the Czech Republic to the NYC K-9 Command Unit located in Queens. Most of Stella's pups were being trained as police dogs, but not Cocoa. In less than a month after basic puppy training, Cocoa would be able to go home with Eva to be fostered during his initial first-year training to become a full-fledged guide dog. Once that year passed, guide dogs like Cocoa would return to the center to train with their new owners.

A few steps into the building, Eva frowned at the loud thumps interspersed between a cacophony of barking. The raucous noise from the various canines contained a level of panic and fear rather than excitement.

Concerned, she moved quickly through the dimly lit training center to the back hallway, where the kennels were located. Normally she was the first one in every morning, but maybe one of the other trainers had gotten an early start.

Rounding the corner, she paused in the doorway when she saw a tall, heavyset stranger scooping Cocoa out of his kennel. Panic squeezed her chest. "Hey! What are you doing?"

The ferocious barking increased in volume, echoing off the walls and ceiling. The stranger must have heard her. He turned to look at her, then roughly tucked Cocoa under his arm like a football.

"No! Stop!" Panicked, Eva charged toward the man, desperately wishing she had a weapon of some sort.

"Get out of my way," he said in a guttural voice.

"No. Put that puppy down right now!" Eva stopped and stood her ground.

"Last chance," he taunted, coming closer.

Don't miss
Blind Trust *by Laura Scott,*
available June 2019 wherever
Love Inspired® *Suspense books and ebooks are sold.*

www.LoveInspired.com

LISEXP0519

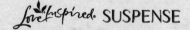

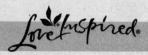
"Dating is so complicated."

"People are complicated, Noah. Every single person you meet is dealing with something."

He asked, "How did you get so wise?"

"Never said I was."

"I'm being serious. How did you learn to navigate so seamlessly through these kinds of interactions, and why aren't you married?"

Olivia Mae thought her eyes were going to pop out of her head. "Did you really just ask me that?"

"I did."

"A little intrusive."

"Meaning you don't want to answer?"

"Meaning it's none of your business."

"Fair enough, though it's like asking a horse salesman why he doesn't own a horse."

"My family situation is…unique."

"You mean with your grandparents?"

She nodded instead of answering.

"I've got it." Noah resettled his hat, looking quite pleased with himself.

"Got what?"

"The solution to my dating disasters."

He leaned forward, close enough that she could smell the shampoo he'd used that morning.

LIEXP0419

"You need to give me dating lessons."

"What do you mean?"

"You and me. We'll go on a few dates…say, three. You can learn how to do anything if you do it three times."

"That's a ridiculous suggestion."

"Why? I learn better from doing."

"Do you?"

"I've already learned not to take a girl to a gas station, but who knows how many more dating traps are waiting for me."

"So this would be…a learning experience."

"It's a perfect solution." He tugged on her *kapp* string, something no one had done to her since she'd been a young teen.

"I can tell by the shock on your face that I've made you uncomfortable. It's a *gut* idea, though. We'd keep it businesslike—nothing personal."

Olivia Mae had no idea why the thought of sitting through three dates with Noah Graber made her stomach twirl like she'd been on a merry-go-round. Maybe she was catching a stomach bug.

"Wait a minute. Are you trying to get out of your third date? Because you promised your *mamm* that you would give this thing three solid attempts."

"And I'll keep my word on that," Noah assured her. "After you've tutored me, you can throw another poor unsuspecting girl my way."

Olivia Mae stood, brushed off the back of her dress and pointed a finger at Noah, who still sat in the grass as if he didn't have a care in the world.

"All right. I'll do it."

Don't miss
A Perfect Amish Match *by Vannetta Chapman,*
available May 2019 wherever
Love Inspired® books and ebooks are sold.

www.LoveInspired.com

Inspirational Romance to Warm Your Heart and Soul

Join our social communities to connect with other readers who share your love!

Sign up for the Love Inspired newsletter at **www.LoveInspired.com** to be the first to find out about upcoming titles, special promotions and exclusive content.

CONNECT WITH US AT:

Facebook.com/groups/HarlequinConnection

 Facebook.com/LoveInspiredBooks

 Twitter.com/LoveInspiredBks

LISOCIAL2018

Earn points on your purchase of new Harlequin books from participating retailers.

Turn your points into **FREE BOOKS** of your choice!

Join for FREE today at **www.HarlequinMyRewards.com.**

Harlequin My Rewards is a free program (no fees) without any commitments or obligations.

MYR18